S T E V E N   H E R Z M A N
TO RULE A WORLD

SWEETSPIRE LITERATURE
MANAGEMENT

Library of Congress: 00000000

ISBN
978-1-964035-62-8 (Paperback)
978-1-964035-61-1 (eBook)

Table of Contents

Preface: Darkness

The night was not like many others in this region of Dracos. The mountains left little to the imagination. The cold kept most people indoors during the latter times of the night and the lack of light kept the public indoors for fear of thieves and brigands. The darkened hillside was not much different from others in the region. It was cold and dark, and a difference that many would remember. History would remember it for all time.

Along the paths and trails, all appeared normal and quite mundane. However, once you ventured deep into the trees and finally reached the clearing usually reserved for the highest of the Druids, you found what would make this hill different. The clearing was covered with the bodies of the dead and dying. Only two people moved among the carnage on that field; a woman warrior, a Tyris, and a small, poorly built and dressed bard, a poet and writer among the Druid clans, as most bards were.

The Tyris did not see the bard, nor did she care to. She had her head bent close to the ground looking for someone or something amongst the dead and dying. Of what she searched for the bard could not tell. As the woman walked her torn Mytan, a form of armor made specifically for the Tyris; a combination of a leather overcoat sewn over top of a steel plate, waved in the reflected light of the full moon exposing quite a considerable amount of bosom, even for the rather flagrant nature of the Tyris warriors. Her simple leather boots and torn leggings gave her the appearance of a lost soul looking for rest after a foul deed. Lost and wounded looking for the rest it knew it deserved. The woman was not wounded however, the blood staining her hands and her clothes was not her own, nevertheless lost and confused she was.

The Tyris searched a long time amongst the corpses of the Demons, men, and beasts that littered that field. It was with great sadness that she found the object of her search. At first, the bard could not see at what she stared. Was it a man, beast, weapon, or one of a million other countless things that littered that field? As the bard neared, he saw what it was and saw as well who the Tyris was. The woman was Athinina, wife of the greatest legend of the bard's time. She stared down upon her husband. He lay amid a circle of the men called the Hands of the Phoenix. How she had hated those men in life. Their rude comments and even ruder manners made living with them almost unbearable. In the sleep of death, she knew she would miss the comments and the mannerisms of these men. At the heart of them, lying motionless was her husband, the Phoenix of legend, Tanis Thalin. At his feet lay the corpse of the largest of the Greater Demons, Potiutios. It had cost her husband his life to rid the world of its evil, and now its demise held little of the satisfaction that she would normally have felt right at that moment looking down at its corpse. She looked down at the body of her lover and removed the bloodstained sword from his right hand. It bore an inscription in a harsh hand down the flat of the blade, "Warmonger." It brought fear to those who saw that blade against them. It had never lost and only one hand could grasp that hilt safely. Quite common in appearance, yet so heavily endowed with magic that all those who sought to own that blade died by it. That is until her lover bore it. As she lifted the blade from his right hand, the edge crossed the bare flesh of her left arm cutting, but not deeply. The curse still lived in that blade. No other hand but his could hold that blade. She quickly sheathed the blade, throwing her own sword down to the now red stained earth. No hand would ever draw that cursed blade again.

In his left hand, the legend bore the "Holy Avenger." Called by most who knew Thalin as the "Demon Slayer," it had lived up to its name. As abnormal as the "Warmonger" was normal in appearance, the "Holy Avenger" held little joy for the young woman. Its snake curved blade etched with a six pointed star, a crossed piece of wood, and a sacred oak tree, the sacred symbol of the Druids, had its name etched down the center in a hand that could have returned to copying bibles as soon as it had finished those two words. She held the blade in one hand as she closed the staring eyes of her husband. A tear formed in her saddened eyes as she stepped back from the shell that once held the man she loved.

"My husband, it is I, Athinina. Please get up. I have collected your blades and we are ready to begin a new life in this beautiful world of yours." It was more plea than a statement. The greatest Tyris stood there over her fallen love and continued to beg. "Please get up and join me in this great victory." Then she whispered, barely audible to the young bard who had come to stand behind her, "What will I do without you?"

At that last statement, the woman turned and burst into tears. The bard placed his hands on her shoulders and she embraced the young man. He tried in vain to pull her from the scene as she continued to call out to her husband. Through her tears she looked at last at the man who held her and told him in a voice that could have frozen the lakes of half the world, "Write well of this day and my husband, Bard. For the greatest of all men lies dead on that field." It was with that the two of them walked from the field, one for greater glory the other to walk into oblivion.

The verse that follows tells the tale of that love lorn couple and how it was that a man named Tanis Thalin would rule a world filled with magic and wonder. A world he would never see. It is a tale that I witnessed personally, for I was that poor bard on that unholy field. I saw the events that led up to that day. I was there at his birth and was present after the final blows of the battle fell. I alone can now tell his tale.

Read on my friends for I am Artitous, bard to the Great Phoenix, and I now will relate the tale of his life to you. It does this old man's soul well to finally release this burden and share the secrets I have held all these many years.

CHAPTER ONE:
THE DRUIDS

The air was a cold damp that was unusual for that time of year. The world had a feeling of darkness to it that even the Druid scholars could not explain.

The young Druid leaned over the embers of the dying sacrificial fire and looked down into the signs left in the embers with confusion. How could it be that one would be born more powerful than he would? Even the spirits could not tell if the one that would be born would follow the light or the darkness that was engulfing their world. A gnarled old man looked over the younger Druid's shoulder. As he gazed over at the dying embers, his breath caught.

"Being of an age that has seen many a strange omen come and go, I know what this thing means. I have seen this very omen before and yet we hesitate even now to speak of it. It is the mark of the Askanitowa. They are the immortal race of humans, elves, and dwarves that guided the world, and the doings of the races. This one appears stronger, faster, and smarter than most. Maybe better than any that was before and may come again. I have never seen the signs this strong before. Gods pray that he will be on our side rather than that of the enemy. I shall give you this task young Artitous. This child has not yet been born. Find him. Care for him. Raise him to be a soldier of the Light."

Artitous looked up at the old man. The older Druid looked a lot older than the younger man remembered. Though the younger man looked pale, he failed to tremble as he looked up into his mentor's face.

"Why should I take on this responsibility? Why should this rest on my shoulders? Why not take this upon your shoulders as you took me?"

"With the rebirth of the Askanitowa, my time here on Dracos is almost done. Soon the time comes for me to move from this plane to the next stage of my life's journey. You must continue where I have left off. Many will need your guidance and assistance in the coming years. The first of many will be the Askanitowa. You must take this burden upon your broad young shoulders because I can simply take no more weight upon these old ones. Know this Artitous. You will not suffer my fate. You will live forever, but that comes at a high cost for you must be a guide to the races of Dracos. You must guide this soon to be newborn child from infancy to his own destiny. You must teach him the ways of the Light as I have taught you!"

At those words, the old man's older form started to visibly age. Soon the old man started to cough violently and his eyes took on a glazed look. It did not take long for the young Artitous to realize that his mentor was gone. The young man fell to his knees at his old mentor's side and began to cry. The boy felt as if he had lost his best friend in the entire world. Sadly, in a sense, he had.

CHAPTER TWO:
BELTANE

As the young Druid left on his journey to find the soon to be born immortal, a young woman by the name of Tasina Thalin was preparing the bouquet of flowers she would wear in her hair that evening during the Beltane's Eve Festival. Her home lay on the bluffs overlooking the Great Sea and shores beyond. As you looked off those bluffs and over the sea, a soul would believe that they could just lift off and fly to that great paradise that lay hidden on the other side. The site of a sunset off those cliffs could bring tears to the eyes of the most hardened of hearts. Not even sea birds would spoil the site of those sunsets. Only the gods themselves had this kind of view.

The young Tasina only matched the view in beauty. Her face compared by many of the local boys to those of the great goddesses. The bloom of her cheeks was comparable to the pale roses that grew in her small flower garden. She had the body that the gods put on Dracos to taunt and tease men but was never to be possessed.

As Tasina finished dressing her hair, she felt the eyes of the young Lord McCryden on her. As his eyes moved up and down her body, she shivered. She saw the Lord looking at her. "Please leave here, my Lord, or I shall be forced to summon my father and brothers to defend my honor. It would not go well for you to have your best warriors facing you in combat now would it my Lord?" The man scoffed and looked her in the eyes, "Your men folk would not stand a moment against my noble blood. Not even for a moment. Besides, I think that you may have enjoyed having my eyes upon you for it took you longer to respond this time. Remember Tasina. I always get what I want!" At this, he strode away and Tasina continued to prepare for the festivities.

As Tasina stepped from her porch to head to the festivities, she stopped for just a moment to observe the sunset over those cliffs. After a moment with a smile on her face, she proceeded to the town of McCryden for the ceremonies. The young lord had just won another of his vile battles and wanted the entire population of the village and the surrounding area to celebrate his great victory over his defenseless neighbors during the traditional Beltane Festival.

The festivals would not be a total loss for her though, she thought. *At least the Elves would be present.* Their presence to provide the blessing of the coming season of growth was as much a part of Beltane as the weddings. The Elves were famous throughout the land as healers and farmers. The elven skills with the healing arts and with husbandry were matched only by their skill with the bow. No other race of people could come close to their true sight and truer aim. For a man be compared to an Elf in archery or healing was indeed a great compliment. At least, that is, if you were not an Elf.

Therefore, it was with a light heart that she left that day to attend the Beltane ceremonies. Beltane was a sacred evening to the Druid people. It was their belief that Beltane was the day the spirit world blessed the earth and those women who were eligible to bear fruit. With that belief, it was also the day that most of the Druid weddings occurred. It was customary for the newlyweds to consummate their unions amongst the villagers of their town so that there would be little doubt as to the purity of the bride. Not all of the couples going off this night were married however. In some of those couplings, one or the other was not a willing participant. This was the case with the young Tasina and the Lord McCryden.

Tasina had mistimed her arrival to the festival. The young Lord had already had an eyeful of the traditional ceremonies, and had gotten more than his ration of wine in his belly. Seeing Tasina enter into the firelight, several of the unwed men called out to her to join them at the fire for the festival with suggestions of what waited her there. Laughing she quickly and firmly turned each down as she moved in search of the Elves who walked amongst the men and women lay upon the earth. Seeing an Elf walking in the distance, she moved rapidly in the Elf's direction. She made it a few feet before the bulk of Lord McCryden blocked her way. Already naked, the Lord grabbed her and pulled her into the wood. Amidst the screams and sounds of the festival, the screams for help and the pleas of young Tasina were unheard by the others at the fires. As the Lord forced his will upon her, he leaned down and whispered into her ear, "I told you, I always get what I want."

Chapter Three:
Danger and Help

Artitous walked into the town of McCryden about midsummer, not even sure, why he did. This little town did not even appear on most of the better maps of the region. Surely, the Lord of the World would not be born here. Yet something told him he was in the right place. As he walked along, he stopped and stared at the primitive huts and hovels these people called homes and nearly ran over the now very pregnant Tasina. She held her head downcast, ashamed of her present condition and refused to meet the gaze of the poorly built young man standing over her steadying her after their collision. As their hands touched, they both looked into each other's face in amazement. Artitous realized that the woman before him was the one he sought.

"Follow me and ask no questions!" whispered Artitous. "Move quickly before it becomes too late."

Artitous grasped the young woman's hands and led her away to a secret place in the groves outside the village and there tended her during the final days of her labors. It was after her disappearance that the young Lord McCryden decided to check up on his unwilling lover. Not being able to find the young woman, inquires revealed that a stranger had taken her away from the village and that the fruits of her Beltane tryst were soon to be born. At this, the young Lord became enraged and killed the man bearing this unfortunate news.

The lord called his most loyal warriors into his keep that evening. Amongst them was Tasina's father. Together they shared a feast that would have sustained many outside that room for many days and the Lord called a quick pause. Standing he told them to find the woman, Tasina Thalin, and destroy her. If she has already born her child, destroy it as well. Preferably, before the child's parentage could be determined. Having given his orders, he told them that the warrior who brought the head of the woman to him would receive a large reward for his troubles. He then dismissed them to complete the evil task laid before them.

Her father knew where to find the young woman and immediately ran for the groves that concealed the hovel where she hid. Upon arriving, he found his pregnant daughter in the care of the young Druid. After excusing himself the Druid left the two to discuss, what he assumed would be a close family matter and headed for the schools of the local Druids. The girl's father begged the girl to run. He relayed that the lord of the village had offered a great reward for her and her child's demise. He begged her to run to the Druids and beg for their protection for none would harm one protected by the Druids. "You must leave here! Go to the great Groves. The Druids there will protect you and the child. I know this was not your fault but now is not the time for arguments. We must go now or we will never get out of here!" yelled Tasina's father.

At hearing her father's words, the girl ran. She ran as fast as her condition would allow her toward the shelter of the Druid woods. Nevertheless, her flight was in vain, for as she progressed down the trails the lord's men overtook her. Greedy for the lord's reward they charged the young woman hoping to take her there on the spot. However, as they moved closer a bright light flashed and blinded the fighters. Taking this miracle for what it was worth, the frightened young woman ran for all she was worth. She knew she could hide down here.

It took her two hours but finally she arrived at the cave. She had never been inside and as far as she knew no one but the Druids had ever really entered the cave. However, enter she must. To remain outside would mean her discovery and destruction. She looked at the mouth of the cave, and she gasped in awe at its great size. The mouth of the cave was large enough to swallow her and an entire army in a single bite. The equestrians would not even have to lower their lances to enter this large fissure into the depths of Dracos. The darkness filling that hole in the earth seemed to swallow all the surrounding light. It seemed to pull all of the light and heat from the very sun. Gripped by fear, she approached the great opening slowly.

Slowly, she looked into the great hole in the earth. Her eyes adjusted to the darkness and a wonder beheld her. The natural features of the cave inside looked carved from the finest of the glassmaker's wares. As clear as crystals were the columns, that held the ceiling high above her head. Everywhere she looked, there was the glass, glowing in time to the rhythm of her heart and the movements of the child deep within her. Slowly she moved a little farther into the cave.

"Come in Child!" said a voice from inside the depths of the cave. "Come in and let me see you. Bring your mother with you. Well, being that you have not yet been born I suppose that you will be unable to leave her behind but come on, come on I have run out of patience many years ago and am now running out of mercy. Hurry now." To Tasina he cried "WOMAN! Enter already. People will question your upbringing lingering in doorways so! I have many a guest within the cave already that does not know you of yet and may believe you have come for their dinner!"

"Please sir. Do not let them harm me!" cried the frightened Tasina. "I meant no harm coming here I simply wished to hide from those who would do me and my child harm." Falling to the floor, she huddled at the feet of the man in the throne of crystal and wept tears she figured would be her last. "You spoke to a child, my Lord. However, my child is not yet born. Why do you speak so?" The woman's curiosity got the upper hand as she approached the throne.

"Do you see the lights around you, Tasina?" asked the man on the throne, "do you notice that they move with the child inside you at this very moment?" Tasina simply nodded her head to each of the questions. "It is your child who will be able to control the magic that has for so long lingered in this cave of glass. He will change the world around us to his liking. Yes, yes woman, I said he. I know a great deal if you care to learn. Come into the light and gaze upon the one who has come to see to the safety of you and your child, if it is possible, and to see that he changes this world for the better. I could definitely use the help having been a young man once myself I think I know how a young man may think."

She forced herself to take the few steps closer to see the man on the throne. What she saw was not at all, what she expected. The man before her was younger than she figured. If he stood, he would have reached a height of about 6 feet and a half. The man looked well-built and very lean with muscle rippling when he moved. A small bull would be an adequate description of him, if handsome could describe a bull. In fact, those of the fairer sex, being what they deemed beautiful, always sought him. The dark hair of his head streaked at the temples with grey gave not the image of age but of wisdom, and the hair of his beard and mustache was as dark as that on his head, again with only a small strip of grey going from the lower lip down his chin in an almost straight line. Tasina stared in disbelief at the man on the throne. This man just addressed her. He was in the white and brown of the Druid order.

"My lord," began Tasina, "I mean no offense, but how should I call you? I am Tasina and your servant. Your look is much different from that I had envisioned from the sound of your voice. Please give me your protection my lord. I have no where left to turn and you are the only hope for my child."

"Young lady, never give your full name to one you have just met. It gives them some great power over you. I have known your name, it being in my visions. As for what to call me, just call me Arty. That is close enough for response and far enough for safety. Never let your mind create for you images. If the sound of a voice can create a picture that will stop you cold in your tracks than what else could the sound of a voice do? Could it distract you at a critical moment? May allow small errors in judgment not normally made? Be careful about what power you allow others to have over you and your thoughts. That will be the first of many lessons that I will give you and your child in the arts of defending yourselves," said Artitous.

CHAPTER FOUR:
SMALL LESSONS

The days passed into weeks and the man who would be a teacher found himself learning from the woman he was supposed to be teaching. Slowly he noticed that a touch of the hand that lasted for a moment now seemed to linger there for more than a few moments. Its break seemed to leave him less full somehow. Like some small part of him was missing. Used to being alone, the Druid did not notice at first that he waited with anticipation more and more every time she was far from him. Finally, he was very strained to be far from her with worry for her safety and her condition. The Druid was not the only one to notice these things. Tasina found herself longing for the lessons in magic, fighting, and wrestling just so she could be near the dark stranger. Letting him hold her down for long moments wondering what it was she wanted from him looking down at her.

One day, Tasina walked in from the stream in the sixth month of her pregnancy. She would usually be in the robes closely tied about her, but today for reasons unknown to her, she left the robe untied and it highlighted instead of concealed the curves of her bosom and shape of herself. Artitous saw her walk into the cave and could not help but stare. Noticing his look upon her and realizing that he would not take her by force, said to him, "Arty, you stand and admire and yet do not try to take the advantage that I offer. I have only been one time with a man and it was not of my choosing. I now wish to give myself to the one I choose. Arty do you not realize that the one I choose is you?"

Artitous stood there not believing his ears for it was what he longed to hear for so long. The woman before him had fallen in love with him. She loved him of all people! *If she only knew, he could not be what she wanted*, he thought. He told himself in a million ways he was doing fool's thing. Yet the fool's thing is what he did and the two found themselves inside the chamber that Artitous used as his bedroom. Tasina moved into the chamber later that very day and the two lived from that moment as man and wife by the laws of the Druid people.

As Tasina came closer and closer to the time of her delivery, Artitous made a surprise announcement. Tasks have forced him to take a trip that should last no more than a few days. He would finish his task quickly and return to take care of Tasina and the child. Artitous warned Tasina with feigned harshness that she was not to have the child while he was away.

Several hours after Artitous had left the cave, Tasina felt the first pangs from her belly. The boy inside her had finally decided it was time. Tasina staggered to the cave in misery looking for the safety of her bed. It was not to be for as she entered the ends of her labor came.

After what seemed an eternity the child was born into the world. What was once a marvelous cave of glass now looked as any other cave? The magic that lived there was no longer there. The child muzzling onto his mother's breast was another story though. For it seemed as the child, now content with a full stomach, was glowing. The magic had moved from the cave to the child. His mother looked down at the sleeping child and smiled.

CHAPTER FIVE:
A CHILD IN NEED

Tasina realized that she had nothing to care for her child. She must return to the village that stood above them. It was a risk she felt she had to take. She needed the things a child newly born would need and desire. She was not going to fail him, and the things she needed lay in the village where she was born.

Taking the game paths that had brought her to the cave what seemed so many years rather than months ago, she finally reached the village. Keeping the hood of her cloak high over her head so none could see into its depths, she quickly moved to the home of an old family friend. Tasina knocked at the garden door as she had so many times in the past when she was growing up. The old woman who opened the door looked at the cloaked figure before her and said, "What do the Druids want of an old woman? Be away with you. Do you not remember the ban placed upon your order put into place by the Lord of the manor? Leave this old woman before both of our heads are forfeit."

Tasina threw back her cowl and the old woman's face exploded with delight and recognition. "You know me then, old spinster? Surely, you have some room for me by your fire for a small while. I sought you out for a reason my oldest and dearest friend. So must I linger in the doorway or are you going to invite me into your home?" The old woman responded immediately, "Child! Child you are home where you belong! Those fools have finally let you leave. Come in; please come in. Come join me by the fire and tell me of your adventures since you have been gone."

At that, the two women walked into the house and the two spoke at length of what had befallen the young Tasina. The woman called Margas gasped at the mistreatment by the lord of the manor and Tasina's voluntary exile from her home. She laughed at the introduction to the Druid in the cave and marveled at the girl's newfound skills. Margas agreed to give Tasina what she had requested including the sword of her late husband that she no longer needed nor desired. "Take the blasted thing if you want it child. It has never been of any use to me and my husband has no more need of it since he perished. Now tell me where you stay and I will bring you more to help you as I can gather it without raising suspicion," said Margas.

With a few brief instructions to Margas, Tasina took her bundle and headed back to the cave where the creatures of the air, land, and sea awaited her return and watched over her sleeping child. Margas waited until Tasina was out of site and rapidly left her house on an errand of her own.

CHAPTER SIX:
BETRAYAL

After traveling about an hour, Tasina turned at the sound of pursuit. She knew that fleeing at this point would only bring them to her child and so decided to make a stand there on the path. Setting her bundles down, she drew the large two-handed sword given her by the old woman.

The first man down the path saw her and immediately charged expecting an easy victory over this small frail woman. Tasina spun suddenly and her blade flashed before the man's eyes. The warrior stopped in his tracks looking at the woman before him with a blade in her hand. Laughing he called to his comrades, "Come and see the Amazon woman! She thinks she can swing that lizard sticker in her hands does she. Take care there now; I would hate to see that pretty head of yours get damaged before I present it to our Lord McCryden."

The other warriors instructed the first warrior to be on with the deed so they could get home and enjoy the rewards offered by the Lord. The warrior swaggered toward Tasina. He had not even drawn his sword by the time he had reached the length of the blade. Tasina struck with the speed of an experienced swordsman and quickly struck the man down before he cleared the sword from its scabbard. Seeing their friend fall two warriors tried to take her from the sides and a quick roll by Tasina found both their blades buried to the hilt in each other. As quickly as a fox Tasina moved from tree to tree and warrior to warrior. However, slowly Tasina tired from the battle so soon after her labors bearing her son. The small wounds she sustained slowly wore the little she had left from her and soon she fell to those who attacked her.

Quickly they performed the butcher's work with Tasina's own sword. Covering the severed head in burlap and placing it inside the game pouch of the senior remaining man; they headed up the path to the castle. After the time it took to get back to the castle, it was of little consequence to them that a cart bore a body from the castle. All that was on all of the minds of these men was the reward. They had survived and brought in the elusive prey. Surely, it would be a great reward. Moreover, the fact that seven of those that left did not come back just meant more for them.

The warriors walked into the main dining room of the castle. The Lord of the manor greeted them like heroes. "Take wines my valiant warriors! You have been the best and most faithful of my men and now you deserve your reward. However, before that, please tell, where are your companions? Surely this child could not have slain seven of my most highly trained, best armed men? They turned traitor and you dispatched them must be the solution to our question then, so drink. Drink! Drink and receive your reward!"

The warriors did drink then and laughed. It did not take long for the poison put into the wine to do its work and the Lord said to the corpses around his table and to the head in his hands, "You now have your reward. You have your eternal rewards."

Margas ran from her home as Tasina left headed toward the keep of Lord McCryden. At the gate, she told the guard that she had come to claim her reward for the capture of Tasina Thalin. The guard laughed and asked her, "Then where was her prisoner? Do you have her hidden in your tunic? Do you have her in your basket? Hidden inside your bonnet maybe?" The old woman waited for the barrage to end and demanded once more entry to the Lord. The guard finally relented and brought the elderly woman into the presence of the Lord McCryden.

"My Lord McCryden," Margas began, "I have found the location of Tasina Thalin, and the boy child she claims is yours. Speak your reward and I will tell you where to find the mother and her newborn son."

"You will tell me what I wish to know, woman. I will give you what is coming to you when I am satisfied that you are telling me the truth. I am not listening to another old wives' tale. Prove to me that your story is legitimate." said the Lord.

"How about the fact that I know the child is yours? This comes straight from her mouth. She resides in the old Druidic cave down by the shore. You should not enter yourselves for she is armed, but she has to exit sometime," said Margas.

"Well done, my faithful fief. I may have had use for your skills at ferreting out the truth, but alas, you have turned on the daughter of your best friend. What is to make me believe you will not turn on me?" said the lord.

"I have done as you asked. What is to happen to me?" asked the very frightened Margas.

At that question, the lord drew his dagger and threw it into the heart of the old woman. "Guards, come in here! Clean up this mess and get the men ready for the chase. I want her head brought back to Me.," said Lord McCryden. The guard replied, "I took the liberty of sending the men just after the statement by the woman my Lord. What is this that the child may be yours? Is that rumor true? How can that be true? It makes no sense." The lord looked at him and smiled, "So you heard that awful rumor, did you?" The lord turned and plunged the dagger just recovered from the old woman into the chest of the guard and kicked him from the podium. "Someone come in here and clean up this mess!" screamed the Lord.

An older man sat watching the lord placing the pike into the earth and walked away. Those who watched him stand there by the road did not know him. He said nothing as he left the village heading toward the forest. He continued until he came to the path on which she had died and followed it down to the entrance to the cave. The sight as he walked in was a miracle in itself. There lay the child, radiating a light that filled the cave. As he looked around, he saw for the first time the fabled cave of glass. Until this very day, the source of a great deal of power that for centuries had gone unharnessed was now in this child. A person looking up into that face would not recognize the young Druid sent to find the Lord of the World. He appeared to be an old gnarled dwarf, whose stocky frame would almost seem natural in a subterranean dwelling such as the cave. Slowly, he picked up the child from the stone ledge where she left him so carefully. The young Druid suddenly felt all the power, wonder in the child flow from the child into him, and back again. The child looked up at the old face Artitous was wearing and smiled as if he knew what he had hidden there, the child then drifted off to sleep. Unbidden the Druid received a glimpse of the future of this child. The child's and Druid's responses were the same, an unholy wail that would rend the souls of any who could hear.

This child would be the strongest Druid ever. The magic in the cave of glass was reborn in one child. Destined by the stars and heavens to be unparalleled in strength and magic, he would shape the world. The only question left to the two sitting holding to one another was whether the child would side with the good or the evil sects of the Druids. This child would either save the world or destroy it. However, could it be that saving the world of Dracos also meant its destruction? This child would live no normal life whichever way he chose. No, this child would have to deal with the temptations of his gifts. He would have to survive many trials until the final days. His passing could destroy Dracos, as we know it. It was for these reasons the Druid did what he thought would be the best. He brought the child to the home of Toirin and Roseper Toirin, the rulers of the Elven people. They would raise him as their own. He also told the Elves to expect a tutor to arrive for the child in a few days, a gnarled old dwarf who was a close friend of the Druids.

CHAPTER SEVEN:
TANIS GROWS UP

Daylight passes into night, and the days eventually become years. Young Tanis, the foundling raised by the Elven royalty, was not immune to the passage of those years. As those years passed, he grew from infant to child to adolescence. He grew not only in the physical sense, but also excelled in the arts, weaponry, archery, and magic as well. He excelled in all these fields, surpassing the young Elves with which he studied. Still the winds of time progressed and soon the child was a young man.

On his thirteenth birthday, his life became irrevocably changed. It was the night of his thirteenth name day that he met her. The young female Elf was the loveliest creature he had ever seen and immediately fell in love with her. The only problem that arose was that he was adopted royalty and she was a commoner, the daughter of the local knife and sword smith. From the time the two young people first laid eyes on one another it was clear that they loved one another. She was a classmate in the same school of magic that he attended and was learning as quickly as he was.

The problem was that royalty and the commoners could not marry. It was a tradition that most would not overlook. The young people were oblivious to this fact and yearned for each other's company.

Charina was her name, and was as lovely as a sunrise. None in the village matched her beauty and she was great in intelligence. Many sought her hand, and she refused them all, even Tanis at first. Time and patience grew a friendship, which the two used to try to hide the love they felt for one another.

Shared glances would linger longer and longer. A stray touch of the hand would linger. He would make excuses to be near her and she would make herself available to him for study dates and other school related activities.

"Charina!" cried Tanis as he ran to her from across the town square. "Charina, you are the smartest person in our class. What do you think of this assignment that I have just been given?" asked Tanis as he tried his best not to smile and giggle with delight. Charina's eyes lit up with delight as they passed over the parchment, but quickly composure once more took over. "My lord prince," said Charina in her most proper and bored sounding voice, "Your sense of humor and childish jokes is less than flattering, but I will accept your offer." She said tossing the piece of parchment over her shoulder.

Tanis looked at the parchment with fallen jaw and moved slowly out toward the library. *I was childish.* Tanis thought as he moved toward the great hall of learning to meet her. Consumed with his own self-pity, he failed to see Charina practically dive onto the paper as he turned his back. Carefully Charina straightened the paper and pressed it between the books she carried. The smile on her face would last for days as she slowly made her way to the library. *No use to appear eager*, thought Charina. After all, it was not as if they were going to wed or anything. It was simply a study date. Then who could tell the future.

Charina and Tanis would spend hours in the royal library. None rivaled the magical texts contained there and none possessed more of them. Tanis would hunt out the titles that Charina longed to read and held them for her at eye level so she would not strain her eyes. One date on a sunny afternoon became two. Two became three. Then it seemed they were always with one another.

You would not see one without the company of the other. Charina was often the guest of the royal family for meals and special celebrations. All spoke of the two of them making the greatest of couples, rivaling even the King and Queen for their perfection for one another. The sun seemed to shine brighter when their eyes met, the air warmer and fresher because they were happy and when the two quarreled it was as if the day became as night and cold as the worst of winters. The traditions appeared to be changing.

The few days the two had attempted to see others were miserable not only to the two of them but to the entire village as well. It was so no surprise to anyone that the two returned to each other. It also was no surprise the day that Tanis asked Charina to marry him. Everyone had expected that the betrothal to have been arranged years since, but since it had not it had to be done the old-fashioned way.

It was coming time for her eighteenth name day when she confided in Tanis that she was going to request of her parents that she wed. According to the Elven customs, it was only proper to request the permission of both sets of parents by both parties wanting to wed. Therefore, Tanis and Charina worked out their requests and enjoyed the company of one another until the time came for them to make their requests.

Now if the parents agreed to the union, then the marriage would happen as soon as they made the arrangements. If the parents did not agree then the couple had another option. Tradition held that a young couple could complete certain tasks and rituals and still permitted to wed. The first of these was that the woman must spend two days and two nights in the Tree of Confinement. A hollow tree transformed into a small cell. Its use in this custom was supposed to allow time for thought on whether the woman was making the proper choice or not. The only problem was that not all the young women going into that tree ever came out again.

The second task was for the man. As the woman lay in the confines of the tree, he was to go to the cave of the great wyrm, the eldest of the dragon, and retrieve a scale from his lair. Though it may seem easy to retrieve a molted scale, you should come to realize that the great wyrm was not overly friendly toward his guests. To pick up a scale would be easy, except that the dragon did not shed. The scales were still attached the dragon and it pained him greatly to have one of them removed. To leave with the scale if you managed to get one was where the problems began. For the dragon could become rather sore at the brave lad trying to remove his scale and in the end would end up with a young man for dinner.

The third and final test was that the couple being bound together. Then the sacred flames of Amon purified them. If this may sound like the least of the couple's problems, you must understand that not many people ever make it that far. The second consideration is that these flames are at the bottom of an active volcano. Once they bound the couple together, they lowered the couple into the maw of the crater, and lowered until they start to scream. The couple remains there until the screaming stops. At that point, the young couples returned to the surface to have the local Druids heal them.

If these tests are all completed, then the couple weds as tradition dictates and their means of getting into that state remains unsaid for the rest of their lives. That is if they can pass one more obstacle. The families of the bride and groom line up between the loving couple who are by now bruised, exhausted, and sore, and the two must fight to one another. The fighting ends when the two's hands meet. It is only then that the two wed.

The day of Charina's birth came and the two young people went as custom demanded to each of their parents. Charina sat at her parents' feet and made her request to wed to the foundling prince. Laughing her father lifted her from the floor and hugged her close.

"If love has made you make this request of me than you have my leave daughter. I cannot however speak for your mother. I leave it in her hands to decide whether your request comes from love, or ambition." Having said this he hugged his daughter once more and walked from the room to give the two women their privacy to speak on the matter at hand.

The mother of the bride-to-be's face slowly grew red. The young people feared the worst as she looked with hatred at the pair. Just as quickly, as her face became red it settled back to its normal hue and a great smile spread upon her face. "My child, my only child. I wished you would one day know the love that your father and I enjoy. The boy you have selected will care for you and provide well for you. I could not be happier for you."

At the royal residence the scene was quite a bit similar to the girl's response. When he asked the royal couple the response was quite the same. They hugged close their adoptive child and heartily agreed to the choice of a wife the boy had made. The whole royal family gathered to escort their child to the home of the smith to congratulate the young woman and her family.

Upon arrival the welcome received was a warm one from the girl's mother. Charina and her father greeted happily the royal family and the young prince that came to court the young woman. The couple looked at each other as if nothing else mattered in the world. As far as they were concerned nothing did at that moment and the families of the two looked at each other with obvious gratitude. The King went to the smith and began discussing a deal for many suits of armor for his new recruits in the Elven army. After all family must aide family. The mothers set about planning the wedding that would come in the following days. The two had never really cared for one another but now giggled and plotted like best girlhood friends.

Chapter Eight: Wedding Plans

As the plans progressed and the date of the wedding came closer the whole village became elated with the joy of the coming wedding. Nothing in the world could spoil the village's glee for their favorite children. It was when the whole place was high on the love in the air that was when the disaster struck. As the festival was being prepared in the great square before the palace, a great beast settled on the roof of the couple's favorite place, the library. The beast of fur, feathers, and scales resembled the great beasts of Greek legend. The body of a lion with the head of one, the head and wings of an eagle, and the head and tail of a dragon looked down on the villagers. A great roar gained it the attention of the entire village. "You choose to allow a bastard child to marry one of your own?" asked the great lion's head. "Feed the boy to us and we shall leave and your village will not be corrupted with the stench of him any longer", said the eagle head. "Beware of one amongst you! For one amongst you intend you all and your children harm. Beware!" cried the head of the dragon as it tried to pull the others from the rooftop and away from the village. "Send them to the trials before the wedding or I will not restrain my brethren from destroying everything here. Force them to the trials or all will be destroyed!"

At hearing the words of the beast, the queen of the Elves broke into tears. The girl's father and the Elven King began shouting in a loud voice for assistance. Had there been some crime committed by the girl?

The thoughts continued and were shouted for just a few moments when Tanis stepped between the warring sides of the discussion.

"I leave at dawn for the great wyrm's lair. I will return within twenty-four hours. By that time Charina's trial in the Tree of Confinement should be completed. Be waiting for me as the sun rises over the bluffs there." Tanis said in a quiet voice.

Saying this he strode away and returned to his rooms to try to get a good night's rest before he would be called upon to go and perform the tasks of marriage. All the thoughts in his head were of Charina and how lovely she would be in her new wedding gown.

CHAPTER NINE: ARMING THE KING

The Elf King had other thoughts on his mind as the young man walked away. The girl's mother had just entered her home when the King approached the smith. The smith led the King into a large storeroom and gave the King a tied bundle. The King gave the smith a pained smile and the assurances that the materials would be paid for. The smith looked at his daughter and told the King that if his young foundling survived to marry his daughter they were paid for.

The King brought the bundle to the sleeping Tanis's room and laid it at the foot of his bed. After a long loving look at his only child, though a foundling, the King went to his own chambers to try to find some rest that he knew would never come.

That morning Tanis came down with the large bundle in his arms and inquired as to whether or not anyone had left the package at his bedside the previous night. The King smiled at the boy and told him to open it and find out what the forest spirits had left him to help him on his way. The kit that lay inside the bundle surprised even the King. The chest plate of a suit of mail and plate armor sat on top of a large collection of items. The chest plate was engraved all over with protection wards to protect the wearer against hunger, fire, and steel. When he lifted off the chest plate underneath sat the Holy Avenger. This blade was assumed lost to the world with the death of the first Elven King so many years before, and yet in his hands sat the Avenger. The rest of the plate armor rested beneath the Avenger, all covered with runes of protection and wards against a multitude of dangers. Also included in the package was a shield of exquisite construction and bore all of the possible wards and runes. The shield read like a book of magic more than a piece of armor. A dagger rested at the bottom of the package and looked to all appearances to be a normal dagger. All the armor and weapons were soon properly strapped to the young man and each bore the wards of protection. Tanis had no way of knowing this at the time, but he would own the armor, shield and sword for the rest of his life. The cloth itself was a tabard with the royal seal sewed to the front of the cloth.

At seeing the items in the cloth now fastened to his soon to be departing son, the King grabbed the boy and held him to himself and cried as if the man faced the final walk to the gallows and the hangman's noose. Tanis smiled at the only parents he had ever known and turned rapidly toward the lair of the great wyrm. The last thing he heard as he walked away was his adoptive father calling after him, "Don't look back!"

At the same time Charina's mother locked the Tree of Confinement's door. It would be a long two day stay for the girl. Witnesses later told that the woman had a smile upon her face as she turned the key.

CHAPTER TEN:
THE TASKS

After sixteen hours of traveling, Tanis arrived at the cave harboring the greatest of dragons. He hesitated just a moment as he looked at the entrance to the great lizard's lair. The sprawling opening nearly forced him to retreat, until the thoughts of Charina in the Tree made him steel his courage and enter the great darkness before him. Tanis believed that all the light in the world had been swallowed by that darkness at the opening to the cave. It was darkness like the deepest night and as quiet as the deepest sleep. As Tanis progressed, he felt the hot breath of the creature wash over him in waves as the creature breathed. As that breath grew warmer his resolve also began to buckle, but one thought of Charina was enough to force him to continue on. He must return with a scale.

It was not long before he neared the fearsome beast. As he approached, he sensed that something was dreadfully wrong. He heard the movement of the great beast deep inside his lair and Tanis felt the blood freeze inside his veins. But the young man continued undaunted. He paused for a moment to tighten the straps of his armor and draw the Holy Avenger. As he finally approaches the ancient creature, he realized that he had forgotten to place his shield on his arm. It now hung uselessly from his back. The creature lifted its great head and gazed upon the now terrified Tanis standing before it.

"SO YOU HAVE COME TO SLAY ME HAVE YOU, YOUNG WANT TO BE DRAGON SLAYER?" roared the great dragon. "OR

ARE YOU ANOTHER OF THOSE LOVES BLINDED FOOLS COME TO STEAL ONE MY PRECIOUS SCALES TO PROVE YOURSELF?"

Young Tanis squared up his shoulders and raised the sword before him. He trembled under the gaze of the great beast, but he still spoke as steadily as he would have to any one of his friends growing up. "Sir Dragon," he began, "I have not come to steal from you nor do I mean you any harm. I seek your permission to borrow one of your precious scales so that I can prove myself worthy of a marriage that a great beast will not permit in its jealousy. If you can find it in your great wisdom to allow me this favor, I will return your scale, and hold myself in your debt for the rest of my life."

"Noble words young man." said the great wyrm. "You are really in love with this young woman? Even coming here is risking death or worse. Come into the light so that I may see you better."

Young Tanis did not know what to do or say so he took a step forward. He stiffened his back as the dragon moved down to peer at him. Its breath stank of sulfur and the boy almost grimaced as the great maw came ever closer. The dragon's great eye never blinked as it passed over the young warrior. After a close examination, the dragon reached out and grasped Tanis and lifted him into the air. The dragon carried the young man to the edge of the nest and set him upon it. The great beast turned around in his nest and reached into it. When the dragon withdrew his great hand in it stood a single sparkling scale.

"For your courage and your manners, I will give you this scale. It is the only one I have ever lost and I soon recovered it. The young man was a good thief but his remains sit at the bottom of that pile of want to be dragon slayers and scale hunters that have tried since." The dragon snickered as he pointed to the pile of bones in the corner. "There are not many any longer that make the attempt anymore and it pleases me that at least they still teach manners to their young out there. I find that law of your precious Elven people to be revolting. All any of them had to do was ask for a scale as you have and I would have parted with one. What was all that death and destruction for? Let no one take that scale from you. It will be stronger in your defense than that one of iron on your back there." At that the dragon giggled again, a sound like the rumble of a volcano before eruption. "Now, tell me of the new Elven King. Tell me of the world outside; it has been a century since I have left the confines of my cave. Do your people still fight amongst themselves outside? War is another of the great wastes you know. Tell me what you know of the world and I will give you another great gift, the aid of the dragons whenever you have the need. Maybe the dragons and the humans can once more share knowledge between each other as we once did at great length with your ancestors."

The great wyrm sat and fastened the scale to the shield on the boy's back with fire from his breath. "Fusing metal with the scales of a dragon, I never thought I would see the day. It was always forbidden but now that the old pacts are gone-maybe some new ones can be forged just as we forged that shield and scale. It is definitely worth a try." said the dragon.

So the young man sat with the dragon and they discussed the news of the world that the boy knew. The two spent the rest of the day and part of that night sitting and talking of the world in general and of the world as it once was a world of peace and tranquility, a world in a constant search of knowledge instead of power. That night both dragon and boy slept in the dragon's nest and at sunrise yet another surprise came to pass.

"Climb up on my back boy. I need to get out and stretch my wings. How about a ride into your village? Today you will ride like the Kings of Old!" The dragon lowered his head and the boy climbed up onto the back of the dragon and the great beast began the short flight to the young man's village.

Back in the village, the elders ran for weapons and called for all those with them to form a line for a dragon approached. They looked on in amazement as the dragon lowered his head and the boy jumped from his perch on the dragon's back. "Be still old men. You asked for a scale but instead I bring you the whole dragon!"

This brought forth many cheers and cries of admiration from all those who had gathered and they quickly began a multitude of questions to both the boy and the dragon. Tanis ran for the Tree of Confinement as he heard the rumbled replies of the dragon behind him. If dragons could smile, this one was smiling from ear to ear.

CHAPTER ELEVEN:
INSIDE THE TREE

Meanwhile, inside the Tree of Confinement Charina was settling in for her two day stay. The interior of the tree was spacious enough for some comfort but not for a lot of movement. She felt the darkness pressing down on her inside the tree and figured it was just her imagination. As Charina settled in, her eyes began to lose focus and before her spread the lives of those around her. First it was her mother's life. It was noticeably missing the end after the wedding of Charina and Tanis. Charina did not understand and did not care to. The relationship there was strained at best.

Then the life of her father was revealed to her and again many segments were missing. How was it that she should not be able to see the lives of herself and her family in detail? Why not show all? Why tantalize with small tidbits of information? She was thinking of these things when her life was shown to her. As she watched the events that were to unfold, Charina fainted into sleep.

After what seemed an eternity, she was awakened by the feel of a hand on her arm. Startling awake she figured her time inside was complete and was to leave. Charina looked around herself and saw that the door was as firmly sealed as before. Leaning back against the trunk again Charina tried to fall back to sleep. Again she felt the hand on her arm and opened her eyes looking at the shimmering figure before her. "Who are you and what would you have of me?" asked Charina. "Speak to me! Tell me what it is you seek!" she screamed at the apparition before her.

"Be still friend. I am a friend. I have lain where you lay. I have been here where you are. Fear lies inside this place waiting for you. If you give in to that fear you will never leave as I have not. I would spare you that fate if I can, child. Listen well. Many of the spirits that inhabit this tree are not as kind or benevolent as I. Listen to none of them for their advice can mean death or worse for you. I cannot linger but heed my warning young one. The tree is full already with the souls of those who have passed before and since I have and I wish no more be trapped here with us. Remember! DO NOT FOLLOW ANY THAT MAY COME TO YOU! Be especially cautious of Him. I must go. Be well and remember true love will get you through." said the spirit.

Charina called after the ghost, "Please do not go. Who are you? Who is the Him you speak of? Please do not leave me tell me more." But her pleas were to the air for the spirit had already faded away to nothing with only a parting wave and a smile. *Other ghosts were to come* thought Charina. She hoped the rest would be a little more forthcoming than this one. She had already forgotten the warning of the ghost.

Charina would see the spirits of several other women. None would speak and all would just shake their heads before they faded to darkness. They appeared to be as benign as the first. But some had a look of fear in their spirit eyes.

After a short time Charina was again awakened by another ghost. This one was a man who looked down at her with a great smile and a shine to eyes and his body. Where the first spirit had appeared as a mist, this spirit looked more solid and appeared to be no more than a man with glowing eyes and a glowing body. Well-tuned and shaped this ghost was as attractive as any man she had ever seen. Holding out his hand he bid her follow him. "You seek to rise above your station in life, child, don't you?" spoke the spirit with a voice so velvety that the words were almost missed by Charina. "You wish to marry not for love but for ambition. You wish to be greater than yourself don't you? You figure marrying a prince will solve all of your problems don't you? Do not try to lie to me. I know all, child. I can help you win your prince. Follow me and I will show you the way to gain your prince for life. You do not believe that he really has gone to the lair of the great wyrm do you? He would not risk his life for you, child. A peasant woman with nothing, a prince wants you only for one thing, he will not risk everything for you. He is sees only a lover, not a woman. He wants you for a toy no more. Follow me. I will show you what you must do to prevent losing your prince."

Suddenly the first spirit's warning rang into her ears, "Beware of the other spirits especially Him." Charina asked the spirit, "Sir, if you speak true, then why did another come to me and tell me to be wary of you? Do you lead me to danger? What is it that you require of me? Speak and I will follow you but not until then."

The male ghost smiled and replied, "She did say to trust no one, did she not? So how can you be sure you can trust her?"

The spirit laughed and pointed to a path leading down from where she stood inside the tree. At the first it looked sturdy and safe, but as she came closer she saw the damage done prior by those who had attempted the path before. Large stones gave way beneath her weight as she shifted near the path. It was definitely a dangerous way to go and she decided not to go. "Spirit is what you lead me to beneath these roots? Where do you take me? Who are you?"

"Child do you really not know me? I am the stealer of souls. I am He Who Would Take You to Death. I am the Betrayer of Fools. I take you to my master, Death, so that he would feed me your soul. A tender treat it will be too. That is the secret of this tree. It houses those who failed to realize the dangers they were in. You will follow me to my master and belong to me. It is too late for you to do otherwise. The few that come out of this tree come out because they were strong enough to resist my charms. I see your looks upon me. I see the dazzle in your eyes when I speak. You will follow me.... another victim of the tree!" spoke the spirit in the silky voice that held Charina in thrall.

Charina took a step toward the path and the spirit moved forward looking and trying to draw her on. Suddenly the words struck Charina. Startled, she leaped to the roots on which she was placed upon entering the tree. "You almost claimed me spirit! But I am wise to you now and will not fall for your pretty face and velveteen voice. It will take more from you to lead me to my death. I have seen the future and you are not in it. Tell your master to come for me if he wants my soul so badly, for he will have to fight to get it from me. You are powerless now spirit. Be gone from me. I have no desire for you, only my prince for whom I wait. Be gone!"

Outside the Tree, Tanis had just arrived.

CHAPTER TWELVE:
ANOTHER TASK

Tanis approached the Tree of Confinement and stood watch over it. He sat at its base for the remainder of the two days that she had to complete inside. The time came for the door to the Tree to be opened and Charina to be released. Tanis stood anxiously beside the door waiting for the woman he loved's mother to appear.

Slowly up the path to the Tree came Charina's parents as well as the royal family. Charina's mother wore a small grin on her face that had been there since the beginning of their trial. The small group of Druids held to the ritual that the Tree be opened with the dawn so an uneasy wait began for the first rays of dawn.

As dawn arrived, the village gathered to witness the release of the girl. Slowly, her mother approached the Tree. She stared at the lock as if seeing it for the first time. After a moment she inserted the key. Surprisingly, the mother laughed. Turning to the crowd she called on all the gods to do their worst and then turning broke the key in the lock. Charina's mother turned quickly and showed to the village the sheered key and laughed again. "So much to you all for true love, for now she will never be released from her prison. The tree holds her forever."

Tanis ran to the Tree and heard Charina's mother calling out to him, "It is hopeless. You'll never get her out of there now, So much for true love!" At that she laughed the harder still and fell to the ground raked with fits of laughter. Her mirth was soon stilled as Tanis grasped the hilt of the Holy Avenger, drew it, and sliced the lock in twain.

Quickly the Druids opened the door and the girl was released. Charina blinked in surprise at the light and smiled as her eyes fell onto Tanis. Charina walked to Tanis and took his hand.

"No!" bellowed her mother. "This cannot be! He has harmed the sacred Tree! He must be slain!"

The Elven people bellowed with rage at hearing the accusations. Tanis picked up his blade readying himself to defend himself and his love, when the dragon intervened. "Stop this!" he bellowed in a voice to make an earthquake seem calm in comparison. "The boy hurt not the Tree. He merely destroyed a lock. Let he who has never committed a wrong come here and try this child before all his family, friends, and peers!"

The Elves stopped in their tracks. "Come now, who amongst you is perfect?" he asked. Finally the head Druid came forward and took the boy and girl's hand. He led the way north. Not to the village but away, to the mountain.

The dwarf who had acted as the tutor and mentor to young Tanis ran up and grasped his hand. "Well done my boy, well done. You have made us all so proud. How did you charm that great beast? Did he really come of his own will? Is he your pet now? Is he a friend? Speak boy teach your old mentor."

Tanis shook the old dwarf's hand and smiled down on him. "I am kind of busy to talk to you now, Artitous. But I promise I will explain all when I am free to do so."

But the fury of Charina's mother could not be so easily quelled. Seeing her chance to kill the young couple she leaped for her belt knife and plunged it for the chest of Charina. Tanis seeing the danger leapt in front of Charina and took the knife to the chest. She withdrew the sharp dagger and was grabbed roughly by several men of the village, her husband one of them.

Artitous seeing the boy fallen to the earth let out a scream flinging back his head and arms. Chanting in the Druidic language he began a weaving of magic so great none would have survived, and yet when he finished nothing happened. Looking around the dwarf spied Tanis standing there his hand outstretched and chanting the ward of prevention. He stood and wiped himself of the dirt and grime and smiled at Charina. The plate mail had worked well in his defense, as did the scale of the dragon that rested around his shield, fused to it by the power of the dragon's own breath. Quietly the couple turned back to the mountain leaving behind all who had not moved quickly enough to begin again the long trip to the mountain.

Artitous called over to the villagers. "See I told you. He is the greatest. He will do great things. I am sure of it." The King walked over to the dwarf putting a hand to his shoulder he said in a voice so all could hear "Artitous, You first said little to anyone, even Tanis, until this very day. Now I begin to believe that there may be some Halfling in you as well, since they are the ones who supposedly run off at the mouth."

All laughed at the King's jest. Yet none laughed harder than Artitous himself.

The world grew quiet as young Tanis led his bride to be toward the great smoking mountain. No one spoke. Nothing moved, not even the birds sang. Amongst this quiet and stillness, the young couple proceeds toward that oldest of the great mountains. The people of the village quickly forgot their fears and let their morbid curiosity lead them to follow the young couple. This curiosity of the morbid, which consumes half the general public, and annoys the rest of them. The curiosity that causes a man to stop to see the aftermath of a battle and makes all people thank the Light that they do not lay on that field, the one that says we survived and wish to look at death as to fathom what we ourselves will be when we pass.

The young couple made it but a few hundred feet before the girl's mother appeared before the couple. Before her she bore a sword of great workmanship, but its weight was too much for the woman as she could not keep the tip but a few inches from the ground. Desperately she attempted to wave the blade before the faces of the young couple, but her efforts proved to be futile for she managed to only move the blade a few inches each way before the tip would again fall to the earth. She raised her voice not in regret but in anger at the young couple.

"You stole your father's affections from me, now you wish to go and be happy with a love of your own! I will never permit this to happen for as long as I still have breath in my body! Leave her here young prince and find one of your aristocratic young sluts to keep you occupied! You don't need common trash such as this cur at your side!"

Hearing the threats of the mother the warrior Druids quickly came and surrounded the young couple, while others of their brethren grabbed the woman and her sword. The rest of the journey went without excitement as they once more set off for the mountain yet again.

The great mountain rumbled as they grew ever closer. The very sound of that rumble kept most of the villagers back away from the summit. The rest stayed behind at the base of the mountain ready to run in an instant if the need arose. The young couple proceeded undaunted by the loud sounds emitting from the fiery hill and proceeded to the summit accompanied by the Druids and her parents.

The couple walked casually to the basket that would take them into the heart of the mountain, and the Druids began the slow decent into the fiery hell below. Slowly the couple drew closer and closer to the lake of liquid rock below until the Elven girl began to moan and cry out about the heat of the mountain.

The basket at this point had weighed greatly upon the two Druids that held the cord and so the two Druids holding the girl's mother went to the aide of their companions, leaving the girl's mother unattended. From the basket all seemed right with the world with their slow swinging decent. Tanis began some old war chants and songs that Charina knew and she joined in with him with a fervor that made her forget the heat.

Tanis heard the sound before he realized there was a problem. From the top of the mountain, staring in barely contained horror and rage, the girl's mother cut the rope securing the basket. From nowhere Artitous came to aid the young man and woman inside the mountain. As quickly as lightning strikes he had a grip on the rapidly spooling cable and made several magical signs. Slowly the cable stopped and held where it was. Pulling hard once he brought the young couple from the hill. The basket seemed to fly out of its own accord. The young couple lay unconscious as the basket finally let down gently on the side of the mountain where their decent had begun. Druids hurried to the young couple but where shooed away as quickly as they arrived by Artitous, who had already started tending to the young couple himself.

Chapter Thirteen: Trials and Truths

From inside the mountain the young ones felt the jolt of the parting cable. Quickly young Tanis gave his shield to his lady love. As she took the shield and placed it beneath her the bit of armor he wore and the shield in her hand began to glow with eerie light. The girl slowly nodded off to sleep surrounded by that glow. Watching Charina fall asleep Tanis soon found himself growing more and more sleepy until he too lay down and slept in the heat of the great mountain.

After what seemed an eternity to Artitous, he bent from his labors and walked toward the girl's mother. Eyes colder than the grave and a heart blacker than the blackest pitch peered from Artitous when he gazed at Charina's mother. She gazed back with even more hate and darkness than Artitous showed. Slowly she raised the blade that had almost cost the young couple their lives. Artitous saw the mother lift the blade and seized the girl's mother and cast him and her into the depths of the mountain.

As the two plummeted into the mountain, Charina and Tanis began to stir. Slowly Tanis lifted his head and looked for the dwarf that was his almost constant companion. Instead of the dwarf the boy saw his in-laws to be approaching with blades drawn. The family approaching with a rage caused by the indiscretion of Artitous, ready to kill for the mistake made by the boy's lifelong friend. Tanis moved slowly to Charina and weakly moved her from his shield. Rising to his knees he strapped the shield to his arm and drew the Holy Avenger. The weight of his arms pulled the young man to the ground. Undaunted, he tried again to rise from the ground to defend himself and his love. Stumbling from the cage he was lowered into the mountain in, he lifted shield and sword in preparation for a fight when the Druids came between the two belligerent parties. The Druids stood facing each side of the growing animosity. At their head was a tall man dressed in the garb of the ancients. Looking from one side of the conflict to the other, the man spoke loudly and clearly, "Enough! I am of the ancient order of Druids. It is proscribed that no bare blades are shown in my presence and if any of you have a problem with that rule speak now! The young prince needs to live, as does the girl. Ask me not how I know these things just suffice to know that I know them. Now lower your blades!"

Explaining the law of the Ancients was wasted on the members of Charina's family for as soon as the Druids moved, the family closed around the Prince. Rapidly he was brought to his knees under the rain of blows from swords, knives, axes, and maces. Seeing the peril of her lover, Charina lashed out using her magic. Seeing the actions of the young girl, she too was quickly set upon.

Seeing the peril of the young couple, the Druids wasted no time in charging into the fray to help the young couple. As rapidly as the rain of blows began, they subsided. The girl's father looking to her with half pain and half love that father always will bear for his daughter, went to the girl and held her as tears filled his eyes. Tanis moved to the front of the crowd and stood before the assembled villagers.

"Why have you interfered in our lives? Have we given you cause to hate us? Yes, Charina's mother is dead, killed by the dwarf that brought me to this place. But that dwarf now lies at the bottom of the river of molten rock at the bottom of this sacred crater with his victim. The two now burn together in hell for their crimes here today. Yet still you attack us, why? We have completed your tasks and requirements for marriage and I now request that the Druids perform the ceremony."

As he spoke, he sheathed his sword and unstrapped his shield. Tanis grasped the hand of Charina who had sustained many wounds from the battle and was not yet being tended by the Druids, who were trying to watch every way at once. The Druid stepped forward and performed the ceremony and the young couple left that mountain that day as man and wife.

The new couple returned to Tanis's boyhood home and was greeted warmly by his adoptive family. As they entered, the news was not all good. They were happy as could be that the boy had come home from his ordeal. The King stood from his throne and kissed his new daughter-in-law and began to relate the story of Tanis's birth. He told of his mother's shame, the chase from the village, and of the human Lord McCryden's attempt to kill the young infant and his mother. He then told them of Lord McCryden's eventual success in killing the boy's mother and the child being brought to the Elves.

This news was more than the boy and his bride could bear. He looked at his adoptive parents asking again for the details of what had happened in the not so distant past, this time in all the details that his adoptive father knew.

After hearing the tale Tanis took Charina up to his rooms and began to rapidly pack the things he would need for traveling. He left the building headed for the edge of town as rapidly as his feet would take him. He still wore the shield, sword, and armor he had worn for his trials and his marriage; he had not even taken the time to change his clothes. His adoptive father tried to talk some sense into the boy warning how dangerous his biological father was. He left the house unswayed. The villagers came out and followed closely as the young couple returned to Charina's home briefly to retrieve her belongings and then as they moved toward the edge of the town. All the village teens hoped to catch a glimpse of the young prince and the new princess's honeymoon night.

Tanis turned in his walk and gazed at the villagers following. He blushed when he realized what they wanted to see. He did not expect that this would happen when he was wed. It was indecent. It was crude. He then admitted to himself that he too did the same whenever a newlywed couple had been wed. If it was possible to blush any redder then he was he did. The thoughts of him and his new wife's first night together made his step lighter and his face even redder.

CHAPTER FOURTEEN:
A NEW PATH

Slowly the young couple moved through the groves and trees that surrounded their home. They had never ventured so far from home and yet they never looked back. It was as if they had ended that point in their lives and they were moving on to the next big adventure in their lives. Traveling mainly at night to avoid notice and sleeping during the day in copses of trees and bushes, they gave the appearance of shades lost between this world and the next. The few travelers met on the road avoided the young pair as they hurried down the paths and roads to their own destinations, rarely even looking back at the pair of lost souls looking for a haven to rest their weary bodies.

The illusion was completed by the dark grey woolen cloaks both wore as protection from the cold night air. The cloaks covered them from the tops of their heads to their knees hiding from sight the armor and sword of Tanis and the Elven features of Charina. Many a time Tanis stopped to ask a passer by the way to the town of McCryden. It was long ago the infant Tanis was carried to the Elven home land from the home of his mother. After a little time the ways all became foreign to him and many times the two foot sore wanderers had to double back to use a different road. Even not knowing the proper way to go, when he was on the proper path his spirits were high and when on the wrong path his spirits would fall to the point of despair. He swore that even in death Artitous still guided him to his proper path and that made him feel that he was doing the right thing.

On the second night of travel the pair found themselves face to face with one of the dangers that they feared. Bandits appeared all around them demanding all their property of value for using their road. Tanis stood before the head of these bandits and spoke to him. "Sir, We are newlyweds and looking for a new home. We have nothing worth stealing. We seek only a safe place to start our family and live in peace. Please sir. Leave us be. We mean you and yours no harm."

The bandit smiled at Charina, "So newlyweds huh. Well you must know that we get the first night with new brides as well. Have nothing of value? I disagree. I see a lovely young lady that will warm all our blankets while your corpse cools. When we bore of her then we will end her life as well. It has been a while since we have had a woman and we do not bore easily. I will warn you of that." laughed the bandit.

At those words Tanis became incensed. Drawing his blade he screamed, "Then let the bravest and strongest that you have be first to taste my steel! You will have my wife over my dead body! Any of you care to taste steel?" Tanis threw his cloak back over his back and cleared his arms for a fight.

The bandits seeing the armor and sword stepped back a moment and looked at Tanis. "You are just full of surprises aren't you? Elven royalty and yet you are not an Elf. You must be the bastard of the Lord McCryden we have heard of. Elven ladies are even better than a human woman. She will last us even longer. Hey boys! I hear that Elven girls are rare treats and we will be treated tonight!" At those words the bandit attacked Tanis. After a few moments the bandit leader lay dead at Tanis's feet, Tanis's blade having severed both the man's sword and his head. Tanis turned toward the other bandits, who saw the death of their leader and picked up and fled at the approach of the young warrior. Charina smiled as she wove the power and switched each of them as they ran. All the pair heard as the bandits ran was the shouts of the men yelling of the murdering Elves. The couple laughed as they continued on the road. The few passers by simply stared and moved faster figuring mad spirits had infected them.

As the two traveled they came upon an old farm off to the side of the road upon which they were traveling. They stopped to talk with the farmer and found that they were close to their destination. The cottage was small and bereft of the ornaments that the homes of the Elves possessed. It had a commonplace set of walls made of the dark clay of the surrounding earth and pine boughs for a roof. Though the cottage had a look of age, it was well tended. The darkened windows held no glass and were shuttered on either side with rough cut boards. The rough door again had the rugged appearance of poverty but was also well maintained.

Walking up to the door, Tanis struck it twice with his mail covered fist. The door gave off two resounding knocks. The door showed some light around the edges as someone inside moved to it. When the door opened Tanis took a step back. The withered form at the door just stared and a voice like sandpaper rasping a piece of wood asked him his business. The withered face was that of a woman and she gazed upon the couple with delight. Her twig like arms came up, one holding a candle the other taking Charina and escorting her into the little hovel. The poor old farmer spoke to them in a voice like cracking parchment. Though old the voice held a strength that only years could account for. The strength was surprising coming from that withered frame.

"What brings you two shades of Hades to my door at this ungodly hour? Are you Demons of death to finally deliver us from the bondage of Lord McCryden? Speak for if I do not like what you are telling me it will surely mean the end of your cursed existence. Do I make myself clear, youngsters?"

Tanis took in the old man's words without an utterance. He had just noticed the crossbow in the withered hands of the old man. "We come from the land of the Elves to exact revenge for a wrong committed many years ago against the very one that has oppressed you. I am Tanis Thalin borne by the young woman that his lordship raped on a past Beltane so many years before. Tell us where to find him and I will leave this very evening!"

The old man quickly held up his hands and said, "No one travels into the village at night. If you are to do what you claim you will, then it is best that you leave in the morning. Let us bed you down for the evening and feed you tonight and in the morning before you journey to your deaths. Here now give me your cloaks."

The couple thanked them greatly and turned over their cloaks to the old woman and man. At seeing Tanis's armor and Charina's ears the farmer and his wife gave a start. Quite rapidly the old man brought forth one of his lambs. It was near death from some disease he could not put a name to. He begged at the feet of Charina to heal it for it and its brothers were all he had after the lord took his ewe and ram for his dreaded tax. Charina was already by the lamb and giving her assistance even as the man continued his tirade. After but a few moments Charina had the lamb licking milk from her fingers and was feeding it from a bowl.

Seeing the lamb's near-perfect recovery the old man grasped Tanis's hand and grasped Charina's hand in warm handshakes and even offered them their bed. The couple quickly convinced them that the floor and some food were thanks enough. The four spent most of that night deep in conversation and some things came to Tanis that he had not thought of prior. The lord of McCryden had a hundred warriors around him, all skilled with the weapons they carried. The town of McCryden was walled and all those entering by the main gate was required to give name and purpose for entering the town. Tanis was counting on surprise for his plan of vengeance to succeed.

The old man was some help on both points for he had a cart loaded and ready for market the next morning. "The guards do not check the carts at the gate," the old man explained. "If it contains nothing that they themselves want or need then they leave it as is. Let's hope none are hungry as I pass through!"

So the four planned through the evening hours and some of the night coming up with a plan for Tanis and Charina to enter into the town of McCryden undetected.

Chapter Fifteen:
Into the Thieves' Gate

Morning came quickly with little rest being had by the old couple or the younger. As the farmer led his cart away, hidden deeply within it, laid Tanis and Charina awaiting the journey to McCryden. Many times on the journey the old farmer stopped to converse, as was his way, with the farmers who lived nearby. Before reaching the gates, the farmer had gathered several other farmers following with their carts as well. Several more led the way into the town with their carts as burdened as the old man's.

As the parade of farmers approached the town's walls, two guards stepped forward and stopped all the carts. Rumor had it that a new group of fighters had formed out in the country and all vehicles coming into the town were to be searched. The old man bit off a curse as the guards approached. The guards went to the rear of the column first and the old man bent to his cart and murmured to the couple under it. "Time to make for the thieves' gate in the east wall, young ones, and the guards are looking for a group of revolutionaries that may be trying to sneak their way into town to perform mischief. Best you away now while they are still out and about."

Hearing of the new obstacle in his path Tanis repeated the old man's curse and led Charina from the old man's cart. Moving as fast as they could stealthily, they reached the wall without being seen. Moving quickly, they soon reached the small door at the east wall that was called the thieves' gate. Tanis went to it and knocked twice on the door. A young strong voice answered the knock by asking what business the pair had in McCryden. Tanis was expecting this and answered the man that he was a soldier of fortune looking for work and that his wife was accompanying him to set up house wherever he found work. The voice at the gate laughed and the door was opened and a young man stepped forth. He was taller than Tanis by a head which was tall considering Tanis was more than six feet tall. Tanis walked up to the man and he put out his hand. "Fellow traveler," began Tanis, "I hope your travels have gone as well as those of my wife and me. I am looking for a place to put down roots and was led to believe this to be the place to do that. So if you don't mind moving I will be on my way." Tanis moved to go around the man but he moved and stayed in front of him.

"So you wish to enter do you, well there is no place for the likes of you here. I will either see your back and your gold in my hand or see your blood here on this soil and have your woman for my own." The young rogue replied.

Tanis stepped back a step and eyed the rogue with his knife drawn. The thief looked at the two young lovers and his posture made him look like a man at his ease. He expected no resistance and if resistance did come he expected to be little problem dispensing the young man. Tanis reached under his cloak and placed his hand on his scabbarded sword's hilt. Taking yet another step back, he drew the serpentine blade. With the point at the thief's throat he moved toward the gate with Charina at his side. Instead of being able to enter he found more men with a variety of weapons waiting for him. Taking two steps back Charina cast a fire spell at the front line of thieves. As these fell others quickly moved toward the couple. Tanis lay about him with the practiced ease of a man used to handling the blade in his hands and had used it often. Rapidly men fell away until once more it was the tall young man who first approached them.

The man raised his hands and looked scared for his swagger. "Hold your hand, my friend. Hold. I am called Perrick Alon and I am one of the best thieves in the world. Surely you can find some use of my skills. If it does not interfere with your quest may I join your little party of two?"

Tanis lowered his blade, he was sick with the killing that had just happened and looked to the man that had caused it. He simply nodded his head and the man began a flowery speech of how he would never let them down and at the wisdom of the young lord and the beauty of his lady wife. Tanis listened with half an ear. He was entering the town and he was as focused as an archer with his bow drawn ready to fire. He was nearing his quarry and he did not want any more interference to postpone the confrontation that was to come.

Perrick spoke aloud to Tanis and Charina, "You come at a much fortuitous time for you have not only found the greatest lover in all McCryden, you have also found her best, I mean her second best, fighter. I will never let you down. I can get you in anywhere you wish to go. I am also the greatest of thieves in this or any other country and you are well served to use my skills. You will not be sorry my lord. Just you wait and see."

Tanis nearly stopped dead. "You can get us into anything or anywhere?" Tanis whispered. "Indeed, my lord," was the young thief's rapid response. "This may be both of our lucky days. You will join us and be unharmed and your skills will be a great boon to me and what I need to accomplish in this town." Tanis said. "Anything you say, my lord. Your wish is my command. You are most generous my lord." rambled Perrick.

Tanis and Charina looked at Perrick and said in unison, "Perrick, Shut up!"

CHAPTER SIXTEEN:
A NEW COMPANION

Tanis allowed himself to be led through the winding streets of the town of McCryden. Perrick proved to be a good guide and knew places in the city where they could stay until they could complete the reason for their trip. Getting to the manor house of Lord McCryden would not be a simple matter of just walking to it. It was the largest building in the town and visible even over the top of the gigantic wall surrounding the town. It was surrounded by guards who would make it difficult for even a small army to take the building. Every two paces stood another guard so it was that no matter where you looked there was a guard. Now knowing what he faced he turned to Perrick. "Good Perrick, since you are the thief, just tell me how we are to get into this great stronghold?" Perrick stood there for a moment then the twinkle once more shone in his eyes. "How good at climbing are you two?" was all that Perrick said.

As they walked several guards spotted the three traveling the streets. "Hey there!", cried the guards, "Show us your papers from the gate and do it now or it will be your bloody head as I will be presenting to our lord, Lord McCryden."

"Papers? Good sirs? What are these papers you speak of, we are new comers to the town and are taking in the sites." said Perrick. "We were never given papers back at the gate. The guards there must have forgotten to issue them to us. We will return now and get them and come right back here to you esteemed gentlemen. Well it may take a moment so just relax and we will be back before you know it."

"Wait a moment now. What did these guards at the gate look like that forgot to give you your papers? They should be put on report and I would like to know who made such a mistake. Be careful how you speak for we would not want the wrong people blamed." said the guard.

"Good Captain! I would never dream of getting one of your esteemed men into trouble over such a small matter, so please allow me to return to the gate and I will . . . ," said Perrick noticing for the first time the papers in the guard's belt. He also saw the sword in the man's hand. "Do nothing is what I will do, cannot speak for anyone else but I will do nothing. That's what I say. No trouble here, No sir, none here."

Perrick looked at Tanis and Charina standing and staring, "For the love of the Light! You two know those weapons on your hips and all that magic stuff, make with it already! Gee, do I have to spell it out for you?" At that Tanis and Charina attacked and knocked out the two guardsmen. Doing so only brought the sounds of more guardsmen on the way though, and soon they were following Perrick throughout the town until he came to a house in the red light district.

"Trust me my lord, I am well known here and they will help us. I swear it. They will hide us out until the guards have given up the hunt. They will sooner or later, given what happened about eighteen or nineteen years ago, killing all those men who did as he asked the way he did. Shameful!" commented Perrick.

"These people know you? I think we will be safer in the street with the guardsmen." laughed Tanis.

"It is to laugh isn't it? A man puts his neck on the line for you and I do not even have the courtesy of a name and now all of a sudden you attack my skills with people? You really can be a headache you know that?" said Perrick.

"Tanis and Charina Thalin" was all Charina said to Perrick. Perrick looked at Tanis and said, "So you're the bastard son are you. You have caused many a good person's death in these parts at the hands of daddy dearest up in the big house. Now I suppose it will be me now that faces the gallows or the headsman for being a fool, huh?"

Leading them to a home that Perrick rented while he was in the city, he laid out his plan. They would enter the town's sewer system and follow it to the manor house. Though not as elaborate as the roman system, it was sufficient for the task of entering the manor house. Trying to sound convincing his new found friends looked askance at Perrick. Perrick once more reviewed his plan as they walked once more around the great manor house in the middle of the town.

The plan was a simple one. Perrick would create a distraction to draw off the guards while Tanis and Charina entered the sewers of the town. They would sit in wait until Perrick arrived then they would move to the manor house where secret passages long forgotten led from the sewers into the manor house. Once inside Tanis would lead them to the Lord of the Manor, Lord McCryden himself, and then the two would fight till one no longer lived. The other would then claim the town and her soldiers for him. The plan was as simple as could be. Only problem was that Tanis was suddenly getting a sinking feeling that for some reason this was not going to be as simple as Perrick let on.

CHAPTER SEVENTEEN:
FINDING THE MAN

The time came and the three gathered near the entrance of the sewers. Perrick ran up and started speaking with the guards near the sewer grate. "Good sirs! You must help me! I am being stalked and set upon at every turn. Bandits are ramped in this town and are setting upon me for my gold and my weapons. See this dagger here. It is older than my great-grandfather and it is worth more than you or I make in a year. I would hate to lose it to these thieves. Help me please!" said Perrick.

"Sir, show us this dagger. And then show us these thieves and we will set upon them. What is your business here in any event? We will need to know that if we are to file the report. So what is your business and turn over that dagger for safe keeping." said the guard.

Perrick saw that his friends were on the move and looked at the guards. "Sirs, you wish to know my business, well it is an old profession. It may be a profession that you are familiar with perhaps? It is called thievery and I am the best of them. And as for the dagger here you go." And with that, Perrick stabbed the two guards.

Slowly Perrick led them from their posts and Tanis and Charina entered the sewer. They waited deep inside the entrance waiting for the familiar shape of Perrick to fill the entrance. Moments seemed hours before Perrick finally entered the sewers; he was wiping his heavy bladed knife off as he walked in. The rag in his hand held the signal of the house McCryden. "Was it wise to kill the guards?" asked Tanis. "They will be found missing. Then they will know something is askew and beef up the security around and inside the manor house."

Perrick listened with only half an ear. He turned to his companions and told them in a flat voice, "And how were we to hide the cut grating? How were we to hide when they inspect every ten minutes? If you want to avoid discovery, you must do what you must do. In this case it was kill the guards then hide the bodies where they will not be found for hours. That is what I have done." Tanis looked taken aback, but Charina just looked thoughtful. Maybe the violence was necessary but he did not have to like it.

Slowly he headed down into the catacombs that housed the sewer system. All around them wreaked the smells of sewage and death. Everywhere they looked rats gouged themselves on things the three young travelers would rather not know what they had once been. They moved quickly so as to make it to the manor house before the missing guards were discovered. Slowly through the dank dampness they proceeded until they approached a steel ladder built into one wall. Above was a rusted hinged door, the wood worm eaten and nearly falling in from disrepair. It was a matter of a few moments for Tanis and Perrick to remove enough of the boards for the three of them to enter the passage above. The great fence of iron that protected the ladder fell apart in their hands. The protection to the passages above long since rusted into history.

Moving into the passage first, Tanis drew the Holy Avenger, the serpentine blade glistening in the half-light provided by light coming through chinks in the walls and around hidden doors. After he started moving up into the manor house, Charina quickly followed him. Perrick came last after replacing the boards in the trapdoor so that careful inspection would not reveal them to have been removed. Slowly they climbed up into the manor, until Tanis stood before a hidden door, and listened to roaring laughter on the other side. "It would appear we have found our quarry," said Tanis.

"Watch where you are swinging that lizard sticker my lord, you have nearly severed me from my head. I am your humble servant and would like to remain so. I would rather not be among the deceased that litter these tunnels and sewers, that is if my lord does not mind," whispered Perrick.

Tanis quickly whispered his apologies and turned back to the secret door. Looking through one of the chinks in the wall he saw a man sitting in a throne like chair laughing at a little man who was about half the size of the man in the chair. The little man held a leather script of papers close to his breast and was giving the latest tax collections and the hunger and poverty seen in his village and estates.

Seeing his quarry, Tanis bent to the handle of the door and turned it with all his might and slowly grudgingly the handle gave way and the door unlocked. Tanis put his weight behind the heavy stone door and the door refused to move. Perrick seeing Tanis struggling with the heavy door bent himself to push the door as well. Slowly the door opened and the three stepped into the throne room of Lord McCryden.

Chapter Eighteen: Into the Lion's Den

Emerging into the light of the throne room Tanis blinked his eyes clear as the other two stood dumbfounded. The room was twice the size they had expected from the view through the chink. Tanis moved forward calling his friend and his wife to follow. Before him led the Holy Avenger still clasped tightly in his hands.

The lord looked up at hearing Tanis and his laughter halted. He looked down at the young party and a laugh escaped his lips. "What is this?" the lord called, "Entertainment?" At that all in the room roared with laughter. Coldly Tanis looked into the face of the one who had fathered him and told him, "Father, I am the child that you sought to destroy so many years ago. It was my mother that you raped on Beltane so many years ago. I have come to avenge her death and put an end to the tyranny you have rained on these good people!" He held his head high as he spoke these words and kept close watch on the guards who stood fingering weapons. "Any who do not wish to perish with this dictator should leave now or share his fate." Tanis said in a voice just loud enough to reach every person in that room's ears. There was sudden motion as all the minor lords and ladies of the conquered territories ran for the doors. It was obvious that though they would move to support the Lord McCryden none wished to die for him.

Standing alone with three guards before him, Lord McCryden sneered and snickered. "Lads, this boy know not whom he deals with. Let me have some fun with him before we begin tearing apart his friends and sharing out their possessions." With that he drew the great claymore that stood next to his throne in a gilded stand. Turning the blade once he charged into the attack with Tanis. Trees falling in the wind met the boar's charge through the brush met parting the silk met the heron flies met by the dragon strikes. Form after form flew from the hands, feet, and weapons of the two combatants until it turned into a match of traded blows. Both men bled from gashes made by his opponent. Slowly the younger man gained the upper hand and he stopped and heaved a breath of relief seeing the weakened Lord McCryden on all fours in the middle of the room. His guards long since had sheathed their weapons in respect for the skill of the young man that faced their sovereign lord.

Tanis stood before the man that had given him life and picked up his head so he could look into the man's eyes. Solid blue death met blue ice, the men locked eyes for just a moment and then Tanis asked "Why should I spare your life? You are the one who had asked for my death when I was no more than a babe at my mother's breast. You, who had raped my mother on that Beltane night and disgraced her before everyone in this village; the one who killed her to cover your own crimes. You have earned death more than once, yet I am not without mercy. Ask for your life and I will grant it. Death is too good for you!" The lord begged for his life and Tanis turned from him and walked toward his now waiting friends. As he approached Perrick, Perrick drew a blade and threw it toward Tanis. Tanis dived to the floor and growled his hate and disgust at Perrick until he looked where Perrick pointed. Tanis saw his father dead with Perrick's knife in his throat. In his hand he held another dagger that he had been meant for Tanis. Perrick had saved his life and he had charged him falsely. Taking Perrick's hand Tanis begged forgiveness. Instead of acknowledging his friend's pleas he called out in a loud voice to all that had gathered to see the fight, "All Hail, The new Lord of McCryden, Tanis Thalin." At that he kneeled before his friend and gave the amazed Tanis his oath of loyalty. After Perrick came the conquered lords and ladies and the local merchants all swearing before the new ruler of their lands.

Chapter Nineteen: A New Beginning

In the months that passed after the fall of Lord McCryden, Tanis worked hard at being the ruler of the little town. He saw an end to the hard taxes that stripped farmers of all they owned and left them to starve. He saw that the guilds finally plied their individual trades with all the fervor they had under the old lord. He even established schools for men and children alike to learn the trades of the town as well as weapons and magic. All seemed right with the world until one day a man in a bright white robe of the ancients appeared in the manor house, escorted by a half dozen of the guard.

The captain of the guards brought the man to kneel before his throne and Tanis rose. "Let him up Captain," Tanis began, "Be welcome to my home, now please tell me what brings you here and under such conditions." The ancient stood there and looked at him. The man slowly looked up and looked at the man before him. "Tanis, do you not recognize your boyhood friend. It was I who aided your mother before your birth. It was I who tutored you as you grew. Do you not recognize me?"

Looking at the man, Tanis did not recognize the youth standing before him. "I think you may have made an error, sir. I was tutored by a dwarf and you sir are not of that noble race. Are you sure you seek Tanis Thalin?" The man simply nodded yes. "Remember I once told you that one with the power can alter his appearance. Let me see if this helps you remember me." The young man's form seemed to bend and twist until before him stood Artitous, the dwarf. Tanis looked puzzled. "If you are indeed Artitous, then why the disguise? If you are that wizened dwarf, then why come to me as an Ancient and a half Elf?"

Artitous just looked at Tanis and said, "I appeared as a dwarf in your youth so that you would have one your own size to relate to, and now that you are grown I appear to you as I truly am so that your studies can continue unchecked. I come now to continue the education you started lad and I am once more to continue as your tutor." Tanis raised his eyebrow again. He was puzzled by the apparition before him. The dwarf had plunged to his death the day he was married out on the mountain. Yet now here he was as a different person. He was a half Elf. Where the Ancients given grown bodies for a new life? He turned back to the half Elf. "How did you survive that plummet into the mountain on my wedding day? I have thought until this very minute that you had died in that fall. Speak man tell me your tale of what occurred that you now stand before me when you should be all but a corpse."

Artitous looked at the man sitting before him. "The magic that you have not touched since my supposed demise is what saved my life. The shield of air that I taught you to weave is what has kept me alive these many days until I could climb from the mountain. But now I have returned and am ready to resume my place as your bard and advisor… if you will have me that." As the bard finished speaking Charina swept into the room. Excitement painted her face as she rushed to her husband and embraced him. She stared into his face and her smile near split her beautiful face in two.

"The Druids have just checked me over my heart. The news is good. My stomach upset is not some disease. It is the birthing sickness. I am to have a child! Your child." Tanis beamed from his wife to his old tutor and then back to his wife. "I hope it is my child, I have not noticed you having another husband around here and I do not believe you would look elsewhere for attention." Tanis said in between laughs. Charina laughed just as loudly as she once more embraced Tanis. This time Tanis embraced her ever so lightly, laughing about not hurting the child.

Charina just held him longer until she noticed the half Elf in front of them. "Hello Artitous, you have finally revealed your true form to us.

I wondered when you would feel we were ready to know the real you." Tanis gaped at his wife. "You knew that Artitous was using a false form and you did not tell me?" Tanis asked. "Of course I did. Did you not know that an Elf can see the magic used by others as if they had made the spell themselves? He did not hide his spell well enough for me not to see it but maybe to your human eyes it was enough."

All Tanis could do was gape as he stared at both the laughing Artitous and Charina. They had both known all along and said nothing. He felt like a horse had kicked his head. No matter how he attempted to clear it, he still was befuddled and confused. The two people he trusted most just continued to discuss the making of the spell and how it could be used to help Tanis in his ruling the town of McCryden. But no matter how much they explained how the disguise was made, he could not understand why they had used it on him. There had to be something there that he did not know there had to be

The time of Charina carrying her child came to a close as it should and she bore Tanis a fine son with powerful lungs and a mighty grip. The child seemed to be an ointment to soothe Tanis after the affairs of his town got the better of his temper. As an infant he relished the time he had to play with his child and as the child grew Tanis taught him both the arts of magic and weapons. The sessions, he taught as games for his young son. It was as good as life got for Tanis and his young son, Paul, and it seemed that life could not get any better.

CHAPTER TWENTY:
TRAGEDY STRIKES

Paradise was not to last for Tanis though. As the child reached his ninth year of life, the family decided to have a family outing in the fields surrounding the town. Charina was take the child out to the field and Tanis would follow with Paul's present. Tanis was supposed to get a surprise of his own at this outing and Tanis could not figure what it could be.

Paul and his mother left the home early surrounded by members of the warrior class assigned to be their bodyguard. In his hands as he hugged his daddy good bye was a wooden blade that Tanis had made him. The small party left and Tanis went to check on his steward to see that all was well before he left to join his family. The steward and Tanis spoke at length on his orders and it was almost noon before Tanis gathered his horse and the new pony for Paul that was to be the boy's birthday present.

As Tanis began his journey, he hummed quietly watching the beauty of the surrounding wood. A bird leaped into the air startled by something but Tanis ignored it. He figured that an animal was hunting and had just missed its meal. As he neared the field Tanis spied a tree with weird looking fruit dangling from it. He was not sure exactly what he was seeing, so he went to examine the unusual tree. A few minutes more would not be amiss when they would have the rest of the day together.

When he made it to the tree, Tanis nearly fell from the saddle. What he had thought to be fruit was in fact the heads of the party that had left McCryden that morning. Amongst the heads of the warriors, also hung the heads of his family. At seeing his wife and child, Tanis leaned against the tree and noisily lost his morning meal. Who would destroy the party of a woman and her child? Tanis rapidly moved to the field where his family should have been. The grisly site before him was worse than the tree had been. Bodies littered the field and only some of them were missing their heads. Tanis searched amongst the bodies looking for clues as to who would have done this unspeakable thing.

Tanis searched for hours amongst the bodies, until in the body of his son he found a spear with a note attached to it. The note read:

Greetings from the Lord of Death, the Dark Knight of Argos.

I have laid waste to your family as you have probably noticed. I am going to tell you once come to me ready to die, and I will let you join your family quickly. Otherwise, you will wish for their fate. I await your arrival.

The letter bore no signature. It needed none. Tanis now knew who and what had committed this atrocity. Tanis took into his head the thought of revenge and of destroying the dark knight. The feelings he had when he had faced his father revisited him as he galloped his horse from that bloodied field and sought his captain of the guard, Perrick.

He found Perrick in the main hall with Artitous. They were debating the best way to defend the castle in the event of a magical attack. Tanis cut their discourse like a knife when they saw his pained face. Perrick placed his hand on Tanis's shoulder and Tanis grasped it and nearly broke his arm except for the flows of magic solidifying the air around his arm. Tanis let out a howl and plopped down into his chair. His arm still supported by the column of air holding it, Tanis took on an almost humorous stance. Artitous released Tanis's arm and the man began to cry. His weeping drew the eyes of all who had gathered to him after his conquest of McCryden.

Through his tears Tanis related the story of what had happened in the field where the party was supposed to be and how he had found the tree with the heads mounted upon it. He also showed Artitous the letter from the dark knight. Artitous studied the letter and then handed it to Perrick. Artitous's face took on a look of hatred Tanis had never seen before. Perrick's face was quickly painted with the same fury.

Artitous took a deep breath and looked at his old student. "Tanis, this is the beginning of a prophecy that began to be fulfilled with your birth. You are the Phoenix. The one destined to rule all of Dracos. The problem is that none, not even you know whose side of the fight you are going to take - that of the good and the Light or that of evil and the Dark. I could not tell you before but now circumstances have made it impossible for me to keep it from you anymore. It is destiny that you must face the great Magus, warlocks, and warlords. The time has come for you to face destiny. I pray that this event will not tarnish your spirit. You have made an excellent start of things and I wish that you will continue to be fair and just."

"Just because of the actions of one man you believe that I will turn into the tyrant that my father had been? I am disappointed in your faith in me, Artitous. What of you Perrick? Do you also believe that I am going to be unable to continue my rule in a fair and just manner?" asked Tanis.

"My Lord, I have not now nor will I ever doubt your abilities. I fear for your well-being in as much as you may not take as much caution due to circumstances. I fear you may inadvertently harm yourself, not that you may harm others." said Perrick. "Besides my Lord, no one could rule as you do. And I would not like to have to train another to take your place."

At that quip by Perrick all three men laughed briefly and started to discuss the problem at hand. The Dark Knight had issued his challenge. The decision now was how to prepare and who to ask for assistance if Tanis truly sought to attack the realm of the man who ordered his family killed. It was guessed that the Elves would come as soon as they heard of the great misfortune that had befallen Tanis. His adoptive father would come to aid him in this battle. Tanis was sure of it. Tanis asked Artitous whether or not they could depend on the aid of the Dwarves when the time came.

"My Lord Thalin, I cannot tell you if the Dwarves will answer your request. The only thing that we can do is ask to them to see if they respond. The Dark Knight is not one to be taken lightly and he already rules a large portion of the dwarven lands. He may use his control of some of the Dwarves to coerce the cooperation of the others against you. Only time will answer these questions. I recommend that we send envoys to both the Elven and the dwarven kingdoms and see what response is given." answered Artitous.

"Perrick! Send out our fastest riders to the Elves and to the Dwarves. I hope the news they bring is good for I fear we will need many new soldiers before this is over." cried Tanis.

"It is already done my lord. I figured that was what you would want and made the arrangements. I hope that this is alright with you, or have I once again overstepped my bounds?" replied Perrick.

"Once again you have shown yourself loyal and foresighted in the face of unpleasant events, my friend. You have called me your lord since the day I met you and I still do not understand it. I have never required it of you. You are my friend and wish you to behave as such. As for your foresight in this manner it is very much appreciated as always. I must learn to cope with unpleasant events it appears. Gentleman, please leave me to my thoughts. I have preparations to make for my family. Excuse me please." said Tanis as he walked from the room.

Tanis stood and left the throne room bound for the apartments that he and his wife had shared. He moved mechanically through the halls not even noticing the servants and soldiers that acted as his bodyguard as they passed in the hall. Tanis stopped before the door and looked upon its carved surface. The door was covered with designs but was dominated by a large Phoenix battling the robed figure of the Dark Harvester. He had never really looked at the door, being consumed with his wife. The detail of the door amazed all who saw it. *My wife had a great eye for detail. She was the one who commissioned this door. Not a line or stone out of place,* Tanis thought as he ran his fingers through the carving and touched the stones.

"Remind me to have this door replaced, Perrick." said Tanis without looking up. "I felt you follow. Do you have something you wish to tell me? I have asked that you please leave me to my thoughts for now my friend. Please do so."

"I think it is appropriate Tanis. I do have something I need to say to you. You are allowed to grieve for them. You are human! Feel for once in your life. You loved them so much and now you act as if their loss means nothing. Are you trying to be a monster? Are you trying to make the world think you are stronger than you are? No one doubts your strength. No one doubts your loyalty to your people. Everyone expects you to grieve the loss of your child and your wife. Everyone expects you to be angry. Everyone expects you to be sad. You are what you are, but you are also a man who is lost and confused from the loss of those closest to you. When you arrived Charina was to give you a great surprise. Well, now I will give it to you. She had seen her mother again. She had come into the village about a week ago. She had told Charina that she wished to be forgiven for her actions on your wedding day. Charina forgave her and was so relieved that she could finally speak to her and find out what had caused this. Everyone thought the woman had died that day. Well, Artitous survived and somehow so did your mother-in-law. Charina found out something the day after she saw her mother. Charina was to have another child. She was pregnant again. The seer had told her she would never see the birth of your second child. We all knew when she swore us to secrecy that this was the end for her. She was going to tell you at the party for your son and bring out her mother to ask your forgiveness. You never mentioned finding the body of an old woman, did you? You did find the body of the old woman didn't you? Tanis?" said Perrick.

Perrick looked to the door to find Tanis on his knees crying into his hands. Slowly Perrick walked to him and placed his hands on Tanis's shoulders as the sobs racked his body. "Come my friend, into your chambers and rest for now." said Perrick.

Tanis looked up into Perrick's face, "How can I rest? How will I ever rest again? My wife and children are gone! I have nothing left in this world. I have nothing left to live for. As to your question, no sir, I found no old woman amongst the corpses of that field, just the guard,

Charina's ladies, and Paul. No one else. No children and no elderly. Leave me now so I may lie in my bed and wait for death take me as well."

Perrick laughed at his friend, "Tanis, you are human after all. Grieve for a while then come see to the preparations to end the monster that caused this pain in you. Remember what it was that is said over our fallen heroes: 'Remember me in laughter for that is how I remember you all. If you can remember me only with sadness and tears, then do not remember me at all.' Your family was heroes. Every last one of them, because you loved them, and they inspired you. They will always be remembered for that. Do not let them have died in vain. Grieve their loss and avenge their passing. Make them not victims, make them martyrs!"

Tanis stood and looked into his friend's eyes. "My family lay dead. You encourage me to grieve. Today I will grieve. Tomorrow, I start the plans to finally end the reign of terror that is being inflicted upon our world. It is over! Perrick! Find my mother-in-law."

"Yes sir! See you in the morning my Lord!" laughed Perrick as he ran for the end of the hall. "And Perrick," cried Tanis after his retreating friend, "don't call me Lord!"

At that Tanis entered his rooms. Seeing the belongings of his wife and child everywhere, Tanis once again fell to his knees and wept. After some time, grief-stricken and weeping, Tanis finally fell into a fitful slumber and slept well into the next day. His sleep troubled by dreams of his family's faces flashing before his eyes accusing him of their deaths. Again and again the images flashed before his eyes before he finally awoke in a cold sweat.

Chapter Twenty One:
Return to Normality

Tanis emerged into the dining hall as the noon meal was being cleared from the tables. Perrick went immediately to the kitchens and ordered a double portion for the lord of the realm. Artitous went to Tanis and Tanis assured him that only nightmares spoiled his rest and those of his own mind's creation. "If you worked so hard in getting me my responses as you do in mothering me, than we march for war tomorrow with ten thousands at my back. Is there any response?" asked Tanis. Perrick came in the tray and sat Tanis down for his meal.

"The news from the Elves was as we expected. They will come when you call. I wish I could say as much for the Dwarves. Our rider has not returned as yet and the land of the Dwarves is closer than that of the Elves. I have taken the liberty of sending out a patrol to find out what has happened to our messenger. The Dark Knight has been tracked by magical means to lands three weeks south of here. His rule extends to the edge of your southern border and has taken up residence in the border town of Tallic Parc. This town as it turns out is mostly dwarven. I fear the worst. Either they have aligned with the dark night or they have been conquered. Either way we can expect little help from them and expect to see them supporting our enemies." rambled Artitous. "I miss them as well my young pupil. May I share a secret with you Tanis? Well no, not now. It may not be appropriate for you to learn this now. Not after everything else we have been through. Definitely not, we have to do."

"Artitous. It is too late to keep it hidden now old friend. Out with it. You know that I can handle anything. It just takes time when the wound is deep as it is now. I know that I will cry myself to sleep many a night before the pain eases. It will never heal, but maybe I can go on." said Tanis.

"Always in a rush to learn what you do not need to know. I will reveal my secret when the time is right. Not a moment before. By the way, Perrick has had no luck in locating your now missing mother-in-law. She appears to have vanished as mysteriously as she arrived. Though some of the guards seem to think she may have headed south two days ago. Others say she left yesterday night late in the evening. Still others seem to think she is still in town reporting having seen her this very day around the market. Which story is correct? I have no way of telling. I have not been able to trace her since I found out that she still lived. I would have sworn I saw her perish in that lava flow. Well, I will ponder more on this. Worry only about figuring how we approach this town three days march to the south. The Dark Knight may flee farther back into his kingdom and we may have to march the entire three weeks to his capital. Well you two figure that out. I must finish figuring out how this woman hides herself so well." said Artitous.

At that Artitous walked from the room and headed to his rooms high in the tower. His mind was heavy with thought. He was sure that day so many years ago that the wife of the Elven smith had died. He had seen her fall. He had seen her heading toward the river of fire. He saw her die. This was impossible to comprehend. He had seen her die. There was no return from death unless... His thoughts were quickly silenced as he felt the blow to the back of his head. The last thing he remembered as the blackness took him was the laughing face of Tanis's mother-in-law.

CHAPTER TWENTY TWO: PLANS FOR WAR

Tanis nibbled at the food Perrick brought him. His appetite had not quite returned yet. Tanis asked for maps of the region to the south, all the way to the Dark Knight's capital. He also wanted maps of the major cities between McCryden and the Dark Knight's home. Tallic Parc was the first map he wanted before him. It was time for serious thought and important strategy. They were to try to save as many people as possible. No unnecessary deaths in this campaign. No one should have to face the loss he had unless it was absolutely necessary. No one died unless it was unavoidable. Some will die Tanis realized, but the losses on both sides could be kept to a minimum. He knew deep down that the fighting would end with the destruction of the Dark Knight. The people would not fight on if the leader was removed. As soon as the knight died so too would the battle.

The maps were brought in and Tanis poured over them. The town was a fortress. It looked about the size and shape of McCryden but the walls were after every few blocks. This would be hard nut to crack, no matter how hard they tried. The best bet to preserve as many of the citizens and warriors as possible would be to get them onto the field before the city. Perrick noticed the lack of any hidden tunnels or sewers. There would be no sneaking into the city as they had so many years ago when they took McCryden.

Tanis felt that the knight would believe him an easy victory and another notch in his scabbard. The Dark Knight would meet him on the field. He was sure of it. The man would not run. Tanis was an untested general and the Dark Knight was the greatest of the world's generals. It would be no contest between the two. The knight's cocksureness may be the very tool that would bring the man down. Tanis could only hope.

They were planning for the possibility that the Knight would run when the rider sent to the Dwarves arrived in the dining hall turned war room. "My Lord," the rider began, "the news I bear is poor. The Dwarves are under the rule of the Dark Knight and cannot openly assist us. They will be pressed by the Knight into service in the battle if you were to pursue it and they cannot go against him. He has threatened to destroy their homes and families if they do not stand with him."

"I have grave news, young friend. It will not be well to face our friends across a field of battle. I hope they are smart enough to think that they must appear but it does not mean they are to fight as well as they can.", said Perrick.

Tanis grinned and sent the messenger back to the Dwarves with this message.

Dear Friends,

In the coming battle, if we find ourselves pitted against each other I ask you only one thing. If fight you must, then fight badly.

Your Friend. Tanis Thalin

A few hours after the message was sent, Artitous came into the room, his head wrapped in a bandage. He looked at Tanis who was about to ask what had happened and all he said was, "I found your mother-in-law."

Chapter Twenty Three:
Step Off

Tanis, Artitous, and Perrick continued for several days to prepare for their attack on the Dark Knight. Many a night was spent pouring over maps and plans of buildings by the three friends. It was three days after Tanis sent the message to the Dwarves that the messenger returned with the reply. It was a simple reply. "We'll see" was all that was written on the paper given to Tanis. Tanis handed it around the table and the all those gathered there laughed with the joke that Tanis had started.

It would be another three days before Tanis prepared his pack to leave for the campaign. As he packed horns sounded outside the manor. Tanis ran to the walls concerned that the Dark Knight had brought the battle to him instead of Tanis bringing it to the knight. Tanis looked out at the coming army and gaped at its order and size. Quickly ordering the defense to prepare, Tanis ran down and donned his armor and weapon. Out the gates Tanis rode to meet the enemy as he approached.

Halfway to the approaching army Tanis drew reign. Standing on his saddle, Tanis suddenly realized what the troops on the battlements were trying to tell him. The approaching army was in fact that of his neighbor and friend to the north, Lord Nargus. Nargus rode up to Tanis and quipped, "Gee sir, if I had known that I was going to be met by the Lord of the manor himself I would have dressed up."

Tanis and Nargus laughed as they rode into McCryden. Nargus's army would camp outside and prepare for the move out in the next couple of days. Lord Nargus would spend those days as a guest of Tanis inside the manor house. As Tanis once more began to prepare for the journey the horns sounded again. Once more Tanis donned his armor and ran for the stables. Riding out into the surrounding field, Tanis called for all those that could follow to do so and be prepared to fight. Several thousand horsemen rode onto the field and the leader called a halt. Slowly Tanis approached the leader with sword drawn and head held high ready to defend his home and people. The leader stood in his stirrups and called out to Tanis, "Sir! Lay down your sword and take me to your Lord. We come to aid him in his quest. Tell him that Lord Feragett has come and demands entry to the manor and space for his men to bed down."

"Sir!" yelled Tanis, "I would take you to the lord of this place but there is one small problem here. You see, I am the Lord of this manor and I would be happy to answer a request for housing. Your men may stay here with these pike men of Lord Nargus who arrived just a few hours earlier. You sir, I will welcome into my home and have you as my guest until the end of this great campaign."

"Quit your fooling man and bring me to the Lord of this place. I grow weary of this waiting game and my men need a roof to rest under, not pike men to keep them company. Mixing foot and horse is never a good idea and a true Lord would know that. So bring me to your lord and quit this foolishness." said Lord Feragett.

"I assure you sir that there is no foolery going on here. I am Lord Tanis Thalin and I am the Lord of this manor. If you have come to assist me in my campaign then you are welcome to my manor and your men here can set camp here amongst the rest of those camped here. I have no place left for them inside the town." replied Tanis.

"I will believe you for now sir. But if I find that you have deceived me, I will see you dead upon my sword." said Lord Feragett.

At that Tanis turned and led Lord Feragett to the manor house. They had barely gained the courtyard when again the horns sounded and Tanis rushed to the field. The sight that met him this time was well welcome and anticipated. The Elven army approached with his own adoptive father at the head. Ten thousand archers stood in straight columns awaiting the word of their King to start assembling camp.

Well-disciplined and rigid, the Elves waited as the King brought Tanis down each rank. Tanis again invited the King in and allowed the Elves to mingle with the horsemen and pike men already on the fields surrounding the small town.

Tanis held his father close as they entered the dining area and wept once more into his father's armor. He kept crying until the Elven King started humming his magic into the ears and mind of Tanis. The magic made Tanis feel less of the pain and less of the anguish that he had felt for the last few days since the loss of his wife and child. He was finally able to once again, for at least a moment, resume with some semblance of the control he had once had. Looking into the eyes of his father Tanis shuddered and knelt at the Elf King's feet.

"Stand man. You are not subject to me nor am I subject to you. No one needs to kneel before another. I have given you back what you lost with your family. We need you at your best my son, not crying for those of us that have passed into the greater existence beyond death. You are still here and your family now watches us from that great land we all wish to obtain. They would not want you to waste away because they have passed on." said the King of the Elves.

"I would not want to think that they were lost forever. They are the cause of this war and they are my reason for destroying those who oppress and destroy for the thrill of it. I want to hurt, father. I want to be grieving. I want to see to it that no one ever suffers the loss that I have suffered ever again." replied Tanis. "Please put me back the way I was."

CHAPTER TWENTY FOUR: ON THE MARCH

After what seemed like forever Tanis and his new found army left for the realm of the Dark Knight. Lord Feragett, Lord Nargus, King Toirin, and Lord Tanis Thalin rode before the column of troops led by Perrick and Artitous, as well as the head retainers of the other three lords. Perrick and Artitous insisted that they ride back with the other lieutenants of the army so as to not appear to be rising above themselves in their peers' eyes. Slowly the column moved to the south. It was reported early on that the army had someone following them. Scouts had been unable to identify the person or group following but every last one of the scouts had seen something following alongside.

King Toirin fell back several times stating that he felt something out of the ordinary. Yet even the Elven King came back with no answers. All he would say is that there was some force at work that he could not identify. Tanis fell back several times looking for any sign left by a follower and always came back empty handed.

At sunset the army made camp and Tanis ordered a larger than normal watch to be posted around the camp. They would not take any chances with security. Lord Nargus was nowhere to be seen as the camp was erected. Well after the fires were lit and the meal was prepared and just about finished, he reappeared. Tanis walked to him and said, "Lord Nargus! Where have you been? We waited for a long while for you before we ate. We finally ate before it grew too cold to eat. Have you eaten? I will order a meal prepared for you if you have not. King

Toirin went to eat with his troops. He said he would return before too late to enjoy a pipe and some ale I had brought for the three of us. He wishes to speak of the coming battle and how we plan to stage it. I had some ideas for it and would speak of them tonight."

"Lord Tanis," said Nargus, "I would love to hear your strategy this evening. Give me time to wash the dust of the road from me and I will speak to you as soon as I am done. I have eaten so do not trouble yourself with preparing anything for me. I will see you all in a few minutes."

Tanis returned to Feragett and sat beside him. Tanis said nothing and just stared into the flames of the campfire. He even missed Feragett trying to give him a tankard of ale and a pipe. Startled, Tanis jumped to his feet and thanked Feragett for the drink and pipe and apologized for his inattention. Before long the two were laughing and rubbing elbows when the Elven King, Toirin, came to the fire. The Elven King looked pale and disturbed as he took his seat.

"Father, what is wrong? I have never seen you so shaken. Please lighten your load on our shoulders. What has happened?" asked Tanis.

"I was going to tell you that your father-in-law had joined our company. It was meant to be a surprise for you my son. Well it has been reported that he was found dead in the forest slightly after we had finished setting up camp. After a thorough search we found about twenty dead Elves, and nearly double that in men were found. They were all killed by daggers and killed in a manner that did not allow for any of them to call for help. I have many Elven trackers searching for clues as to the killer's identity, but in this I think we have a lost cause until the killer or killers reveal themselves." said Toirin.

"Father, do not look so lost. The Elves will find our killer or the dragon will. If he does not then the men will. One way or the other, we will have our killer. Now sit and enjoy a pipe and ale. Relax your mind and rest." said Tanis. It was here that Lord Nargus returned to Tanis's campfire.

"I hope I have not missed much," said Nargus as he approached the somber gathering. Looking around Nargus dropped his eyes. "Obviously I have. Someone please inform me of what has happened so that I may share in your despair. Has our coming been detected?

I had hoped it would not. I have brought word that our ranks have swollen as we passed to the realm of the Dark Knight. Local lords are flocking to your banner, Lord Thalin. Though this does not look the time for rejoicing."

"Many of our troops were slain this night. About sixty. The Elves and the riders search for clues to the murderer or murderers. They will be found but still it pains me to see so many lost in the hours before the battle begins. There is a traitor amongst us and that traitor must be rooted out." replied Tanis as he lit the pipe in his hand. "Nargus, sit and have an ale. It is a fine draft and it would be a shame if it were to go to waste on the likes of these poor sorts that surround this fire!" laughed Tanis, "Besides, you know it will be impossible to live with the Elf if we let him out drink us. We really must catch up for I believe he has already had his third cup and we have not even started our first."

"How could I refuse an offer put in such a manner," said Nargus and the whole company around the fire burst into laughter that lasted deep into the night.

CHAPTER TWENTY FIVE: MURDER!

The next morning brought more poor news. Several other troops had been found killed as well as a number of the local lords who had joined the army. The lords though had been set upon by the horse of Lord Feragett. The leader of the patrol had overheard them speaking of the bounty they would collect for the betrayal of the army moving south to the border.

"Tallic Parc prepares now for a war to end all wars. The Dark Knight has called in all of his forces from around his realm and asked that all his vassals bring in all their troops as well lest he be forced to march on them when he is through with us. We have learned that the Dwarves have been moved into a position to attack our right flank as the battle begins and that he has his own dragon prepared to attack on our left. My lords it is not too late to call this off. We are still hopelessly outnumbered and now surprise is no longer ours. I am afraid and so are the men." said the patrol's leader.

"I will address you all as we move onto the plain just after noon. I need time now to collect my thoughts if we are to continue. I need a moment my friends and father." said Tanis to all those gathered around him.

With that Tanis moved away from the rest and sat upon a log and appeared lost in thought for many a moment. After what seemed an eternity to those awaiting his word, Tanis stood and did as he often did when he was troubled. He went to speak to the dragon.

"Old one!" cried Tanis to the dragon. AI need your counsel, please, lean down your ear so we may speak." The dragon leaned down to the young man and the Elven King and other nobles of the lands suddenly found themselves unable to hear the conversation between the two.

"That is a fine how do you do," said Nargus, "He hides behind a wall of magic to keep us from eavesdropping and what does it do? Prevents us from listening in too! Some things are just too rude."

The small group laughed quietly and failed to hear the approach of Tanis and the dragon, which at that precise moment choose to release a booming laugh that stopped all conversation and laughter as he leapt into the air and flew away to the south. In the stillness Tanis climbed to the top of a small boulder that littered the roadway that the army passed upon.

"My faithful friends and troops. You have come far to fight a battle with evil and a great deal is being asked of you. You go now into a battle many of you feel is a lost cause. If this is your true feeling, then leave. Open a path to those who choose to leave for home. I apologize but we will have to retain you armor, weapons and horses for the coming battle though. There is no disgrace at leaving. If you will leave, leave now. Once this begins any who try to leave will be struck down for cowardice. None will look less on you for your decision.

To those of you who stay to fight, do not taunt or hinder those who leave us. They are our brothers and they have their own priorities. We march into a battle and war that may very well be our last. There will be neither any quarter given nor any received. I will not lie to you, many of us will not return from this battle. Many of us who do return will be too injured to ever return to what we were before this battle began. But know this; whether you stay or go, you are a hero already. Just for coming this far you are heroes. It will be as an army of heroes that march on our enemy, not an army of men. This is the advantage we show to our enemy. So prepare and make your choice, the avenue home or the avenue to war. The final leg of the march begins now and I for one will march to war."

At that Tanis climbed from the rock and began preparing for the last leg of the march. Picking up his own belongings and packing them was one of the few chores Tanis preferred to perform for himself. It made sure he could still fit into his helmet he said to all who would ask why he would choose to do such labor when so many would do it for him willingly.

Picking some dirty stockings from the ground and shoving them into his bag he noticed the small trail of blood trickling under the tent. Dropping the bag, Tanis ran around the tent to find the source of the small puddle of blood that had stained his tent. On the ground near the tent he found the source of the stain. A dagger lay discarded amongst the twigs and dirt that had been moved when his tent was erected. On the handle, the mark of Lord Nargus stared back at him. The blade was covered in blood.

Tanis scooped the blade from the ground and ran to the other leaders gathered awaiting their servants to complete folding the tents and packing their gear. The others saw Tanis running toward them and waved in anticipation of the young man joining them. Tanis ran to Nargus and dragged him off to the side leaving the others dazed and confused. "Where were you last night before you joined the rest of us at the fire?" demanded Tanis. "Tell me where you were and how I came by this dagger wet with blood and I will spare you."

Nargus looked at the dagger and looked confused. "Lord Tanis, This is not my dagger, but a well-made fake. Here, look to the mark. All my daggers are made by the same dwarven smith. This is not his mark. Only the Dwarves could make a piece of beauty out of so much gaud and gold. Also this piece is a front balance dagger. I use only the rear balanced type of daggers because I am no knife fighter. I use it solely as a tool, not a weapon. I assure you sire, this is not my dagger, nor has it ever been my dagger. I would look to another who knows my daggers well to find your murderer. This piece misses the part of the crest that is my own. See. My dagger has my initials engraved under the crest. This has only the crest. The initials are missing. I will swear under any oath that you choose that the knife in your hand does not belong to me. I will also obey whatever edict that you choose to pass on me. I will accept it, but I assure you I have had nothing to do with the deaths of last night or this morning."

"What deaths this morning?" Tanis asked, "How do you know of deaths that no one else knows of and I find your dagger near my tent. You must be the one who has performed these killings. Tell me now why I should not mingle your blood on this blade with those valiant men you have sent to their graves. Tell me why I should not kill you now!"

"My lord, do as you wish but I know of the deaths of several dozen more of our troops only because a patrol of Elves reported them a few moments before you burst from the tent. I was with Toirin this morning since the fire broke last night. I could not sleep and spent the night with the Elf. He seems to not need sleep." replied Nargus.

Dragging Nargus to the others Tanis threw him into the dirt and asked his father, "Was he with you last night father? The entire night?"

"Allow me to help you to your feet, Nargus. My son has forgotten the manners I taught him as a youth. Tanis, he was indeed with me. What is the meaning of this?" demanded King Toirin. "Have you completely lost all grasp of your senses?"

Tanis slumped to the ground beside his father looking abashed into the flames of the fire. Events of the past few days where beginning to weigh upon him. If things continued as they were, there would be no army to continue with. "Lord Nargus, please accept my sincere apologies. My mind has been troubled by the recent attacks that have occurred along our path. Finding your dagger at the scene of the latest crime made me jump to conclusions that I should not have. Please allow me to return your blade to you." Tanis stood up and handed the ornate piece to Lord Nargus and returned to his seat around the fire. Lord Nargus turned the jewel encrusted dagger round in his hand and looked at it. Nargus rose from his seat and tossed the blood soaked dagger into the fire and watched as the false gold and gems popped and melted into ruin.

"If only it was as easy to remove the problems of our world as it is to destroy one instrument of the pain that rules our world," said Nargus as they sat and watched the remaining pieces of the murder weapon destroy itself.

"Prepare to march!" screamed Tanis as he lifted his pack and moved toward the empty field that would be the scene of the coming battle. Looking back along the path of those who would leave showed that none chose the easy road. They would all move forward together.

CHAPTER TWENTY SIX:
THE FIGHTING STARTS

The army of Tanis Thalin moved out onto the field and stood staring at the great city laid out before it. The sight of the turrets on its walls touching the sky caused a sense of awe even the Elves felt. The great stone blocks of the wall shone with the rising sun as the men and women warriors marched onto the field. Tanis was dumbstruck as he walked to the front of his army and joined his foster father and closest friends.

"Father, what have I led these men to? I fear the worst for us all." said Tanis to his companions. "I should have thought with my head instead of my heart. Now all of these good men and all of us will lie dead on that field. The Dwarves will not respond. We stand alone against the power that created that."

Toirin looked down at his foundling son and smiled. "My child, you have learned the last great lesson of battle. You are now looking at what you think is undefeatable odds. But do not fear my child. The day is always darkest before we begin. I will tell you this, the surprises this day will not be yours, but of your enemy. Lead your people into battle with confidence in your victory. Let them see you proud and unafraid as we begin this day. For this day will be yours my son. Do not show your people fear or that is what they will take into their hearts. Show courage and strength and that are what they will take. Give your soldiers the strength that they will need this day. Do your part and allow me to handle the details!" screamed the Elven King.

"Father. You are right and this is not hopeless, I think. I will take the field today and the Dark Knight will fall at my hand! Men draw arms and follow me to Glory or death!" screamed Tanis. All around him men started screaming out replies and making ready for battle, lining themselves for the coming battle.

The troops of Tanis Thalin moved slowly toward the walls looking in trepidation as the wall loomed high above them. As they grew closer to the walls, the enemy's troops began to emerge from secreted tunnels under the walls. Rapidly, Thalin's troops sat outnumbered upon the field and even the Elven King looked concerned. Suddenly, a loud sound pierced the air and from the wall emerged the Dark Knight with his dwarven escort. "So you challenge me? You child? You think to bring down the most deadly of the Dread Lords? My, have the Druids run out of want to be heroes so now they recruit children? Men make this quick so I can enjoy my now disturbed lunch."

"Order the archers to draw arrow but not to loose." whispered the Elven king, "then prepare the long arms for a charge. Hold them all in place but do not fire or move. I will tell you the proper moment."

"I will make it so Father; our lives are now in your hands. Archers! Draw arrow and hold! Long Arms! Prepare the charge! Hold until you are ordered to move!" screamed Tanis to his troops.

The enemy moved closer and closer and soon the commanders of the archers and the long arms men were looking to him for orders and were told to continue to hold. Soon the leaders of his men plead for the orders which would allow the men to move against the ever advancing enemy. "My Lord Tanis, the enemy is within easy bowshot now. Why will you not allow us to fire? Soon the enemy will be right on our doorstep. They are within 500 meters my lord. Please give the word. We will let loose and at least give ourselves a fighting chance." said the commander of the archers.

"They have moved to within 400 meters!" shouted a man from the rear of the army as more enemy troops advanced from behind Tanis's troops. "Be still and hold your drawn arrows. Fire when I say and no sooner." said Tanis. "Let them know what courage is."

But a few moments later again the commander of his archers came and pleaded with Tanis, "My lord, they are within 300 meters. We could practically pick them off with our slings. Please give the order and boost our men's spirits." Tanis simply responded, "I will give word when it is time. Stay with your men and trouble me not again."

When the man left, Tanis looked to his foster father and whispered, "Father they are within 250 meters I dare not wait much longer. When should I give the word?"

Toirin whispered back, "Laugh as if I have made the greatest of jokes then look startled at having laughed. This will give the men courage. You are unafraid then why should they? When they reach 200 meters give the word that the archers should fire only on those before us. Your surprise that I promised comes soon."

Tanis laughed as loud as his lungs could be forced and himself to appear for the world at his ease though he still felt like his insides would twist and break apart. Tanis suddenly felt a strange relief pour over him as he laughed and found he wished to continue. As he laughed so did some of his men, and soon the entire army have broken out in laughter. Looking about Tanis saw men who were jumping and flailing about and yelling out to the advancing army. They held their lines but within them they hurled insults and unpleasant sentiments to the advancing enemy.

At 200 meters, Tanis gave the order to fire. Arrows filled the air and rained down on the suspecting enemy causing no great injury to the sturdy Dwarves that advanced still in their lines. Tanis seeing the lack of effect looked to the only father he had ever known with confusion. Again and again the arrows rained down and again and again the Dwarves where ready for them. The enemy army had advanced to 50 meters when a rumble began such as had never been heard. Tanis looked around to seek out the old wyrm that traveled with them assuming that he had finally roused himself to assist in the coming battle but the truth startled him further.

Deep in the distance Tanis saw what looked like great birds approaching across the horizon. It was from this direction he had heard the sounds. The King of the Elves looked up with happiness in his eyes and ordered all of the Elves and men to lay down their weapons.

Screaming up and down the line he called for all the warriors to step from their weapons and lower their eyes from the sky.

Tanis ran to his foster father yelling, "What is that father? What comes here? Why do we flee from the battle instead of standing and fighting?"

Tanis had only enough time to gasp as his foster father knocked him to the ground and he lost consciousness.

Chapter Twenty Seven: New Allies and Battles

Tanis jolted upright from his sleep and looked around the tent he was in and saw his foster father sitting with a tall stranger. Confusion spawned in his mind as he listened to the account of the battle unfolding. Tanis jumped to his feet and search for his weapons. "How dare you betray me!" screamed Tanis at the top of his lungs at the men seated across from him.

"Who betrayed you?" asked the man speaking to the Elf King. "You were protected from what was coming. Your father is an astute man who is very good at keeping himself and his people safe. That includes an ungrateful young man who has grown too powerful too quickly." said the unknown stranger.

Tanis looked closer at the man in front of him trying hard to pierce the shadows and darkness surrounding the stranger. The man was tall, standing about six foot three or four, and slim of stature. The man looked as frail as a fallen twig on a winter morning. The black cloak the stranger wore covered his body and face completely making any further identification impossible. The deep red bands around his wrists looked as if stained there by vast amounts of bloodshed over many years. The man moved with a grace that marked only the most skilled of warriors but this illusion was dissuaded as the man appeared to stumble upon the cleared smooth ground.

"Sir, Father, tell me what has befallen our brave men and women. How did the battle go?" asked Tanis. "The men and women of your command acquitted themselves well little one. My people helped to even the odds and keep the balance in check. We have not yet attempted to take the great city. I felt it more important to take the surrounding fields and paths and force the lord of this land to come to us, rather than lay siege to a city that cannot fall." said the dark stranger.

"I fear my manners are lacking today. My friend, this is my foster son Tanis Thalin, My son, this is Gargomel. Gargomel is the leader of the Faerimouth people. They are warriors of the fairy folk and usually do not involve themselves in the petty wars of men. You were knocked unconscious because they fear and despise weapons and armaments. They fight with weapons wrought of the power that you yourself were taught as you grew. They are not a force to be trifled with and when you did not drop your weapons and avert your eyes, I took action to protect your life. They are part man and part gargoyle. They are intelligent people and well-schooled in all the arts. They are shunned by those they protect, and hunted by men as Demons and portents of evil. I assure you they are neither Demons nor evil. They come to help us in our darkest of hours and they come at my request. It is they who I had told you were coming." said the King.

"Father, you mean that you knew they were coming from the beginning? Why did you not say something? Why did you not tell me that these fair folk were coming to join us in battle? I would have welcomed them with open arms as brothers and allies. Why did you hide their presence from me?" Tanis inquired as they sat around the fire. "What difference would knowing have made to you? Would you have done anything different? They came at my request and do only as they feel appropriate. They do not take orders. They do not take commands. They only do what they will and then they go. Gargomel remains only to speak with me and to introduce himself to you. I fear you have not made a good first impression upon him, though as he seems a little upset right now."

"You misunderstand me, old friend," began Gargomel and was then suddenly interrupted by the sounds of chaos outside the tent. "They come! They come!" the shouts from outside the camp said. Gargomel spread his leathery wings to full stature and Tanis saw that what he mistook for a cloak was indeed his folded wings. The horned, scaly face of Gargomel at first caused Tanis to shudder in an uncontrolled fear. Tanis spied his weapons under his cloak and spoke to Gargomel, "Sir, I mean you no offense, but allow me to fight at your side this day. We may need every blade and sword we can muster. Leaving my blades behind may not do us the justice that your people fought so hard to obtain."

"Take them up and follow me, youngling. You are right to ask my leave but now we must fight. I fear if they brought forth all their might against us that we may need the might of the dragon hoards to save us." said Gargomel as he stepped from the tent and looked at Tanis.

It was as Gargomel feared. The Dark Lord rode at the head of the coming army and it appeared as if all breathing beings not with Tanis had taken arms against him behind the great Dark Knight before him. Even Gargomel was taken aback by the enormous force flooding the field and coming toward the army of men and Elves. "I fear what we have accomplished yesterday is about to be undone," said Gargomel. "You fear quickly for one made of stone," quipped Tanis "Look to the heavens and behold my own present to our forces."

The pair looked where Tanis pointed and beheld the approach of many winged beings flocking down toward the army. The look of confusion upon the Elf King and Gargomel's face was almost humorous to Tanis. "I had thought that your approach yesterday was the approach of my friends early. By the way, didn't one of you order dragons?" laughed Tanis as the shapes grew into the form of hundreds of dragons, led by the familiar face of the great wyrm.

"My lord Tanis, I have brought the dragons' clans to do battle for you. It would appear we are none too soon as the battle is about to begin. Dragons attack the armies of the Dark Knight and teach him a dragon's fury!" screamed the great wyrm.

Gargomel leapt to the closest of attackers and a glowing blade appeared in his hands. "Well young one," he called over the din of combat, "just don't stand there get in here and do battle."

The warriors of the light moved with speed never before imagined as they entered the fray with the Dwarves of the Dark Knight. The enemy pushing hard toward the command tents of Tanis and his followers. The lead dwarf moved as if possessed by some dark force as he moved closer and closer to Tanis. Gargomel moved to intercept the dwarf and soon a one on one contest was observed by both sides as the battle came to a standstill while the two lords of their peoples stood locked in combat. The great axe of the dwarf met with the power wrought blade of the gargoyle again and again as they danced in the deadly game that is combat and all stood entranced as the two fought. The sturdy dwarf moved harder and faster into his foe and soon both were covered in each other's blood. As the fight continued both dwarf and gargoyle slowed and soon it became one combatant trading blows with the other.

The Dwarves watching this fight cheered and yelled their encouragement to their master while the Elves and men screamed to Gargomel. The forms of their weapons spun and connected then parted and connected again. Again and again one tried to finish the other and soon both combatants' endurance was spent. In an attempt to finish the combat, Gargomel lunged into the dwarf as the dwarf leapt into the great gargoyle. The effort of both seemed wasted as both men's attack landed with chilling effectiveness. The power wrought sword of Gargomel pierced the proud heart of the dwarf just as the great axe of the dwarf severed the head of the powerful Gargomel. As the two fell to the blood stained earth, both sides of the conflict stood in wonder at the scene that had played out before them.

Tanis ran to the fallen body of the gargoyle and drew his weapon yet again. Looking to the Dwarves he charged into their lines and slew several of the now stationary Dwarves. Moving to follow the lead of Tanis, the troops he led moved into the lines of now confused and distressed Dwarves. Men swung about themselves and the Dwarves fell back still dazed at the loss of their leader. As it began to look as if the Dark Knight's forces had been defeated a trumpet blast from the walls brought every eye to the great gates. The gates were slowly opening and advancing from the gates came the Dark Knight and his minions that were not yet fighting and to those who had already been in combat against him, it seemed he brought forth all the minions of darkness with him.

"Did you believe it would be that easy to defeat me? You have killed my slaves, the ones forced to fight for me. Now face my true might and power, now meet the shadow army from which you have so many times run and hid. Now you face my true legion!" screamed the Dark Knight as he led what appeared to be Demons from the city into combat.

Tanis saw the knight riding forth and turned to face him. Dismay filled his face as he watch the Demons spread onto the fields. "No more of this," whispered Tanis and he lifted his arms above his head and closed his eyes. A dim light began to spread amongst the Demons and men on the field and slowly grew brighter. Soon the light grew to blinding and none on either side moved wondering what new surprise came upon them. Tanis whipped his arms down and the field erupted in geysers of light enveloping many of the Demons that had started fighting. The bulk of them still remaining with the Knight were yet unaffected but those in the lights wriggled and wreathed with pain and agony. Tanis opened his eyes and looked at the Demons and soon all that were enveloped in the light were not but piles of ash before the men and Elves on the field.

The Dark Knight's smile was almost sincere as he watched Tanis approach him. The Dark Knight held back the remaining Demons and rode forward toward the standing form of Tanis. The knight swung his blade and moved through form after form as he approached Tanis who still stood looking at him. The Knight laughed as he came within a few short meters from Tanis and drew back to execute a killing maneuver. Tanis saw him draw back and grinned as he pulled the small crossbow from under his cloak and fired at the now exposed form of the dark knight before him.

Time stood still as the bolt flew from the crossbow and found its mark just beneath the helmet of the Knight. Ever so slowly the knight stopped and his hand dropped the weight of the great sword he carried. Surprise showed on the face that could be seen beneath his helmet as he fell from his horse and landed face down onto the blood covered earth. Tanis moved forward and drew his sword to finish the knight and remove his head but saw there was no need for butchery. The Knight was dead. Tanis quickly turned to the rest of his army remembering the

Demons stacked against him and gazed in amazement as those Demons that had emerged from the city with the Dark Knight now lay on the blood soaked ground wriggling in their own death dances. "The knight had obviously not trusted his own minions," said Tanis to King Toirin as he approached him, "He linked them to him even in death. Now his death is theirs. Bring together the men and Elves that still live, Father. Tonight, we sleep in the city of the Dark Knight."

CHAPTER TWENTY EIGHT:
A NEW EVIL

As the fall of the Dark Knight was taking place, another battle of sorts was taking place on the opposite side of the world. It was not a battle of swords and spears but of words and policy. In a darkened country on the opposite side of Dracos, in the highest room of the highest turret, a meeting was taking place.

The castle belonged to one of the darkest of the Enrine. The Enrine being the dark wizards and lords that ruled many of the lands, one can only imagine what it was that the darkest of them possessed. The turrets reached a full thousand meters into the air with the appearance of incompleteness about the tops. The jagged forms at the tops looked as if the workers just walked from their work and never looked back. The wall thick enough to withstand even an attack from the dragon hoards. They were thick enough for the entire army of this dark wizard to stand upon and look out over an approaching army.

It was not the size alone though that made this structure impressive. The walls of this keep were the darkest of reds. It appeared black as you rode toward this keep from the bowels of the planet, but as you approached you realize that you were looking at the deepest color of blood. The dark lord was known for taking his enemies and spilling their blood upon his walls. It was a feel for the power, he would explain to his armies as he would lower the dagger to his squirming enemy's throat.

In this castle, the dark lords and wizards met. The room was large enough to house a garrison of men and women comfortably, and it was doing so at the present as many of the Dark Lords went nowhere without their compliment of servants and guards to protect their interests. Though only twenty were called to this meeting, well over two thousand sat along the walls awaiting their masters' whims.

The eldest of the dark lords, Elfinous, stood and walked toward the center of the large room. Raising his hands and his voice he spoke to the gathered crowds, "My friends and colleagues, it is my pleasure to announce that the time draws near for our complete victory over the world of Dracos. Lord McCryden is not here? Where is that man? Was he not summoned with the rest of you? And the Dark Knight? He too has failed to answer my summons. Can anyone tell me of this strange occurrence? Never before have they missed out on the opportunity to prove their loyalty to our cause. Well, no matter. I have looked upon the signs and symbols. I have seen that the Askanitowa have been reborn! There is one out among the lesser out there that probably does not even know who he is at this point. We must find him! We must train him! We must see him be our partner in this great undertaking. With his power we will be unstoppable!"

When he has finished a small rumble of approval spread amongst the people in the room. Their rewards would be coming after all. The old man was going to see his promises through. People were muttering approval at the old man's statements when a dark cloud entered the room. From the middle of this cloud a figure emerged and a small ball of flame shot forth and consumed the old man. The dark lords and wizard stopped dead in their tracks looking at the figure shrouded in darkness. The figure had the size and stature of one of the hated Elves. Many reached for weapons only to find they were unable to move.

The figure moved to the place where the old man had stood and surveyed the crowds. "The old man was a fool, and so too are all of you. Lord McCryden will never again be present at any of your petty gatherings. He has been slain by the newest of those light blinded fools. The Dark Knight too has fallen to this young stag of a Druid. Two of your great number dead at his hands and you feel that victory is ours? And what will happen when he comes for you? Will you be the ones to destroy him and his growing power? I have placed myself near him.

I will see it through that he becomes our minion. First we must weed through the chaff that fills our number. Now here is our plan. I will give you our means and ways of doing what must come. I will lead you all since it would appear that our fearless leader is no longer able. It will be I who will lead us to our great victory and give us control over this great land. Do any of you have an objection? Just show your hand and I will step aside and allow you the command. What, no takers? Have none of you the strength of will to challenge me? I am not surprised. So before we begin are there any questions?" said the mysterious figure before the assembled evil.

Many were trying to move their arms and bodies but none were able. One wizard opened his mouth and spoke to the figure, "Who are you, dark lord? How should we call you? I for one would like to know to whom we should bend knee." said the dark wizard, Garrick.

"Garrick, you will know me in due time. It is not yet the hour for my identity to be revealed for it may compromise what is to come. Just suffice it to know that I will be aware of each of you. I will give each of you your orders in turn. Just know this, we prepare for war. Go back to your respective lands and prepare for war. Garrison your troops and make ready for we will march. And we will march soon!"

"Garrick makes a good point. We should know who we follow. Surely you do not fear us, great one?" said the Dark lord Mardoc. "Never press for more than I am willing to give, Mardoc." said the figure. "In due time all will be revealed. Until then do as you are ordered. Make ready for war!"

With that the figure disappeared as fast and mysteriously as he had appeared. The council found that it was able to move and work again, no longer held by the mysterious figure's spell. Most stood and moved toward the door. There was work to be done and a strong new leader to see it done.

CHAPTER TWENTY NINE:
INTO THE CITY

The gargoyles came early the next morning to collect the remains of Gargomel. Reverently they moved to the site where he had fallen and collected him into his wings and carried him away. A young gargoyle came to Tanis and King Toirin, "My lords, we gargoyles are now without a leader. Tanis it was you Gargomel said to follow in the event of his demise. Yet we must first go to our home and give proper burial to our beloved leader. I feel he knew this was coming. He made too many plans for it to be otherwise." said the young gargoyle.

"It is with heavy heart that I take your care into my custody. I was unable to protect him. I failed him. I fear that I will fail you all as well. But do not fear and do not have care of abuse at my hands. The war is over. The Dark Knight is slain and evil has once again been destroyed on our world. All may live free and work as we have to see our lives pleasant and full. I pray that there is no more need for fighting in my life time." said Tanis.

"Over?" asked the young gargoyle, "are you sure of this, My Lord. I am called Ruark and am Gargomel's son. I have it from good sources that we are just beginning. Over? I think not, for there are many other folk in this land who would like to see you destroyed and this world in their evil grip. Over? It will never be over. The best we can hope for is the balance of power that once controlled this world. Victory? For today there is victory but the darkness comes. It is spreading and only through vigilance will we ever truly be safe. The Dark Council will not be overjoyed to hear that their champions are falling. I fear war is still on the horizon, and it will be for all of us."

"The gargoyle is wise in his young years," said the great wyrm. "Tanis, you were equally young and jaded when you came to my home those many years ago. You feared that all was lost and would never be as it should. Well you saw that happiness can come from strife and it did. You have to work for it. Is that not right my young friend, Elf?"

"Young?" replied King Toirin. "Surely you jest an old friend. Yet to you I suppose even the earth we stand upon is young, my ancient friend. As for your question, happiness must be taken when it can be. To assume that it will come to you is fallacy. We are all subject to whims of fate and sometimes they are kind. At others, let us just say that they have a warped sense of humor. But come. This battle is over and no more loom in our near future, let us celebrate the lives of the fallen and the futures of those who have survived!"

"Once more your wisdom astounds me, Father. Tell me when our celebration starts and I shall be there. But for now I have a city to put right. Perrick! Get over here I have a task for you!" yelled Tanis.

The group moved into the city together to the screams of approval from the people. The likeness of Tanis was hung from the buildings lining the entry to the city and people lined the sides of the streets to catch a glimpse of their savior. "Father, why do these people line up and shout in this manner? Who is this hero they call for?" asked Tanis.

"Their hero is you, child. It is you they yearn to see. You have delivered them from the rule of the Dark Knight and now they see a bright future awaiting them. You have brought them a greater life, whether you know it or not. Enjoy the honors today for tomorrow it is likely that you too will be unreasonable and uncaring for their welfare. After all, they are Dwarves." said the King.

"Father, are you prejudiced? I sense a distinct dislike for the Dwarves in your voice. And I was hoping that I could give them into your care. Perrick, my old friend, it is you who will rule here in my name. I hope that you will take them to your bosom and love them like a father. Can you do that for me?" asked Tanis.

"My lord, it would be my honor but is there not any better suited for this task. After all, I am not the most well-known ruler. My kingdom is of another nature and I suspect if my loyal subjects found out the other nature I follow, that you might find your steward hanging around upon the walls that await you in his grand palace." said Perrick.

"Then I guess you had better be sure they do not find out. Perrick go to the palace and make ready for me as I come now to see to the great beginning we have made here." laughed Tanis as he spurred his horse forward and caused his bodyguard to mutter expletives as they moved to surround their charge. The older folk were right. Happiness must be taken when it was available. It was so now and he was going to take it.

CHAPTER THIRTY:
NEW ARRIVALS

Tanis stood upon the ramparts of the City of the Dark Knight, after what seemed like an eternity, with Perrick and his foster father, Toirin. Looking out onto the field they had fought upon a year earlier brought a little sparkle to Tanis's eye. The land was green again. Farmers moved upon the sprouting rows with a spring in their step that had for a long time not been there and for some it had never been there. People were stopping every so often and talking in the fields and men and women laughed and enjoyed their lives.

"Look at those people. Throughout the kingdom this is the scene. People are happy. People are enjoying life. They no longer live in fear nor look at each other as a spy to their lord. Why Perrick, I had even heard talk that the people think you were Elven trained yourself. This scene just shows you what it is we are fighting for." said Tanis to Perrick.

"It is true that the people are happy, My Lord. They produce far more in a year than they have in centuries according to the records. I am grateful for your trust in ruling your people. I only hope to fulfill your expectations." replied Perrick.

"It is hard to miss expectations, young one, when none are placed on you!" laughed the King of the Elves. "Why, Tanis himself could not do a better job and could expect no more than he, himself, is capable of. By the way Tanis, I have a gift for you. It will seem weird but it is truly a gift that you will see benefit from in the near future. Come with me, the two of you. Come see the latest in a long list of things I have arranged for you. I give you this before I leave for home, my son. You can handle the rest of your life without my holding your hand. My people need me now. So you will have to give me leave to go to them. Besides, your mother is definitely not happy that I have been gone so long."

The King of the Elves brought Tanis and Perrick down a hallway and down to the courtyard. In the center of the courtyard a group of warriors stood talking to Artitous and Lord Nargus. The leader of the band stood in what appeared to be heated argument with Nargus, and large groups of his men that at first appeared to be lounging at their ease suddenly took on a more deadly calm. Though appearing at ease they truly were ready to spring to their Lord's aid at a moment's notice.

"What is going on here?" asked Tanis as he strode into the courtyard.

"Someone let these heathen monsters enter our keep! Imagine letting these savages into your presence. It would be my eyes and my tongue if I were to allow such a thing to occur!" said Lord Nargus.

"And I tell you Nargus that we were invited and your prejudice against my people needs to end. We come at your Lord's request. We really do not know even why we are here. There has not been a battle here in over a year. Now if you will move aside so we can approach your master, maybe we can all get some answers." said a distinctly female voice.

"Woman warriors of the Tyris, you are welcome in my son's home. Nargus, you fool, get your men back to their posts and stop this foolishness right now. These women are our guests and need to be treated as such. Savages you call them? Why is that Nargus? Because they do things a little differently from what you are used to? Remember the day we took this fine city? I refused to take the command of it because I felt that the Dwarves were not worthy of my help. I know now that I was wrong and hope that they forgive me for my blindness that has for so long kept me from working hand in hand with our brothers." said King Toirin.

"Toirin, you said that there was need of me here and yet I see no wars, no battles. What is the meaning of this?" asked the woman's voice again.

"Athinina, please forgive the urgency of my letter. It was necessary that your arrival was in the greatest of haste. I apologize if I have misled you. There is a great deal that must be done and it must be done shortly. I feel a shifting in the air and I feel that time grows short for us again." replied Toirin.

"The name is Lady Targul. And I will not be addressed so informally by the likes of you without my leave. I have never been as slighted as I have just been and I am hard pressed to remain here with the likes of your total primitive ignorant. I have seen better manners from the crows and vultures after a battle. My ladies! Prepare to ride!" said Athinina.

"Please wait, my lady. I apologize for the behavior of my man and for the forwardness of my father. Please accept my hospitality until we can all get to the bottom of this mess. I am Tanis Thalin and these are my lands. I wish to know his reasoning and know why it was he summoned a group of beautiful women such as you to my present home." said Tanis.

"Well, insults as well as ignorance. Beautiful? Would you call Nargus there beautiful? How about that horse there? Is it because my reproductive organs are on the inside rather than out that you call me beautiful? I and my people are warriors! We are not something to be ogled and adored. We are for the purpose of disposing of the dark powers that are consuming this world. If this is the last hope of the free people, I fear all is lost. Mount and Ride my Tyris!" shouted Athinina.

"Please wait and join me at my table at the least. Let me make up for my insults. And as for your questions, well yes, I call Nargus beautiful all the time and especially my horse there. It has done well by me for many a year. As for where your reproductive organs are, well that matters little to me, but of what I can see, you are definitely well endowed and truly blessed amongst your kind." grinned Tanis.

"I may come to like you yet," said Athinina, "But do not get your hopes up. Tyris go to the mess and get yourselves some chow. I go to the hospitality of these people. Be ready since these people do not know our ways. Do your best to blend in. Now Lord Thalin, shall we go?"

"My name is Tanis, my Lady Targul. And I welcome you into my home." said Tanis.

"Oh no, my lord, call me Athinina." said the warrior queen.

CHAPTER THIRTY ONE:
MIDNIGHT TALKS

Athinina left the meal with Tanis confused. She had never let her guard down with the handsome lord, but her head spun with the events. The meal was simple yet elegant and he was nothing but polite. He had spoken mostly of trivial matters and a little of his lost family. How one man could bear such tragedy was beyond her comprehension. After all, in her kingdom men were so much weaker.

He had excused himself after the meal was finished and retired early speaking of seeing her the following morning. He even begged her forgiveness again for the actions of his follower. "What kind of people were these that took insults to heart?" she wondered briefly. All she knew for certain was how strange these outsiders were.

Slowly she entered her rooms and found her attendants already waiting. Her dearest friend and confident was standing beside her bed waiting as always to dress her for bed and fix her hair for sleep. The woman was dearer to her than any other person she had ever met and she would be lost without her.

"Clairine, please excuse the others and come fix me for sleep. I am weary from our travels. See the others bunked with the other soldiers for the night. When you are through, come back here for a time. Just hurry." said Athinina in her best command voice. She could still control her emotions like a true warrior at least.

The women jumped to obey her commands as they always did. They were well trained in that respect. They followed her orders to the letter. They could do no less.

Clairine came back into the room shortly after leaving with tears of rage in her eyes. "They insist on bedding down our women separate from the men, my lady." began the woman. "They would not even consider how it would degrade them to be placed such! How can we remain here with that kind of insult?"

"Clairine, it is for but a few short days. They mean no insult. They are just uninformed outlanders who coddle their women. Let it be. I will discuss it with Lord Thalin in the morning. But to other discussions, please. These outlanders make my head hurt." said Athinina.

"A few days, my lady?" quipped Clairine. "Just this morning it was only overnight. Have you found something to entice you to remain? I will have to pull out some more of your lovely gowns for your meetings then. Shall I?" she was giggling as she finished speaking.

"Why would I dress in those foul things?" laughed Athinina. "Besides, if I choose a mate here, he will have to grow accustom to my Mytan sooner or later."

"A mate, my Lady?" smiled Clairine knowingly. "Is there a man in mind or have you just decided to start looking here among outlanders instead of our own stock?" asked the serving woman.

"Well, no one strikes me as strong enough yet, but you never know. One of these men may have the manhood to satisfy a Tyris." giggled the warrior queen.

"That young lord looks attractive. Should I arrange for him to meet you in your bath? I firmly believe he may suit you. He is rather too handsome though. You would have to scar him some, I believe." smiled the younger woman.

"In my bath? Hmmm, that is a little forward of you but maybe while dressing. Enough to show interest, but not saying I am weak like these outland women." smiled Athinina.

"My lady, now who is being forward?"

"Just undress me and arrange for him to be here after my bath in the morning." smiled Athinina. In the back of her mind she started wondering why she had just arranged things the way she had. These people really must be getting to her.

CHAPTER THIRTY TWO: STRANGE CUSTOMS

Athinina woke early the next morning and summoned Clairine. Preparations were made for her bath and she sent Clairine to summon the young Lord Thalin to her.

Athinina moved quickly through her morning cleansing and prepared for her dressing. Clairine came in dressed in the Mytan that marked her as a Tyris and spoke rapidly to her queen. "My Lady, the young Lord is on his way. He speaks like the poets of old. You must really work on him to make him suitable for you." smiled the younger woman.

Athinina blushed as she finished toweling herself. What was she thinking? The young man was not old enough to have seen much war. He was probably unblooded. "These things are correctable I believe" she said to the air. The question was whom was she trying to convince?

Tanis knocked at the door and waited a response. He was nervous being summoned so early. Had he offended this potentially powerful ally? He would have to work hard to correct it if he had. The door opened to a scene he had definitely not expected. Athinina sat in her padded chair clothed only in her skin. She was well toned and strong, he could see and bore many scars on her well rounded body. It seemed she had no modesty about her present state. Tanis stopped short as she rose to greet him. This was definitely not what he had expected when being called to her.

"My lady, it would appear as I have come at a poor time. I will return a little later when you are better suited for company." said Tanis.

"Come in and be seated, My Lord." Athinina said. "I will be but a few moments. Would you come over and do up my straps. My ladies in waiting do such a poor job of it. Do not be embarrassed for me. It is not our way to be ashamed of how the creator made us." said Athinina as she moved to her Mytan and pulled it over her head.

Tanis noticed again the scars that covered a portion of her body and turned the conversation to them. "It is not usually our way to see a woman unclothed amongst us. At least one we are not wed to. You have suffered many wounds. Your people allow women to go into battle? We try to protect our women as well as we can. Not many of them go to battle and those who do usually are healers. Those wounds must have pained you terribly." sputtered Tanis as she moved to him to tighten the straps of her leather armor.

"This armor suits you; of course the covers must be beautiful for such a woman as yourself. Why this armor covers barely more than our women's undergarments. You would look stunning with the proper outer garment, maybe embroidered with your crest. I can set people to it immediately if you would like." said Tanis.

"An outer garment?" replied Athinina. "That would hinder my movement. Is there something wrong with my Mytan? Do you find me unpleasant to look upon? Be away with you. I would not want to trouble you with my appearance if you do not find it pleasing. We will discuss our treaty later. I was unaware that you outlanders were so weak. Clairine! Show this fool to the Remove him from my presence, NOW!" shouted the queen of the Tyris.

"I meant no affront my lady. Please, I am just unused to your ways. Forgive my ignorance. Let us speak further in the great room of our alliance. I seek to learn more of your customs." said Tanis, now visibly shaken.

"I will consider it." was all Athinina replied as Tanis was hustled from the room. As the door closed, she turned to Clairine, "So do you believe I was suitably forceful with him? Do you suppose he was impressed? I hope he does not find me weak and prudish. It may have been a mistake to have done this so rapidly. What say you, Clairine?"

"My lady, it is hard to read these outlanders. Come here my lady. He has left this so loose that you will come out of it as you walk. I assumed that these men would be stronger. Do you think he believes you weak? He barely cinched the strap. I think you should allow him the next move. It is only proper. After all, you have shown a little interest. Now let us see how he responds. I have arranged for practice in the courtyard so that your workout and training schedule will not be interrupted by our travels. You really need to maintain your skills if you are to proceed with this alliance." said Clairine.

"Right as always, my friend. Perhaps the young Lord will be present to see how real women are. Arrange it so for me." responded Athinina.

"As you wish, my lady." said Clairine with a small inward smile. In her mind she thought that her plans for her lady were working out perfectly.

Chapter Thirty Three: A Little Sparing

The scene inside the courtyard was one to be remembered. Athinina was squared off with three of the better swordsmen in the castle. The men moved with the fluidity of experienced warriors if with a touch of hesitation toward the warrior queen. They moved simply and without the gusto they may have employed with each other. They were still in shock at the way the very attractive woman in her very scant armor moved and fought. Two of the three were trying without any success to avoid staring at the amount of bosom she had exposed by the Mytan. The other had experience dealing with the Tyris and expected an easy, brief exchange of blows before the lady quit.

He moved into the queen with the boar rushes through the brush to find that the queen was no longer there. He stopped and looked around for the missing queen just to find her standing behind him leaning on her blade. Quick wits spared him a blow that would have split his skull. The man moved quickly putting the swan's call to her. The queen met form for form and soon the man found himself giving ground to the warrior queen. Slowly the warrior moved back and back until he found himself butted against the wall with the queen's blade at his throat. "You have a dagger, why have you not drawn and attacked me while I held you with my larger harder to wield blade?" asked the warrior queen under her breath.

"My lady I am aware that I would be dead before it cleared the sheath. I am man enough to know when I am defeated." replied the warrior.

"Any true warrior draws anyway so at least he would die with a blade in his hand." replied the queen of the Tyris.

"We do not waste men or people here, my lady." whispered Tanis. "Athinina, we value the life of every one of our men, women, and children. It is not so with your people?" asked Tanis. "Of course it is but we also value bravery and skill which I have yet to see here. Maybe there is one better for me to spare with, my Lord, to redeem your people?" replied the warrior queen.

"You press a hard fight. It will be difficult to find your match. Perhaps maybe myself?" asked Tanis. As he spoke he removed his jacket and scabbard and drew his blade not realizing he drew the Warmonger. The queen barely waited for the blade to clear his sheath before she attacked. She hit with the power reserved for the gods or the insane. Tanis was pressed hard from the start. Slowly though the strain of travel and the weariness of her past sparing caught up to her and her berserker strength started to fail. Tanis pressed home the advantage until finally the warrior queen lay at his feet with his blade tip at her throat. The fight had not been pretty and the blade in Tanis's hands seemed to move of its own volition. Many a strike was blocked that should have severed the life from the warrior queen. Tanis found himself turning some of the blows himself that would have proven fatal to the queen of the Tyris.

The queen looked at the blade and her eyes grew wide. "You are a fraud!" she screamed looking at the blade. "You use magically altered blades to defeat me? Are you afraid to face me without the aid of major magic? Do you feel yourself that poor a man and warrior that you must cheat to face a woman?" she challenged Tanis.

"Athinina, I do not know of what you are speaking. This is the blade my stepfather gave to me as child. It is no more magic than you or I." replied Tanis to this tirade. "If you must accuse someone of cheating in a fight do not look to me. Perrick, maybe, but not me, I must beg to differ." almost screaming at Athinina.

"Do you not bear the Warmonger? Is that not what you wave before my face right this moment? I would rather deal with the scoundrel. At least him you will not be surprised when he does something dishonest. I expected more from you, Lord Tanis Thalin. But considering your bloodline I should not be surprised. Sired by one of the Dread Lords themselves. It must be hard to try and be good and civil with that kind of evil within your soul. I hope it destroys you like it did your father."

"Lady, you wound me. I could have struck you down just now but I stay my hand. I never knew the man that sired me, I killed him. I was raised by the royal family of the Elves. I was never his man. I destroyed all that he tried to do with his evil influence and tried to make things better for all of my people. You believe me to be an evil, lying, cheating monster than you had better pack your things and leave for you are not welcome here any longer. I have tried my best to do what is right for all my people. Every one of them! You may depart. When you return do so with a more civil tongue in your mouth!" screamed Tanis.

The look on the queen's face went flush as Tanis screamed but Clairine knew it was not with anger. It was as she feared. Her lady had fallen for this young upstart. To everyone's surprise the queen jumped to her feet after Tanis spoke and silenced him with a deep passionate kiss. Tanis reeled back with its passion as she pressed herself to him but finally fell into her embrace. All those watching the scene could not tell if he was reaching for a blade or trying his best to hold her to him. Men looked around for instruction from their officers and they looked to the women of the Tyris. No one had seen this kind of display before and did not know how to respond. It was Artitous who finally reacted to the scene before him. Gently coughing at first then loudly to get the pair's attention he moved closer to be heard well. "My Lord and Lady, shall we call an end to the day's practices or shall we begin them again?"

Tanis jumped back and straightened his shirt and tunic. "By all means my friend, end the practices. The heat must be affecting our ability to think. Let the men go to be refreshed before we work further. Is this your wish my lady?" asked Tanis. The queen smiled down at Tanis, "Whatever my lord feels is appropriate. I await the orders of my liege."

CHAPTER THIRTY FOUR: HAPPINESS

The days stretched to weeks and soon a year passed without incident as the two Lords of their people continued to spend time together, learning from each other. Growing together, Tanis was often away to see to the government of his lands. Athinina was often away to see to her people's needs and to prepare for the coming conflicts which were sure to happen. Clairine traveled with her mistress and tended to her needs as she traveled. The servant acting more the lady then the lady on many of the occasions the two young people were together.

Clairine combed Athinina's hair and leaned to her ear, "Mistress, why do you spend so much time with the young lord? He is brash and young. Tell me, my lady, what do you see in him?"

"He makes me feel as a lady should, Clairine!" said Athinina. "He makes me feel as if there is nothing else in the world but the two of us when we are together. He moves with the grace of the ocean and the power of a waterfall. He is gentle yet strong, powerful yet vulnerable. Does this make him wrong for me? Just tell me if I am losing myself to gain nothing, my dearest friend."

Clairine looked at her queen and the trace of a smile crossed her lips, "My queen and my friend. He is the reason your heart beats is he not? It is the tradition of the Tyris that the women ask the men for their hand. If you feel that he is the one who will inspire your future battles and your future control, then propose to him now! He is young. He is impetuous. But he is the one for whom you wish to live your life. If you do not ask him soon though, I am thinking I will."

The queen and he handmaid laughed until they cried and then laughed again. The world was as it should be for them at that moment, and life was good. The two women rolled around on the bed and floor laughing and giggling throughout the night. All thoughts of the young Lord left their heads as the two laughed and talked deep into the night. Neither had enjoyed a night such as this since they were youths, and the companionship served the two of them well.

As the two laughed and conversed a shadow showed near the open door. The shape of a woman was seen coming from that shadow. Tanis's mother-in-law moved slowly, with a blade drawn, waiting for the two to separate. A wave of her hand and the shadow disappeared. She walked slowly as to not alert anyone when she saw the maid. It seemed as if she stared right at her. The maid would have to go first. Something was not right with that one. She would have to wait once more. But her time was coming. It was coming soon.

While the queen of the Tyris and her maid talked and laughed a much different conversation was going on far from the palace of the young Lord. The serpentine man walked slowly into the room and walked to the hooded man in the tower. "Master, it has been prepared as was instructed. We await our orders to move before the next stage begins."

"Beast. Tell the others that the time is not right. When I am ready you will all be informed. Have your men ready to fight as soon as we march. It comes close to the time of reckoning and we must be ready. Our enemies cannot be allowed to survive." said the hooded man. "Soon, beast, Soon."

Still further in the dark lands another conversation was being held. The winged beast looked down at the Dark wizard and smiled. "We are ready, master?" asked the beast.

"We are ready, animal. Gather your forces and move to the east. Bring me Young Thalin's head." whispered the wizard.

CHAPTER THIRTY FIVE: THE WAR BEGINS

In another place to the east, Toirin sat up in his bed and looked down at his slumbering wife. The sweat beaded up upon his brow as he looked down at his wife and smiled. It was a sad smile as he leaned down and kissed her sleeping eyes gently. Rapidly he leapt from the bed and moved to the men who guarded his door outside. "Move quickly and call up the forces! Get the commanders out of their beds and bring them to me. We march by the dawn!"

The king of the Elves moved rapidly down the hallway to find his armor and prepare himself for combat. War was returning this day to the world and Tanis had to be warned. Battle would be on his doorstep rapidly and he was probably unaware that it was coming. The Elf King ran for the stables as soon as his armor was fixed to his body. He could waste no time getting to his son.

The King made it to his stable and came to a sudden stop. The eerie silence that surrounded the building gave the King pause. There was something not right here. The King moved slowly into the stable looking to the rafters and stalls. The silence became oppressive as he moved deeper into the building. The silence was broken momentarily as two young troopers in the King's guard ran to open the doors to his horse's private paddock. The only sound heard was the creak of the hinges as the doors opened. The young soldiers looked with pride upon the King as he moved to enter, his senses still reeling. There was something wrong here. The troopers moved closer to the paddock when the world erupted before the gathered bodyguard of the King.

The King was thrown to the walls as the paddock flew apart before him. Gigantic Demons poured from the remains of the paddock and moved toward the prone form of the King. The guards who had entered the paddock lay dead at the feet of the great beasts, their bodies looking as if the bones had been removed and the rest left to rot. The armor they wore had not even slowed the animals. The Demons had torn them apart without hesitation.

The prone King reached for his sword. If he could draw the weapon he may be able to fend off the beasts long enough for help to arrive and drive them off. The King reached his hands and knees when he realized his sword was missing. A quick glance around showed that the blade had been thrown into the side of the building opposite where he had landed. The force of the explosion had also removed part of his armor. Defenseless and weaponless the King struggled to his feet calling out to his soldiers waiting for him outside the stables.

The beasts taunted and teased the King as he struggled to reach the doors. The horned creatures moved rapidly to keep the King separated from the exit. They herded the elder Elf left then right. Never allowing him to move forward toward the safety of the night and his troops, nor allowing him to retreat to the safety of the stalls. Desperation set in as the King moved again to the left and the right. Fear kept the King pressed into the small corral the enemy was closing around him.

Images began to swim in the mind of the Elf King. He had images of his family and peoples being torn apart by the beasts as he fought to save himself. Images of Tanis being killed trying to save his life. More images of his dear wife being torn asunder because they wished information from him. He saw all that he had built being destroyed as he continued to fight for his existence. The meaning had finally become clear. The Elf King had finally reached the blade that had wedged itself into the wall. Pulling and straining he began working the blade from the wall. The largest of the Demons moved forward and swatted the Elf and sword sending both flying to the floor, raising large amounts of laughter from his companions. The King crawled slowly to the blade lying in the dirt, reaching slowly for it so not to raise the alarm of the gathering Demons.

A look of serenity came upon the face of the King as he finally realized what he had to do. The Demons were not trying to finish this. They waited for something or someone. He could not allow himself to become the pawn for this other greater power. The King moved over the sword and got himself to his hands and knees looking down at the blade. He would at least send some of these animals back to their master in pieces. Snatching the blade from the dust he leapt at smallest of the creatures cutting the horn and part of its chest from the left side of its body. Again he swung severing the wounded Demon's head from its body. He turned in time to see the closest Demon ram his blade into his chest instead of his back. The King staggered back looking at the blade protruding from his chest. Spurred on by the blood that now poured from their fallen colleague and that which flowed from the Elf King, the beasts rushed in toward the Elf. They disregarded the whips and screams of the great Demon that led them, charging in to finish the old Elf. Again and again the King struck killing another of the beasts before he finally succumbed to the merciless attacks of the Demons. As the Elf fell, the great Demon roared in anger, killing the closest of his minions in his anger.

"The old one was supposed to remain alive. The Master wished him. Now what do we tell Master?" asked the Demon to the others.

"How about the truth?" came the reply from the far end of the stables. The great Demon turned and looked to the source of the sound. A cloaked and hooded figure moved toward the gathered Demons looking at the corpse of the once proud Elf King. The figure bent to the body and looked at the damage to it. "I believe I told you I wanted it alive, is this not true?"

"Yes Master." whispered the Demon.

"Is this alive, my pet?" asked the cloaked figure.

"No Master." whispered the Demon.

"And why is it not alive, slave?" inquired the hooded form.

"I do not know, my Master." replied the Demon as he moved to lie at the feet of the cloaked figure.

"Should I punish you all? After all you have failed me and destroyed a very carefully laid plan." said the figure.

"The slave does not know, my Lord. The slave begs for understanding being weak and lacking the great knowledge of the Master. Forgive your slaves my master for we do well in removing the other Elves. We have done the other things you ask and do that good right master?" said the now groveling Demon.

"Be gone from my sight. This may work to our advantage in any event. Be seen as you leave. I want them to see you flee. It will cause a great call for revenge from one that is unready to exact such an overwhelming task. I think this may be the very thing that could rid me of several enemies. Go on you idiots. Be gone just remember, flee slowly." said the figure as it turned to move toward the door to the stable. As the being turned its cloak came open and revealed a small portion of the being beneath. The small bit of leather told the Demons a great deal. As they fled the Demon had a great smile upon his face. *Much may yet come from this error* thought the Demon. *Much may yet still come of this.*

Chapter Thirty Six: Gathering His Forces

The envoy of the elves had found Tanis in the training yard practicing the sword and short spear with Athinina. Rapid movements back and forth between the two were barely able to be followed by those watching. The two had fought in this manner so often that one knew what the other would do three steps before the other moved. Tanis would strike with Light of the Moon only to find the Eagle Flies waiting his blade. Athinina would strike with the Glass Shatters to be blocked by the Boar Rushes. The two were so evenly matched that these mock battles would continue for hours before either ever landed a strike on the other.

The Elven envoy moved to the edge of the circle and called loudly to Tanis, "My Lord! I must speak with you!"

Tanis turned ever so briefly to see who had called him and it cost him as Athinina slammed home a strike to the abdomen. Raising her blade Tanis called for a halt. "Please dear lady, mercy. I appear to have some business to attend to." he laughed "How can I help you, my dear Elf? What brings you here in the stead of my father? He usually bears messages from your people to me. All well, tell me, my friend, what brings you so far from your precious wood?"

Tanis's laughter stopped short as the Elf recounted the battle and the death of his father. "Dear Elf, join me inside. Athinina summon your war council. Did you bring the Elven generals with you? Artitous! Now where did that Druid get to?" Tanis screamed. "Find the Druid and bring him to me. Also send people to Perrick. He must also come here with the Dwarven War Council."

To Athinina he spoke gently "My dear Lady, it would appear that our private battles here are at an end. It is time now for the real battles to come into our lives. The time for play is at an end. Forgive me the lack of time I will have for you in this time for now I must face the unbeatable. I now go to face Demons."

"You do not face them alone" replied Athinina as she turned and left the practice yard to gather the Tyris War Council.

"A wise woman," said Artitous to Tanis as he watched her leave. "She may not be your Charina, but she still has the fire and the will to be as great at your side. You linger with her more and more. I think it will not be long before I hear church bells, hmmm"

"All those close to me are murdered Artitous. My father is dead. Murdered by Demons. Again and again, I allow people close to me and they are killed. I cannot take it anymore. Why am I tortured so? I just wanted my life to continue as it had. I was happy. Things were over. I had defeated all those who came upon me. Again and again fate throws these things against me when all I want is to live unmolested by the forces that control the world and universe. Why would they not leave me be?" he asked the Druid.

Artitous smacked Tanis in the back of the head. "Artitous why did you do that?"

"It feels good when that is not happening does it not? Fate has a way of teaching us things, like how can you truly be happy without knowing the occasional anger and sadness? How can you ever rule without first being ruled? How can you control events without first submitting to them? I once told you that fate has a purpose for the things that it does. I say this again. We may not see the reason fate does what it does, but we must trust in it. It will always see that what must be done is done. Remember we are but pawns in an ancient game. Fate knows what it is doing! Your father would not want you to mourn him. He would not want you avenging him. You move on emotion. Let your logical mind control you for a moment." said the Druid.

"Right as always my friend, but I cannot follow your council. This time it has to happen this way. I must go and face these creatures. Someone summon Ruark. I will need the gargoyles in this coming battle. Also someone find me the old dragon. I have need of him and his people." said Tanis as he moved toward the keep and the council he knew awaited him there.

"Even dragons have names" boomed a great voice over Tanis's head. "And mine is Mastol. I wish you to know that and please call me by it. I feel you have earned the privilege of having my name. So what do you need from the dragons? Is there a problem here? Speak little friend and we will see it fixed. Please, why do you seem so tired and in so much pain?" whispered the dragon. Even the dragon's whisper sounded like a hive of bees buzzing…. bees the size of buses.

"My father is dead. He was killed by a horde of Demons. I seek to destroy them. They will know what pain is when I am through with them. I need all of the dragons that are available to help, for I move as soon as possible on the Lands of Darkness and the Heart of the World." said Tanis.

"Toirin was a good man and father. He will be missed by all who knew him. I will summon my brethren but it may take time for them to gather in numbers sufficient for your purpose. In the interim, think of a means of protecting yourself. If they attacked him, then an attack on you will soon follow. I propose that you join me in my lair. None will come for you there, at least any with sense." said the great wyrm.

"I have an idea for that as well, old friend. I will discuss it with everyone inside. Will you take your place at the window as usual?" asked Tanis.

"Of course I will. This I would not miss. I have said you needed protection more than the few you have gathered for years. Now I see the great thoughts of the great King." laughed Mastol.

Chapter Thirty Seven:
An Unexpected Proposal

The groups gathered quickly in the keep of Tanis's palace. The gathering took some time as they had to await the dwarven and Elven envoys. Tanis's eyes lit up as he saw Perrick riding at the head of the dwarven column. "Welcome back old friend. Good to see you well." said Tanis.

"Almost wasn't well. I took on a dwarven wife. When I told her I was summoned to you, let us just say that I had to do some fancy footwork to keep from being here in multiple pieces. She is a great cook and wonderful woman, but a little on the controlling side. She told me that I had better come home straight away from this war because she was not going to act in my stead for too long. Typical women, huh. Still mooning over that dangerous one of yours? She would be even worse than mine I wager. At least mine can cook." laughed Perrick.

"Still can't shut you up, huh Perrick? Married huh? You mean some woman decided she could handle you? She must be some saint of a woman. Come we have a great deal of business to discuss and already you are the last to arrive. Even the gargoyles are here already. Ruark sends his regards. He did not know you would be here. You can return them yourself." replied Tanis as he led everyone into the great hall. As promised the dragon's snout could be seen peeking into the keep window as they all took their seats.

"We have a grave problem. The forces of evil have struck. Demons were seen at the assassination of my father. I have now taken the reigns of the Elves, along with the rule of all the others who have put themselves under my rule. The list grows longer by the day. I hope I can live up to their expectations. I need to bring our troops to the West where the wizard, Marzioa, lives. He is the one with the power to summon and control Demons. It must have been him who sent these creatures after my father." began Tanis.

"The wizard has not caused any harm or concern up until now. How can we be sure it is him?" asked Artitous. "Could there be no other with such ability? If they are strong enough to summon and control a pack of Demons, they are strong enough to hide themselves. We must also face the fact that we may not have a face to place on this enemy"

"How could be any other? A cloaked figure was seen leaving the scene of the crime. It seemed that the Demons were playing with him until he fought back. This figure has to be the wizard. He does nothing to be a part of our coalition. He has not even bothered to answer the invitation I sent to him to come speak with Me." said Tanis.

As he spoke the doors to the room blew open. All eyes focused on the figure in the dark robes walking into the room. Slowly it walked into the room and moved to the front of the table where all the leaders of Tanis's people were seated. The dragon just watched in silence as the cloaked figure moved around the table. When it reached the end of the table, the figure lowered the hood of its cloak, revealing an Elven man. "I have not responded to your requests for I have not had reason to do so. I am always very busy so I leave my home only when it is necessary. You request for a dinner visit left me lacking in desire. I heard of the passing of the Elf King. Toirin was not my best friend but neither was he an enemy. I will grieve his passing when time permits."

"You had him murdered you false ally and friend. You murdered my father. It had to be you." said Tanis.

"I had no hand in the death of your father. I sensed the portal open. That is what woke me from my sleep and brought me here. I am sure that your father sensed it as well. It is why he was in the stables I would wager. He probably was on his way here when he was ambushed. Did you not know he was in armor and on his way here when he died? I found this out by sending my draconians to find out what had happened. They reported rapidly on the cause of the excitement. He apparently killed three of the Demons before he was killed. That is no small task. So now I am here. I hold no blame for your father's death, but I will loan you my minions of draconians to fight alongside your other allies. I too will join you on the field of battle. A limitedly trained wizard such as you will need some help if the wizard who summoned those Demons does show himself." said the wizard.

"Does someone hold the power now?" asked the wizard. Looking around the room his eyes fell on all of those who could wield the power as well as a couple who until this very moment were unaware of their abilities including the maid of Athinina. "Clairine does not have the ability to wield the power." said Athinina. "I would have known about it. We have no secrets. She would have told me. All of our women who have the ability are collected, taught, and placed in service to the people. None are left to learn on their own. If she had the gift she would have been taken and that is all there is to it. Your senses are wrong good wizard."

"As you say dear lady. As you say." said the wizard.

"I now need to assign a bodyguard for myself. It should consist of a combination of the peoples who follow us. No group left out. I suggest all of you select three men each from your armies. The best warriors you possess. This should show our enemies that we do not fear them by over-protecting. Nor do we leave us vulnerable to attack. I even have a name for this group, The Hands of the Phoenix. This group will have the safety of me and those close to me in their care. Choose carefully as these men will have complete access to me. I would not like to have to worry if I will come to harm while I bathe. Does anyone have any idea where we travel to? We must find out who caused these attacks. We must find out and eliminate them before all is lost. Anyone any ideas?" said Tanis.

"I believe I know where we can begin." said the wizard.

"My lord, please come to my rooms this evening after the dinner hour." asked Athinina. "I have something of which I wish to speak to you about in private quarters."

"My dear lady, as much as I enjoy your company alone and in public I have no time for revelry now. But speak now and we can settle what makes you uncomfortable. Most of us present here are dear friends and will think no less of you regardless of what you have to say." said Tanis.

"Tanis, you misunderstand me. We must speak in private for I have something important to ask you. This has nothing to do with this assembly. Please, meet me later so we can speak." said the Tyris Queen.

"Once more I say just speak your mind, dear lady. Speak your mind." said Tanis.

"Fine then, you will marry me. I wish it and require it of you." said the Queen of the Tyris.

"My lady! I had no idea! But the manner in which you present this. I don't know...." began Tanis.

"When I first arrived here you told me that anything I required I would have. You told me to command what I needed and I would have it. So now I stand before you and I say this. I need you. I require you. Beside me forever. You and me together for all eternity. I love you and know that you love me. So I say again I require you and by your word, if I require it you will deliver it. So do you say that you will not honor your word?" said Athinina.

"Athinina, those near to me die. I do not wish to lose you as well. How can you ask me to allow you to place yourself in harm's way? That is the last thing in the world I would allow." said Tanis.

"You placed no restrictions on your statement. I say again. I require you. So what say you before all these witnesses? Is your word good or is it worthless? The choice is yours."

"Athinina, I will live up to my word. But I fear you may regret your request. I do love you Athinina, and I will give you what you ask." Tanis replied.

"See I told you this was worth leaving my tower for. So now I get to attend a wedding and a war. Who says you cannot get any better. Shall we go prepare?" said Marzioa. "I know the perfect draconians for your new bodyguard. They are more than adequate for the task you are looking to perform. A wedding, wow. Not what I was expecting. Let me go and make my preparations."

"Let us all go and make our preparations. Time is going to move quickly from here on. I suspect that we will be seeing the first battles as we move. I hope you know what you are doing Marzioa. I hope you are right in your assumption that you know where to start." said Tanis.

"So do I" was the wizard's only reply.

CHAPTER THIRTY EIGHT: PROPHECY

The wedding was planned for the coming week. The entire palace and all of the visiting dignitaries and their troops assisted in the preparations. Athinina stood on the ramparts and watched the commotion going on beneath her. Clairine moved up beside her and looked on with her queen. Athinina kept looking on without speaking as they continued setting up for the big day. Tanis wanted everything perfect for his bride to be. As for her, she could not understand why there was so much fuss made by these people.

"He does not know what makes a coupled married in our culture does he?" asked Clairine. "Should I tell him?"

"I think I will enjoy showing him after his ceremony. He is definitely in for a surprise I think." giggled the Warrior Queen.

"He is definitely in for a surprise, my queen." Snickered the maid.

Meanwhile Tanis ran all over the palace. His head full of the wedding that was coming. He had almost totally forgotten the war that loomed on the horizon. He had been running all day when he paused by a wall to catch his breath. He stopped and leaned on the wall to collect himself before moving on to his next task when the wall he leaned on gave way. Looking around him he found himself in a chamber he did not even know existed. Slowly he moved around the room looking at the paintings and books lining the walls.

Dust covered the table in the middle of the room and the table contained an open text. The book looked as if it had been pulled out and left momentarily then utterly forgotten. It sat in the stand open where it had been whenever it was pulled from the shelves. Dust covered it almost from top to bottom and the layer of dust was so deep that Tanis almost missed the book.

After a few moments of cleaning Tanis could read the text so long left there waiting to be read. Slowly he moved his eyes over the text and read the lines left for his eyes to find so many years later.

"And In a time ruled by evil and darkness,
One will come to rule us and to save us. He will
Rule the world, but he will never ascend the throne.
Demons at his feet will lay dead, slain for their evil
And at their feet he too will lay dead, slain for our lives.
He will never own a throne, yet he will forever rule our lives.
The Phoenix will come to save us all. Aided by his wife and family
He will push his life to save us all.
His widow will bear the new rulers of our world
And it is their offspring who will truly rule this world from on high."

Tanis looked at the text in confusion as he continued to read. It made no sense. He studied history and he remembered no ruler whose children ruled the entire world. *Artitous may know*, thought Tanis as he picked up the book without further thought and shoved it under his arm. He looked around and finally found the lever that released him from the room and moved down the hall looking for the ancient Druid.

It was not the Druid Tanis found as he moved down the hall. Marzioa nearly ran over Tanis without realizing as he moved down the hall knocking Tanis to the floor. Marzioa bent to assist Tanis to his feet when his eyes fell upon the text. "Tanis, where did this text come from?" asked the wizard.

"What text? Oh that. I found it in a hidden chamber in the side wing the wedding will be held in. I leaned upon a wall and nearly fell into the room. It was laying there wide open when I entered the room." said Tanis.

"Show me this room and I suggest you move this wedding." said the wizard.

"I will show you but what harm can one text do? It is so old that no one remembers even who wrote it. What good would it do to see the chamber? It is not even an accurate measure of history. The man it speaks of never existed. I know history and this King never existed." said Tanis.

"The King does exist. You are too close to see it is all. He stands as close as your shadow don't you know. This is prophesy. It is not history. This text could be dangerous in the wrong hands. For this is a guide to absolute power for good or evil. With this text anyone could take power over the entire world. The whole future of our world is written here. The other texts in this room must be as powerful lest they would not have been hidden." said the wizard as they moved briskly toward the hidden space.

Artitous moved toward them and followed them in their hurry. "Where do we fly to my good men?" asked Artitous.

"We have found a hidden cache of the great texts. This is stuff right up your alley Lord Bard. It is history and present and other topics close to your heart. We cannot speak here. We are not alone." said Marzioa.

But as he said his piece the fact that they were followed became apparent. Several men separated themselves from the wall and moved toward the apparently unarmed trio. The men moved rapidly toward the three men. Tanis was the first to see the black blade in hands of the closest man. Shoving the wizard to the floor, Tanis let fly with a fireball that tore the man in two. Two more assailants jumped over the corpse of their fallen fellow and moved closer for the attack.

Artitous lifted his arms to attack but never got the chance. As he lifted his arms the men fell to the ground. Each with weapons through them. Weapons of many different societies. The Hands of the Phoenix stepped from where they hid and moved to retrieve their weapons. "This one is Tagarin if I do not miss my guess" "This one is Malgorian" "This one is Draconian" "This one is Talick" came the calls back and forth as the men looked at the fallen.

The wizard looked down at the fallen enemies and shook his head. "Hunters, my Lord Tanis, Death Hunters. It is a good thing we killed them, or they would have kept trying until you were dead or they were. They were focused on you. Tell me again. You found the book open to what page? Show me the text. I suspect our enemy also knows this text. Followers of the dark lords come here looking for you. But I would swear that the Dark Knight would not have anything to do with texts. So how would the text have been opened to this segment? I suspect that we have a spy amongst us." said Marzioa.

"Tell us everything my Lord. And show me this room. Something tells me there is more there than a text that predicts the future." said Artitous. "I suspect this is the study of a great wizard. Tell me Marzioa, who owned this palace prior to the Dark Knight?"

"The Druid council owned this castle. They owned it for millennium before the knight took it. They used it only as a place of research and study. They did nothing else here. It was once known as the Druid's Keep." said the wizard.

"Then we are in more danger than we ever believed. Many seers lived amongst and taught the Druid priests and elders. If this is a repository of the secret knowledge which they hid from their own initiates, how much more dangerous is it in the hands of our enemies? This could be disaster beyond our imagining. We must keep this room to ourselves. No one else must know of it." said Artitous.

"Can it not be sealed?" asked the younger man. "After all, magic can be protected by magic."

"Yes and alert every creature capable of using magic that there is something there to hide. Are you mad? Tell me, young man, when in battle how do you hide your ambushes?" asked Artitous.

"You hide it in plain sight, blending it in with the surrounding environment. But what does that have to…… I think I see. By doing nothing it makes it harder to find." said Tanis.

"Eventually even a blind squirrel finds a nut, huh Artitous." said the wizard.

"Yeah, everyone gets lucky sometimes. Even the young." laughed the arch Druid.

As the wizard and druids moved away a shadow detached itself from the wall and moved into the chamber. This is where she would find the magic she required. She search for a moment and removed a single text. Then she moved to the door and again melted in to the shadows. She would be ready this time.

CHAPTER THIRTY NINE: WEDDING NIGHT JITTERS

Three days after the attack in the palace, the wedding of Tanis Thalin and Athinina Targul took place. The grand hall of the palace was filled with people from every corner of his kingdom. Many came to see the new couple as they left the hall and maybe touch the hems of their garments. The hall was decorated with flowers by the thousands and with fineries that rivaled the very palaces of Olympus themselves. No expense was spared as the tapestries and silks were placed about the hall. Great vats of flowers white as a new fallen snow were placed with care at close intervals making it appear as if the ceremony occurred in a vast flowered meadow.

The columns were covered in silk imprinted with the sigils of the Targul and Thalin Houses. The white backgrounds stood out strongly against the dark grey stone of the columns. The seats covered in a soft padding of new white wools. The bride presented herself for the ceremony in a fine new gown made for her by the palace seamstresses. The cloth of the gown could have produced enough shirts to clothe half of the soldiers in Tanis's army. The veil covered her face was so light that the gentle breeze of her breath caused the veil to stir before her. She felt distinctly uncomfortable in her gown and swore that it would be a new shirt for the troops as soon as she could be out of it. She would not have worn it, electing to marry in something much simpler, except for the statement by Artitous that appearances were all important to the people. The people prefer to see something extravagant by those who

123

lead them as a show that they can and will provide for their people. It made little sense to her.

Tanis arrived at the wedding in the same simple tunic he normally wore for special occasions. The velveteen of the tunic was made to match the fabric that covered the entire hall. Tanis had the tunic made for the wedding in white so that he could tell Athinina that it was indeed a new tunic. When Athinina saw Tanis in his new tunic, her eyes opened wide with surprise. Here she was draped like a huge gift and there was her husband to be standing there as comfortable as could be. The look she gave him promised a firm speaking to when the ceremonies were complete.

As Athinina came down the aisle to meet her husband and for the ceremony to begin, all the anger and distress over her garments disappeared. A feeling of butterflies in her stomach, so foreign to her, suddenly hit her as she moved to Tanis's side. The feeling grew worse as she looked at him and she realized that this would change her world forever. She could no longer think for herself alone. There were two of them now. She would never have to walk alone again. She looked over at Clairine at her side. The woman had been at her side for years. Now she would have two rulers. No more answering to her alone. True amongst her people men had few rights but she was no longer amongst just her people. She would have to think as these odd outsiders thought now.

Clairine smiled at her and the butterflies settled. She was doing the right thing. Clairine would not allow her to do otherwise. Clairine looked at her mistress with pride in her eyes and her heart. She was doing what was best for her people and for herself by marrying the young Lord. Athinina would now lead the largest land force ever assembled. She truly was the greatest of the Tyris Queens. Clairine watched the long ceremony with great boredom and nearly fell from her chair when Tanis interrupted it by grabbing Athinina and kissing her deeply before the entire crowd.

"I couldn't wait any longer, Lady. Please forgive me for spoiling such a great ceremony." said Tanis to the queen.

"Trust me, my lord. I was almost tempted to do the same to you if this continued much longer. I was kind of hoping that this would be over sooner than later. Now please explain something to me. Why am I burdened with all this fluff when you get to wear clothing as you always do? I think you and I are going to have to discuss this more closely later." warned Athinina.

"Just be gentle with me my lady. That is all I ask." said Tanis as they moved from the hall to the banquet that awaited them out before the palace.

The Druid Priest presiding over the event look puzzled and amazed as the couple walked from the hall and left him standing before the startled crowd alone. Once more the young lord had amazed them all and done what they had least expected.

Chapter Forty:
Celebrations and Surprises

Out in the courtyard where they had set the banquet, large kegs of wine and beer had been set up with stewards standing by to serve the guests. Large tables of food were spread around the entire courtyard piled high with such dishes as roasts and pork and venison. Large quantities of fruits and vegetables filled other tables and stewards waited there as well for the guests. There were no tables to sit and eat as Tanis wanted the food and drink available to any who desired some. As platters emptied chefs refilled them with fresh food from the kitchens. The locals who farmed the land brushed elbows with the lords and ladies who ruled their lands in Tanis's name. Shepherds mingled with bankers and beggars with lords. Class meant nothing this day and Tanis ensured that it remained that way by stopping and speaking to every one of the people who had come to this event.

By the end of the day Tanis and Athinina were hoarse from the well-wishers and those who would see the bride and groom to a very happy honeymoon with suggestions for the wedding night. Athinina assured her warriors that the wedding night was already well taken care of. Tanis would blush whenever he would hear Athinina speaking to one of the Tyris warriors. After all, this was not something that would be discussed in proper company. This was not discussed in any company!

The couple walked tiredly and a little drunkenly toward the suite reserved for the two of them. The Hands walked slowly around them, doing their best to avoid noticing the state of their commanders. The

Hands of the Phoenix moved carefully down the darkened hall. Tanis tried to send them away stating they needed no more protection but for some unknown reason the head of the guard ordered a closer guard. As they approached the doors to the bedding chambers the doors flew from their hinges.

The guard had been waiting though. The dwarf that led jumped at the first being to move toward them through the door scoring its chest with the blade of his axe. Athinina fumbled clumsily with her gown as she struggled to draw her sword. Tanis managed to draw his but, in his state, ended with it upon the floor. His attempts to call upon the power resulted in the same failure. Athinina finally had her blade up in time to see the fallen creatures around her. The Hands had done their work with brutal efficiency. Around them lay the bodies of Demons and spiders. The spiders were large enough to consume a man with barely a hesitation. The Demons appeared to be of lesser castes and only to see to the behavior of the spiders. In the bedding chamber fine webs covered it in its entirety. Everywhere the group moved they found themselves becoming more and more entangled in the webs of the now deceased spiders. Slowly the group moved deeper into the chambers looking for more danger when the danger found them.

From the ceiling of the inner chamber a deep rumbling emerged. The group found themselves almost stuck fast by the webs that they had had to cut through. As they became trapped, they saw the cause of the sound. A huge queen spider moved toward the now trapped group and moved toward the lead man of the Hand. The man pulled and strained against the webbing trying to release him to protect himself and his master when the spider fell upon him. It was over in moments. The spider had drained him to the bone and was moving on to her next victim, a dwarf directly behind the man. The dwarf had managed to free a hand but had not managed to free a weapon. He too died rapidly as he tried to use his freed hand to clear his weapon and fight back against the giant monster.

The giant spider moved slowly toward the now stuck fast figure of Athinina and the blood of her previous victims dripped from her mandibles as she advanced. Tanis and Athinina watched in horror as the spider moved slowly across the web toward her new victims. Athinina wiggled in her dress trying to get unstuck from the webbing that now held tight to her dress. The more she squirmed the more the spider seemed enticed. Slowly Athinina seemed to become enveloped in the web as she wiggled and moved within her gigantic dress. The spider moved forward faster than Tanis thought a creature of its size should be able. Tanis was still trying to clear his mind enough to use his power to destroy either the webbing or the spider, but nothing would come.

As the spider reached the still squirming Athinina the room filled with a flash that drowned out the vision of all those who continued to try and fight. The world went dark to all those in the room as the room faded.

Chapter Forty One:
Why did it have To Be Spiders

The wedding had gone off without a hitch and Artitous and Marzioa were slowly moving down the corridors discussing the room in which Tanis had found the text. Something just did not seem right that the room was hidden and never found by the prior occupant. The discussion had gone to things such as magical protection, but they agreed they would have sensed its presence. They speculated on dumb luck, but Artitous calmly reminded his companion that there was no luck. Marzioa then countered that it was convenient that the knight had not used that wing for so long. What could possibly have kept the Dark Knight from that wing?

Artitous was looking around and thinking when Marzioa suddenly stopped. "How much cob webbing and spider webbing did the stewards say they removed from that wing?" asked the wizard.

Artitous looked confused for a moment then realized what his friend was alluding to. "Where would they have gone? Why would they not have attacked? There would have to have been an entire colony of the beasts to have created that much web." said the Druid.

"They did, we just did not realize it. Remember we assumed that several of our workers left before the work was done because no trace of them could be found? Remember how many of the workers complained of being bitten or stuck by things unseen as work proceeded? We have been blind! They did protect them. They placed the spiders here as a security system that would appear natural. The only question now is where they would have gone since they were not crashing the wedding?" asked the wizard.

"Spiders like the dark, high, damp places of our world. They would not have traveled far from their usual hunting grounds, especially if they suddenly became very lucrative to them. So where would they hide until all was cleared away and they could return?" asked the Druid.

"The bridal suite!" they shouted in unison as they turned around and ran for the high dark chambers that the newlyweds had chosen for their honeymoon. Rapidly they traversed the halls calling for every soldier that was still fit to hold a weapon to follow behind them. The two learned magi called to anyone with the strength of will or the ability to wield the power to come after them to the bridal suite and to make haste.

The outer doors where closed when the now huge party of men, Dwarves, Elves, and every other sort of creature that followed Tanis reached them. Artitous's first thought was that the honeymoon had commenced and that this was a false alarm. Marzioa looked at Artitous and smacked him in the back of his head. "Artitous, learned friend, one thing causes error to your theory. There are no posted guards." Marzioa moved through the outer doors and cut a path with his power toward the inner chamber. He arrived in time to see the giant spider bearing down upon Athinina's now helpless form.

Marzioa let fly a spell no one present had ever seen before. At first it blinded everyone in the inner chamber and startled the spider. Then at near the same time it turned into a ball of light that slammed into the body of the spider sending it sprawling. The spell stayed with the creature and continued to pummel and beat against the great arachnid until finally the spider tried a final time to fight back and was once more beaten into submission. With a great heave the spider curled it legs beneath it and slowly stopped its breath. Marzioa took no chances with deception and ordered several spearmen to bring in very large spears and see to the destruction of the creature. His orders left no room for interpretation. No one was to get near the spider.

Artitous looked around the carnage in the inner chamber and saw the remains of the two soldiers who had been killed by the spider. One of the two fallen warriors was a ranger. A ranger was a long-range scout who used disguise and subterfuge to hide and learn information which he then returned to his lord. The Druid looked to the wizard and asked "Marzioa, a question. Don't these great spiders take on the intelligence and capabilities of those whom they feed upon?"

"My friend I believe you are right. That would mean that the spider would have some idea of tactics and fighting having killed the two soldiers." said the wizard.

"You make a mistake. Only one of these was a soldier. The other was a ranger which would mean that..." began Artitous.

"Run you fools!" screamed both magi at the same time. "It feigns death!" And both the magi ran toward the curled form of the great beast. Their warning came too late for those closest to the giant spider. As the magus screamed to them the spider made its move. Quickly it was upon the two closest soldiers and had killed the two with her mandibles spearing a third with her stinger. The spider slowly circled the two magi standing before it back to back. Both bore flames around their hands and looked at the spider with unbroken attention. "Remove everyone from the room." called Artitous to the surrounding soldiers. "This is our fight now. Just get everyone else out of here before any others can be killed."

Rapidly soldiers started moving to clear away the webbing and release their lord and lady, as well as their comrades-in-arms. Several Tyris arrived in time to be shooed from the room with the rest of the newly arrived soldiers who had heard something was occurring on the upper floors. The wizard and the Druid moved to keep the creature from moving toward those who were trapped, keeping themselves between it and its intended victims.

Finally, the all clear was given and the two magic users looked at each other and then the beast. Marzioa struck again with his abusive ball of light while Artitous struck with fireballs. Rapidly the spider succumbed to the combined attack of the two wielders of the power and it fell to the floor. To ensure no further subterfuge from the spider, Artitous cast a further fireball to incinerate the great insect while Marzioa swept the burning remains on a flow of air into the fireplace.

The two magi remained until the remains were reduced to dust, just to ensure that there could be no further mistakes on any of their parts.

"Artitous, I do believe after this, we need and deserve a drink." said the wizard.

"Why my good man, whatever do you mean? A drink? I had more like four or five in mind myself." laughed the Druid.

"Well let us begin with one and add them from there." replied the now laughing wizard.

Tanis and Athinina finally awoke as the two magi walked down the hall laughing at talking of how they had underestimated their adversary. Tanis looked to Athinina and Athinina looked to Tanis. The two moved from the floor and began down the halls. They did not speak only looked at each other and shook their heads. One of the Hands of the Phoenix who came to replace those incapacitated in the fight looked at Tanis and asked, "What is wrong my Lord?"

"Can anyone ever figure wizards?"

CHAPTER FORTY TWO:
THE FIRST WAVES

The couple never did get their honeymoon for soon after the wedding the wars began in earnest. It was but a mere week after the wedding that the first battle occurred before the very walls of the Dark Knight's city. Great bands of men and reptilians attacked aided by packs of werewolves and vampires. Trolls dotted the battlefield fighting for the werewolves and vampires, keeping their distance from the reptilians that ferociously tore into the men, Dwarves, Elves, and draconians of Tanis's army.

Wave after wave attacked the defenders of the city and was repelled again and again. The Tyris joined the fray and managed to assist in driving back and destroying a small portion of the Trolls that had joined against the forces of Good.

Again, and again the battle grew in fierceness then waned. It would grow then wane. Finally, it appeared that the defenders had defeated the men and their allies. The defenders pushing their enemies further and further back from the city. Just as they thought the final blows were being struck, the next wave appeared.

This wave was different than the ones that the allies had faced before. This wave included minor Demons and firedrakes. The firedrakes called themselves dragons at one time but were cast from the species by the other dragons. The firedrakes were not as smart as their cousins the dragons and they had no sense of justice or compassion. The firedrakes killed for fun and pleasure, not to survive.

On came the firedrakes and minor Demons. The already tired and battle-weary soldiers of the city fell back to the walls of the city and were pushed hard to keep the invaders out. The last few of the city's reserves flew to the fight but soon it looked as if they too would be overrun. With certain victory now appearing to be in the hands of the enemy, once more the enemy pushed the downtrodden defenders. From the sky above came a sudden shrill call. Looking up into the sky showed that help for the allies had arrived in the form of the gargoyles and their allies the giant rocs. The Rocs were great eagles that measured enormously in size and girth. These seven or eight hundred-pound eagles could sever the neck of a dragon with a single well placed bite. Their talons could tear through the strongest steel plate.

Once more the battle turned and soon the firedrakes and Demons were the ones in flight. Sensing a lull in the fighting Tanis sent out a pair of Rangers from the Tyris to scout the enemy and try to discern their next intention. Tanis had suffered a large slash early in the fighting and was been treated by the healers when word of the Rangers' return reached him. Trying to move from the healer's tent, Tanis was stopped and restrained by members of his own guard and his wife. Athinina had been in the thickest of the fighting and was completely unharmed. Tanis could only look at her in wonder and try to determine what kind of power looked over her like a cloud.

The Rangers flew into the tent and stood before the table Tanis had been wrestled down to. It had the air of a bit of a poor timing to the Rangers, walking in with the Lord's wife resting upon him in a rather unseemly way. Tanis bid them to give their report and to disregard the performance going on before them. He assured them that it was definitely not what they believed it to be. The new Lady of the land simple wished to prevent him from further harming himself. Tanis blushed as the Rangers turn their backs on the couple. "This is not the way it appears!" He cried to those in the tent.

The Rangers merely snickered as he protested. Athinina smiled knowingly as the Rangers finally moved into a position where they could give their reports. This caused even more red faces and even more laughter as the Rangers moved quickly to have their backs to the pair.

"Please give me your word good people. Please I need to know what information you bring here. What have you seen? Is it over or are more on their way?" queried Tanis of the Rangers.

"My lord, the enemy moves from the lands of darkness to the fields of Gennii. They seek to set camp in our sacred fields. They come from the three major Dread Lords left alive. I fear this may be the battle that we have been waiting for. Thousands of men, firedrakes, Demons, and dark creatures flood onto the plains daily. We watched the approach and we have seen more clans present than I have ever thought to see in one place. The Dark World comes to war!" said the first of the Rangers.

"My lord, the news is as bad from all directions. They are coming. They move with an efficiency I have never before seen. It may be a very short time before more attack." said the second ranger.

"Thank you for your information. I will debate on what should be done. Artitous and Athinina, please come to me here. I have a large favor to ask of the two of you. I need you to travel north to the lair of the great wyrm. Tell him I need all the dragons that can be mustered. Artitous I ask that you go to the gargoyles and see to it they are moving. Marzioa, I need you to see to the draconians. I will muster and lead the main body already assembled. It will be up to me to see that this battle is fought well and to hold until our full might may lend us victory. Go to your respective assignments and bring these warriors to our aid. We need this more than a few more capable warriors on the front lines. No arguments from anyone. Just go. We all have our assignments. Go!" said Tanis as he managed to move himself from beneath his wife. Already he had documents and maps being brought to him. Tanis was pouring over them when a sound filtered into his hearing.

"I already sent you all out on your errands. What do you need?" asked Tanis as the flap closed behind the figure entering the tent. "I come to speak to you, Lord Tanis Thalin. Son of the Lord McCryden and the local flip skirt. This is the young bull and wizard we are to fear? I never suspected a mere child would claim so many of the others. You are what, twenty or thirty summers? My god, at this time in my life I was just starting magic. The dark power is a strange bedfellow I will warn you. It promises great things and delivers. Have no doubts about that, it delivers, but it also comes at a great price. Only the strong are able to pay that price to make themselves strong enough to face a true dark sorcerer. It is the dark power that makes us strong you know. I can teach you this power. It will prevent you from growing old. It will protect you from harm. All it demands is blood. The blood of your family. All you need do is ask and I will teach you the ways and means of this dark magic. I will teach you how to destroy your enemies with a wave of your hand. All you need do is bow!" said the robed figure.

"I have recently injured my knee, so pardon me if I do not kneel at your feet. I fear I have stretched my neck as well, for it will not bend to bribery. I know what your dark sorcery can do, for I have seen it. I also have no desire to see it again. Tell me, how long did you plan on waiting to reveal yourself? Did you feel that waiting until now would help your cause? Tell me what have you gained from your charade? You hide amongst us and act as if you are one of us. You believe we allow you information that may alter the final event that is to come to pass. I know you have found the storeroom. I also know that you know the prophecies of the Phoenix. The final battle is not ours, but much further down the road. Maybe our heirs will be the ones to settle this? So, do you wish to lower your veil now or do you wish your face revealed after one of us is dead?" asked the Lord of the Land.

"You believe you know so much. I offer again this great gift. You have no other options than join me or die. So, what is your choice? You are immortal, and yet you would throw it away for these things? Join me. Give me your gift and I will ensure that you are raised high in the dark legions. This is not instant, unlike these foolish beings. You start at the bottom and work your way up. In a few hundred years you may even be the top dog. But for now, do you live with me, or do you die alone for these things?" asked the cloaked figure.

"To think I counted you amongst my friends and advisors. You believe that you control me? You believe that you have the power to force my hand? I have not shown my power. If you seek to see power never doubt that I will dispense it without fear upon my enemies. I will give you the option now, stand with us against these hordes and assist us in their destruction, or stand against me, and be destroyed with them,

Clairine. Won't your mistress miss your services one way or the other?" asked Tanis. His voice trailing to a whisper as he spoke her name and turned to face his adversary. He drew his sword and moved toward the standing form of the maid. "You killed my father. You killed all of those close to me. The Dark Knight and Lord McCryden both answered to you. You killed those whom you believed to be of most threat, yet you never came close enough to Artitous or myself to allow us to see the real you. Did you think we did not know? How long did you think to conceal your true form from all of us? Are you planning on running now or maybe attacking me and hoping that you may overpower me? You may start a battle that was foretold by that seer so many years ago and see either a new beginning or an end to our world. The choice is now yours. A new battle or a lasting peace chooses well, for your choice now will decide the fate of our world. Whoever wins this battle will rule this world in its entirety. Choose and let us be done with the games and the charades." said Tanis.

"Choose you say. View my true form and then I will give you my choice. War is here. Now I tell you. View my true form then hear my choice." said Clairine. As she spoke the maid suddenly swelled and became larger and more muscled. Horns sprouted from her head and wings from her back. The woman's face distorted and changed to that of the monster within. As she changed, she grew larger and larger until the tent no longer was able to conceal the events within it. Flinging her arms into the air Clairine threw the remains of the tent to the ground and shouted to all those around her, "Hear me forces of the light. For too long my people have been imprisoned and enslaved by those who knew the ways of our kind. Now is the time of freedom for all Demons and those who follow and revere us. Those who follow the ways of justice and goodness will now feel the yoke of our reign. I say to you all, take up your arms! The battle is upon you and I will see to the destruction of all who oppose the forces of evil."

CHAPTER FORTY THREE: DEMONIC BATTLE

With that the Demon produced a blade of flame and attacked the smaller form of the man at her feet. Tanis met stroke for stroke, every move the Demon made. Potiutios, the greatest of the Demons once hidden as a lady's maid, moved harder and harder toward the leader of the free world. Tanis moved side to side using his speed and agility to stay out of the range of the greater Demon's reach. As the fight began with the Demon, a great roar came from the surrounding forest. More Demons poured from the trees assisted by those who had chosen to follow the fell beasts. Firedrakes and Trolls burst onto the fields and tore into the defenders trying to prepare for the battle. The forces of evil and the forces of good moved back and forth along the field pushing to keep and protect their respective leader. Each battle seemed tied to the other. As Tanis gained the upper hand and pushed back the great evil, evil retreated and lost ground to the defenders of the light. As Tanis fell back to regroup and regain his composure so too did the forces of the light.

Back and forth the two parties moved up and down the field. As the battle progressed more warriors from both sides of the battle arrived. Dragons suddenly dived down and attacked the Demons from the air, while the horned winged harpies attacked them. Draconians fought the men and firedrakes fending off the miniature dragons preventing them from attacking the men and Elves. As more troops on both sides of the battle arrived the battle escalated and more combatants on both sides fell.

Tanis threw his shield to the ground and drew the Holy Avenger. Both blades sung as they attacked the now tiring Demon. Tanis also felt the fatigue settle upon him. Knowing that the battle between the two of them was nearing completion, Tanis moved suddenly into the attacking Demon's path. Caught unaware the Demon raised its blade to finally finish the young Druid who had harassed and challenged it so. Potiutios moved to finish the young attacker and felt the burns of the other's attack. She moved forward trying to gain her footing again and tried to spread her wings as she felt the pinch of the second attack. The wings on her back refused to move as she commanded. Again, she tried to launch herself into the air and again her wings refused to respond.

Tanis was struck as he moved in to finish the dark lord, tearing the meat of his arm so deeply he nearly lost the Holy Avenger. As the arm failed from its wound it fell and tore away the wings from the fell beast. Both combatants severely wounded, they paused to look around them. Rings went forth from them of the dead and dying. Fighting was still erupting where the living found the living. Everywhere the two warriors looked they saw death and destruction. The great Demon looked down at Tanis and smiled. It raised its arm and swiped Tanis through the middle sending him to the ground. Like a spider the Demon pounced on the fallen form of the man. Potiutios hoped to finally finish the creature that had caused it so much pain and suffering.

As Tanis watched the fell beast falling upon him, he realized that he could not keep the beast from finishing him this time. He watched in slow motion as the beast jumped upon his prone body. His reaction was to lift the Warmonger toward the Demon as it crashed down upon him. He felt the blade bite into the body of his foe as he felt his enemy's weapon bite into his chest. Tanis hoped his blade had caused the wound his enemy had caused him. Tanis fought to stand and found his body not responding. He tried to move his head and found it impossible. As the world began to fade, he saw a figure approach him.

As the hooded figure looked down upon him the figure came into focus as the rest of the world faded. The face that looked down upon him suddenly relieved his fears and worries. His dear Charina's face stared down at him from the cowls of the robes. Charina reached down a hand and took his hands in hers, "It is time my love." said the apparition before him. "Do not fear, your wife and your children will continue where you have finished. It is time for you to rest now. You have done your part. Your children wait for your coming. It will fill your son with pride when he hears of your deeds this day."

"My children? I have had no more children since our children. To whom to you refer?" asked Tanis.

"She never told you? She is pregnant. She will bear you twin sons before the year ends. They will be the ones to continue where you have finished. Now come. You will be reunited with them all in time and we will all celebrate the world you have created and the peace you have begun." said Charina.

"Will this hurt?" whispered Tanis as the world once more faded from grey to black.

"Never again my love." replied Charina as her face faded and disappeared.

CHAPTER FORTY FOUR: AFTERMATH

Artitous made it back to the battle in time to see the final blows of the battle between the great lords of this world. The great Demon fell upon his master only to find his blade waiting and his own life expired. Rushing to his master's side he realized that his master no longer was here. The two had finished each other. Looking around he saw that the battle was over. Both sides had suffered great losses, but the forces of the light still had a leader. The forces of darkness had fallen away and dissolved with the coming of day. He felt the world moving from the darkness that had enshrouded it to the new day.

It was over. They had won but the cost had been extreme. The Lord of the World lay dead, as did most of the armies of the world. The great Demon and most of his legions lay dead, and again there were none to move into the void created by their loss. The side of light had won. The war was over. He sat down and prepared a fire to perform the rites of seeing. As the flame moved and grew, he looked deep within and his breath caught. It was not finished, just a pause, for now.

A new battle was coming. A new war was coming. His family now ruled this world, but now they would be forced to keep that rule. It would not happen tomorrow. But the time was coming. Artitous looked down at the flame and smiled. He still had much to do.

CHAPTER FORTY FIVE:
THE DAY OF LOSS

The night was not like many others in this region of Dracos. The mountains left little to the imagination. The cold kept most people indoors during the latter times of the night and the lack of light kept the general public indoors for fear of thieves and brigands. The darkened hillside was not much different from others in the region. It was cold and dark, and yet there was a difference that many would remember for the rest of their lives.

Along the paths and trails, all appeared normal and quite mundane. But once you ventured deep into the trees and finally reached the clearing usually reserved for the highest of the Druids, you found what would make this hill different. The clearing was covered with the bodies of the dead and dying. Only two people moved among the carnage on that field; a woman warrior, a Tyris, and a small, poorly built and dressed bard, a poet and writer among the Druid clans, as most bards were.

The Tyris did not see the bard, nor did she care to. She had her head bent close to the ground looking for someone or something amongst the dead and dying. Of what she searched for the bard could not tell. As the woman walked her torn Mytan, a form of armor made specifically for the Tyris; a combination of a leather overcoat sewn over top of a steel plate, waved in the reflected light of the full moon exposing quite a considerable amount of bosom, even for the rather flagrant nature of the Tyris warriors. Her simple leather boots and torn leggings gave her the appearance of a lost soul looking for rest after a foul deed. Lost and wounded looking for the rest it knew it deserved. The woman was not wounded however, the blood staining her hands and her clothes was not her own but lost and confused she was.

The Tyris searched a long time amongst the corpses of the Demons, men, and beasts that littered that field. It was with great sadness that she found the object of her search. At first the bard could not see what it was she stared upon. Was it a man, beast, weapon, or one of a million other countless things that littered that field? As the bard neared, he saw what it was and saw who as well the Tyris was. The woman was Athinina, wife of the greatest legend of the bard's time. It was her husband that she stared down upon. He lay amid a circle of the men called the Hands of the Phoenix. How she had hated those men in life. Their rude comments and even ruder manners made living with them around almost unbearable. In the sleep of death though she knew she would miss the comments and the mannerisms of these men. In the heart of them, lying motionless was her husband, the Phoenix of legend, Tanis Thalin. At his feet lay the corpse of the largest of the Greater Demons, Potiutios. It had cost her husband his life to rid the world of it evil, and now its demise held little of the satisfaction that she would normally have felt right at that moment looking down at its corpse. She looked down at the body of her lover and removed the bloodstained sword from his right hand. It bore an inscription in a harsh hand down the flat of the blade, Warmonger. It brought fear to those whom that blade was raised against. It had never been beaten and only one hand could grasp that hilt safely. Quite common in appearance, yet so heavily endowed with magic that all those who sought to own that blade died by it. That is until her lover bore it. As she lifted the blade from his right hand, the edge crossed the bare flesh of her left arm cutting, but not deeply. The curse still lived in that blade. No hand but his. She quickly sheathed the blade throwing her own blade down to the now red stained earth. No hand would ever draw that cursed blade again.

In his left hand, the legend bore the Holy Avenger. It was called by most who knew Thalin as the Demon Slayer and it had lived up to its name. As abnormal as the Warmonger was normal in appearance, the Holy Avenger held little joy for the young woman. Its snake curved blade etched with a six pointed star, a crossed piece of wood, and a sacred oak tree, the sacred symbol of the Druids, had its name etched down the center in a hand that could have returned to copying bibles as soon as it had finished those two words. She held the blade in one hand as she closed the staring eyes of her husband. A tear formed in her saddened eyes as she stepped back from the shell that once held the man she loved. "My husband, it is I, Athinina. Please get up. I have collected your blades and we are ready to begin a new life in this beautiful world of yours." It was more plea than a statement. The greatest Tyris stood there over her fallen love and continued to beg. "Please get up and join me in this great victory." Then she whispered, barely audible to the young bard who had come to stand behind her, "what will I do without you?"

At that last statement the woman turned and burst into tears. The bard placed his hands on her shoulders, and she embraced the young man. He tried in vain to pull her from the scene as she continued to call out to her husband. Through her tears she looked at last at the man who held her and told him in a voice that could have frozen the lakes of half the world, "Write well of this day and my husband, Bard. For the greatest of all men lies dead on that field." It was with that the two of them walked from the field, one for greater glory the other to walk into oblivion.

"Lady, your children will need a tutor." said the bard.

"Who better than the man who taught their father?" asked the Tyris.

"Then back to the shadows of oblivion for me." smiled the bard.

"Right where you love to be, old friend." said the Tyris as the two walked off into the coming dawn.

Chapter Forty Six:
A New Beginning

The night was dark and quiet on the mythical and magical world of Dracos. The stillness was a welcome change for the residents of the area. The trees that once hid brigands, murderers, and thieves no longer caused fear to these simple people. The One had come and made their existence safe once more. The people could go out to their neighbors' homes after dark without fear of being harmed or robbed on their way home to their simple homes. The night was almost over as our tale begins. Most of the people were sleeping in their beds as the light of the new day was dawning. Some who worked the land were already awake and waiting for the sun to begin their day's work, while others were just beginning to stir.

The sun fell upon the fields of battle that had raged nearly a year before and a glint was seen by the old man leaning on his staff looking over the great battlefield. *How many died out there that day?* Thought the old man. Such a waste of life and time was how he saw it, but it was not his call. He had followed the man here so long ago. He remembered the night he watched the hero's widow search that broken field like it was yesterday.

He had walked onto the field and seen her bent almost to the ground searching for something. He did not recognize her at first. The way she walked, and the poor light gave her the look of a spirit more than a human. She became recognizable as she drew the great man's swords from his now dead hands. He knew she was speaking but could not hear the words.

He had walked to her and she had admonished him to write the story of what had happened there. Athinina had lost so much that day. The woman she trusted more than any other person in the world had attacked her husband on that field. It had turned out that Charina was truly a greater Demon, Porthious, bent upon taking over the world. She had nearly succeeded had it not been for Tanis. He had been the one who had caused him to leave his precious Druidic Groves so many years before. The signs had been so strong that he would unite the world under one banner and rid it of the evil that had plagued it.

The signs were right, of course. They were rarely wrong, just misunderstood, or misinterpreted. People just were not meant to know what the future held. He thought that Tanis would be his companion throughout eternity. The boy was as he was, Askanitowa. The Askanitowa were the legendary immortals of the Druid lore. The stories of these great men and women were told far and wide as a means of teaching people the value of morality and kindness. They were taught as lessons in being what all people should be; kind, pious, self-sacrificing to aid his fellow being. Most people did not believe that these people had ever truly existed. The old man and women who had lived with them were long gone now. The immortals had gone into a form of hiding preferring to keep their gifts hidden. They aided their fellow people from the shadows now. It was better that way. Recognition would definitely make things much more difficult for them. People just were not meant to live forever.

He looked at the monument raised to his friend and pupil and a sad smile came to his lips. Tanis would never have approved of the gaudy display. It did not even resemble him, but the people swore it was him in all his glory. They had never met the man. They never truly saw what his existence was about. It always brought tears to his eyes to think of his old friend. Things could have been much different, but he had made his choices as all of us have to. He did not know of his unborn children growing within his wife. He would not have taken the chances he took. He would not have done the things that had cost him his life. But then the war would still be raging, and the darkness would still cover the face of Dracos. The evil that had a death grip on the world would still be there. Nothing would have changed. Men were just not supposed to know the future. The changes that come from that knowledge could be catastrophic. The very seams of existence would just fall apart. *The Creator knows what He is doing after all,* thought the old man as he began to morph into his true form. Artitous looked once more into the face of the monument and turned toward the castle in the distance. His new pupils awaited him, and it would not do to allow them to grow unguided. *Much harder than their father,* thought Artitous as he walked from the monument's field. He really needed to stop coming here. It did no good for him or anyone else to dwell on the past. As he left, he saw the rodent damage near the base of the statue. "Druids are neglecting their duties again, there is some dug up earth at the foot of the statue."

Instead of walking back to the castle, Artitous turned and placed his hands on the cold stone. He just looked up into the hard face looking out into the field. Artitous once again thought of his waiting pupils. They really would look like him. Not easy to instruct, nor as likely to be as eager as their father to learn. It was going to be a challenge to teach them everything they needed, but he would do it. He had no choice; they were the future not him. Back to the shadows was where he was headed. From there he had fought his war before, and it was there he would continue to shape things to come. *Maybe just a brief look into the future of the children might not hurt,* thought Artitous, *just a peek to see if I am on the right path.*

Again, he caught himself and smiled. Children were a gift and a challenge. He would continue as always. The same as he did with their father. Turning from the statue he walked slowly from the field. None of the scars from that day remained upon this field. To look upon it now you would not believe that thousands were buried there; buried where they had fallen because there was no other place to take the fallen. Most of the locals did not even remember that the field was also a graveyard. The Druids did their work well. They would keep the farmers and squatters from taking the land as their own for their crops as long at least as the order existed. At least they knew the truth.

Slowly he moved toward the keep deep in thought. Without looking up he addressed the trees to his left, "Athinina, you may as well come out from there. I have felt you there for some time. Do not attempt to run and hide, you know it is impolite to hide and spy on your friends."

"Still can't hide anything from you, can I?" asked the queen of Dracos.

"Gave the Hand the slip again, huh?" asked the Druid. "You will cause Captain Martin such grief he may not be able to stand for a month. You truly live to torment the man, don't you?"

"Arty, if I do not do this once in a while the men would think me soft. Besides if Martin was so good, I would not be able to slip past him. There are no more threats anymore. No one would harm me. I am their queen after all, and all is as it should be. What reason would compel them to harm me? Besides I needed to see his face again. It has been weeks since I have been here last. I begin to forget his face. Is that wrong? I fear I forget him more every day, falling in with the stories and tales. They are more real now for me than the truth. What am I to do?" asked Athinina.

"Just remember. That is all we can do." whispered the Druid as the gates to the keep rose in front of the couple and members of the Hand of the Phoenix, Dracos' elite fighting force, quickly closed ranks around the queen and the Druid.

CHAPTER FORTY SEVEN: TWINS

Athinina looked out the windows as the time of her pregnancy came to a close. Soon the child would be born, and she would be able to give her new born child all the wisdom to rule her kingdom once she was done. The pains had started in brief spurts here and there; it would not be long according to the midwives and Druids. The child was enormous, one of the midwives had commented. She had been the only one to predict twins. That would double the challenges of motherhood if that were the case. The others had simply said she retained water which was normal for a woman in this condition. Holding her now swollen belly she smiled and began thinking of the lone dissenter. Maybe she should send the midwife who had predicted twins a small gift. It was too much to hope for but still she hoped.

Walking to the small desk in her rooms she sat and started writing yet another entry in the journal she kept. Since it had happened that her best friend turned out to be a Demon in disguise, she trusted no one. She would never again allow anyone to get close. Just Artitous she smiled. He was a constant from her old life. He was all that remained of the life before that awful battle and that terrible war. He had been away from Thalinburg for months and she had worried for his safety. She knew he would return though. He would not miss the opportunity to teach the offspring of his protégé.

Picking up the journal she began to write as was her habit now when she was troubled or just needed to speak to someone or something.

Seclusion changed nothing and her public audiences to govern and settle matters of state kept her occupied much more than she truly wished to be. Perrick was never around to aid her in her duties. His wife and children needed him as much as she did, so she shouldered the burden and continued without him. Perrick had said he would return to run things when the baby came. He was still a great friend to her husband and her. He had promised to be here by week's end. It would be nice to see him and his family again.

Looking to the journal she realized that it was nearly full. This was her third journal since she had begun them at the end of that battle. She finished her entry and placed the journal on the bookcase near the other two. What would people think of her if they knew? The most powerful person in the world wrote to a stupid book. That would shake the kingdom to its core. She would have to get another one; she still needed an avenue to vent.

Moving back to the window she looked out over the castle. People moved happily around doing their assigned tasks and moving with a bounce in their step that had not been there before her husband came. Life had indeed improved for these people tremendously since the war. It was good to see people happy again. It had been so long since they had known happiness. They now had happiness, but she wondered if she would ever know it again.

The infant inside her moved again, bringing her attention to it. How she longed for a girl to teach all she knew. She longed to see her grow up into as great a woman as she was. A boy would be nice, but in her native land men were just not as revered as women. They had their place in the home, but they were not the important figures that you saw in this land. A boy would require too much coddling and care. A girl she could make strong and independent. Again, the infant moved within her and her thoughts drifted to the rooms she had prepared for the infant. It would want for nothing; the people of the kingdom had seen to that. If the toys that filled the rooms were any indication, the people would expect the child to heal with a glance and walk on water. This child would definitely want for little in this life.

Athinina rubbed her bulbous belly and moved as best she could to her bed. The child's motion had caused her some discomfort and cramping, and she decided it would be a good time to lie down. It was as she was lying there that the first wave of pain hit her, and she screamed to the ceiling. Could it be that the child was arriving? The midwives and Druids said at least another two or three weeks. How was this possible? As a second wave of pain wracked her body, she screamed out again in agony. *It was not possible that this should hurt so badly* she thought, *Women do this every day, and they suffer no ill effects. There must be something wrong.* Again, the pains came and again she let out a wail that was finally heard by the guard outside the door.

"My Lady are you alright in here?" queried the guard. "Shall I send for the midwives and Druids? Tell me what is needed, and I will fetch it, My Lady. Be calm, my missus just gave birth to my child and she was a nervous wreck. But everything went nice and smooth and she was back on her feet in a couple of days. She is quite the scrapper, your majesty, but you are stronger than she is so you should come through with very little problem I am sure. These people you have here are the best in the …"

"Sir get me my midwives and call for the Druids. And please when you return do me a small favor." said the queen, cutting off the man's rambling.

"Anything my Queen." said the soldier.

"Be silent upon your return. Now go, quickly!" screamed the queen as yet another wave of pain swept over her. Alone once more, Athinina tried to get out of bed and walk through the pain and cramping. 'Surely I could get by the pain if I could get up' thought the queen as she tried and failed to pull herself to her feet as yet another wave of pain shook her. "Where are they?!" She screamed as yet another wave of pain shook her body and she started to weep. "Come on already you slugs move yourselves. I am in need of your help in here!" Athinina screamed at the door.

As yet another wave of pain shot through her, the midwife walked through the door. "Be still now. The child has decided to arrive, and it is time to make you ready for it. Just lie still while I get the bed prepared.

Guard! Go and hold her majesty's hand for this. She will need some comfort in the coming hours. Ah, Mica, it took you long enough. Bring those things in here so we can begin. So now Majesty, just clamp down on your man's hand there whenever the pain becomes too great and we will get through this just fine."

"This man is my guard, midwife. And if the pain is great, the reward is greater. I know how to handle pain. I have lived with it all my life. I will handle this just fine." said Athinina as another wave of pain wracked her body. The queen of the world grabbed the hand of the guard and squeezed with a fury that bent the metal gauntlet on the man's hand. As the pain subsided, the queen told the midwife, "Yes, I will be fine." The look upon the midwife's face caused the Druid who had just entered the room to cover a laugh. Especially after seeing the face of the young man as he shook his now bent hand and attempted to remove the metal glove.

"I would leave that on if I were you, it may provide some small protection." smiled the Druid. "How is our new mother to be? She appears to be having a little problem with this birth. You poor man. It will be over soon. Besides it should be the father there not this poor whelp. How long is there to wait good woman before the child arrives?"

"Not long now, sir. The child moves even now to the birthing. It should not be long before it makes its appearance in this world." said the nurse. Looking down at her queen, she spoke in a hurried voice, "Hurry now, get me something to wrap the child in for I believe it is about to come. I need warm water and towels to cleanse it. We would not want our queen to see the child in a poor state. Hurry now! Move! Move!"

And come the child did. The young boy was born moments after the nurse called for the materials to clean him. "My lady, it is a boy. A strong young man to carry on your great and noble line." said the midwife as she cleaned the child and prepared to place the child on his mother's breast. "See, he responds to you already. He will be a strong one, he will, the great prince of our people."

The queen looked down at the child and a small, disappointed smile crossed her lips. *A boy,* she thought. *Weakness and no small lack of mental capacity to rule.* She looked down at the child now being placed on her breast and her first real affection for him emerged. "You are much like your father. How I wish he were here to see this." As she spoke a new wave of pain wracked her exhausted form. "What is happening? I thought this was over." she cried. The midwife and the Druid jumped to the Queen's side as she convulsed with yet another wave of pain. Looking over the prone woman the midwife grabbed at the men standing around her and called for more toweling and more water. "My lady, it appears I have made a misjudgment. You are about to give birth again. This is definitely a good surprise. Quickly now I need those items I asked for."

Moving quickly and with practiced ease she was soon placing the second child on its mother's breast. "My lady, you have another perfect little boy. Twin princes to rule after you. You must so proud." spoke the midwife. "What are you going to call them? Surely you will name one of them for their father. They are identical in every way it appears. This should be a new challenge for your majesty just keeping them straight. It is a rare treat to bear two children at once, but you are well-deserving of it."

"Two boys... who would have thought? Find the midwife who predicted that I would have twins and give her great rewards. She must possess some form of premonition to have predicted this. As for names, I will name them for the first two men who enter that door. I would not feel right naming them for their father as only one could bear his name and the other would feel the lesser. These children will know that they are equal in my eyes and in the eyes of the people." spoke the queen as if she sat on her throne. "You there, sir. What is your name?" spoke the queen.

"Torlin." replied the man that walked through the door as the queen was finishing being cleaned up after her labors. "And you?" she asked the second guard that followed Torlin into the room. "Thomas." said the second man.

"There are the children's names. Thomas and Torlin. Torlin to the boy born first with the raspberry mark near his left ear. Thomas to his brother with the mark near his right ear. You said the boys were exactly the same and yet you missed these small marks. I guess it is something only a mother would notice. Torlin and Thomas, what does the future hold for the two of you?" asked the queen as she looked down on the babes now nuzzling into her breasts. "Look Torlin barely eats while Thomas has a healthy appetite. These boys will be the death of me one day. I can see that now."

As the queen was making her observations, Artitous walked into the room. "I see that once more I missed an important birthing. My timing is, as always, terrible. Let's see these young ones. I see there are two of them. Speak woman, are they boys, girls, or a mixed batch?" asked the Druid leader.

"They are two perfectly healthy baby boys, my lord. I will remain until I am sure they will prosper then I will return to the groves. If you will excuse me, Lord, I must return to my charges." replied the midwife.

"And how is their mother?" asked Artitous to the now exhausted queen lying on the bed squeezing her newborn children. "What names have you given them?"

"They are Torlin and Thomas. And as for me, I believe that I have just fought my way through a thousand dragons in only my skin and with my only my bare hands." replied Athinina.

"That is common to feel exhausted after such an effort," said the midwife, "after all it is a great deal of work to bring life into the world."

"I will remember that." whispered the queen as she looked down on her sons. It seemed as if they almost glowed with an eerie light as she looked down on them. But obviously it was a trick of the light. After all, how could one glow with a white light and the other with a dark light. Looking at them made her forget the eerie lights and she stroked their little crowns and smiled. His sons, his children. He would live on in them and continue his work through them. The boys moved and wiggled, snuggling deeper into their mother's breasts. They had strength she would not have dreamed a boy child would have. They were definitely their father's sons.

At the statue, the rodents had cleared a section of gravel and the earth had dipped were there had not been a depression before.

Chapter Forty Eight: The Adventures of the Young

As the wind passes through the trees and over the plains, so pass the years. The young ones found first their feet, and as they grew found their voices and their strength. Young Torlin showed an affinity toward the arcane and learning. Many a day he would sit and watch the children, men, and women of the Wizard Academy, watching their movements and imitating their words. This of course led to no small amount of problems. When Torlin was only a year old his babbling nearly burned the city had Artitous not been there to stop the flames.

Thomas on the other hand followed the soldiers and Rangers and learned all he could of their ways and the ways of battle. He would arrange his toys as armies and fight faux battles in his rooms. His skills even then amazed the generals and elite Rangers.

Artitous started both of the boys' educations early. Torlin would be brought in to observe and listen to the other boys as they learned the control they must utilize with their abilities. Torlin would watch spellbound as they learned new magic but would rapidly grow bored with the lessons on the morality, responsibilities, and reasoning to use magic. He would often doze off during the lessons on magical items and premonition, his talents lying in other avenues of magic.

As he slowly grew and learned more of magic, Artitous made sure that the boy watched all of his lessons. He would see to the proper instruction of Torlin if it killed him. Artitous often found himself dodging the temper tantrums that the boy would often display. One nearly saw Artitous with a chair materializing inside his skull. *The boy was learning to use his powers rapidly, but he is still young and unschooled,* thought the Druid, *He will outgrow these tantrums, I hope.*

It was not long before the boys turned ten that a decision was made by the queen and Artitous. The boy's abilities would be bound until he was ready to use them responsibly. The boy would be brought to an arcane circle and there be surrounded by a number of the Druid order.

He was brought into the circle by his mother and made to sit while twelve of the Druid order rapidly surrounded him. Artitous joined the circle of Druids and the Druids began their chant. After a small period of time some of the Druids were found kneeling, the exertion beginning to wear on them. By the time the chanting had been going for a while all the Druids were on their knees with the exception of Artitous who stood like an oak tree amongst the others in the room. Artitous raised his arms and began a low chant of his own in an ancient language known only to the Druids.

Torlin looked at the people around him and a small grin passed his lips. The boy sat and watched the people's movements and listened to their words. Athinina watched the boy with fascination. The boy was not throwing his usual temper tantrum at being left out of some magic or other, quite the opposite he seemed to be enjoying it. Torlin's grin grew to a smile as the Druid's chant progressed. The boy found this humorous. Athinina did not understand the child's thoughts and grew more confused as Artitous raised his voice. She was not interested in the Druid's speech but what did concern her was the sweat beading on his brow. Artitous had said that this was a simple thing. Artitous said this would be over in a few moments and it would not take any effort on anyone's part.

Looking around the circle she realized that something was dreadfully wrong. All of the people circling the boy were now covered in sweat as they continued their concentration and chanting. Several had gone from being erect around the boy to sitting on their legs. The strain was beginning to get to them. Artitous again and again repeated the words in the old tongue, nearly shouting them at certain points. *What could be the problem?* Thought the queen of the world, *surely it could not be this hard to bind one little boy?*

Again, and again Artitous repeated the phrases of power and again and again, he was showing signs of weakening. Surely this would be over soon. Torlin stood and laughed as the Druids kept to their work. Soon he was dancing around the circle and laughing at the people surrounding him. He moved around the circle and found he could not pass closer than a foot toward the kneeling Druids. The boy became enraged. They had placed a barrier around him. He would not let this go.

Artitous watched the boy as again and again he tried to place the binding upon the boy. The boy was powerful but that was not what was keeping the binding from falling into place, something was definitely amiss. He changed his chant to a probing spell to see what was causing the problem. When he thought his strength was spent, he found the problem with the binding. The boy had woven a shield against the binding. It was strange that the boy knew what was happening as they had been careful not to mention this to him or around him. They spoke of it only when the boy was far away. This should not be happening.

Artitous changed the spell yet again to attack the shield trying to bring it down quickly. The boy stopped his dancing and his anger and looked at the man he considered a favored uncle, "Uncle Arty, what is it that you are doing? Do you need some help? Why are all those people looking so tired? You are working great magic no doubt. I want to learn this magic. Uncle Arty, will you teach it to me?" said the boy to the now wavering Druid. The smile on his face told the truth of it though the boy knew what they were doing.

Artitous found he had only one option. He again changed the spell this time aimed at the boy's mind rather than at the boy's power. A face of rage and fear showed on the boy as he slowly fell first to his knees then to the floor. The sleeping spell had been unexpected by the boy and the shield between the Druids and the binding was released. Quickly the Druids put the binding in place, some showing blood coming from eyes and ears. The shockwave from the binding knocked the Druids that had remained on their knees to the ground.

Artitous fell to his knees as the spell took hold and many of the Druids fell asleep where they had knelt. Almost all of the Druids had blood flowing from eyes and ears; some even had blood flowing from their noses. Artitous waved Athinina to him and had her help him to his feet. "The boy is stronger than we could imagine. He instinctively erected a barrier to the binding. He is more dangerous than we first believed. He should never have been able to accomplish this at his age." said the Druid master.

"What are we to do?" asked Athinina. "This could cause no end of problems for all of us. Should we check his brother as well? If one is this strong in the arcane, the other may be as well."

"My lady, I have not even felt the ability in Thomas. The boy just has no arcane abilities, his talents lie on the battlefield. I hope we are able to harness it as we have harnessed the powers of Torlin." replied the Druid as he limped from the room leaning on the queen. "My lady, please help me to that chair."

"What do we do now?" asked a nervous queen.

"We can simply wait and monitor the boy. The binding should hold until I start to lessen it. But the boy has shown abilities he should not possess. I am afraid all we can do is to wait and see what the future holds for us."

CHAPTER FORTY NINE:
DIFFERENCES

Thomas was the opposite of his brother. Thomas watched the warriors down in the courtyard and was amazed by the agility and prowess of the warriors as they seemed to dance from form to form. Thomas sat in admiration of the Elves as they fired their arrows at the practice targets. No matter how far from the targets they moved, the Elves never seemed to miss the bull's eye. The leader of these archers was an older Elf named Martin. Martin led the Elven Rangers who patrolled the area around the great cities of the empire. The Elves could move without detection and apprehend those who were terrorizing their communities.

Martin took upon himself the responsibility of defending the capital. He held himself responsible for the events that had cost Athinina's husband his life. He had been the head of the Phoenix's Hand. He led the bodyguard for Tanis Thalin and had been on patrol scouting the enemy when the battle between Tanis and the great Demon had taken place. He still would not step foot on the ground surrounding the statue on the battlefield.

Martin took to the boy rapidly. For his third birthday, Martin bought the boy his first bow. Athinina thought the boy's interest in battles and the art of war was wonderful. It was great that the boy wanted to learn of the great battles of the past. He studied the tactics and the outcomes of these ancient battles until he could recite them verbatim and then interpret what those ancient generals had done right and how to improve upon the way those battles had ended. The battles lost he studied more than the battles won. He told his mother often of these ancient battles and how the generals could have won them. He studied the terrain and the enemies in those battles so he could almost predict what the outcome would be and how it would be obtained.

Athinina found Thomas often in the company of wizards and Druids learning of their abilities. Thomas knew he had no disposition for magic, but he would say that to fight a wizard one must know how they would fight and defend themselves from attack. One could not depend solely upon other wizards to see an end to a magic user, he would say when asked. Many of these men and women would not do what was necessary to end a battle when it came to fighting one another. Their hierarchy depended solely upon strength in the power and if an enemy was the stronger, the others would simply fall into line with the enemy. There lies the problem with magical folk, he would tell his mentors. He would say that there just needed to be a better chain of command amongst the magical.

Chapter Fifty:
Great Adventures

Thomas and Torlin were as close as two people could be. One rarely was seen without the other except when it was time for their studies. Torlin would often take the lead on their many outings, and as boys would, they got themselves into trouble. Thomas would always plot out the actions that Torlin wished to perform while Torlin would add his input on the ways of using his special abilities to ensure that the stunt went off.

One day the boys were in the local village pilfering pies from windowsills of the houses. They were caught later with their hands and faces covered in the juices of the berries from the pies. The boys suffered a great scolding and Thomas returned to each of their victims and reimbursed the people from whom he took the pies for their losses. Many of them reimbursed with much more than the pie was worth. Thomas showed a generosity that would define him to the people. Torlin became defined with a cruelty that would also mark him.

CHAPTER FIFTY ONE:
RUINS

The boys had just turned thirteen when a great discovery was made in the hills surrounding the great city of Thalinburg. After the death of the boys' father the city he had made his capital was renamed in his honor. The local Druids charged with understanding and learning of the past had found the entrance to an ancient city. The boys and their mother went to the site to see the ruins which were being unearthed. The boys saw this as a new play area for them and were scolded again and again as they tried to enter the ruins to hunt for relics or to play hide and seek amongst the columns.

Athinina spoke to the Druids responsible for the dig and inquired to their progress. The Druids explained that the city sprawled for what seemed like miles. They had mapped out the surrounding areas looking to see if they could find the edges of the site. They were as of yet unable to determine the ends. More time would be required to find the extent of the ruins. Athinina congratulated the men on their good work and called for the boys.

The queen called out for the young princes again and again getting no response. After what seemed an eternity, she found a small opening in the earth and called down into it. If the boys had managed to find their own entrance into the city, they could be anywhere within it. "Martin!" Athinina cried, "Fetch me my weapons and armor. Prepare a team of your best Rangers the boys have gone into the city."

Martin ran for the supply carts that held their supplies and equipment handing out weapons and armor to the Rangers and providing the queen with her kit. Screaming for individuals he quickly had a team of twenty Rangers fully armed and equipped to be lowered into the city below. Martin insisted that he be the first to enter the cavern. Who knew what may be lurking in the streets of the ancient city? Martin told the queen that he would take no more chances in losing anymore of his charges.

Martin leapt into the opening, drawing his blades as he fell the short distance to the floor below. Looking around he called out for a torch for the queen as well as a rope ladder to be lowered. The next person into the cavern was no less than Athinina herself. She came down on the rope ladder as it was lowered, riding on the bottom rung, looking as if she were descending from heaven. Martin seeing the queen's descent cursed and grabbed the guide line to control her descent, ever watchful of the surrounding area. The queen jumped from the ladder and looked around the cavern where they stood.

"Martin, what is this place?" asked Athinina, "It looks like the remains of a city square. Look at the statues there. They look almost human."

"My lady, it looks like the remains of the city center. The boys left tracks all over the place. They are looking around and playing hide and seek it looks like to me. There does not appear to be any danger as of now. The tops of the towers are up into the bottoms of the hills, the basements are buried beneath our feet. It looks like there is some kind of platform above us creating this air pocket, but I do not believe it will fall. It appears to be solid enough. I see no other signs of life down here except the boys so we should be able to track them easily." replied the ranger as the rest of the Rangers quickly entered and surrounded the pair.

"Then let the search begin." whispered Athinina.

Chapter Fifty Two:
A Familiar Adversary

The small group moved slowly out from where they had entered, looking at the marks left by the boys as they explored. Their search was temporarily interrupted by the arrival of Artitous. He surveyed the ruins with interest but refrained from comment.

"So silent, old friend?" asked the queen.

"We are not alone, My Lady. Something lurks in these halls, something dangerous." replied Artitous.

"We have seen no other signs of life, dear Druid" said the ranger leader, "If there were anything alive down here I would know of it."

"No disparagement upon your skills dear friend. This thing that lives here does not yet wish to be seen. It is biding its time, watching for weakness. It is going out of its way to keep from being seen. I feel it watching us from these empty windows." replied the Druid. "We must use caution."

The queen once more took the lead as the Rangers fanned out looking for signs of the boy's passage. The tracks finally led them to the building closest to the place they had first entered. Artitous moved to examine the door looking for traps or devices that may have been left to cause mischief on the unwary. Artitous stood and shook his head. The boys had gone this way but the door had a form of trap attached to it. The boys had crawled through the missing window and not set off the trap. The adults were just too large to enter the same way. "We need someone to disarm this trap before we can continue." announced Artitous. "Someone get Perrick."

"I believe I can be of some assistance there, sir." said a small voice from the back of the group of Rangers. The youngest of the Rangers stepped forward and approached the door.

"This may be beyond your skills young man. This is a job for a master thief. I just do not know where we will get one here." said the Druid.

At Artitous's words the Rangers, queen, and Druid began to argue over who they should have brought here to disable traps. Each of them had an idea of who should be called and the name coming up the most was Perrick. The queen turned to Martin and was ordering him to go for Perrick at once when a small sound caught their attention.

"My Lady, the job is done. I have even opened the lock holding the door closed. If you would like to keep the trap, I took the liberty of taking it. It looks like some weird magic dough, but now we can look at it and figure out how it works." spoke the young warrior.

Martin laughed as he slapped the young man on the back. "Boy, have you been in the company of Perrick? Obviously you have picked up some of his most unsavory skills. Tell me your name boy."

"I am Paul; Perrick has had a large influence on me for no more reason than he is my father. He taught me everything he knows. I just chose not to follow his lead and join the ranks of rogues and thieves. He does not influence me that much." replied Paul.

"Well, at least one member of that man's family has some sense." said Artitous. "But Paul, in the future please allow us to observe your work. We would like to keep the only one with sense in the Perrick family in the same condition in which he entered this place." Even as he spoke laughter began.

Martin was the first one through the now open door and moved a short way into the building. Looking from wall to wall he noticed for the first time the signs of giant spiders. It had probably been the spiders that had broken the windows when they came in. Martin called back to the rest of the group, "Be careful. We may have giant spiders lurking about. Be ready for them should they come. It appears I owe you and apology, Old One."

"None required but that is not what I am feeling. Something else lurks amongst these ruins. Just be wary. Spiders are a danger we are accustomed to, are they not my Queen?" said Artitous. The queen responded only with a blush that turned her face a deep crimson as she remembered being attacked on her wedding night so many years ago.

Martin looked at the Queen puzzled then looked to Artitous. "You had to have been there the last time we encountered these beasts." said the Druid.

CHAPTER FIFTY THREE: DANGERS OF THE RUINS

Slowly moving forward with Paul in the lead looking for traps, the group approached a doorway on the far side of the room. The boys' tracks continued forward but they had definitely entered a few steps into the room connecting to the hallway beyond. Paul went first looking for traps that may be waiting for them and jumped from the room. The group raised weapons preparing for an attack when Paul said "Sorry. I thought I saw something." The people around him lowered their weapons except Martin who drew and fired his bow. Paul hit the ground screaming of the Elf trying to kill him when he noticed the dead spider on the floor next to him. Paul regained his feet long enough to faint back to the floor.

"Heart of a lion, huh, boss?" inquired another of the Rangers.

"Ready arms! They are coming! To arms we are under attack!" screamed Martin.

The ranger drew again and fired into the room. Dropping his bow he drew his swords and set himself in the doorway in a classic Florentine pose. The queen moved toward the entrance they had used only to find more of the beasts coming from behind. In moments her short spears were out and the spider lay dead at her feet. Martin called for the Rangers to protect the queen but she waded into the combat to the rear as more of the creatures charged at their backs. Martin fought his way forward into the room looking for the source of the beasts. As he entered yet a third wave of the beasts attacked from the direction the boys had gone.

The queen's group finished their enemies first and moved to assist those clearing the way forward. Martin fell back into the room screaming that there were too many of them this way and that all of the people in the room were needed to get through them. Artitous, who to this point had refrained from the fighting, raised his arm and pointed toward the doorway. Seeing the Druid's movement, Martin and his group dived to either side of the door. Moments later the room erupted in flames and the screams of the spiders filled the air. Those that attempted to flee the magical flames through the door where cut down as they entered the hallway.

As rapidly as the attack began, it subsided and at last all the beasts lay dead or had fled. Martin and a few of the Rangers entered the new room and stared in amazement. All of the spiders and their webs were ash, but the papers and artifacts that littered the room were left unharmed. Artitous entered the room and picked up one of the sheets of paper littering the floor. Looking at the paper briefly, he again waved his hand and a ball of light appeared next to his head. "That's better." remarked the Druid as he looked at the sheet before him.

"Can you read it?" asked Martin.

"My lady and dear ranger, we are in a city of people we thought destroyed millennia ago. These are the ones who laid the foundations for our own fair city a few miles from here. The ancient Druids finished it, as the original builders left it unfinished according to our records. The records speak of a rumor that there was three cities that were within miles of each other. We had never found any evidence of the other two so we just assumed it was rumor. Well we have our evidence now, don't we? This paper speaks of a war between this and another city. Since ours was not complete I can only assume it has to be the other city we are missing." said Artitous as he read and fell deep into thought.

"Artitous, though this history lesson is fascinating, please remember why we are here," said Athinina, "We are looking for my children remember?"

Searching the room briefly revealed another door but it led only to a small storage cabinet. Leaving the room, the group moved down the hallway following the boys' footsteps. After what seemed like an eternity the hallway opened into a large clearing.

Chapter Fifty Four: The Golem

In the center stood a giant steel statue of a warrior in full armor and bristling with weapons. The boys where standing at its feet and playing with something that none of them could identify.

"HALT!" said a voice that shook the very walls of the surrounding buildings. The boys ran to their mother, dropping the device that had so engrossed them. "IDENTIFY YOURSELVES AND PREPARE TO BE CHALLENGED!"

Artitous moved to the front of the group and looked at the huge statue. "This should not be here. This just cannot be. We must leave this place now. I do not know who these people were but they created a steel golem. It is time we left before it decides we are a threat and decides to destroy us. I fear without its key we are powerless to stop the golem."

"The box by its feet is the key," said Torlin, "It says so on the rear. It speaks of the guardian and its abilities."

"Torlin did you press anything upon this device?" asked Artitous.

"I don't think I did," said the boy, "I may have, or maybe it was Thomas. I do not know what he did with it when I grew bored with it."

"I did not press a thing, Uncle Arty, I swear." said Thomas. "I was careful just to look. I'll get the device and maybe you can turn it off."

As he spoke, Thomas ran again toward the golem. He reached where they had dropped the device in time for the golem to turn around and look at the boy. Again the voice filled the clearing; "IDENTIFY YOURSELVES OR BE DESTROYED!" spoke the golem. Thomas ran as fast as his legs could carry him back to the Druid and handed him the device.

"Is this the key you seek, Uncle Arty?" asked the boy as he stopped at the Druid's feet.

"It is indeed, but there is a problem. This thing should have no knowledge of our language, yet he speaks to us in our own tongue. That should not be possible if this city has indeed been buried for millennia. I wish to try something, My Lady. Move the queen and princes toward the exit. If I come running, it means we must make a hasty retreat if we are to live. Now go." said Artitous.

The group moved slowly toward the exit in an attempt to avoid the great machine before them. Artitous moved toward the golem with his arms raised above his head. "I am Artitous!" screamed the Druid. "How is it that you understand my speech?"

"YOUR PRIMITIVE TONGUE IS EASY FOR US TO UNDERSTAND. WHAT PURPOSE DO YOU HAVE HERE, ARTITOUS!" asked the golem.

"We have found your city. It has been abandoned for thousands of years. Can you tell me what happened to your people?" asked Artitous.

"THEY REMAIN HERE. BE GONE OR I WILL DESTROY YOU." said the golem.

"What do you mean they remain here? Surely this city has been empty of life for thousands of years. How can they remain?" asked the Druid.

"YOU HAVE BEEN WARNED AND YOU DID NOT HEED IT. NOW PREPARE TO BE DESTROYED." spoke the steel statue.

Seeing the golem taking steps toward him, Artitous looked at the device he held in his hands. He briefly looked over the control panel looking for a means to shut down the creature. Seeing nothing of help on the device he turned and ran for the entrance. "Run!" screamed Artitous as he reached the group slowly working its way up the rope ladder. "It comes. It comes."

Artitous turned toward the square to see the golem entering it. Artitous raised his hands and fireballs flew toward the golem. Obvious damage showed on the exterior of the machine, but still it moved forward. Martin appeared as if by magic at his side and fired off three or four arrows into the hole created by the fireballs.

"Keep up with the fireballs. If we can make enough holes in the exterior, we should be able to take it down by attacking the interior." said the ranger.

"I will as long as I am able. The last battle tired me but I should still be able to launch a few more of these things at that brute." replied the Druid.

"String some of this rope out across the plaza." said a voice from behind them. "It moves slowly and will be easier to kill if we can get it off its feet."

"Thomas, please get up the ladder! You are the future of our people. You and your brother must survive." screamed Martin as he fired two more arrows into the interior of the golem.

Thomas ran past the two fighting the golem and headed for the statues that surrounded the plaza. Rapidly he tied the ropes around a statue and said a silent prayer that this one would not start moving as well. Running across the plaza he tied the other end high enough onto the statue to trip the lumbering giant coming toward them.

Running back to Artitous and Martin he snatched up his bow and added his arrows to those of Martin. The three that now fought the golem jumped as a huge fireball smashed into the front of the beast. "Not you too!" said Martin. "Run! Both of you run!"

But the boys remained and continued to add to the barrage that rained down upon the giant behemoth. Slowly it moved toward them until it reached the ropes that Thomas had tied to the statues. Trying to continue its legs found themselves wrapped in the ropes. Instead of tripping the giant, the strength of the golem was so great it caused the statues to come off their bases and wrap around its ankles like a pair of bolas. The golem attempted another step and found itself toppling to the ground.

With a crash the golem hit the floor causing the helmet to fall from its head. Seeing the weakness all the warriors rained down weapons and fire upon the golem's head. After several moments of fire and a nearly exhausted pair of magic users, the golem stopped its movement. Slowly

Artitous moved toward the fallen golem. He feared deception from the beast and moved toward it slowly.

Artitous approached the creature and looked down on the prone form of the golem. Suddenly the monster opened its eyes and looked at the Druid. "IT HAS ALL BEEN FOR NOTHING. I TRIED ….. TO STOP……. IT FROM HAPPENING……….AGAIN." At that the light left its eyes and the monster died.

"I do not believe it was trying to protect an extinct people." Artitous said to the group standing before him. "I believe it was trying to protect us."

"That thing tried to kill us! How can you say it was trying to protect us?" said Martin as he looked down on the now prone form of the beast. "It probably was still trying to lure us in is what I figure."

"I don't believe that. It specifically spoke of failing to protect us from it happening again. I am not sure what it means, but I will find out. I will have to study these ruins more." said the Druid.

Torlin spoke up at that point, "Just let's not talk about it or study it now shall we. We have more company coming."

Looking were the boy pointed showed a large number of giant spiders slowly moving into the light of the plaza. With a start, Martin shoved the queen and princes up the ladder. "Get them out of here now!" He screamed. "We are under attack! Get troops down here now!"

Before he finished speaking, three dozen more archers and Rangers fell through the hole and prepared a battle line to combat the advancing spiders. Three more Druids came down as well and forced Artitous up the ladder as well. From below they heard the sounds of arrows and fireballs. Screams of men and spiders filled the air and several of the insects made it out the opening just to be cut down by waiting warriors. Thomas grabbed up a sword and joined in the attacks on the spiders that made it out of the caverns below.

Soon the rest of those who had gone down into the ruins were being pulled up from the hole. The insects had stopped streaming from the hole and the spiders below were dead. It was reported that all the spiders and the queen that lead them were also slain. They should trouble the people and the workers no more. With a great sigh of relief, the royal party that came to the ruins set off for home at nearby Thalinburg to rest and recover after the ordeal of the day.

As the golem died, a machine deep within the ruins of the city suddenly turned itself off. In the tubes surrounding the machine, beings began to shift. In a tube containing a rather large individual, an eye opened.

Chapter Fifty Five:
The Boys Get a Job

Several years after the discovery of the first city, the Druids announced that through research and knowledge gained from the first city they had located a second one. From Thalinburg, the boys could stand on the tops of the walls and see the towers as they were being excavated from the surrounding hills.

Thomas had recently been installed as leader of the armies of Dracos. His prowess in battle was unmatched by any of the other commanders and his fame for keeping the peace was known around the world. Everywhere he traveled the people flocked to him for fair judgments and his ability to end most conflicts without bloodshed. He was known as a peacemaker even though his prowess on the battlefield was also legend. He could fight when he had no choice, but preferred the peaceful resolution of problems.

Torlin was installed as the leader of the Wizard Academy and the Order of the Magus. He spurned the rules and regulations of the Druid order and decided that the Magus offered more freedom. He was known for his fiery temper and his sharp tongue, making him unpopular amongst the people of the kingdom. His wisdom was unmatched among any order of magic user, but he was prone to using it to his own advantage instead of to the advantage of all. The binding placed on him in his youth was removed and his full strength was finally available to him.

The boys had grown apart as they aged. Torlin's selfish nature conflicted often with Thomas's generous nature. Thomas began to argue with Torlin about the purposes of rule and their practices in governing. Their mother often played referee as the two would end up in physical confrontations about their differences.

It was because of the fighting and problems that their mother finally decided the best course of action would be to send the two boys to the separate ruins of the two cities. If the boys could not work together and cooperate in a mature manner then they could do the tasks of common laborers to assist in the search and recording of the ancient ruins. Torlin would be sent to the first city found, while Thomas would be sent to the other. Thomas and his troops would be needed at the second metropolis to assist in the removal of giant rats that occupied the great city. Torlin's people would definitely be needed for the removal of the spiders that still held most of the city.

The morning of their eighteenth birthdays, Athinina called both of the boys before her. "My sons, the fighting between you tears apart the kingdom. Half support one of you the other half follows the other. It is too much for us to continue this way so separating you is the only option I have left. Torlin, you will be going to the first discovered ruin I have found out is named Metra. It will be there you will help remove the spiders and complete the research into the people who built it. You will also help to discover whether there is anything that may benefit our people. Thomas, you are to be sent to the other ruin called Tetra. It is there that you will do the same as your brother. Find whatever you to help us. Get those ruins cleared and when the tasks are complete perhaps the two of you can live in some kind of harmony. You are both to leave immediately."

Thomas rode out with his soldiers within an hour of his mother's request. He would be condemned to the pits of Hades if he let his brother get the jump on him. Torlin left within moments of his brother. This could be the opportunity to learn some new kind of magic to give him an even greater advantage over those who oppose him.

Artitous followed the boys as they left the city for the ruins. As he watched them his second sight came to him. Franticly he turned and galloped his horse back to the city. The queen would have to be told of this immediately.

Torlin reached the ruins and rode through the now cleared gates toward the foreman of the digging. After five years most of the city remained buried and work progressed slowly trying to remove the soil from the city. The location of the side entrance where the golem had been fought was also clear now. The golem had been removed and was being studied by the Druids within Thalinburg at the Magical Academy. Spiders remained the biggest problem at the dig site and more showed themselves daily.

Torlin grew impatient with the man and silenced him with a wave of his hand. "I will deal with your vermin problem, good man. I even know a few ways we can clear the dirt from the city even faster using different magical formulas. Why get our hands dirty when magic can be set in place to do it for us?"

"Magic is not meant to be used to complete tasks like this, my prince." replied the man, "Do you not fear being corrupted by the power?"

"Corruption is for the weak. Do I feel weak to you man? Do you believe you know more of magic than I do? I should blast you from the face of this kingdom and spare us your cowardly view of what makes us powerful. In fact, I think that is just what I am going to do." said Torlin.

He raised his hands and began the incantations that would allow him to destroy the man in front of him when his voice suddenly went mute. No matter how he tried to speak he could not. Looking around he saw Artitous standing and shaking his head.

"Have you learned nothing youngster? I thought I told you never to waste your abilities on the unimportant and NEVER to attack those who could not defend themselves or were not attacking you? Have you forgotten these lessons so soon?" said the older Druid.

"I have forgotten nothing old man." replied the young wizard. "I simply know that the weak need to be removed for the benefit of the strong."

"Is that a fact? Who decides the weak from the strong? You perchance?" asked Artitous.

"Maybe we need to find the truth of strength between us? Uncle Arty, I have been a thorn in your side since I was ten years old. What gives you the idea that I could not crush you now? Do you think you are able to defeat me old man? I am younger and stronger!" The prince was losing control. The boy lifted his arms and sent lightning arching at the older man.

Artitous just stood there as the lighting came at him and disappeared in the glare of the bolts. As the lightning dimmed and people could look at the spot where the Druid stood, people gaped in amazement as the Druid just stood there. "Haven't you learned anything from us?" said Artitous.

"How is that possible?" asked the prince.

"You still have much to learn, don't you?" whispered the Druid.

"This is not possible!" Torlin screamed as he launched attack after attack at the older man. Spell after spell flew at the Druid but nothing came close to harming the man. Finally the spells slowed down and stopped. Torlin stood spent looking at the older man who just stood and shook his head. Torlin became enraged when he saw the older man was not even winded. Torlin stood up to his full height and once again was about to launch another spell when the air around him solidified and the Druid's voice seemed to resound off the building so loudly the young prince tried to cover his ears for the pain it was causing him.

"Torlin! That is enough! This is not the place for your spoiled nature or for your temper! We all must work together here if we are to complete this daunting task. You will cease this nonsense now or I will be forced to do something we will both regret!" Artitous seemed to scream at Torlin.

People seeing the reaction of the prince looked around to see what was causing his discomfort. None of the people heard the comments of Artitous nor did they know of the restrictions he had placed on the younger man. Finally Artitous released Torlin and looked at him with pity in his eyes. Artitous went to the young man and held him. The boy needed to learn but he still needed compassion. Maybe by the display of compassion the boy would begin to learn.

Torlin shook with rage as the Druid pulled him close. After a few short moments the boy had settled down and hugged the older man back. The man was like a father to the prince after all. How could he remain angry with him? Torlin stepped back and looked around the ruins seeing just how much had been cleared of debris.

CHAPTER FIFTY SIX: TWIN CITIES

Towers stood proud and tall where the hills once stood. Years of blowing dust and dirt and debris had buried the city and caused the towers to look like a field of rolling hills. The towers were now clear and the beauty of them took the breath from the young man. Every inch of these towers was covered with intricate carvings and relieves of animals and people. Plants that could have been growing on these towers were actually fine wrought stonework that even the greatest of stonemasons could not replicate. These could have grown here and turned to stone under the gaze of a medusa. So real you almost expected to smell the aroma of the flowers and see the plants sway in the breeze. The animals appeared to have been frozen over time and adhered to the walls.

Torlin moved to the walls and moved his hands along the carvings. How could these have been formed by the hands of mere humans, Elves, or Dwarves? He followed the carvings until they reached the soil waiting to be removed. As his hands moved down the carvings, they tripped a lever hidden on one of the carvings. The platform around them looked out over the central plaza of the city. It had two exits one to either side allowing access to the building. When the lever was activated, an outline of a door appeared amongst the carvings on the wall.

Torlin pushed on the door and it swung easily into the building. He called for Artitous and the warriors who had accompanied him to follow him as he entered the doorway. A small, narrow corridor led down into the tower. Two Rangers got ahead of the prince and Artitous joined the younger magus in the middle of group. The passage closed behind them but was rapidly reopened by Artitous and blocked open with some fallen rubble from the building. The passage led only twenty feet before it ended at a spiral staircase.

The first two Rangers moved onto the stairway and slowly began their descent. The air was surprisingly fresh, not smelling of the musk and decay much of the rest of the city reeked of. The passage was also surprisingly clear of the webs and small creatures that covered a lot of the city. It appeared as if the passage was untouched by time as they progressed down the winding steps. The passage remained claustrophobic as they moved lower into the tower. The first Ranger stopped as he heard something just below them in the stairwell. Signaling the others to remain he moved down the stairwell followed a few feet behind by the second Ranger. Artitous and Torlin were on the heels of the second man waiting for some word from below.

After a few moments the first ranger reappeared in the stairwell. "The way is safe. There is some form of room a few feet below us. The magus will have to determine what it is, but there are preserved bodies here in tubes that stretch as far as the eyes can see. This must be were the original inhabitants of the city ended. None appear to live in the tubes. Bubbles floating in the fluid surrounding the bodies cause some movement but I believe it is merely the bubbles."

"We will determine what the devices are and what the situation is young man." said the Druid. "These things are better left to those who have some idea of what they are looking at."

The group moved into the room and looked around at the tubes that lined the walls and filled the giant chamber. Thousands of beings appeared to be interred in the room connected to a machine that seemed to regulate the fluid levels. Torlin noticed that one of the tubes was open and the occupant missing. Artitous looked at the tube and stood in quiet contemplation. Someone must have been down here already and just did not report the mausoleum. But why did they remove one of the beings especially without first consulting the Druids. Decisions such as this were to be made by the entire staff of Druids and Elders, not by one individual.

As the ranger had said, the beings appeared to have some movement within the tubes. Bubbles of what appeared to be air floated through the liquid inside the tube. Some of the beings seemed to be more active than others, but Druid and wizard agreed that the ranger's assumption was correct, that they moved with the fluid in the tubes. Torlin looked at the control panel with obvious fascination. It was lit by some kind of power that he had no knowledge of. Artitous followed Torlin to the controls and looked them over with rapt fascination. "Do you have any idea what this panel does? I have never seen the like before." breathed the Druid, "I do not even know what this is even working with. Have you read of anything like this?"

"I have never seen the like of this," breathed the awestruck Torlin. Torlin remained at the control panel as the rest of the group searched through the room. He looked at each of the plates and inserts in turn. He tried again and again to read the text that covered the device and silently wished he had spent more time studying ancient languages. Reaching under his tunic he pulled a piece of paper and a bit of charcoal from its place of concealment. Torlin placed the paper over the first patch of symbols on the control panel and pressed the charcoal to the paper making an impression of the symbols. As he moved the charcoal over the paper the symbols moved into the panel and a screech began throughout the chamber.

Artitous rushed to the controls and looked upon them searching for the cause of the sounds. "What have you done?" he asked the prince.

"Nothing, Artitous. I took an impression of some of the symbols. That is all I did. Just copied some of the symbols." said the prince.

"The symbols must have been on some kind of switch. Which symbols did you take the rubbing from? Show them to me so we can shut off that sound." Said the Druid.

Torlin took the paper from its concealment and showed the Druid. His head was hung in shame for the damage he thought he had caused. He looked around the chamber as the Druid reviewed the rubbings. Torlin thought he saw that other tubes in the room had been opened and remarked about it to the Druid. Artitous quieted the boy with a wave and telling him he had to concentrate on the rubbing to interpret the symbols upon it.

"I do not believe you have caused any harm, my prince. It is labeled completion. This should have no effect on what we are seeing. I think simply repressing the symbol will silence this awful sound." said Artitous.

Artitous move to the controls and pressed the symbol again and the alarm was indeed silenced. Artitous called the party together and suggested that they return to the camp for a meal and sleep. The alarm had frayed the nerves of all of them and rest would do them good.

"What do you think was meant by completion?" asked Torlin as they moved from the chamber and headed back to the surface of the city. *Metra can wait until morning* thought the prince. Sleep really would be welcome after that annoying ringing in that chamber. The group though tired walked quickly to report its findings to their appropriate groups.

"It could be no more than an on and off trigger, Torlin. You have caused no real damage this time but I must ask you, do not touch anything without first consulting the Druids. It could have been a lot worse down there. You may have activated another of those beasts that we encountered all those years ago and I believe we do not have any rope lying about this time." said Artitous.

They laughed their way to camp with funny stories of past exploits and prepared the report they would give to the scholars. It had truly been a great day.

Deep within the tower a new sound began. The beings in the tubes moved in rhythm to the sounds. Slowly the tubes began to open until all were open and the beings now stood looking at one another and about the room.

One of the beings moved to the control panel and checked some readings upon it. The year made no sense. How could they have slept in those stasis pods so long? Surely the war could not have lasted all of those years. The being moved to the others, blinking at the light and slowly watched the others begin to move. It briefly explained the situation to the others.

The beings looked at each other in amazement and prepared for the ascent from the chamber. The world must be a little different since they slept and most were very excited to see the differences. Maybe their descendants awaited them with open arms and worship as they had 10,000 years before. Surely the creators were still remembered and a superior world awaited them. As they prepared to move to the surface, smiles came to their faces. They must have won the war and now they would rule Dracos.

CHAPTER FIFTY SEVEN: THOMAS ARRIVES

Thomas entered the grounds of Tetra, the second of the ruins, quite a bit more reserved than his brother had entered Metra. His first action was to go to the site foreman to inform him of his arrival. The gnome who was running this dig site was a wizened old being named Brogan Killbear. He was a leader amongst his people and a leader in the area of history. Brogan was also known for his violent temper and his lack of tolerance toward those who did not know what he knew. Everyone on the dig site avoided the old gnome, some out of fear of his temper, others out of sheer disgust at his poor attitude.

Thomas entered Brogan's tent and sat at the desk that was the tent's only furniture. Sitting in the chair, he was looking at the maps littering the desk when the old gnome came into the tent. "Who do you think you are sitting in my chair?" asked Brogan. The archeologist moved to the young prince and practically dumped him onto the floor.

Thomas jumped to his feet, "I apologize, good sir. I was simply awaiting your arrival and became enthralled with the maps that you have recorded of the dig site. Are these truly accurate? Is the city really this large?"

"Apology not accepted. Enthralled with maps, ehh? Should not have been snooping and you would never have seen my maps now would you? But in answer to your question it is truly that large. And a carbon copy of Metra on the other side of Thalinburg. The only difference is that Tetra has no ornamentation. It is devoid of statues, carvings, or any other decorations. Your mother warned me that you were coming and I was to assist you in clearing and cataloging the city. She has the grand plan of rebuilding and using these cities again. Phah! Leave these ruins alone and let the dead keep them I say. Phah and Phah!" said the gnome.

"Surely there is good reason to rebuild these walls is there not? These ruins seem to hold millennia of knowledge and wealth to aid our own society." answered the Prince.

"We gnomes were once thought of as mongers of money and knowledge. We became known for our magic and our spells, ehh! Wizards would come to the gnomes from miles around to learn our magic craft. We became revered for our knowledge of the ancient world. You tall ones liked to pick on us for our size and hording ways but now who do you come to? Ehh? The gnomes that's who! You big'uns come to us gnomes and beg us to come to these dead places you do. You ask us what we know. Tallies like the gnomes when they need knowledge. Phah! Why we left the comfort of our homes is beyond me. Small and green are we who see and we who do. Eyes like cats and fingers like snakes and teeth so long and sharp. Isn't that the nursery rhyme? Long fingers and noses, yes? Small? No, no. You are just too big. See well in the dark though. Oh yes. We are opening up the first of the buildings today. Dead center of the first street. If you hurry, you and your men may earn your meals today protecting my gnome workers. Go now. Must earn your meat. And do not touch anything that is not trying to eat someone! Leave that to me and me alone!" smiled the old gnome.

Thomas smiled as he left the tent. He liked the old gnome and he already found out they were not opening anything without him present. The gnomes were extremely intelligent but were weak in the arts of war. They could lift their weight easily and then some. Strong as most bulls but just did not know how to fight. That was why he was here. Brogan left the tent right behind him and followed him to where the rest of the digging crews awaited their leader and the soldiers.

Thomas quickly arranged the troops around the doorway and he himself would be the first one in. After all, what could be in there? A few spiders maybe? A dead body ages old? Maybe a few shredded pieces of paper? Thomas pulled his swords and waited while the gnomes opened the door. The old one moved over the door several times and stopped to work on parts of it before he finally opened it up. "Traps." Brogan whispered to Thomas.

The door pulled open and Thomas flew in followed by two of his Rangers. After a moment his eyes adjusted to the dim light and Thomas got his first good look around. His Rangers had already fled the room screaming and he could not see why at first. Looking around showed him the reason they fled and he moved right after them.

"Skeletons!!" he screamed as he ran from the door. His Rangers looked at each other then and then the three that had entered the room. Most had thought their young leader had finally lost his nerve. Just behind their leader came the first of the undead creatures. The animated skeleton pulled itself through the doorway and looked around, covering it sockets where the eyes should have been as if the light was blinding it.

CHAPTER FIFTY EIGHT:
THEM BONES

Brogan was the first to move. Shoving Thomas toward the moving skeleton, he told Thomas, "Take off its head with that meat cleaver you've got there. That will put an end to it I wager!"

Thomas reacted instinctively and swung as the old man instructed. As soon as the blade severed the neck the creature stopped moving. Thomas moved forward to see if there were more creatures coming and ran headlong into three more fighting each other in the doorway trying to get out. The Rangers moved quickly and Thomas killed one while the others took care of the other two. A torch thrown into the room revealed that the entire room was filled with these things.

Thomas looked at Brogan and said, "Are you really sure you want to go in there?"

Brogan did not respond instead he shoved Thomas into the room. The Rangers followed quickly and the fighting began in earnest. The Rangers became amused as the skeletons fought each other as much as they fought them. The Rangers found themselves often watching as the skeletons would attack each other. One would attack its fellow and tear its head from its shoulders just to realize the Rangers were there and attacked the living. Thomas allowed the skeletons to have at each other as much as he allowed his men. The Rangers often found themselves locked in combat and bumped rear to rear with what they thought was one of their own just to find out they were fighting back to back with a skeleton. As soon as the skeleton finished with the skeleton it had fought it turned on the man fighting beside it.

After what seemed an eternity the final skeleton fell with a scream of defiance upon its toothed lips. Miraculously not one of the Rangers perished in the battle, but all were exhausted and cut and bruised. Thomas quickly surveyed his men and found them all still alive and breathed a sigh of relief. With so many enemies it was amazing that none had perished in the battle. Brogan came into the room and looked around at all the fallen skeletons and took Thomas by the hand, "Took you long enough boy, didn't it?" He surveyed the fallen and looked at the arch that led deeper into the building.

Thomas and his men sat down as the gnomes entered and Thomas looked at the old gnome with a smile on his face and replied, "Well, you can have the next set and see if you can break our record."

Brogan did not reply but smiled and pointed toward the arch. Thomas turned slowly figuring the gnome was simply teasing him to see more skeletons marching through it toward his men. The difference between the skeletons was that these were armed. Brogan pointed again and said to Thomas, "You may want to deal with those before you decide to take a little breather don't you think? Ehh!"

Thomas lifted his weapons again and looked at the aged gnome, "This is your turn, isn't it?"

"We are lovers not fighters, dear boy. Go and kill something won't you? Ehh!" replied Brogan.

Thomas charged into the new wave of skeletons and killed the first few to move through the arch. These moved with a greater determination and surprisingly did not attack each other. This group was smaller though and took less time to dispatch. Even though they were armed it became apparent they did not know how to use their weapons. Though they did not attack each other a few died at the hands of their fellows as one would swing at a ranger and accidentally sever the head of one of its colleagues.

The Rangers moved swiftly to finish off the skeletons and again moved to sit down as the gnomes began their work. The Rangers were now tired and in no small way injured by the two preceding battles.

Thomas again took inventory of his troops and found them all tired and battered, but alive. Only one of them had suffered a serious injury and it appeared he took it by one of the other Rangers. Two of the Druids who traveled with them moved to tend to his wounds as the rest sat and tried to relax.

Brogan again moved around the room and looked at the remains that lay on the floor. He moved deftly for a creature of his age and his fingers found bits of paper and writing scattered throughout the room. He quickly assembled the larger pieces and was reading them when his ears once more perked up. Thomas did not need the old gnome to tell him another wave of skeletons was coming this time. He heard the creak of armor and the clank of weapons on bone himself. Jumping to his feet again he threw a torch down the archway to see just how many were coming this time.

Thomas's eyes widened as he saw the quantity of enemies moving toward the arch. These moved with military precision and were protected by collars of steel and leather. Thomas quickly assessed the situation and blurted to those around him, "Run!"

Everyone in the room responded. The gnomes moved to the walls as the Rangers formed their battle groups. Thomas looked around shaking his head and thought, *don't these people know what run meant?* Drawing his swords again he joined his group and tried to usher them toward the exit. The men did not fall back though. The Rangers stood awaiting the enemy whom their leader had seen.

Quiet greeted the warriors who had rapidly deployed for the next wave. They stood ready and prepared to meet their foe. After a few moments, the first group started to get antsy and looked as best they could down the darkened alley. They could see no movement. What had scared their leader so? They began to loosen armor and lower their weapons when the armored skeletons burst from the silent arch. The group in which Thomas fought moved quickly to protect the group that had let their guard down. Rapidly all the groups were pulled into the battle and again the enemy was defeated. Thomas bore a wound running from his ear to his neck earned while defending Brogan. Thomas noticed there were many more injuries after this battle. The skeletons were much better with the weapons they carried and the armor made it much more difficult to dispatch them. Thomas checked on his men and found that they had suffered their first casualties. Three Rangers lay dead and six more were grievously injured. The Druids moved quickly amongst the injured and worked to heal the damage caused.

Thomas again looked around the room and saw with dismay the damage done to his troops. These men were exhausted and well beaten. Many were nursing multiple small wounds and some looked to bear broken bones. These attacks were becoming more coordinated. The enemy grew smarter and less messy. Thomas looked into the supplies he had brought with him and found the lengths of fine wire he had brought. He had planned on using these to keep off spiders and other such animals from his camp. The creatures of nature did not like the smell of metal and the fine wire would give them warning of the creatures approach.

Thomas took the wire and ran a length about the neck level of the skeletons. 'It is a long shot,' he thought, 'But if any more of those things come through there at least some may lose their heads to the wire.' He sat once more with his soldiers and the gnomes and moved amongst them with water and bandages. Brogan joined him and smiled, "You move well for a tally! Ehh! I think I rather like having you around." said the old gnome.

Thomas smiled back at the old gnome and replied, "I just need to teach the little folk to fight and we'll get along just fine! Just keep that water coming, will you?"

Brogan and Thomas were still laughing when the next wave tried to pass through the arch. Both jumped to their feet and the Rangers had weapons drawn just to see that the trap had worked much better than planned. Thomas looked at the pile of bones that now littered the archway and realized that they had run headlong into the wire not even realizing it was there. Not a single one made it past the arch and into the room. Both Rangers and gnomes breathed a sigh of relief, when Thomas saw the blade move through the arch and cut the wire. Hearing the twang of the wire being cut Thomas jumped up and said, "OK, Who taught them to do that?!", as once more enemies streamed from the arch.

The gnomes moved among the combatants banging on leg bones and pulling skulls from the skeletons they could bring down. They were careful to avoid the weapons brandished by the skeletons and the Rangers moved to protect them from the enemies who refused to fall. Brogan grabbed up one of the skulls and charged into the battle using it as a bludgeon on anything getting close to him. Unfortunately he brought down two Rangers with wild swings and found himself being dragged from the fighting by two Rangers. Just as quickly as he was released though he was back into the thick of it swinging his skull with all his might and Brogan took down two of the enemy skeletons ending their threat.

Soon this wave too was over and the aftermath proved it had been a costly victory. Around the room three more Rangers lay dead and one gnome gazed into the ceiling. The gnome had perished trying to kill the skeleton that had been pinned to the floor beneath it. Thomas moved to finish it off when Brogan placed his hand on Thomas's arm, "Let us see if we cannot learn where our friends are coming from shall we?"

"These things cannot speak and even if they could, do you believe they would reveal anything?" screamed a now angry Thomas.

Brogan moved between Thomas and the skeleton and kneeled by its head looking down at it. "Sir it appears you may be having a little problem there. Ehh! Maybe a little help here? Wanting to stand again I would say. What do you think my Prince?"

"Kill it and be done with It." said Thomas.

"Kill it, me thinks that first it may want to speak to us, yes?" said the gnome.

"Kill and eat the bones so sweet. Kill and eat the deep red meat. Master sends and we come to eat the meat." said the pinned skeleton.

Thomas jumped back with surprise. "Who is this Master?" asked Thomas shaking his head with disbelief that he was speaking to a skeleton.

"Master comes next time he says. Came along after the others left. Very few left when he sent us. Most you already kill. Few more left. Me smart. I cut the tricksy wire you left for us I did. The rest come and I eat the meat." said the skeleton.

"You did not answer his questions, ehh!" said Brogan. "Once more who is the master?"

"Ask him yourselfs. He stands in the arch now. He tells you tale maybes. Or maybes he just eats the meat." said the skeleton looking with admiration at the beast that indeed inhabited the arch.

The arch was inhabited by the face of a dragon looking over the room and the Rangers within it. After a few moments the Rangers wearily pulled themselves to their feet and drew their weapons. Thomas threw down his weapons and ran to the dragon. "Mastol! You old worm, still hiding in the dark places of the world I see. It has been ages since last we met. How goes the dragons, dear friend?"

"Ever like your father, Thomas. Always meddling in the affairs of dragons. Be wary of that young friend, some of us find you crunchy and tasty in stew." laughed the dragon. The sound of its voice and laughter shaking plaster from the ceiling and walls. "Sorry about that. I forget the age of this structure. The caverns beneath are beautiful though. Come down and see them. Sorry about the welcome. I am afraid I have had some visitors through the years who have been less than friendly so I figured a little defensive force was in order."

"Never fear me old friend. I thought that you had finally passed on when I hadn't seen you in so many years. Mother would love to see you again. Have you seen Marzioa? Mother asks of him whenever anyone comes to the castle. Seems he disappeared the same time you did." said the prince. The Rangers around him stared in confusion as the prince stood rubbing the ears of the fierce beast before him. Some lowered their weapons while others eyed the dragon with fear and mistrust.

"Your friends don't seem too happy to see me. Shall I chew one or two to soften the rest for you?" smiled the dragon knowingly.

"You are always the kidder. Lay down your arms men. This dragon is a friend and a lord of state. Mastol, please do not kid that way. Some of my men are a little touchy about being chewed and we lost a few to your bodyguards." said the prince.

Brogan spoke up and moved toward the dragon. "Your bony friend there is still moving. Ehh! Maybe do away with him now? Dragons indeed. Never friends to the gnomes. Chewed quite a few of our kind, dragon. Maybe we leave now and run from evil creatures? Ehh!"

"Brogan you old fool. How many nights have we sat and discussed the state of the world? No friend to gnomes. Why if you were at my front door instead of my back door I may even have chewed you! You tough old bird. How goes your work here? Looks as though you have cleared some of the city already." said Mastol.

CHAPTER FIFTY NINE:
SAGE ADVICE

"What do you know of these cities, Mastol? They are ancient and we know so little of them still." asked the prince.

"How old do you think I am little one? These cities predate even me. I wish I could tell you of them but even the spires were covered long before I was born. The dragons used to speak of the race makers. Rulers who played with things they should not have and produced many of your peoples. These may belong to them." said Mastol.

"No offense old friend." said Thomas.

"None taken. And as for my skeletal friends there. I will correct that problem for you as well." said the dragon. With a wave of his head the skeleton stopped moving and no other sounds came from the archway. "Had you let me know you were coming I could have prevented this from happening."

"Next time tell me where you're living and I will send advance notice." laughed Thomas.

"This reunion is all great but we have much to do. Much to do yes." said Brogan.

Mastol looked down at the gnomes and the others sitting in the room and just laughed. "Gnomes!" As he spoke he withdrew his head and went back to his lair deep under the soil of Dracos.

CHAPTER SIXTY: HIDDEN SECRETS

Thomas and the gnomes moved quickly in clearing the first building of all the items it contained. Brogan spent many a night sitting at his desk looking at torn pieces of parchment. Thomas would join him often inquiring as to the contents of one piece or another just to be shooed from the tent so the learned could work. Thomas would often wander the ruins of the ancient city near the camp, looking at the huge towers that rose from the soil. Even though they were unadorned they still possessed a quiet beauty in and of themselves. He would run his hands over them in amazement that these structures had lasted so long without anyone maintaining them and with a dragon living in the basement.

Mastol often came from his lair to visit the prince and his old friend in the camp. Brogan would ask his opinion of some of the texts they had found but he could tell Brogan little to nothing. "Marzioa would know of these things." he would often tell the gnome and the prince. But the wizard never made an appearance.

Thomas was wandering the ruins one night while the dragon and the gnome discussed some new thing when his hand brushed a niche carved into the wall on one of the towers. He was sure it was intentionally placed there for none of the other towers possessed one and you could not see it. It could be felt but it could not be seen. Thomas rushed to the camp after quickly marking the tower and rushed into Brogan's tent. Mastol still had his head in the tent talking with the old gnome and the speed with which the prince rushed into the room caused both to jump startled. Mastol ended up with the tent covering his head as he moved upward rapidly and Brogan fell into his chair.

"Sorry to scare the both of you but I have found something. I've found something big." said Thomas.

Mastol was still trying to dislodge the tent from his head and Brogan just glared at the young man. "You come charging in here like you have the armies of the Dark Lord on your heels because you found something! Phah! Give it here."

"It is quite attached to one of the towers I'm afraid and I am sorry I startled you. Mastol come down here and I will help remove that tent. You there Rangers! Help get this tent put back to right. Come you both must see this." said Thomas.

It took a few moments to get the tent off Mastol's head and his mood was a bit sour when he heard it was over a supposed discovery. Thomas led them quickly to the place and showed the old gnome the niche in the wall. Thomas looked proud of his discovery until Brogan looked up from it.

"This is it?" asked Brogan, "A hole in the wall? This building is millennia old and you do not expect to find a hole in the wall? You scared the life out of us for a hole. Come Mastol, what were we discussing before the prince overreacted?"

Brogan and Mastol moved back through the camp and Thomas kicked the wall in disappointment. He had thought it interesting. It looked intentional. Thomas decided he would continue to look at the niche even if the elder gnome decided against it. Thomas drew his dagger from its sheath and pushed the tip into the niche. As the blade entered the niche a sharp click was heard and Thomas quickly withdrew the dagger expecting to see the tip of the weapon missing. Thomas was amazed to find the weapon whole and even more so to find it unharmed. Thomas shook his head in confusion trying to figure what the click he had heard was when he looked up and saw the section of wall he was looking at had swung in. He had found a secret compartment! Thomas again raced down to where the gnome and dragon spoke as they awaited the reconstruction of the tent. Brogan again jumped as the prince rushed up to the two elders.

"I have discovered a passage! That hole turned out to be a passage. I stuck my dagger into it and it opened a door into the tower. Come you must see." said the young prince as he again headed into the ruins.

"I swear if you have scared me again because you knocked over a part of a wall, I am going to use your guts for garters." mumbled the gnome, but his pace was faster than that of the young prince as they headed for the opening.

Mastol was looking down in the opening as the others arrived. His face looked like he had smelled something odd. "I do not like the looks of this." The dragon mumbled, as the rest of the party headed slowly down into the opening. Slowly Thomas led the way down into the tower following the spiraling stairwell, followed by the gnome and several of his Rangers. The stairwell went on for what seemed hours until they came to the bottom. The bottom opened up into a large chamber filled with metal cylinders and a huge mechanism covered with levers and buttons and lights.

Brogan moved rapidly to the mechanism and looked down at the controls before him, "I cannot make out what any of this is," moaned the gnome, "This goes way beyond my knowledge it does."

Thomas held the torch for the older being so he could see better, but he kept shaking his head and worrying about not being able to decipher the language. Thomas looked at the text and noticed that it was different than what they had found above them. In the buildings above they had found script that appeared to flow together like a river, down here the characters resembled some sort of picture writing. "Could this be the same people's creation?" asked the young prince. "Look at how different the symbols are. These had to be made by two separate peoples."

"It took you that long to notice the obvious, boy? Well, we know a couple of things now. These were made by two sets of peoples and one of them possessed much greater knowledge than ourselves." said Brogan. Looking at the prince he added, "Don't touch anything!"

Thomas stood idle behind the gnome archaeologist. It would not be him that triggered some form of trap or some other kind of unpleasantness. His eyes wandered the walls and the cylinders that lined them. Each bore an inscription across the top and was otherwise unmarked. Thomas moved to the closest of the shining metal tubes and lightly ran his hand s down the front of it. The tube stood a foot and a half taller than Thomas's height. Silvery in color it reflected the young prince's image back at him as he brushed the dust of ages from the front of the column. Brogan busied himself with the control panel as Thomas looked at the cylinder. The mutterings of the gnome filled the chamber as he looked from device to device on the panel.

"Boy! I need more light here!" Brogan called out to the young prince. The gnome turned to see where the prince had gone and nearly leapt upon the younger man's back. "No, No, No! I told you not to touch!"

"Dear master, I told you I would not touch anything. It can cause no harm to brush some cobwebs from one of the cylinders can it?" replied the prince.

"Mm mm yes. It could have. What if the tube had a hidden device? You move the dust and activate it, then what I wonder?" replied the wizened gnome. Though concern filled his eyes, the gnome's face reflected a pride in the boy's curiosity. "A good digger you would be. If you would just bring me more light. Just don't touch anything until I say!"

Properly chastised the boy moved behind the gnome and watched as practiced fingers moved over each item in the control room. The gnome's long fingers gingerly lifted and brushed to remove the accumulated dirt and cobwebs from the panel. Thomas once again grew bored and looked around the room. From deep in the shadows Thomas thought he saw something move. Begging the pardon of the old gnome, Thomas slowly moved forward toward the darkened corner of the room.

As Thomas moved forward he scanned the ground looking for indicators of something moving that way. He moved slowly and used his ranger training to watch for signs that anything had passed that way. Thomas reached the corner and saw nothing. Looking behind the cylinders and around the pillars in the corner revealed nothing of any consequence. Yet still the small hairs stood up on the back of his neck. He could not shake the feeling that he was being watched by something or someone.

CHAPTER SIXTY ONE:
HUNTER OR HUNTED

The ancient creature looked down from the top of the chamber wall looking down at the man who had invaded his territory. Slowly it followed the man as he walked around its lair. Looking down on the man it could not determine what it truly was. It did know that he had sharp eyes. The man had seen it move from the shadows to the wall. It must take more care not to be seen. These things in its home might yet prove valuable as food. How long since it had eaten? The creature did not know but the thought of food brought drool to its lips.

Slowly the creature inched forward toward the very unfamiliar light. Was it always that bright? It must be careful as the light hurt its eyes. Moving slowly upward, the creature moved to the ceiling and looked down upon his unsuspecting prey. The man had moved beside the smaller man. The two looked down at the box in its home as if it were something of great importance. The creature did not concern itself with such matters. Slowly the creature moved across the ceiling looking down at the variety of men in its house. There were six of them. But which to eat first?

The creature moved slowly down the wall toward one of the men who had rested there for a nap. The sleeping one would make a good beginning. But before it could eat it must inform the colony. The creature was torn between feeding itself and feeding its colony. Indecision caused the creature to freeze where it stood on the wall. It could not decide what it should do. To bring more of its kind meant sharing the food.

Eating before it went for the rest would scare the others and would mean sharing its kill. The decision it had to make was not an easy one.

One of the Rangers who had accompanied the young prince down into the tower leaned on the wall. It had been a long night the day before and this was turning into a long day. They had not been attacked by anything in quite a while, so the ranger decided it was time for a nap. His fellows moved slowly amongst the columns and cylinders searching for signs of danger as he sat with his back to the wall watching the door. The man nodded off again and again but woke rapidly looking at the doorway through which nothing had passed since they had arrived. He decided that there was nothing that would harm them in the tower and settled back to try and catch a few moments rest before Prince Thomas decided to press forward with the exploration of the chamber they were in and the surrounding rooms.

The man leaned back and set the back of his head against the wall. The rest would do him good and it would only be for a moment. The man leaned back and looked around him one last time before closing his eyes.

The creature saw the man close his eyes in sleep. This was its only opportunity. Slowly the beast moved down the wall giving its victim time to fall into a deep sleep. Turning itself slowly, it preceded bottom first over its target. As it neared its target a long shining stinger emerged from its sheath. How long had it been since it had used its sting? Slowly closer and closer the creature moved toward its new food. As the man leaned in sleep, a hairy appendage moved into the light followed slowly by a striped abdomen tipped with the large stinger. The creature continued down toward its target and another appendage emerged into the light.

Ten feet above the man it paused as its abdomen and lower arms reached the light. Fear caused the beast to stop its downward movement. It did not want to be seen as it took the first. Maybe if it took all of them, then it could get the colony and move back to the surface. Once more the animal moved down the wall careful not to awaken its prey. So close to its new food it could not help but drool openly.

Slowly it progressed and soon the tips of its wings showed in the light. Its solid black back supported the crystalline wings that no longer worked. They had forgotten long ago how to use them and they had broken as time progressed. A second pair of legs moved into the light as excitement pushed it to move faster towards its prey. The second pair of legs bore the appearance of fingers at the end that held the creature to the wall. The third set of appendages came into the light and these resembled the arms of the man below it. The hands gripping the wall as a spider clinging to its web.

A foot above the sleeping man the creature stopped and raised its abdomen. The stinger gleamed in the light of the torch as it raised it for the strike. Poison leaked from the tip of the stinger as it prepared to strike. Finally the beast's head moved into the light revealing a head that was part man and part wasp. The huge eyes of the wasp looked down as the abdomen raised to strike. The human mouth opened revealing rows of sharp canine like teeth ready for ripping into its prey. The mouth was drooling uncontrollably as it moved the last few inches to its intended victim.

Finally the creature reached its victim and plunged the stinger into his neck. The man jerked awake and attempted to rise to his feet. The beast moved quickly and grabbed the man by his mouth and throat using its middle arms. Using the rest of its appendages the creature moved rapidly to the ceiling and began to feed.

Thomas saw the ranger sitting against the wall and could not blame the man for his fatigue. Nothing was happening here. The gnome was busy trying to categorize the devices on the pedestal and Thomas was feeling tired himself. Thomas turned back to the gnome and looked over its shoulder, "So good sir, how much longer?" asked the prince.

"When I am done, you will know. The young man must learn patience, I think." replied Brogan.

"Do we know anything yet about this device?" asked Thomas, his impatience was beginning to show and he rapidly regretted his question.

"Mm mm yes. We know that it is a machine. What it does, we do not know yet." smiled the gnome.

At least the old gnome had a sense of humor. Thomas turned around and walked away from the gnome and the device. The ranger who was napping had disappeared. Thomas looked out the door to see if the ranger had gone to relieve himself and found the doorway empty. Looking around Thomas could not find the ranger anywhere in the room. Thomas looked down where the man had been sleeping. It seemed normal enough to his eyes. There was no sign of a struggle and no signs that anything was wrong. Thomas decided the man had gone back up the stairs to the surface.

As Thomas turned to head back to the device, a drop of liquid hit his shoulder. Wiping it off with his hand he did not even look at it until he entered the light around the machine. Looking down at his hand he saw it was covered in blood. He drew his sword and searched the ground for signs of the source of the blood. Looking around the room he saw no signs of the source of the blood. Moving out of the light he looked for signs of the ranger's passage. Holding the torch above his head as he searched the floor, Thomas heard a sizzling of fluid hitting his torch. Looking around for the source of the liquid, Thomas became more and more concerned about his missing man. It was unlike his soldiers to wander away.

Slowly he raised his eyes up the wall. A thin trail showed on the wall as his eyes moved up to the ceiling. Thomas rushed to the wall and felt the red stain. The blood was fresh. Something must have been dragged up the wall. Thomas began to wonder if a silent battle had taken place looking at the thickness of the stain. It indicated that a severely injured being went up the wall. The soldier would have put out an alarm if anything had come into his range of vision. Thomas shook his head with confusion. Looking up at the ceiling, Thomas's torch reflected off a shiny surface. Thomas had not noticed the ceiling before and the flash caught his attention. Moving toward the center of the room, Thomas kept his eyes glued to the ceiling.

Sudden movement caught his attention as something moved from the torch light. Thomas finally noticed the trail of fresh blood that moved with a strange sound. Thomas sheathed his sword and drew his bow. Something had pricked his instincts. There was definitely something wrong with this scenario. Drawing an arrow and lighting it on fire from his torch, Thomas aimed at the edge of the darkness and loosed the arrow.

The creature watched the fancy one move around the room looking at the floor. The bright lights they carried still scared the beast and it eyed it wearily. The *fancy one never looked up*, thought the creature. It would be able to finish its meal after all. He moved across the floor with the creature watching carefully between mouthfuls. The fancy one was looking at where it had taken its prey. *The animals do not know how to look.* Thought the creature. A laugh almost escaped its lips. The beast almost felt sorry for these creatures. Looking around the room the creature saw the small ones still looking at the shiny thing in its home.

Again the creature began to move toward its lair. It was time to alert the others. Food had come to their home. As it picked itself up to move the beast noticed the fancy one looking toward the ceiling. This could not be good. How could they have grown so smart so quickly? A brief moment in the light perked the fancy one's attention and it began to pursue the creature.

Cursing itself as it moved outside the range of the light, the creature determined that it must dispose of the fancy one before he alerted his people. Slowly the creature moved around the edge of the light. Planning its attack would be difficult because the fancy one was not leaning against the wall. If it dropped onto him it would alert the rest of its prey. It could not do that.

The creature watched with curiosity as the fancy one put away his sting. Why would the prey do that if it realized he was being hunted? Perplexed the creature watched the fancy one point the long stick it carried at the ceiling. The creature was confused as to the purpose of this act but just watched enraptured. The fancy one moved his light near the stick and then a strange occurrence happened. Part of the light came up to the ceiling and stuck into it. The creature jumped back as it connected, looking at the new item in the ceiling. The light now clearly showed the creature to its prey. The light had stuck only inches from the beast.

Looking down at the fancy one the creature decided it had to take him. It was too late now. The animals down on the floor had seen the beast and now it was time to fight. Lifting its meal for one final bite it threw the carcass at the fancy one. The battle had finally arrived.

CHAPTER SIXTY TWO:
BUGS

Thomas jumped back as the creature on the ceiling threw the body at him. It had to be his missing ranger but he did not have time to confirm that as the creature fell from the ceiling right behind the man. Thomas attempted to raise his bow for a second shot but the creature closed before he could get the shot off. Something so large should not be able to move so quickly. Thomas dropped the bow and drew the sword on his hip.

Holding the sword before him he began to circle the beast before him. The beast rose up on its hind legs and swung with very human looking forearms. Thomas moved back and swung blindly with the sword. He was rewarded with the feel of the sword biting into the limb of the creature. The beast let out a scream that could only be called a human cry of pain. Thomas backed away from the creature again and lowered his weapon. "You there. Hold your hand. I would speak to you if you are capable." said the prince.

"Nothings to says, says I. I do not speak to preys." responded the beast.

"Then speak to a friend. Please hold your hand. I do not wish to destroy you." said Thomas.

"Noooo. I speak not to preys. You preys. I say no more." said the beast. It reared up again and Thomas saw the stinger sliding from the bottom of the creature's striped abdomen. Thomas raised his blade and tried to speak to the creature again.

"Please, I see your stinger and you see mine. Let this come to a peaceful ending and not to another violent confrontation. I would hate to have to harm a great creature such as you. It would be a shame to have to destroy a beautiful creature such as yourself. There are many more of us than there are of you and it would not be possible for you to survive. Let us end this another way." implored the Prince of Dracos.

"No mores! You die now. Many mores to feeds. You will be the firsts." said the beast and once again lunged at the prince. Thomas jumped away from the probing stinger and swung his sword up and under the beast to find it hit nothing. Thomas lunged into the beast and swung the sword again, this time being rewarded with a strike on one of the middle limbs. Thomas spun away from the beast and swung his sword backhanded connecting with yet another of the beast's arms.

The bloodied creature reared up and looked into the face of the man who had caused it so much pain. None of the wounds were dangerous but the pain was getting to the creature. The beast moved toward the far wall of the room to find its way cut off by the human. Thomas moved slowly toward the creature the creature again trying to soothe it with words. His words just seemed to agitate it further for it reared up again and renewed its attack.

Thomas knew he would have to kill it. If it were to get away it would alert the others of its kind and who knew how many of them there was. Two more Rangers moved into attack positions around the creature and the beast feigned an attack on the closest of the Rangers. The soldier moved to counter the beast to find it leaping onto the second ranger. The second ranger had lowered his guard slightly when he saw the beast move to the other ranger and was startled to find it flying toward him. Thomas jumped to the man's aid just as the creature raised his stinger and thrust his blade in between the segments of the creature's body.

The beast jumped away from the man ripping the blade from Thomas's hand. Thomas rolled away from the fight looking for another weapon. The Rangers swung and hacked at the beast as it charged their leader. Thomas moved on all fours away from the monster still searching for a weapon as he dodged the creature's attacks. Thomas continued to move away from the fight pursued by the creature when his hand fell upon something on the ground. Not looking Thomas thrust upward vat the monster to see an arrow in his hand pierce the creature's eye. *At least I got off my second shot,* thought Thomas as he searched the ground for anything else he could us to defend himself with as the creature tried to remove the broad headed arrow from its now destroyed eye.

Thomas called out to a ranger not yet in the fight for a weapon and the ranger threw a sword to his prince. Thomas reached his hand up to catch the blade just to have it knocked away by the now enraged beast. It pressed its advantage forcing the prince into a corner. Rising up onto its rear legs the beast moved forward.

CHAPTER SIXTY THREE: MEETING THE METRADON

Torlin lay sleeplessly upon his cot. The city lay not two hundred feet from him and he slept in a rag. This was no way for the next ruler of Dracos to sleep. He was royalty. Surely his brother got to sleep in one of the buildings in his city. Torlin lay a few more moments before using his powers to light a lantern and get up from his cot. Artitous entered the tent shortly after the prince lit the lantern holding the paper Torlin had used to get the rubbing from the control panel.

"We still have not been able to decipher the text from the panel." began the Druid. "It is just such an obscure dialect that I am not sure we will ever know what it says. It resembles so many languages but it makes no sense in any of them. I wish Marzioa were here. He was always the linguist. Maybe he knows this language."

"Then let me look at It." said a voice from behind the Druid.

Both men in the tent jumped to their feet preparing spells of a particularly nasty sort and looked toward the source of the voice. Standing in the entrance to the tent stood the wizard. Marzioa looked at the prince and smiled, "Got your hands full with this one don't you Artitous? Stronger than the last time I was here. So what is this language you wish deciphered? I really am a busy man and I don't have all night."

The wizards and Druid shared a brief laugh and then set to work. The wizard held the rubbing up to the light and squinted at the text. Turning the paper round several times and looking at the markings he shook his head. "This is a base language. It is ancient. But these symbols have been given new meanings so many times since this was written, it could say anything. See this symbol. It means 'to begin' in Elfish or 'To Finish' in Dwarven. But it has a different meaning in the more ancient texts. It is impossible to translate it unless you have someone who spoke the language to translate It." said the wizard.

"Start" said a gravelly voice at the front of the tent.

"What?" said the wizards ready to flay the hide from the person interrupting the private meeting.

The man styled reptilian creature walked into the tent and pointed to the paper in the man's hands. "It means start." said the reptilian. "Now why are the slaves reading?"

"There are no slaves here." said Torlin. "May I ask who you are and why you have come into my tent in the middle of the night asking such things?"

"Much has changed since I went to sleep I see. I did not even recognize my home when I awoke. I am Horned Carl, first Centurion of the Metradon. When I went to sleep, the scale-less were the slaves to the scaled ones. If the panel is correct we have slept for many years. Much has changed. Tell me, did we win the war? Did we destroy the Tetradon? Are they dead?" asked the scaled visitor.

"We know nothing of whom you speak. We do not even know who your people are. Our testing shows that you have been down there for ten thousand years. Just the fact that you can stand there and speak to us is a miracle. Please sit and speak with us about your people and what the machine down in the ruins is and what it does." said Artitous.

"Please do not refer to the city as the ruins. It was yesterday that I walked across the great square and entered into the stasis chamber. Where is the guardian? It should have prevented you from entering the chamber. It was designed to survive forever. It should have been there to defend us. Otherwise it must have been destroyed. Now for you, have you found their city? It would have been twin to this one. Now tell me is it exposed or does it still lie beneath the earth?" asked Horned Carl.

"If you are asking if the other city has been found, it has been. Your people can soon be reunited if any sleep in its bowels as you have slept in the bowels of this one. How many of your people sleep in the chamber below? We will do what we can to provide you all the necessary items to survive until we can create suitable arrangements for you." said Marzioa. Looking to his companions he said, "I do keep informed of these things."

"Those who dwell in the other city are not my people. As for how many sleep below, none know. There are over seven thousands of the Metradon awaiting my order to come to the surface. As for those in the other city, you will destroy them all, slaves. Your masters have awakened and we intend to take back all that was ours. Now you three will be the first to kneel to your masters. Now kneel! Do not attempt to kill me for it would spark a war you have no way to win. Kneel and do as I tell you! I have little time to lose and little patience for your kind." said the reptilian.

Torlin rose to his feet and took a step forward, bringing his hands to his waist looking as if he were preparing to kneel. The one called Horned Carl smiled as the young one moved to show the proper respect. They still feared the Metradon. This was a good thing. Still smiling he moved to give his scaled hand to the young man to kiss when he felt the searing pain in his head. Looking around he could not tell which of the three was trying to attack him. How they assaulted him he did not know. Any who were found that could wield the power were put down amongst the slaves. Had things really changed so much?

Torlin rose to his feet as the Metradon before him went to its knees. Squeezing the skull of the creature with the power, he looked into the creature's eyes and smiled at its confusion. "I kneel to no one! What ails you? You look as if something is squeezing your skull. Oh, wait. There is. Now know this, your day is done. We are no longer your slaves. You are now our slaves, and your obedience will dictate whether or not our yoke will be difficult or light. Now that you are on your knees, why don't you kiss the hand of your new master?"

"Never!" replied Horned Carl grabbing his head in agony. Artitous and Marzioa moved to block the spell of the younger man just to find they were unable to move. Torlin smiled at them as he looked at the reptilian creature before him and he waved his hand. A sharp crack sounded throughout the tent and the man on his knees fell to the carpets lying on the floor of the tent.

"Do be a dear gentleman and clean up this mess. I have a new people I must go and enslave." said Torlin as he left the tent and walked toward the chamber. The others in the tent found themselves able to move once Torlin entered the tower and the wizard and Druid looked at each other for a brief moment and flew from the tent. One moved toward the center of camp, the other toward Thalinburg. War had come to the land once more.

CHAPTER SIXTY FOUR: MEETING THE TETRADON

Thomas stood looking at the monster moving toward him and tried to force himself deeper into the corner. His men hesitated when they saw their commander pinned directly in front of the creature. Fear kept them from firing afraid they would hit their prince. Thomas searched around him with fingers and eyes looking for anything that may assist him when his hands found purchase on the wall. Pressing up with his arms he kicked out with his feet, knocking the beast into the control panel. As soon as it had moved away from their commander, the Rangers opened fire and the creature fell heavily onto the panel.

Thomas moved to the creature just as the alarm sounded. The gnomes jumped to the panel and searched for the source of the sound. The creature rapidly moved from the panel and the sound stopped. Thomas recovered his bow and sword and quickly formed his men for the assault he figured would be forth coming. After a few moments, he moved amongst the Rangers and had them start evacuating the gnomes who were down in the chamber. The remaining Rangers formed a rear guard as the others moved up the stairwell to the surface. Slowly they made it to the surface and the little group gathered at the doorway looking down into the stairwell. Silence greeted the men as they waited by the doorway. Thomas looked around the first landing and then returned to the others. "We do not appear to have been followed. I want a guard posted on this door. Rangers! I want nothing to pass this door without my knowledge. Now get those Rangers on this door and no one opens or enters without a full platoon of Rangers." said Thomas.

Chapter Sixty Five:
Stories and Meetings

Thomas turned to leave the scene of the commotion when someone tugged his arm. Thomas expected to see a ranger pointing to more of the creatures but instead found the old gnome at his elbow pointing to the doorway and the reptilian creature standing within it. Thomas went to his sword, but the old gnome prevented him from drawing the blade. "Speak to it before we start carving it up. That is better I think, yes. Maybe we will learn something." said Brogan.

Thomas once more was humbled by the old gnome's wisdom and compassion as he moved toward the creature in the doorway. Thomas looked upon the reptilian looking man and felt a knot of fear in the pit of his stomach. Where were these beasts, and were they watching them all along in the lower chamber? Mastol had moved to the assembly by the door and the reptilian looked up in amazement at the great wyrm looking down on him.

The reptilian man looked to be the same height as the young prince and of a muscular build. Lean and with the look of great strength the creature seemed to move with a grace that implied great speed and agility. Thomas decided that if these beings meant them harm, the group that had gone below would be dead. Thomas moved forward and took the reptilian man by the hand and moved him away from the door so it could be closed. Thomas looked into the creature's face and smiled gently to the man before him. "I do not know you or your ways so please forgive me if I offend. I hope you can understand me. I wish to introduce myself; I am Thomas, Prince of Dracos and heir to the throne. Welcome to our camp."

"I am Dagmar, First of the Tetradon. It is a pleasure to awaken not to war but to a new peace and tranquility that did not exist before I went to sleep. Tell me did you find another city by chance? One inhabited by a race similar to my own? They call themselves the Metradon. They are prone to be warlike and thus very dangerous, we are more the peacemakers and prone to talks. But do not mistake me, in war we give as well as we receive. We went into our slumber so that we might survive the stalemate which had threatened to destroy both our peoples." said the reptilian.

"My brother works there now. As far as I am informed they have found no trace of another people. But that was days ago and much may have changed since then." replied the young prince.

"My you have grown large and strong have you not youngling?" said Dagmar to Mastol. "Your kind grew no larger than my knee before I went into the long sleep."

"Much has changed since you have slept. The world is no longer as you remember it. Humankind rule here, with the aid of all the species of the world. I am sure your peoples would be welcomed into our councils as well. But it is to Thomas you must direct your inquiries, for he commands here. I am merely a family friend, and have learned long ago to keep myself out of the intrigues of politics." replied the great dragon.

"The humans? The slaves? Which of them did you say was leader here? Thomas? Which of you is Thomas?" asked the creature.

"We are no longer slaves nor do we keep slaves. All are equal now. We work together to accomplish our goals. I welcome you to our councils, your wisdom and insights will be very welcome. Your people will be helped to establish yourselves anew. Everything you need, we will give to assist you." said the prince.

"Many thanks, Thomas. Your words are kind. I apologize. You see, the world is so much different than when I went to sleep. I am going to try to grow accustomed to the way things are now. With your kind help we will be great neighbors." said Dagmar.

"Bring your people to the surface and we will find shelter and food for you all." said Thomas.

"There are about eight thousands of us. I will go to them and lead them up here. Together we will assemble our camp." said Dagmar.

Dagmar moved slowly down the stairwell toward where the rest of his people waited. The Tetradon waited for him to return and give word as to the safety of the world. Dagmar entered the stasis room and looked around. His entire people waited for him and perked their heads up when he entered.

"My people, the slaves now rule. Our ancient enemies still sleep for now, but it is time to move to the surface and reclaim what is ours, and prevent the return of our hated rivals. Retrieve the storage pods and prepare for war!" screamed Dagmar as he moved to the hidden chambers which contained their supplies and weapons.

Chapter Sixty Six: Needs and Wants

Daybreak found the two camps in a state of disarray as the gnomes, Elves, and men scrambled to accommodate their new found allies. Together the three races moved to provide shelter and food for the masses that came from below the cities.

Torlin's camp moved rapidly to create shelters fit for not much more than animals. These beings now belonged to Prince Torlin and it was his order that they not to be made too comfortable. Torlin screamed at and threatened the new found beings and used his immense powers to keep the beings in line. Food was brought to the creatures and many set to it with a fervor while others stood in disbelief at the circumstances which caused these current events.

An hour after daybreak, Artitous returned to camp with a dozen of the Tyris. Slowly the warrior women moved throughout the camp and settled upon the pens which held the reptilian peoples. The Tyris are a people accustomed to hard lives. Their women are the warriors and their men the homemakers. A Tyris warrior wears a Mytan or a piece of leather armor in the shape of a one piece bathing suit. It is low cut and fitted with steel plates to protect the vital parts of the woman wearing it, but can be considered a little risqué to the people and warriors of Thalinburg. The Tyris enjoyed flaunting their bodies, if only for the response it received from those around them. In a fight however, there are no better soldiers or allies. It is said that they do not know the meaning of surrender and it is hoped by most of the people that that theory remain untested.

The Tyris and the Druid entered the camp and quickly secured every aspect of it. Artitous moved to Torlin and pulled him to the ruins where an unheard conversation took place with heated gestures from both men and much hand waving. As the two men conversed, the Tyris had gone to Torlin's slave pens and pulled it open. Rapidly the creatures within moved to the opening and tried to push their way through. A large male roared and spoke to the advancing mob in a strange language and they all stopped moving. The male moved forward and examined the women destroying the reptilian's prison.

"Just don't stand there looking, big guy," said the Tyris who stood at the gate trying to cut through the ropes that held the gate in place, "grab hold and lift so I can finish getting that gate out of the way."

The Metradon male moved to the gate and lifted it. Before the woman could raise her blade though, the reptilian creature tore the gate from the post supporting it. "I am not big guy. I am Two Horns. I am considered unattractive to my kind because instead of having four huge horns I only have two. But I am strong and ready to serve the mistress."

"No mistresses here, Two Horns. We are a rescue party. Our queen will not tolerate slavery of any kind. We are here to set you free and to see if your people require any other assistance." replied the young woman warrior.

"I am ashamed to admit that our new role seemed to come easily to me. If you do not wish to be mistress, please how should I call you?" asked Two Horns.

"I am Roanda Steelhand. I lead this group of Tyris warriors. As to your physical appearance, better not ask me about that. I am no judge of your people's good looks but I must say that you look pretty good to me for a giant lizard." said Roanda.

"Giant lizard? I am afraid I do not understand the reference. But if our conversation is through, I wish to get my people back to our city." said Two Horns.

"By all means and if your people require any assistance, please let us know." said the Tyris as she turned and walked away leaving the hole wide open and clear for the Metradon to pass unhindered. Two Horns walked past the Tyris, still carrying the gate, heading for the buried city. "By the way Two Horns, anytime you want to dispose of that is fine with me. You can just lay it anywhere." said the young woman.

"Many apologizes, dear lady. Forgot I was holding It." replied the reptilian as he flung the heavy gate to the side of the road. "Was never considered the brightest of our people."

CHAPTER SIXTY SEVEN: A NEW ALLY

In Tetra the scene was slightly different. The Tetradon moved to the surface carrying large containers which they refused to open. Thomas moved amongst them with his new found ally, Dagmar, and saw to their comforts. Tents went up rapidly as men, Elves, and gnomes worked together to raise a temporary city for the reptilian creatures. Dagmar was polite and rather informative as Thomas, Brogan, and Mastol moved through the ruins of the once proud city. It was agreed as they moved through the remains of the city that all of their peoples would share the burden of reconstruction. Together they should be able to unearth the city and restore it to its previous wonder in short order.

Thomas spoke often to the leader of the Tetradon making inquiries as to the function or design of one item or another. Dagmar would often reply to him, "Do you know the designer of the first sword? I just used the item I do not know its history." Mastol was another story. As work on the city of tents progressed, Mastol began to pull into himself. He did not participate in the conversations which occurred amongst those around him but was there whenever the prince and reptilian creature were together.

"Mastol is something the matter?" asked Thomas one day as the two sat looking at the ruins which now resembled a city instead of a hillside.

"I do not trust those things. They smell funny, like something is not quite right." said the great wyrm.

"Many would say that you smell funny too, old friend. Does that mean we should mistrust you?" laughed the prince.

"Ever the comedian. My Prince, I fear that something is not right here and that when these things have recovered we may have a problem with them." said the dragon.

"Ever the worrier. Do not fear old friend. We will see this through and we will be greater for our alliance with them. Dagmar is of great heart and spirit and rules them well. I have not seen one even look like it was going to go against his wishes." said Thomas.

"I still do not trust these things. Do not be alone with him. I fear what may be the result of his counsel. Thomas, how do you think your brother is doing with his boring city?" asked Mastol.

"I don't know old friend. It must be slow going without the extra aid we have received. He must be bored to tears out there. I would ride over there to tell him of our discovery if I thought I could get away for a while. Just right now, the project is still in its infancy and not yet far enough along to leave to the supervision of others." said Thomas.

"You worry too much, young one. But you are right. Your place is here for now. Maybe your brother will visit us here when the work on Metra is stable enough for him to depart." said the dragon.

"My brother leaves something he may learn from? Heaven forbid. The only reason he would leave that city is if he completed his work and learned all there was to learn of the city. Besides the way my brother behaves it may cause some bad blood between our two races to have Dagmar meet Torlin." said the young Prince of Dracos.

"You boys really should patch up your differences. It may happen soon that you may need one another. The way things are now, neither of you would work with the other. This may cause a problem. I just fear for you and your brother's safety and the effects of these things on you both." said Mastol.

"With you looking over my shoulder, old friend, what can possibly go wrong?" asked Thomas with a bit a laugh.

"Yes, what indeed?" replied the dragon. The difference was that Mastol was not laughing.

CHAPTER SIXTY EIGHT: TYRIS WISDOM

Torlin was livid at the return of the Druid to his city. How dare the old fool come back here and tell him how to run things. Releasing his slaves and moving toward diplomatic relations. These things had not seen the light of day for how many thousands of years? And to send those women to oversee everything was just an insult. They were just his mother's eyes and ears. They would report to her everything he was doing here and ensure that his brother won the contest between them.

Thomas was always her favorite, thought Torlin. *She wants him to be the heir apparent. She would like to see one of her little women warriors shove her sword through him.* His thoughts were interrupted by one of the Tyris' approach. "Lord Torlin, I am Roanda Steelhand and commander of this unit of the Tyris. I look forward to working with the greatest wizard in the world. You are a little thin for my tastes but you are a handsome man all the same if I may be so bold. You and I are about the same age you know. Well, I have to set guards and got things moving along if these people are to be back in their city in our lifetimes. I will talk to you later with the progress. You look tired and should rest while I deal with these minor details." said the woman.

"That will be fine. I will be in the ruins of the library should you need me... What was your name again?" Asked Torlin.

"Roanda." replied the Tyris as she turned and moved toward the mob of people and creatures standing near the ruins.

Maybe there was something to be said for having the Tyris here after all. Thought Torlin. "There is always a benefit to everything, you just have to find It." said the young wizard.

"Pardon my Lord, I did not catch that." said Roanda.

"Nothing, nothing. Just try to get things going will you? I do not wish to spend the rest of my life living in a tent." replied Torlin.

"My people live their entire lives in tents, sire. What is wrong with living in a tent?" asked the young woman, flames seemed to burn behind her eyes as she spoke.

"Nothing, just not my idea of a great and pleasant existence." said Torlin as he moved rapidly toward the ruins to escape the glare of the young woman.

Another of the Tyris walked up to Roanda as she walked toward the waiting group. The Tyris looked at Roanda with confusion as Roanda laughed at nothing as they walked. "Is everything all right, commander?" asked the Tyris.

"Fine," replied Roanda, "what do you know of men?"

"Not much I am afraid, commander. I try to avoid them whenever it is possible. After all, who needs those whining, weak, and scared people around? Worthless in a fight and only good for two things, bringing up your children and seeing to the household." Replied the woman warrior.

"Still clinging to the old ways even after all of these years living amongst the others. You know that these people do not think like we do. They even have the roles of men and women reversed. Their men go to war while their women tend the home. Well, maybe when the time is right I will find one of their men and coerce him to our way of thinking." smiled Roanda knowingly as she watched the young prince making his way to the ruins.

"Commander, these men are only good for one thing, and that is not really appropriate talk in pleasant company." said the warrior.

"You're right. Come, we have details to arrange. Let us chatter like draftees later. At least the prediction of Artitous was incorrect. War has not returned to our land. I was not even born when the last war ended. I hope we never have to see it return." said Roanda.

"Don't tell me you are going soft on me!" said the Tyris.

The two women laughed at the private joke as they made it to the group standing around waiting for them. It would be a long project and harder still because they would have to work around the meddling of Prince Torlin.

CHAPTER SIXTY NINE:
HIDDEN PLANS

The group of Metradon stood apart from the others who awaited the pink skinned woman. Two Horns had assumed the command after the death of Horned Carl and he had been holding them in an iron fist. To think that the woman believed he was concerned about what she thought of his appearance. Two Horns moved amongst his chief warriors and told them of his plans. This should work to their advantage after all. All they needed to do was keep their stockpile from the primitives until they could set their plans in motion. They would play along with these slaves for a while. They had to. But soon it would be time and they would claim what belonged to them.

In Tetra, a Tetradon moved through the human camp. His head and face were covered; it was vital that he warn the humans without anyone knowing. Dagmar would kill him if he knew what he was doing, but he had to do something. The reptilian reached the tent of Thomas and slid the parchment he was carrying under the fabric. The reptilian ran toward his own camp when three Tetradon stepped before him.

"Out for a midnight stroll?" asked one of those who stopped him.

"Just out for some air is all, I beg the pardon of the patrollers for disturbing them." replied the cloaked reptilian. He had forgotten about the patrols. He had to be more careful if he were to aid their new allies.

"Mind telling us what you were doing by the human chief's tent?" asked a voice from the shadows. The cloaked being recognized the voice immediately as that of Dagmar.

"Just happened to pass that way, First." he replied.

"I believe he lies. Soldiers, kill him." said Dagmar and turned back toward the tents of his people. The resistance had managed to survive and now they were plotting to aid the slaves. This could lead to trouble as their plans moved forward. Maybe he should have spared the man's life, if only to learn of his comrades. He dismissed the thought as soon as he thought it. The resistance trained their people to die before revealing anything they knew. He must keep this from the pink skins. They would not understand and may even stop trusting him if they knew.

Over his shoulder he heard the muffled scream of the man as he was slain. Dagmar turned around and moved rapidly to his men. A little discretion would be necessary for the time being…. but only for now.

CHAPTER SEVENTY:
THE MUSEUM

Torlin was confused. The woman from Thalinburg was annoying him to the point of distraction. How dare she come here and tell him what was going to happen. She had released the slaves he was going to use to see that the excavations moved even faster than he had originally planned. He was moving through a section of the city that lay under quite a considerable bit of sediment that had accumulated since the city had been abandoned. The darkness was lit by a small sphere of light he had magically produced so he could see and make his way deeper into the ruins. He was searching for the library the one called Horned Carl had described before he had killed him. It should give him some comfort being amongst the texts that supposedly lay within its walls.

Torlin finally found a likely building that could pass as a library and entered through the huge front portal. He had no one accompanying him so he simply blasted the doors off its hinges with a blast of air he conjured to prevent a trap from harming him. These gnomes wasted too much time trying to preserve all the pieces of the city. It was a ruin after all. He noted with satisfaction that no blasts occurred except the doors shattering. Too many precautions for his taste, but these gnomes thought too much. Everything was dangerous.

Slowly he entered the foyer of the building and looked around at the surrounding passages. Three hallways left the foyer and any one of them could lead to his goal. He was mentally berating himself for having so quickly killed the Metradon. He really did need to learn a little patience.

Looking around the foyer he decided on the forward hallway. It was as good a place to start as any and he was anxious to find the tomes. Who knew what magic lay within those texts. Maybe some skills that they had forgotten they had forgotten. It would truly make him the most powerful sorcerer on Dracos. Let Artitous think he was most powerful. He would teach the old Druid. He would show them all.

Moving along the hallway, he noted many rooms off the main hallway. A few magically erected barriers would keep anything unfriendly inside those rooms. Why wait for soldiers to clear the building when all you had to do was block everything in? Torlin finally made it to the end of the hallway and found a huge chamber lined with cases. He had found a museum. Not what he was looking for but it would be a pleasant distraction for a short time. Going to the first case he peered deeply into the now darkened glass case.

The skeletal remains of a large creature was reassembled and displayed within the case. The description of the creature was in the same ancient dialect that had stumped him in the hidden chamber. He still did not know how to read it. *It doesn't matter what the card said anyway.* Thought Torlin. He would simply rename it himself later. After a few moments he moved to the next case and the remains of a dragon stared out from behind the glass before him. He recognized this creature having grown up with Mastol looking over his shoulder. Not interested in things he already knew of, Torlin moved on to the next case.

Inside the case was a series of objects laid out in neat rows. They looked commonplace enough. Cups and rods and necklaces filled the neat rows, but he could not take his eyes from them. Lifting the top of the case with another flow of magic, he reached into the case for one of the necklaces. Maybe a gift to the Tyris commander would get her to allow him a little more freedom. Knowing his mother and her people it probably would not help, but he would try anyway. Women always enjoyed gifts. As his hand was about to close over the nearest necklace a voice behind him startled him out of his contemplations.

"I would not touch those if I were you. They are very powerful magical items. Too powerful for you to handle maybe." said the voice from the darkness.

"I know what I am about." said the young prince as he swung his light around to locate the source of this new irritation. The only thing that he saw was in a far corner. A pair of what appeared to be glowing yellow eyes.

"If you could lessen the light, I would be extremely grateful. I have been in these ruins for so long that light bothers my eyes now." the voice pleaded with Torlin.

Pleading was better. That was what the prince was used to and he was not about to allow some creature from the dark to call the shots with him. Bad enough he had to listen to that stupid woman. He would not allow some unseen creature the luxury of commanding him as well. Torlin increased the brightness of his light illuminating the entire chamber. A catlike man raised his arms to his eyes, protecting them from the glare. Torlin moved toward the creature, speaking in his typical condescending manner. "Afraid of a little light? I would think something of your size would not let a little brightness intimidate him. Come and make me lessen my light if it troubles you so. If you dare that is."

"You are a young fool, kitten. Do you not know who I am? I am Pan Thor, wizard extraordinaire of the Catarel People. I became lost searching these ruins three years ago and am now eager to be free of them. Do not make me destroy the one hope that I may leave this place, rather than join the exhibits that surround us." said Pan. "A kitten does sometimes require a lesson in humility, but right now is neither the place nor the time for that lesson. Do not force battle between us. I fear the shockwaves of it would bring this building down around our tufts."

"Are all of your people such cowards and fools? This building has stood here for millennia. Do you believe a little magical play will bring it down? Give me your best, cat. I will teach you humility." cried Torlin.

"So be it then. But when I have you showing your belly and you have your tail between your legs, maybe you will show a little more respect." replied the Catarel wizard.

Bolts of lightning sprang from the corner occupied by the catlike creature. Torlin dived behind a case of objects he could not identify to protect himself from the blasts. 'That was a trick I will have to learn' thought the young prince as he sent fireballs toward the cat. Lightning and fireballs met between the two combatants and the shockwaves from the two connecting caused plaster and rubble to fall from the ceiling. Maybe this building was not as strong as Torlin thought.

The two continued their magical battle and an occasional stray blast would strike the walls around them or a case would explode when struck by a fireball or lightning strike. Torlin began to grow tired as the battle progressed and he could tell by the slower attacks from the cat that it too was tiring. Torlin decided to make one last ditch effort to kill the beast and sprang from his hiding place lashing out with a huge fireball. The blast struck the wall above the cat, who sprang away from the attack. Unfortunately for both of them the blast was enough to bring the ceiling down upon them both.

Torlin lay on his back with a large chunk of the ceiling across his chest and waist. Breathing was difficult due to the weight and the fact that he had probably broken at least a couple of ribs. His left arm was pinned by the debris as well so he could not use magic to remove the rubble. Looking toward where the cat had leapt, he saw his adversary pinned beneath a slab of marble fallen from the wall. All that showed was the beast's head and it too showed signs of having problems breathing and moving. Torlin tried to lift his head and found that his body would not respond. Turning his head he called to Pan, "So Pan, are you happy now? We are both trapped down here and we both will perish here. And here you thought you were so intelligent. Well done!"

Pan responded in a weak voice, "I am not the one responsible for this disaster. Look to yourself if you seek blame for this catastrophe. I believe it was I who tried to speak to and guide you."

"Guide me? Why would I take any advice from you? You shot first. I retaliated. If you desired peace you have a funny way of showing It." said Torlin.

"What choice did you leave me? You had insisted on being a spoiled kitten. In my culture the young respect their elders despite what they think they know. If you had listened to me, we would not be in this predicament." hissed Pan.

"Well now that we have so short a time to live what do you propose we do? We are both unable to do much beyond look at each other. I hope you have a plan as for me I have nothing." Sneered the prince.

"Can you move your hands?" asked the cat wizard.

"Only my right hand. I cannot work any magic without both my hands." replied Torlin.

"Only if you think you can't. You can work magic without both your hands, just believe you can. Now use your right hand and control the air to lift this rock from me so I can remove it from you." replied Pan.

"And even if this works, you will come here and slay me. How can I trust that you will not kill me at your first opportunity?" said Torlin. "Besides, the exits are now sealed with debris. We are not going to be able to remove it all and escape before we succumb to hunger and dehydration."

"You still do not trust anyone or anything do you?" said Pan. "I know that we are sealed in, but there is water running into the room near the rear of this room where you found me. As for food, there are many creatures that I am sure you attracted with this battle. They may not be the most pleasant food source but we will survive. And if I had wished to kill you, I would have. We have greater problems to deal with than each other. Once this is over, we can go our separate ways and never again have to look upon each other if that is your desire. But for now, we are stuck in this together."

"You tried awful hard to kill me. I saw what you were throwing at me. You are moving rather well by the sounds of it. Release me first and then I will decide whether to reciprocate the favor." said Torlin.

"What are you saying? I am unable to move or I would have already released you. I assumed it was you that was making that racket. What are you chipping at the stones with? I would almost swear it was spider feet." said Pan.

"I am not chipping at the stone. Spider feet? There are no spiders here in this building. We cleared them out of some of the other buildings but this one had no webs that I saw when I entered." said the young sorcerer.

"Did you check the side corridors? I found traces of those things everywhere." said Pan.

"Side corridors? No, I suppose I didn't. So now we must contend with spiders. They are the normal spiders I hope and not the giant variety." said the prince. Something was dawning on him. He would not survive this without the cat. The cat would die if he did not help it. Never had a situation like this arisen for the young prince. Something else depended upon him for its survival and he depended upon it for his survival. His mind suddenly lit up like a great sun. They all depended on each other. Maybe his goodie two shoes brother was right. People of all kinds and types did matter. He would definitely have to try harder to be kinder if he survived this.

Torlin lifted his free arm and focused on the slab holding the cat when he noticed the movement to the cat's left. It was a giant spider moving slowly toward the great cat. Torlin focused again on the stone willing magic to flow and move the stone. "I can't do it! One handed I cannot control the power." cried Torlin.

"You can young one. You just have to believe. Focus on my voice. Forget you have hands. Just focus your mind on the stone and the magic to move It." said Pan.

"I am scared Pan. Have you ever believed something for so long and finally realized you were wrong? I fear the spiders have already found us. I can do nothing. Forgive my arrogance if you can before we die." said Torlin, his voice cracking with tears.

"For one so strong you are giving up very easily. The spiders will not have us. Now focus on the stone. You can do this. Focus and believe in yourself! Don't think you can do it, know you can move it. Tell it to move and it will move! Believe it!" said Pan.

Torlin raised his arm again and closed his eyes to block out the image of the spider moving onto the slab holding the cat to the floor.

CHAPTER SEVENTY ONE:
RESCUE

In the camp Roanda heard the explosions. Searching for the source she saw nothing but she was sure they were coming from the ruins. Torlin must be taking out his rage on some unfortunate piece of masonry somewhere. Roanda sought out Artitous to stop the destruction. What good would it be to unearth the entire city just to destroy large portions of it? She found Artitous down at the ruins edge. The Druid looked into the ruins but his eyes were glazed as if he were standing there but was a million miles away. Roanda turned to leave when the Druid spoke, "Roanda, assemble your warriors. We must go and rescue the young prince. He is in danger."

"Why should we risk our necks to save him? He deserves what he gets. He has done nothing but be rude and insulting since we have been here. If the man is in danger, and I stress if, let him deal with it himself. That's what I say to that." said the Tyris commander.

"I think you will find a changed man under the rubble of the ruins. He has never had to deal with anything like he is dealing with now. I suspect he may be a very different man than the one who went into the ruins." said the Druid. "Now follow your orders and go into the ruins to retrieve the prince. Make haste, he does not have a lot of time before he will be killed."

Reluctantly Roanda called for her weapons and her warriors. It looked like she would have to babysit the young man after all.

CHAPTER SEVENTY TWO:
UNKNOWN FEELINGS

Torlin closed his eyes so he would not see the spider and fear overtake him. Raising his hand he again tried to summon the magic. At first he felt nothing and the fear of failure crept into his mind. Swallowing the fear, he once again tried to summon the power and he felt with surprise the stone through the power. He felt it wiggle under his influence and it strengthened his resolve.

"Keep it up kitten. It is working. The spider was frightened by the stone's movement but it will not hold him long. Try again. Focus. You can do it." said Pan.

Torlin opened his eyes and focused again. The stone wiggled and slid slowly off the pinned cat. He had moved it halfway off the cat when he dropped it. The cat's hands were free now and he felt the stone try and move from him. Torlin looked down and saw both his arms were free and lifted them to move the stone from the rest of the cat. As he lifted them though he felt a sharp pain in his arm. Looking up he saw the multi-eyed face of a giant spider latched to his arm. Screaming he turned the power toward the beast and found he was unable to call the power. He tried to lift his arms again and found them unresponsive. The spider moved slowly toward the now inert prince with venom dripping from its open mouth. Clicking its mandibles in anticipation, it moved slowly up the remaining stone holding the prince.

Torlin's vision came as if through a fog and he could barely hear anything. He knew Pan was calling out to him, but he could not hear what he was saying. Torlin's vision slowly came back into focus and he looked down to see the spider approaching him over the slab holding him to the ground. Once more Torlin tried to lift his hands to strike at the advancing monster, and once more he found himself incapable. Watching helplessly, Torlin stared in wonder. This was how he was going to die. The spider had finally reached his head and shoulders and was lowering its mandibles to the prince's throat when Torlin saw the spear materialize in the creature's head.

Torlin felt rather than saw the hands of the people lifting him out from under the slab. He tried to call out to Pan but all that came out was a croak. The spider's venom had really crippled him. Again he tried and this time managed to utter one word, "Pan."

From behind him he heard a voice telling him to be still, but again he tried to speak, "Pan" was all he could utter. The person holding him lowered him to the ground and he heard the sounds of fighting and felt himself being dragged from the ruins of the building. After what seemed an eternity in the dark, he finally saw starlight above him. He had never realized how much he actually enjoyed looking at them. He lay immobile staring at the sky when he heard voices around him.

"He was bitten on the arm by one of the spiders. He was right where you told us he would be. He had a strange looking companion with him. The spiders were descending on it like there be no tomorrow." said a woman's voice.

Torlin felt a tear fall from his eye. Why was he so hurt? Had the creature not tried to kill him? The cat had been derogatory toward him since the two had met. Yet the cat had proven something to him. It had been his encouragement and his strength before the spider had bitten him. Now that influence on him was gone. It was breaking his heart. Torlin felt something being laid gently at his side but he could not move to see what it was. Around him he saw women warriors and Rangers rushing around and heard the sounds of battle once more surrounding him. Artitous stood above him launching fire and lightning at the approaching enemy. He could not see what was coming but he could imagine it was probably the reptilians or the spiders. The two races were the only ones who would attack the camp. And the reptilians would not be attacking if it were not for him. *How many would die for his vanity this day?* The thought kept running through his mind. One had already died and that was already too much.

Torlin felt himself being lifted and carried once more. The sounds of battle receded as he was moved and finally quiet surrounded him. He saw the Druids moving around him, covering him and making him comfortable. A weak smile was all he could manage. It would have to do for now. Slowly sleep over took him and his world faded from color to grey to pleasant dreamless sleep.

CHAPTER SEVENTY THREE: ADVICE AND CHANGES

As Torlin lay sleeping in Metra, Thomas was wide-awake and speaking with his newfound advisor. The two had become close in the last few days. Dagmar whispered his advice to the young man almost constantly since he had made himself known to the humans. Dagmar traveled with the prince and advised him on which buildings to open and which to avoid. He told of things found in the ruins and explained the daily life of the Tetradon.

Thomas moved through the ruins looking around the now nearly unearthed city. The Tetradon had many ways to clear the accumulated soil from their city and he marveled at their tireless work ethic. Earlier in the day, Tyris had arrived in the city led by one of his mother's friend's daughters. Meka Paron was a young woman about his age with a will of iron and the looks of a goddess. Thomas fell head over heels in love with her the moment he saw her. Thomas went to her tent often with the evening meal in the guise of ensuring she had eaten. Meka would graciously accept the food and then reenter her tent shutting him away from her. Her ways intrigued him even more and caused the prince to watch for even more opportunities to be near her.

Thomas often went to her asking for instruction in the Tyris's ways with weapons. He would fake a lack of knowledge to get the woman to spend time with him. The woman seemed to know he was lying but humored the young prince with his daily lessons. Meka did not understand the prince's motives and really did not care. It broke up the monotony of her days and it would not be long before she could return to Thalinburg and the young guard she was seeing.

Thomas was very happy to see his good friend, Paul, amongst the newcomers. Paul Alon was the son of Perrick, Thomas's mother's governor of the Dwarven people. Perrick was a reformed thief and spy, yet people in court still kept a close eye on their belongings when it was known he was in court. The man had passed all of his knowledge on to his son on locks and traps. Paul had decided on ranger training and had earned his place to stand at his friend's shoulder on many occasions. Paul's problem was he did not deal well with stress or fear. It was known to cause him problems as they had seen at the opening of Metra. Now Paul marveled at the greatness of Tetra.

Thomas spoke to Meka and Paul about the city on their frequent walks through the ruins; Dagmar always close to hand to explain the function of some obscure building. On one such walk near the perimeter of the city, they found a part of the great wall that had once surrounded the city. The section they saw gave the impression that the walls rivaled those of Thalinburg. "It must have been near impregnable when it was whole." Mused Thomas to his friends. Meka just shrugged off the thought of walls. The Tyris did not use them and really felt it was cowardice to hide behind them. Thomas thought them the greatest thing in the world. It would make his city indomitable if they were restored. The only one who encouraged this was Dagmar. The reptilian made both Paul and Meka nervous.

Thomas decided to try to attract the woman's interest one evening by having her brought to him while he was bathing in his tent. His servant ran to find Meka as Thomas slid into his tub of water. Meka entered unaware of the prince's intent. She rushed in and inquired as to the urgency of his request. Seeing Thomas in the tub of water, Meka laughed and rapidly removed her clothing. Thomas knew from his mother that the Tyris felt that seeing another in their bath was a sign of interest, but if the other was also in the buff, it spoke of a lack of interest. Thomas's heart sank in his chest as the young Tyris spoke to him of weapons and fighting sitting there in her skin. Though he was happy to see her body, he was also downhearted that she had not remained clothed and not remained standing to get a better view of him. She was merely being polite. It was considered rude to be clothed while another was naked if you lacked an interest in them. She sat and washed herself with a cloth as she spoke of little things and of the skills; she wished to see him master.

Thomas dismissed her after a time and finished bathing himself. He was so embarrassed. How could he have not attracted her attention by now? He felt anger rising within him as he rose and dried himself. He was attractive. He was kind. He was a skilled warrior. What was wrong with him? The anger filled him as Dagmar entered the tent. Dagmar seeing his state of dress turned and walked from the tent until Thomas had dressed. A small smile now rested on his lips, the prince was ready. Dagmar seeing the prince's interest in the female followed her to her tent and listened for a while at the rear of it.

Meka returned to her tent from Thomas's; her mind thinking still of weapons and war, not love and affection, when one of her warriors approached. "Leader, why were you called to the prince's tent?"

"He was in his bath. He wished to speak of weapons and war. You would think that the prince would grow weary of it after a time," replied Meka.

"His bath? Meka could he be trying to gain your interest? It was quite forward of him. You would think he would have called you to his dressing room first. Didn't he listen to the courting lessons of his mother?" asked the woman.

"Interest? You do not think that the Prince of Thalinburg and Dracos would have interest in me do you. That would be something would not it. Ragan would get a laugh out of that wouldn't he? Royalty looking at me. Well, even if he is interested in me I showed him I am not interested in him. That should settle it.," said Meka.

"The prince has been acting strangely since that reptile has been hanging around with him. I do not believe he will stop there. I think he will try again. Meka have Ragan be wary. It may become very dangerous for him if the prince should learn of him," said the Tyris.

"That I will, dear friend. At least Thomas does not know of him yet so at least he will be safe until then. I think this will blow over rapidly, but we will have to wait and see." said Meka.

"So you got to see him in his bath, Meka. Tell me everything!" said the woman.

"Now I see who he should have summoned." laughed Meka and related the details of her visit to her friend. Unbeknownst to the two women the reptilian known as Dagmar sat listening to them. The information he had just gathered would greatly assist him. He now had the final piece to turn the prince to his cause. Smiling, Dagmar returned to the tent of the prince.

Dagmar waited until he was sure the prince was properly clothed and entered the tent again. Thomas's face was a combination of pain and fury. Dagmar went to the stand in the tent and poured two glasses of what these people called wine. Handing one to the prince he settled down on the cot and waited for the prince to sip on his glass. "Dagmar, what do you want of me? I have not had a very good night. Make your request quickly and leave Me.," said Thomas at last.

"I saw your mate leave. She is attractive for your kind is she not?" said Dagmar.

"She is not my mate and probably will never be my mate. She totally spurned me. But she is very pleasant on the eyes isn't she?" replied the prince.

"Not your mate? My apologies. I overheard her speaking of Ragan and assumed she was speaking of you. My mastery of your language still leaves a great deal to be desired. I take it Ragan is a rival for her affections then?" asked Dagmar.

"Ragan? The guard Ragan? I would think that he would not be much of a rival to me, but obviously, he is. Dagmar have a runner summon Ragan here. I have a plan to remove the competition. You will enjoy this I think. Hurry and get the ball rolling and I will explain my plot," said Thomas.

CHAPTER SEVENTY FOUR: EVIL PLANS

After a few moments, Dagmar returned from his errand. Things were progressing nicely after all. The prince was falling deeper into the dark nature of the slaves. Soon Thomas would have none near him to influence the boy away from him. His very nature would be his undoing. Dagmar returned to the tent to listen to Thomas's plan and determine just how far under his control the prince was.

Mastol watched the Tetradon enter Thomas's tent. He had seen a difference in the prince since the reptilians had been uncovered. More and more the prince turned to this thing for assistance rather than that of those who had been so much his guides in the past. Mastol feared the influence of the scaly one, but he kept his mouth shut. It would not do to turn the prince against him if the creature was poisoning his mind. Mastol needed to consult with Marzioa, but the recluse was nowhere to be found and that troubled him as well. Mastol figured the wizard would be in Metra, but he had not been seen for two days. He was last seen heading toward Thalinburg. Mastol had gone there to find that the wizard had spoken to the queen briefly and the two teams of Tyris where sent. Afterward no one had seen hide or hair of the man. Mastol would continue to try to find his friend for guidance but he held little hope he would find the man in time. Until he could though, he would watch the little one and his new friend very carefully.

In Thalinburg, Marzioa entered the dark inn. He had seen the man he sought enter it a few moments before. If he were right, this would make a great deal of difference in the coming days. He walked in and located the man he was looking for and walked over to his table and sat down. "I have been looking for you for a while. Glad to have found you. We need to talk you and Me.," said Marzioa to the cloaked figure. The cloaked man ordered another drink and said, "So let's talk."

Morning came early for Thomas. He awoke often in the night with strange dreams haunting his sleep. Dreams that found him chasing something he could not catch. Dreams that had his heart tearing out of his body and flying away. Dreams of him falling into a great abyss. Thomas moved sluggishly to the morning meal and sat secluded from everyone. He would glare at anyone who came close to him, chasing them away with his eyes. His temper increased every time Meka passed by him. The woman caused such pain and passion within him. Thomas started to rise when she passed by him, but his stubborn streak kept him from calling out to her. He wanted her to come to him. At this point, he did not care if it was as a lover or a supplicant. Either way she would be his.

He was brooding over these thoughts when Dagmar approached him with news of the new building the Tetradons had finished clearing of debris. Thomas listened with half an ear to the reptilian until he heard of the problems the Tetradons were having. Thomas's head shot up from his thoughts when Dagmar mentioned the wasp-men pouring from the building when they attempted to open the door. Thomas's eyes lit up as he described the minor battle and the retreat of the Tetradon workers. Ten of the Tetradon had perished and seven of the wasp-men. The battle had been hard fought just for the Tetradon to escape.

Thomas grinned as he motioned to Dagmar to follow him. Things could not be any better if he had planned them. Thomas led Dagmar back to his tent and held the flap for the reptilian. After the two were in the tent and Thomas was assured there was no one to hear, he began to speak. "So there are large numbers of these wasp-men in that building? Did your people have an estimate as to the numbers within the building?"

"No, my Lord. Only that they swarmed the moment we approached the door. There were so many that the ground was darkened by their very presence. But there appears to be a very large number of the enemy." said Dagmar.

"Dagmar, has Ragan arrived from the city? If he has, I have a mission for him to complete for me. Go and collect him and bring him here for me if you would be so kind, my friend." said the prince.

"Certainly my Lord. Give me a few moments to find him. He apparently arrived from Thalinburg this morning. Will there be anything else while I go for him?" asked Dagmar.

"Yes, try not to be seen," replied Thomas. As he spoke, a small smile came to his lips and darkness seemed to fall upon his eyes.

It took the creature a little more time than he had figured to find the man, Ragan, but find him he did. Dagmar spoke quickly to the man and made sure he would speak to no one until he had entered the tent of Thomas. Ragan stood at attention while waiting for the prince to enter. Dagmar became impatient as time progressed and Thomas did not appear. Where could the man have gone? After what seemed an eternity to the two men in the tent, Thomas returned. Ducking into the tent, he closed the flaps and tied them off. He could not risk a guard overhearing what he was about to do.

Ragan snapped to full attention as the prince entered the tent. Ragan admired the skills and diplomacy of the younger man. If all their warriors were like Thomas, maybe the wars that had once plagued their world may not have happened. It brought great pride to serve Thomas however, he asked. It was even better that Thomas had asked for him personally. Now he was serving under the greatest commander and was near his Meka. Could life be any better? Ragan stared straight ahead and spoke to the prince, "My Lord, it is a great honor to serve you here. You have been an inspiration to many of the men, me included. It is an honor to be here at your disposal."

"Is that so?" asked Thomas. "What do the men think of me?"

"They speak extremely highly of your prowess in battle and of your kindness to all that cross your path, friend or foe." replied the ranger.

"I have need of you for a specific mission, Ragan," said Thomas.

Ragan's heart skipped a beat as the prince spoke his name. 'The man even remembered all his troops' names. What better man was there to serve under?' thought the ranger as his chest swelled with pride. "What is the mission, Lord? I will endeavor to complete it in as timely a fashion as possible."

"The rewards will be great. I would even finance the wedding of you and Meka if you complete this mission. I would promote you to my second in command so that you can give Meka all she could ever desire. Does this sound acceptable to you?" asked the prince.

"My Lord, that is more than generous. What is the mission and it will be done. The sooner I have it the sooner it will be complete. I will not let you down." said Ragan.

"It is simple, my friend. I need you to take five men and clear the new building we just uncovered. I will even select the men for you," replied Thomas with a sinister smile upon his lips. "Clear the building and you shall have your reward."

As the man saluted and ran from the tent, he ran into Meka. The brown haired Meka looked as if she were a common farmer's daughter. Nothing really stood out about her. Few knew she was the daughter of one of the Tyris nobility. She was well built and strong but the ranger's uniform she wore covered much of the curves and beauty of her body. She preferred the heavier ranger garb to the traditional Mytan of the Tyris. It was more protection and she blended in better with the crowds. Her face gave away her hidden beauty and the few who had seen her without the armor appreciated the fact that they had been given such a glimpse. Ragan threw his arms around her and lifted her skyward. Meka caught off guard gave him a well-placed knee to the kidneys for his effort but the pain did not even sway him. "I am off on a mission for our lord, and when I return I will have the means to give you the life you so richly deserve." said Ragan

"You obviously do not know me well if you think it is money that attracts my eye. You are a fine warrior good and noble. When you return from this mission, I will decide if I will wed you. Until then keep your focus on the mission and not on what you expect from me in the tents afterwards," replied Meka with a laugh.

"Right as usual, My Lady. But I will return soon and when I do I will hold you to your promise." smiled the ranger.

"What promise?" screeched the Tyris. "Why I should just.… If you do not leave now I will ensure that you are under the camp instead of a part of it. My promise? I will see you later when you return. Hopefully after I have calmed down."

"As you say, My Lady. As you say." replied Ragan backing from Meka. A broad grin covered both their faces.

CHAPTER SEVENTY FIVE:
CLOSING THE CITY

Mastol finally was able to corner Thomas later in the day as he walked to survey the city. Thomas moved as though in a trance not really seeing what he was being shown. Mastol finally blocked the prince to a wall with his tail and spoke to him. "What has taken your thought, young one? Is there something bothering you? Please speak to me and let us see if we can correct this dark mood that has taken you."

"Do you see the wall there, Mastol? It could withstand the assault of tens of thousands and yet time has laid it to ruins. What do you think of rebuilding that wall, Mastol? Only making it better and stronger. What say you to that, Great Wyrm?" said Thomas.

"Are you mad? That wall was plenty fine in its day. There is no reason for a wall now. We have stopped the Dread lords and we face no enemies now. There is peace, so why waste the time and effort to build a wall you will never need?" asked Mastol.

"We do not need it now, but who knows what lies ahead. Why be caught unprepared, Old One? Better we be ready and not need them then be caught without a defense should the need arise. Wisdom obviously does not come with age does it Mastol?" said the prince.

"Thomas, I meant only that there are other projects that need your attention at this point. Why expend the resources for a wall, when most of the city still lies buried beneath rubble and debris? It is foolhardy to do too many things at once. Do you not see that?" said the old dragon.

"Mastol, you challenge my authority? I cannot have that. Not even from a friend of my mother's. Leave now and maybe I will not set Rangers to see you off. Your aide here is no longer needed nor is it desired. You shall see one day I was right, Mastol. You will all see one day." smiled Thomas as he pointed toward the horizon where Thalinburg lay. "Go visit Mother and inform her that Tetra is now under my sovereign control. I will be sending no more reports from here and I will consider anyone she sends from this point spies. Everyone knows the penalty for a captured spy. So warn her to take care whom she sends for I will execute anyone she sends. Moreover, I mean anyone. Safe journey old one and may we never meet again." said Thomas as he turned and walked away calling out orders for the stonemasons in the camp to get to work on the walls.

As Thomas and Mastol argued, Ragan approached his mission. The five men with him moved with the skill and abilities of seasoned Rangers. Slowly Ragan moved to the door of the building filled with thoughts of his reward to come. As Ragan pulled open the door, his last thoughts were of his lord's great miscalculation. Why would he send six men when there were so many? This thought did not last long as his vision quickly turned to blackness and his squad was pulled into the building, never to be seen again.

Within the stasis chamber deep under the ruins, the first wasp-man encountered by the men of Thalinburg was finally found by his people and his fate reported to the queen. The queen listened to the report and closed her multifaceted eyes to ponder the circumstances. A new enemy has come to their home and now they would have to defend it. The queen called her general into the throne room and ordered all the others out. They would have to defend themselves from this new threat and they would have to do so now.

CHAPTER SEVENTY SIX: HEALING AND CARING

Torlin slowly awoke in the medical tent. His body felt as if he had been beaten to within an inch of his life and his head felt as if it were stuffed with cotton. He slowly lifted his head and saw the Tyris, Roanda, sitting on one of the camp chairs. Her eyes were closed in sleep. Torlin tried to think why she would be there but his mind just would not respond. To distract himself from the woman, Torlin turned his head the other way and his eyes rested upon another person covered in blankets on the next cot. The person moved and squirmed under the pile of blankets keeping it warm. Torlin could not figure who or what it was, but he assumed it was a soldier from the fighting at the entrance to the ruins. As he thought of the ruins his thoughts returned to what had happened down in the building itself.

Torlin felt his eyes begin to water as he thought of the cat-man, Pan Thor. In the end the creature had tried to save his life and it had cost it its own. Torlin could only blame himself for being too slow to learn the lesson the cat was trying to teach him. Torlin decided to retrieve the wizard's body and return it to his people. It was the only right thing to do.

Torlin once more turned his head and saw that Roanda had opened her eyes once more and was looking down at him with concern in her eyes. Torlin wondered briefly, where she was when everything was going down in the building. A brief rage built within him as he thought of her not being there but it rapidly subsided. He found it difficult to remain angry.

Roanda stood from her chair and moved to his cot. She dipped a cloth into a basin and gently mopped his brow. Fear and affection filled her eyes as she methodically washed his brow and face. Torlin turned his face to her and a small smile came to her face. "So you're awake, are you? Good. Now you can wash your own face." Standing she strode from the tent. When she was sure she was out of the prince's sight, she let a large grin come to her face. He would be all right. She would have to keep a better eye on him apparently. He had a knack for getting himself into trouble. She walked along thinking of the curves of his face and the way he looked as he slept until she reached her tent. 'It would be nice to get some real rest,' she thought as she lay down on the pallet of rugs she used for a bed. She fell asleep thinking of his eyes looking at her after he woke and the look of his face when she had found him under the ruins.

CHAPTER SEVENTY SEVEN: ADOPTION

Torlin propped himself up and looked around him in the tent. His roommate still slept fitfully under its pile of blankets and Torlin decided it best not to wake it. Torlin sat there for a few moments when a Druid entered to check on the two of them. Seeing Torlin awake, he moved quickly to the prince. Surprise filled the man when Torlin pointed to his sleeping companion to be seen first. The Druid had expected that the prince would be shouting demands and making himself the center of attention in the medical tent. "How is it?" asked Torlin.

"How is that being? He is getting better slowly. He was bitten multiple times by the spiders so it will take him a little longer to recover," replied the Druid.

"He must have been one of those that entered the ruins to find me. I must see to it he is given great rewards when he is well," said Torlin.

"He was not one of the rescue party. Do you not know who this is? Well it is understandable you would not, you have been asleep for three days and been nearly dead for two weeks. That woman has been here since she pulled you from the ruins. Her and her team went down there after you. The Rangers just kept the spiders from over running the camp and a good thing they did. I have never seen so many of them in one place before," replied the Druid.

"Is Artitous here? I would speak to him when he has a moment," said the prince.

"I will fetch him immediately. Please do not harm me for lack of haste," said the Druid.

"I will not harm you. The being I was trapped down in the ruins with has seemed to cast some kind of spell on me. Do not rush Artitous. If he is busy, leave him alone. He can come here when he is available and not a moment before. Tell him to come at his leisure. I have much to make amends for. Thank you for your kind ministrations for my care. I see that you have changed and bathed me while I slept. I still cannot believe it has been two weeks. Thank you." said Torlin with one of his rare smiles.

"I wish the thanks belonged to me, my Lord. However, the young woman tended to you. She would allow no one to come close. She said that she was there at your mother's order and was to see to your care. She even gave you your medicines and your meals. You would have thought she was tending her husband rather than her charge. Well, I will go and let Artitous know that you are awake and let you regain your strength," said the Druid, still watching for a sudden attack from the young prince's temper.

"Then have her come here to me when she is rested so that I may thank her as well. Now go so that you can get back to your other charge." said Torlin.

From next to him a familiar voice came from under the blankets. "Be still kitten. How is a person supposed to rest with you meowing like that? Good man, could you please bring me something to eat? I feel as if I haven't eaten in a week," said Pan Thor.

"It has been two weeks you overgrown fur ball. And could you bring two meals instead of one? I would like to eat with my friend here and thank him for his kindness down in the ruins. Pan you must tell me what happened after I was bitten down in the ruin." said Torlin.

"The kitten has learned to ask nicely. Because you asked nicely, I will tell you the last few minutes that I remember. You were bitten on the arm and I was just able to move my hands. I sent a blast of air to try to move the bug from you to find I could not move. Looking down I saw one of those great bugs had latched its jaws around my chest and was biting for all it was worth. As I was falling into darkness, I saw a spear pierce the head of the bug on top of you. The blonde-haired woman that held the spear thrust it so deeply into the beast you would have thought the beast had attacked her mate or kitten. She drew her sword and was hacking on it when I finally succumbed to the venom of the spiders. A dark haired woman was killing the spider that bit me but I saw little of her before I fell into darkness," said Pan.

"I thought you had perished down in the ruins. I felt like I had failed you. What have you done to me? I have never worried about anyone else before. I did not care if a woman mopped my brow while I was ill before. If it did not affect me, it was not worth my attention. Now I find myself caring about others and not being the demanding, self-centered person I once was. Tell me cat. Please. What have you done to me?" pleaded the prince.

"I did nothing to you, kitten. You have grown up emotionally due to your ordeal. Sometimes seeing one's own mortality is enough to cause a major shift in your life, and in this case, it was for the best. You have grown and now understand what those around you have known for a long time. That it is those around you who mean something, not just you and your desires. Some never learn that lesson amongst my people and yours. I pray that future generations of both are born with that lesson ingrained in them and that they will make this a much better world than the one we now live in." said Pan.

"Amen." responded the prince.

"Ahhh, the two adventurers are awake!" smiled Artitous as he entered the tent. "You sent for me, my Lord?"

"Artitous, I was wrong. I tried to use my abilities to force you to be submissive and subservient to me. I treated you as if you were nothing when I should have sought your counsel and advice. Please find it in your heart to forgive me?" said Torlin to a dumbfounded Artitous.

"Forgiveness is yours, my pupil. I must say, a monster went down into the ruins and a man has returned. I worried about you when you took the Metradon as slaves. I figured all-out war would erupt when your mother sent the Tyris. Now I am confident a happy ending may come of all of this," said Artitous.

"Dear Sir, who are these Metradon you speak of? I saw reference to them deep within the ruins. Do they still live?" asked the Catarel.

"They lived in some kind of machine for thousands of years. I have never heard of the like. They are reptilians by nature and have strange tattoos upon their cheeks. Now please come out from under your blankets and let me have a look at you," said the bard.

Pan Thor removed the blankets covering him revealing to Torlin for the first time the cat's black fur streaked with gray. About five feet tall he looked more like an overgrown housecat, than a vicious killer and wizard. His deep yellow eyes Torlin remembered from down in the ruins, and his quick, sharp tongue as well. Artitous looked at him for a moment and made a strange circular movement in the air. Pan repeated the movement and bowed low.

"You are a Catarel," said the bard.

"You know of us? Tell me are the rest of my people well? We are the last of our kind and I hope we thrive as all of you have. I am anxious to return home. I have been away for years and now I seek the company of my kind. Are they still a few miles to the south of here?" asked the Catarel.

"I have sad news. During the last few years your people have been attacked by multiple different groups." stated Artitous.

"Battle does not bother my people. We just go and lick our wounds if we lose and move forward again. The clan must have their fur ruffled in a terrible way," mused Pan.

"I am afraid that my news is direr. They attacked a clan of dragons." began Artitous again just to be interrupted by the cat once more.

"So they got some singed fur did they? Serves them right for going after such a large prey as a dragon. Moreover, not just one dragon, but also a whole clan of them. They really should have known better. So where are they camped now so I may return to them?" rambled the cat. Tears began to well up in his eyes as he spoke to the Druid, reality dawning on him as he rambled. "They are not camped anywhere are they?"

"No sir. They were killed by the dragons in a very bitter battle between your two peoples. If the prince will approve it, you are welcome to remain here. It depends upon him and his decisions on you," said Artitous.

"Well, I appear to have no home to return to. I fear now I will travel for the remainder of my years and see the end of my people. We were already few enough. When I am healed enough I will depart, kitten," said Pan looking down at his cat like feet.

"Well you know we already possess too many wizards and sorcerers here. We can learn nothing about your people now that they have wiped themselves from existence. I have wondered what the custom for adoption with the Catarel people is. Now I will never know," said Torlin.

"One does not adopt lightly in our people. However, if we were to, we would clasp the child or person by the arms and state in a loud voice three times that the person was of your clan and under your protection. After the third time, all would know it was so and it would not be questioned. Is it not that way here?" asked Pan.

"It is a bit more complex for some of our people less so for others. Are you up for a walk? I feel restless and want to walk off some of my pent up energy. Join me please the two of you," said Torlin, a sly grin crossing his face.

"Of course we will." the two in the tent with him replied. Pan rose slowly to his feet and Torlin himself supported him as he recovered his balance and was handed his staff.

Torlin led the two out into the common area of the camp and all present looked on in awe at the cat-man amongst them. Torlin stopped suddenly in the middle of the common area and grasped the cat's arms looking around at the rest of the people. In a loud voice so all could hear him, he shouted out three times, "This man is of my family and under my protection. Let none question his word when he says he is my brother!"

Pan's eyes shot open and he stared at the young prince. "Kitten! Do you know what you have done? You have named me your kin and your brother. That cannot be taken away! Now that it is done, it is done. I am bound to you now. I have done no great deeds to deserve this. Now I am once more in the debt to your people. Your kindness has been great but to make me one of your family. That requires great deeds and I have none. Why Kitten? Why have you done this?" The cat-man rambled.

"You foolish feline. I adopted you for what you have done for my people and me already and what I am sure you will do in the future. Your honor does any of us proud and your skills are legend. I would learn all I can from you and as my brother; you may be more willing to teach me the great secrets of your magic. Did you think that I had no ulterior motive when I adopted you? You need a home and I need another teacher. Now we both have what we need," Torlin grinned in a mischievous way. "Besides, my brother and I have not seen eye to eye for many a year now. Maybe I also wanted a little company."

Pan looked at Torlin and tears came to his eyes. Moving so fast even the quick Rangers could not move between them, Pan wrapped his tail and strong arms around Torlin. Torlin waved off his protectors as they moved to assist him and stayed trapped in a one sided hug for many minutes, unsure how to return the affection being shown. Torlin had always been the distant one. He did not endure physical contact well. Slowly Torlin wrapped his arms around the shaking Pan. At first, it was an awkward hug between the new brothers, but slowly Torlin relaxed and true affection could be seen between the cat and the wizard. Slowly Pan pulled away and patted Torlin's back. Looking up at Torlin with his salt and peppered hair covered face; he grinned and spoke lowly to the man next to him. "I guess it will not do to call my brother kitten. I am assuming you have another name?"

Torlin once more put the mischievous grin on his face and responded to Pan, "It is Kitten. I thought you knew me. You mean you were poking fun at me?" Torlin said with feigned hurt in his voice.

Pan just stood and stuttered, Torlin laughing at the wise old Catarel wizard tried in vain to recover from his assumed blunder. Torlin roared with laughter as the cat tried harder and harder to recover his dignity. Finally, Torlin leaned down, his sides hurting with laughter, and spoke to Pan, "My brother, my name is Torlin, not Kitten. I was poking fun with you. Come let me show you the project I am working on. I only fear one thing Pan. Telling my mother she is a mother to a cat." Both men laughed as they moved toward the ruins of Metra.

Chapter Seventy Eight:
Rebuilding a City

Thomas moved slowly over his newly finished parapets and battlements. Construction had gone quickly with the aid of Dagmar's people. Though not entirely complete, the rough work was finished and the final additions were being started. He smiled as he looked at Dagmar's people scurrying from place to place building his walls. As Thomas looked toward Thalinburg and his mother's palace, Meka joined him on the wall, "My lord Thalin." she began.

"Meka, how are you? I have told you repeatedly it is Thomas. What aid can I give you?" said Thomas. "You seem troubled."

"My Lord, I mean Thomas, my friend, Ragan, was sent down into the ruins a few days ago and he had yet to return. I was wondering if we should send out another patrol to see if his patrol can be located," said the woman as she looked out over the city.

"This man is a friend of yours? It is rumored he was more than a friend. However, since this means so much to my mother's emissary, I will send out a series of patrols into the ruins to see if he can be located. You of course should remain here. Your instructions on the combat techniques of the Tyris are most fascinating and I would like for them to continue," replied the prince. As he spoke, a sly smile came to his lips. "We will do our best to bring him home or return his remains to the city proper for burial."

"Let us hope we are not too late." murmured Meka.

Thomas smiled broadly and replied, "Let us hope."

Meka ran from the wall after speaking to the prince. She must arrange for the search parties. Since to get the parties to go she must remain, she was going to ensure people she trusted were amongst the searchers. Something in the prince's manner made her wonder if there was not something she was not aware of. She slowed suddenly and thought things through. She must use caution on whom she asked to join the search parties. She must not make it appear she was including many of her people or more may become mysteriously lost. Walking back to her camp she entered her tent and tied the flap. She needed time to think things through.

She turned from the flap and found that she was not alone in her tent. Dagmar sat on her sleeping pallet licking his scaly lips and smiling as she turned. Instinctively she had her sword in her hand and at the creature's throat. Quickly regaining control, she returned the sword to her scabbard. It may have slammed home a little harder than she had intended but she was now not just concerned but angry. "Master Dagmar, Do you not ask permission to enter another's tent anymore? You nearly lost your head for that indiscretion. Be quick, what business do you have here?" asked the woman warrior.

"My lady, I meant no disrespect or affront. Oh no. I merely sought to inform you of your friend, Ragan, was it? It seems his patrol came upon a group of creatures of some sort. We do not know what or who they are at this point," said the reptilian.

"So he is in bad shape then. I cannot wait to rub it in that he still needs me to watch his back," laughed Meka.

"My Lady misunderstands. You may have to wait a long time to tease your friend. It seems that this report came not but a few moments ago from a lone survivor. It would appear all the others have perished. I am truly sorry and I am sure the prince will wish to convey his condolences once he is aware of the situation." Dagmar hissed. The reptilian seemed to have a satisfied smile upon its face as he watched the warrior fall to her knees in tears.

"Are you certain of this, Tetradon?" she asked as she regained her feet, "I swear on all I hold holy that if you are concealing something from me I will see you dead on the end of my sword! Now tell me everything you know about this and leave nothing out. I will give you one chance to tell me the truth and if you know what is good for you, you had better make me believe you the first time." Her voice trailing off as she drew her blade and put the tip of it to the reptilian's throat. It may have been her imagination but she almost believed the creature grinned at her. She swore to herself that if this beast were lying to her it would be the last thing it ever did.

CHAPTER SEVENTY NINE:
SEARCH PARTIES

Back on the wall of Tetra, Thomas found himself briefed on the survivor's story. It had amazed him how fast the woman had flown from the wall. It seemed as if she had somehow grown wings. She was definitely showing all the qualities he wanted from his mate. Funny thing thinking of her as his mate. Thomas was sure it must have been some kind of mental trick his mind was playing on him. Thomas moved slowly toward the tents formulating in his mind what he was going to say to the woman. She was probably going to be crushed by the report of what happened to her friend. Thomas almost relished the thought of being able to tell her of the occurrence. Her pain would be most satisfying.

Thomas approached the tents and was nearly knocked off his feet as Meka flew from the tent. Spinning away from the attack, Thomas grabbed hold of the woman. "Hold there, warrior! What is going on here? I must speak to you at once." Thomas said.

Meka stopped and looked up at the prince and then threw herself into his arms, sobbing into his tunic. Thomas looked down and slowly wrapped his arms around her shaking form. Stroking her hair until the tears subsided, cooing gently to her and making soothing sounds, she finally eased her tears and looked up into the Prince's face. "My Lord, Ragan is dead. It was confirmed by those beasts you keep here. I do not trust them. It had to be them that have caused this. Please send them away. Another colony of them was found in Metra. Surely they can meld with their own kind." wept the young warrior woman.

"I think that would be premature, my sweet. I do not believe that the Tetradons had anything to do with Ragan's death. I was coming to inform you of it as I just heard myself. Tell me what you know and I will fill in what I have been informed of." replied the prince.

"Just that he died on that patrol you sent him on. The entire patrol wiped out by some unseen enemy. It must be the beasts. It must. Who else would wish to destroy one of our patrols and could do so as completely as it occurred?" said Meka. "Surely you do not favor these beasts over men such as us."

"Let's not let bias determine our opinions, Meka. You may yet find that the Tetradon are not the enemy you expect. They have skills, which are most useful. Behold our new wall. They built it in a quarter of the time and at twice the quality of the gnomes. Moreover, best yet they charge us nothing to do so. What more could you want from a people than sheer loyalty and devotion to their tasks?" asked Thomas.

"Sounds more like slavery to me, but I am a lowly warrior and am not involved in the affairs of state. I will be with the Tyris preparing for battle. Your mother sent us here to protect and protect we shall. We will accompany all the patrols from here out so that these things do not happen again. Pardon me as I take my leave," whispered Meka as she walked toward the center of camp and a waiting group of the warrior women he despised so much.

Thomas watched her leave and a small smile crept onto his face. He may have her yet and that would cement the witches to him. This would definitely work well should all go as planned. Thomas moved further into camp and headed to the foot of the ruins. His next task once the wall was complete was to rebuild the fortress. It would be his palace and let the outside world attempt to penetrate it. The wall would be complete in a few more days and he was assured by the Tetradon that it would be strong enough to withstand even the strongest of magical attack.

Thomas was concerned about his dear brother, Torlin, bringing his dear wizards to his walls. If the beasts were right, let them come. His mother would send wizards as well and they would break their strength against his walls. Tetra was his now. No one would order him here. No one would look down upon him here. It was here that his word was law. Thomas would have to send the Tyris away before too long. They were entrenched with his mother, and he was not ready to attempt that overthrow. Soon, but not yet. Torlin was another story. Taking over both the ancient cities would give him the strength he needed to take the seat of power in Thalinburg and secure his place as ruler of Dracos.

Thomas found himself lingering amongst the tents as evening approached. He walked amongst them as night fell and found him watching Meka's tent. The shadow through the fabric walls showed that Meka was preparing to go to her blankets for the evening and he stood enraptured as he watched her shadow removing first her armor, then the small quantity of fabric beneath. He stood staring as each piece came off the shadowed form and desire grew within in him as each piece went into its evening storage place. He could barely control himself as the shadow moved to the pitcher of water and the basins and he watched the shadow cleanse itself of the dirt and grime of the day. How he longed to go into the tent and force his will upon her. He would not yet, of course. It was still too soon. She was to be his but not yet. He wanted the young minx to come to him. It would happen. As he watched, the shadow lifted the evening clothes and donned them slowly. He could stand it no more and he moved away from the tents. His thoughts raced as he devoured the memory and yearned for her to perform the same before him. It would come he thought. It would come.

CHAPTER EIGHTY:
WALLS

Torlin moved slowly through the continued work of clearing the city. His thoughts ran through his experience down within the catacombs of the ancient museum. It was unreal how he had allowed himself to be trapped there and yet he had learned something. He was not the all-powerful wizard and sorcerer he believed himself to be. He still had so much to learn and yet he did not even know where to begin. He found himself spending a lot of time with the Catarel and yearning to hear the words of wisdom, which the old cat had to offer. Pan had taken to his new clan so profoundly and had no compunction against revealing his inner most powers. Torlin would sit amazed by the cat's abilities and found himself asking questions he never knew he had.

Artitous would sit in on these lessons and offer advice to both of them. He felt himself grow closer to the old bard, as the days grew longer and as time passed into weeks and even months. His own abilities he learned to keep in check as they grew with each passing lesson. He had not realized just how close to losing himself he had come. No more man-god for him. He was strong only when he remembered that there were powers much stronger than him at work here.

Torlin sent a runner with progress reports to his mother often and the returning news from Tetra disturbed him. There had been no news from the other city in weeks. Spies sent to observe the work had gone silent as the weeks passed and his mother grew concerned. The Metradon continued their work, but you could sense the pain and anger within them as they labored. Torlin knew they deserved their anger. He would try to ease the labor and increase their benefits as time progressed. He had already begun this but he would have to increase the efforts. The creatures deserved so much more than he was giving to them and the death of their leader made them all the more deserving.

Two Horns moved to the young prince's side. It would have to come soon if his people were to rebel and take back what was theirs. Torlin's actions had shown he was willing to work with the Metradons but the damage was already done. Some of his people grew soft and wished peace with the young man. This could not be. He had killed their leader in cold blood and promoted him in his place. He was supposed to gain the leader's trust through this action. Well, the boy needed to be taught a lesson, but not until the armory was uncovered. The years had buried most of their beautiful city. Could so many years have passed and no one had won the war?

The man's people had found out that the Tetradon still lived as well. Removing the boy would have to wait until that enemy had been eliminated. The warlike Tetradon would surely come after them before long and when they did, he would have to be ready with his people. The way to do so elude him at this point but it would come to him. Maybe if he convinced the young man to reconstruct the walls? That would supply the protection his people would need in the coming conflict. Maybe reconstruct the entire city? Only time would tell, but overthrowing the slaves would have to wait for now. Just for a while, he would play as if the slaves and the Metradon were allies. Just for now, while he needed them.

Torlin looked at Two Horns and smiled at the Metradon. "Your people deserve a well-earned rest. I would give them a two-week holiday if they desired it and would see them have what they desired for a full festival. I have been wrong to your people and we started badly. Tell me what your people desire and it will be yours," said the young man.

"What we desire you cannot deliver," hissed Two Horns. "It would require much sacrifice for your people and you would not willingly give it."

"Try me and see what I would be willing to deliver. You may be surprised," replied the prince.

"Give us our freedom and old stature. Make us the masters and you the slaves once more and then peace may reign within the city," said the old lizard man.

"Your freedom is yours, but I cannot give you the other. Equality must be our compromise on that point. No one ruling any other. It is the best I can do. In Tetra, another colony of your people has been discovered and if your people choose to they may join them. This may help your people's spirits. What say you to that?" said Torlin as the two walked through the ruins that had finally been totally cleared.

Two Horns stopped, his lips quivering with rage and torment. "Tetra is inhabited by the most devilish of our people. They are evil incarnate and you would suggest that we join! You wish us to go to our life long enemies on hands and knees and turn ourselves over to them for sacrifice and destruction. We would remain slaves to the slaves before we would allow such a thing to happen! You insult us with every breath, human. In my time, it was we the masters and you as slaves. It must be so again or we are lost. Do you believe that the Tetradon have allowed your kind to order and instruct them? Never! Your people there probably lay dead and the Tetradon feast upon their rotting corpses. It would be so here but we do not have the ability to do so. Trust that one day we will regain our status. One day we will rule and take the two cities as our own. I swear it to you. I swear it!"

"Do all of your people feel this way? I would have hoped that my actions had made small amends for the anguish I once caused them. Their freedom is theirs and I will not ask them to do more than they are willing, but we must somehow come to some form of agreement as to our equality." the prince replied calmly. "I wish to apologize if I have offended you. I did not know that such hatred existed between your peoples. I will not refer to them again."

"Be sure not to. My people will take their freedom, but the work will continue. We need neither festival nor any rest days. We are not weak and require no rest." Two Horns said.

Torlin did not know how to respond to this tirade. The creature's earnestness took him by surprise and the veiled threats gave him pause. The creatures wanted a war. How could this be the case? They have been in a slumber of some kind for millennia and they emerge not looking for peace but for retaliation. Surely, they learned from the first time their peoples fought that war was not going to solve this. Torlin shook his head in confusion and left the creature to its work.

Torlin moved slowly toward the camp and sat in wonder. How could this be the case? How could the people who created these cities be so warlike and destructive? He could only shake his head and hope that the beings in Metra were of a more peaceful nature. *Thomas would probably have them all singing around a campfire soon after their emergence.* Thought the prince. That was just how Thomas was. How did he not see that Thomas was right? Fighting and backstabbing was just not rewarding. Maybe his brother had been right all along and doing the right thing could bring more rewards. Confusion reigned heavily upon the young prince and his mind spun from the thoughts running through his head. Pan Thor moved up to the prince and sat down next to him as he sat in thought. "Thinking again?" asked the Catarel.

"Always. I have not been the best of people of late, have I?" asked the prince.

"Everyone has their moments of darkness. It is how you recover from them and how you fix those errors that mark a man.," replied Pan.

"I just don't know what to do from here. The Metradon seem to harbor some major grudge and I do not know how to correct the error I have caused them. I wish to befriend and aide them and all they want is to rule and fight. What can I do to settle this problem?" the prince asked the Catarel.

"Those beings have their own issues to overcome. They have been in hibernation longer than anything on this world has existed. They have a great deal to overcome and you must only give them the time they need to do so. I for one do not trust them though and would suggest keeping both eyes on them. I fear there is a lot to come with these creatures and I would not want to be caught with my tail between my legs." Pan said. "I fear we have much to concern ourselves with these creatures yet and

I will not allow them to cloud my judgment of them. It is only a matter of time before they prove they are unworthy of trusting and I will not be caught in a snare of lies."

"Wisdom once more from your unbiased eyes. I wish I could separate myself from this and see so clearly. I fear for my softhearted brother. I hope he is doing well if he has beings such as these to deal with. He may be more vulnerable to them than I Am.," said Torlin as he surveyed the city. "The work moves quickly with the help of the Metradon. I hope to have the city rebuilt and ready for my mother in a few more weeks. The Metradon want to build a wall around the city, but I denied the request. Walls are for war and that is where I least want to go."

"I think that the kitten has finally learned the error of his ways and is finally showing his true colors. You do your clan proud youngling and you do me proud. You may be a man yet if you keep up the way you have been going." smiled the cat.

"I've still a long way to go, old friend, a very long way," grinned the prince as he stood and strode toward his tent.

CHAPTER EIGHTY ONE: BATTLE PLANS

In Tetra, the wall surrounding the city was nearly completed. Thomas stood on the parapets and looked toward the city of Metra. His thoughts had been of strategy of late. The city his mirrored was ripe for the plucking. His spies had reported that there was no wall surrounding the city. Basic defenses were not in place and the people were more concerned with excavation than with war. Perfect for him to take over and run both races. Dagmar moved to the prince's side and whispered in his ear, "The Metradon do not even suspect. We can take them with little problem and we can rule this world unopposed. It would take little to do this."

"You are right as usual, Dagmar. How go our preparations? Surely we have uncovered more of the city?" asked the prince.

"No more of the city. Enemies have blocked our progress. Perhaps we should send our army as a training exercise. It may prove our might to the enemy and end the war before it is started?" said the Tetradon leader. Unseen to the prince the creature turned a small smile onto his lips. The plan was working so smoothly the Tetradon would rule these people alone in no time. Patience would be the key. Pushing too hard would ruin the plan and all their work would be for nothing.

"I hunger for some action. I think I will lead an offensive myself. If these creatures think that they can keep me from my objectives they will learn quickly the error of their ways," said Thomas as he fingered his sword's hilt. "I think I will enjoy this."

In another part of Tetra, Meka Paron entered into the meeting of the Tyris. She surveyed her sisters and moved slowly speaking briefly to each of them. Trouble was brewing within Tetra and she had to somehow get a message out to Thalinburg and the queen. Meka sat and spoke to each woman finally settling onto a cushion reserved for her. Slowly she took in the sight before her and shook her head. The creatures held the gates and there were too few of them to fight their way from the city. It would be a slaughter to send a visible envoy from the city. Stealth had its own problems. The creatures seemed to see in the dark as well as the women saw in the middle of the day. They were ever vigilant and watched inside the walls as much as they watched the outside.

Meka stood and spoke to her sisters, "Lady Warriors, we have the problem of getting a sister out of the city and getting her to the queen. Thomas has made it impossible for anyone to enter or exit the city and he has enslaved the workforce sent here from Thalinburg. The warriors of the city follow him blindly and our movements are watched at every turn. We need a plan to get one of us from the city and at this point, we have nothing. Do any of you have any ideas? It will take a miracle but maybe one of you has a thought that I missed."

As she finished speaking Thomas walked into the tent. He walked directly to Meka and spoke to all the Tyris, "We march in the morning to clear enemies from the excavation site. I expect you all to be there or there will be repercussions. I hope I did not interrupt anything of importance but my mother's soldiers will be a great aid in my work here."

After speaking, he walked from the tent not awaiting an answer. He knew that they would obey or be killed. So did the Tyris, they knew their numbers were too small to do more than a minor annoyance. Even their fabled skills would not be enough to stop the plans of the prince. Knowing all of this the Tyris sat and set plans for the morning.

Morning dawned on Tetra and the prince moved to the head of two hundred warriors including the Tyris. The plan was laid out to them all. They would move to were the patrols were routinely being destroyed and destroy whoever was killing the warriors of Tetra. They would take no prisoners and they were to leave none alive to return and report the offensive.

Thomas strode off toward the still buried part of the city followed by the warriors gathered for the purpose. Rangers drew arrows as they approached the buried buildings were the patrols had sent their last communication. The Tyris eased their weapons as they moved further into enemy territory. Nerves were beginning to show on every person there except the prince. Thomas finally stopped at a sealed door, and waited as Paul inspected the door for traps, as was his routine during the excavations. Finding none he moved away and two Rangers forced open the door.

As the door opened, three beings swept onto the Rangers and quickly tore out their throats. Arrows flew quickly toward the creatures and one was killed as a dozen arrows peppered the being. The wasp-men fell and two more streamed from the door to replace them. Thomas drew his sword as one of the beings charged him and severed its head. The creature fell dead in its tracks just to be replaced by more of its brethren. The women of the Tyris drew their weapons and entered the fray. At first, the warriors of Tetra seemed to hold the higher ground and they moved toward the door. However, the creatures seemed to multiply as they were slain and soon the warriors found themselves being forced back.

Thomas laughed as he killed one creature after another. He seemed to grow more energetic as enemies fell to his blade. Twice a well-placed set of arrows spared him from being killed by creatures attacking from behind. After only a few moments Meka found herself back to back with the prince, fighting for her life. The warriors of Tetra were reduced by half and more of the creatures came and attacked the beleaguered warriors. Thomas took no notice of this and called for a harder push toward the door. The warriors soon found themselves surrounded and being pressed into each other.

The numbers were soon down to fifty and still more of the creatures attacked. Thomas stopped in his tracks and raised a whistle to his lips. Sounding one long blast from the whistle, Thomas turned and continued the fight. No sooner had he blown the whistle than several hundred of the Tetradon rained down fire from strange weapons down upon the surrounding enemy. Enemies and friends fell to the strange fire as the Tetradon fired repeatedly into the fray. They seemed to have no care as to whom they killed as long as someone fell to their unique weapons. In a moment, the momentum once more changed. The warriors joined by the Tetradon were soon pushing the enemy back to the door and the door was sealed once more.

Thomas screamed at the Rangers who had sealed the door, "Open it! I want them all dead. I swear upon this city that if that door is not opened I will say the men holding it."

Meka still being back to back with the prince turned and struck him on the head, knocking him senseless. Turning she called for the warriors to gather the wounded, including the prince, and return them to the camp. The day was lost as far as she was concerned. As she fell back, she counted the warriors remaining. Twenty remained of the two hundred. So many dead for nothing as far as gaining ground. Only ten of her Tyris remained of the thirty she brought with her and many of those wounded. Two would never fight again and others would be out of commission for weeks while their wounds healed. Meka shook her head as they moved back to camp. The deaths were senseless. How many had died to the Tetradons' weapons? Only Thomas and Meka seemed to miss the spray of weapons fire that had killed so many.

Thomas woke as they approached the camp. His temper seemed to be intensified by the retreat. Thomas screamed at men and Tetradon alike as they moved and as he tried to rise from his litter, he was forced back down onto it. Thomas screamed louder and threatened all who came close the further from the door they went.

They finally arrived at the camp and the wounded were taken to the medics. Many died from their wounds as they were tended and some were released quickly with only minor injuries. Thomas was checked and released immediately. They found no wounds upon him and so let him leave. Thomas moved from the medical tent and went to Meka. "I am sorry about your people," he said to her as she watched the medics carry out another unfortunate soul who had succumbed to his wounds.

"It was senseless. I do not know where they all came from. We did not even seem to bloody them. So many dead or wounded, for what? Only twenty lived and were able to fall back to camp. They bore out only fifteen wounded. Thirty-five came out of that blood bath and more are still dying. How do you fight an enemy like this? They just seemed to kill and kill. The more we killed the more came. How many of them are there?" said the Tyris. Her eyes welled with tears and she turned into the prince and wept in his arms.

"We will avenge them all. I swear it to you." smiled Thomas as he wrapped his arms around the shaking form of the Tyris leader. "I swear it. The next time we will be prepared. I will bring twice as many soldiers and we will be victorious."

"Twice as many or ten times as many we will not be able to defeat so many. How can we defeat someone who has no fear of death?" cried Meka.

"Let me worry on that. Let me worry on It." whispered the still smiling prince as he rocked the crying woman.

CHAPTER EIGHTY TWO:
BAD ADVICE

Torlin walked the paths of Metra and watched as the excavations continued. Giant spiders plagued the efforts and were dispatched quickly. The head Tyris was foremost in his thoughts as he walked. He could not shake the thoughts of her and found himself finding reasons to be around her. He invited her to sit in on meetings about the clearing of the city and found he was anxious to hear her opinions. He had never experienced this before and he found it disconcerting.

Torlin stopped before the tower leading down to the chamber where they had found the Metradon. Something troubled him about Two Horns. The creature was too forthcoming, too cooperative. He had told the prince that his people once ruled the world and yet now they were more than pleased to work and act as labor for those they once ruled. Two Horns was more than happy to show him the technology of the Metradon and had allowed him to handle the strange tools and weapons on several occasions.

As if thinking of the creature summoned him, Two Horns walked up to the prince. "The city nearly stands free of the earth," hissed the Metradon. "We should think of protecting it as we rebuild. What of building a wall?"

"What do we need protection from?" asked the prince. "Surely you do not fear anything in this time. Besides our largest threat is from the giant spiders that attack us on a regular basis and a wall will not keep them at bay."

"Spiders may not be the only enemy we may face. In the twin to this city lay, the Tetradon and they are as evil as it is possible to be. A little protection would not be amiss." said the Metradon.

"Continue with the work and do not trouble yourselves about protection. My brother excavates the city of Tetra and he would have reported anything like the awakening of these people. He is not so far gone as to hide important facts such as that," said Torlin.

"As you wish, My Lord. As you wish." replied Two Horns as he moved away from the prince and headed back into the city. In his mind, he prepared for the coup that he and his people would pull after the city was restored. No more would the Metradon bow to the slaves of old.

Chapter Eighty Three: Puppy Love

Pan Thor sat at the dinner table across from his adoptive brother and smiled. "Something is amiss, brother. Tell me of it so that we can make it right."

"It is nothing. I am just considering. What do you know of love?" asked the prince.

"Does the kitten have a particular mate in mind or do you speak in generalities? I, for one, have not seen you to be particularly close to anyone," said the Catarel.

"I do not have a person in mind. I was just making conversation. So what do you think of love and have you been in love before?" asked the prince.

"You lie to me. So which female do you fancy? As your brother, I would approach her for you and let your interest be known. It is custom and I would be happy to do it for you," said Pan with a great smile across his face.

"I do not fancy anyone. I'm telling you that I merely speak I generalities," replied the prince.

"It is the lady warrior is it not? She seems lovely for your kind. I prefer a little more hair myself, but she seems to be the one that attracts your eyes," said Pan.

"Roanda is not interested in me and I do not want you to approach anyone for Me.," squeaked the prince. "Is it that obvious that I am attracted to her?"

"I think so. I think she returns the affection though. Just my observation, but she seems to enjoy talking to you," teased the Catarel.

"Do not tell her anything. I will tell her in my own time. Please promise me that you will not approach her.," squeaked the young prince.

As the two spoke, they had neglected to notice the woman warrior come in. "Approach me or not, I already know how you feel, young one. As for my interest, let me make that decision."

Torlin jumped up out of his seat and nearly fell over. "Roanda! How much have you heard? Please forgive me if I have offended."

In response to his blundering, the leader of the Tyris grabbed the prince and enveloped him into an embrace and passionate kiss that drew the prince into a state of nirvana that he had never dreamed of. His head swam as he lost himself in the woman's embrace. The moment lasted for only a few brief seconds but to him it lasted forever.

It lasted only until Pan coughed and giggled.

"What do you find so funny, fur face?" the prince sniped.

"For someone who does not favor someone you seemed to enjoy yourself."

Replied Pan Thor.

CHAPTER EIGHTY FOUR: YOUNG LOVE

The Tyris and the prince were nearly inseparable from that day forward. They did everything together and were soon often distracted by each other.

The Metradon noticed the distraction and began to secretly build the fortifications that Two Horns had lobbied so hard for. At first, it was a block here or some timbers there. However, as the two human leaders became more distracted the building went forward in earnest. Before long, the walls reached ten feet tall and about eight feet thick.

The prince came out of his tent one morning and noticed that the walls were in place. He searched for the Metradon leader and found them working on clearing a small section of the city they called the Scholars' Square. The wall already stretched around the section and dirt was being pulled from the square and piled outside of the wall. Torlin walked to Two Horns and pulled him aside, "What is the meaning of this, Two Horns? I believe we discussed fortifications. I told you not to build them and yet here they are. How do you explain it?"

"My Prince, I was told that you had changed your opinion on the wall and wished it built. See it is nearly complete now. Soon we will be ready. So soon." said Two Horns.

"Ready for what? The city is only three quarters cleared. You act as if we are going to war!" declared the prince.

"War is not a word I am familiar with. Please explain." hissed Two Horns.

"War is conflict, fighting, and death. We are not getting ready for it do you hear me?" screamed Torlin.

"Conflict comes on ravens' wings, My Lord. Ready or not, the Tetradon will not wait for us to complete our work. You will see that they will come soon." Two Horns said to the now irate prince.

Flames built up on the prince's hands as he stared face to face with the Metradon. Not until the soft touch of Roanda's hand did, the fires slip away and finally die. "Maybe a little protection is a good thing. I have not heard anything from my sisters in Tetra. I am concerned but not enough to go there yet."

As the two conversed, a now very concerned Two Horns tried to slink back into the shadows. As he moved, a dragon flew down from the skies and lighted in front of the prince, Tyris, and Metradon. "Hail Prince Torlin. I have word from Marzioa. Danger comes from the south. The Dread Lords are in motion once more. They have mobilized a small army but it is more than you have here. The dragons will not intervene in your conflict this time. You should move to the city of Thalinburg and there wait for the armies of your enemy." said the small dragon.

"What is your name, young one?" asked Torlin, forgetting his manners once more.

"Who do you call young? I am 200 hundred summers old. How many have you seen? My name is Jasper and am in the service of the great wizard, Marzioa," replied the dragon.

"Who do you think you are addressing, dragon? I am the head of the Mysteries of Dracos. I could destroy you where you stand. Apologize for your insolence." screamed the prince, hands starting to glow with power. Again, a soft touch from Roanda calmed the young man. "Perhaps you are being too hard on this fine young dragon. He is a messenger from your mother's close friend. We should discuss his warning and have him give his message to your brother. The two of you together would be more than a match for this horde," said the Tyris.

"Dragon forgives me…" started the prince when the dragon stopped him and said, "I have a name, Prince. Use it."

"Jasper forgive me, it has been a long day, and I am tired. Your words are indeed dire. Please get word to my brother and I will prepare to leave the city," said Torlin.

At that, Two Horns jumped in. "My Lord. We can hold off a much greater force for a much longer time here in Metra. Do not allow this harbinger of doom and gloom to chase you from your mission. They will be no more trouble than the giant spiders that roam the city."

"I forgot you were there Two Horns. You say stay, this dragon says go, my heart says go and my head says stay. My Love, please give me the deciding vote. I need to see this logically." said Torlin as he bent over and kissed her hand gently.

"This decision is yours, I am afraid. None of us here can make this decision for you. Use your best judgment and I am sure all will be well," said the Tyris.

"I will send word to Marzioa in a few days. Thank you for the warning. I will take all your words under advisement. For now, I will ponder my decision," said Torlin.

At that, the little gathering broke apart, the dragon heading into the sky, Two Horns to the edge of the city, and the humans to the Prince's tent.

At the city's edge, Two Horns met with the leaders of the Metradon. He explained briefly the situation and when he finished, the leaders discussed the options. Two Horns was adamant that they stay and prepare for the real battle. He explained that the humans' usefulness was ending. The city was nearly clear and the wall built as well as it possibly could be built. They just had to clear the factories, they could produce the weapons, and supplies they needed to annihilate the Tetradon and the humans.

The Metradon slowly slinked toward the buried section of the city and began once more to work. To the outside observer they seemed to move with a renewed vigor and the leaders had strange smiles upon their faces.

It took two days before the prince of magic appeared from his tent with the Tyris leader in tow. His decision made.

CHAPTER EIGHTY FIVE:
TRAITORS AND SPIES

As Torlin debated his decision, Jasper approached the city of Tetra. He was coming in for a landing when the first arrows flew by his head. Veering sharply he landed behind the walls of the city and found himself surrounded by Rangers and Tyris. "The prince allows none to enter or leave our city. Identify yourself so that you may be recorded as the spy that you are." said the ranger in charge.

"I come from Marzioa with a dire warning. I am Jasper and must speak to the prince," said the dragon. He was about to move forward when he felt the chains clasp around his legs. They had chained him to the walls.

"I will let the prince know that a guest has arrived. He will decide if he speaks with you before your execution," said the ranger.

"Execution?" screamed the dragon. "You threaten me with execution? I will let you know that I have ambassadorial status with the crown and I will have the heads of the people who have clamped me in irons."

"The crown is not recognized here, dragon. Now you will be drugged until the prince decides your fate," said the ranger.

"You will do no such thing. Come no closer to me than you are now. I warn you that I can breathe ice and I am not shy about doing so. Do not think that I will suffer your indignities," cried Jasper.

"You have no choice. There are too many of us to stop us from doing to you what we will. No shut up and take your medicine," said the ranger as he approached the now very shaken-up dragon.

As the ranger moved, the dragon kept his word and let loose a barrage of ice. The ranger fell frozen and the others took a step back. Two Rangers raised their bows and the dragon froze them too. As they fell, two more Rangers came into the dragon's limited view. They pointed to the dragon's sides, he saw all of the Rangers and Tyris with bows drawn, and they had moved into a semicircle around him. Closing his eyes, he sent a mental message to Marzioa. His mission was about to be a failure.

The ranger in charge was about to order the troops around the dragon to shoot when the prince arrived and ordered them to lower their weapons. "Dragon why have you come here?" asked the prince.

"I have a name. It is Jasper. I come with a dire warning from Marzioa. Release me and I will relate the message," said Jasper.

"No. I think not. You are now my prisoner and you will do as you are told. Now tell me this dire message and I may decide to let you live," said Thomas.

"Release me. I will tell you my message and leave. No one else need get hurt," said Jasper.

"No, you will tell me this message and I will decide your fate. I warned everyone not to send anyone here or they would be killed and now you have come. I must be a man of my word, so I may rebuke myself and let you live, tell me your message and if it is that dire I will let you live. You may not leave but you may live," said the prince.

"Fine. It is the Dread Lords. They march once more and the dragons will not intervene this time. You are best advised to return to Thalinburg and await your enemy there. It will take more than you have here to defeat the coming army," said Jasper as he lowered his head in defeat.

"I hear your words and you think that is dire news. I will break them upon my walls. I have the aide of my allies the Tetradon and we shall rain fire and death down upon the coming enemy. As for you, Rangers, continue what you began before I stopped you. Put this beast down," said Thomas.

"But you said if I told you…" Muttered the dragon.

"I said I may," replied the prince. "And now I say that you will perish. Good bye dragon."

The Rangers lifted their bows once more and suddenly a great wind blew up around the dragon. The chains around his legs broke and his wings stretched out to the sky. The Rangers fought and failed to keep their feet in the wind and the prince screamed into the wind. As the wind died down the dragon had already struck off and was flying away. The prince ordered a pursuit and some of the Rangers mounted up and tried to follow the dragon.

It took a few miles but the Rangers quickly lost their prey and returned to the prince. The prince walked up and down the line of Rangers, asking each of them in turns why they did not pursue faster. Their answer that they could not keep up enraged the prince and he called for his sword. Meka came from his tent carrying the sword and handed it to the prince. He stood all the Rangers up and started at the first ranger. Again, he demanded to know why they still were not following the escaping prisoner. The first ranger declared that the dragon had outdistanced the horses and was lost. The prince stood before the man for a moment then raised his sword and removed the man's head.

He moved down the line of men and demanded repeatedly why they let the dragon escape. After he had killed the third of the Rangers, Meka stood beside him and whispered into his ear. Her whisper brought his sword down and he turned and walked away with Meka. The palace was nearly complete and he was going to move into it soon.

He related the dragon's warning to Meka and she laughed. "The Dread Lords fight more against each other than us. An army of theirs will destroy itself before it even reaches our walls. They have no one to lead them anymore."

"They may be a good warm up for the main events to come. Shall we entrench the city and prepare for war?" asked Thomas.

Meka looked down at her feet, thinking of Ragan. Since his loss, she had been drawn to the prince like a moth to a flame. She yearned to feel the release of death so she could be with Ragan again but she still wanted to find out how he had gotten on that patrol. She had killed the order sergeant who had arranged the patrol but he had claimed before he died that the orders had come from someone else. She still did not know who had given the original order but she would find out.

Thomas spoke to her but she just let it pass her. He spoke of his plans and how he was going to finish clearing the city then clearing the world of his brother. Meka did not care as long as there was battle. He spoke of the remainder of the city that still required clearing and how the wasp-men had made that impossible. He was going to get a whole army of the Tetradon to go to the area and clear the wasp-men with their magical weapons. Dagmar had promised that they would do whatever they could to aide in the clearing of the city. Meka grew to detest the Tetradon leader, but he was unavoidable.

Meka and Thomas parted ways at the foot of the palace stairs and Thomas went in. Meka went to prepare her people for the coming war. They still needed to get a woman out of the city and into Thalinburg. Thomas was not wrong, but a report needed to be made. Meka found herself thinking of the Prince more and more and she came to a decision. It had come to her in a dream of the prince and had felt right. She would marry the prince and learn of all his commanders that had feared Ragan. She would then have the power to see the murderer executed.

She discussed he plan with the other Tyris and some of them seemed to think she might be going a bit too far. She dismissed their concerns and spoke of the wedding he would give her if she asked. The ones who supported her decision imagined with her the flowers and gifts. It would be a grand occasion. She just hoped that the prince still felt the same way for her as he did. She was slowly coming to care for him and that would have to do for now.

Meka left the gossiping women and sought out the prince. She had to do this before she lost her nerve. She wandered the ruins in search of the prince and found him in his nearly completed palace. He sat upon a carved throne of deep, dark wood. On one leg, he had a dragon. On the other, he had a person. On the back legs, he had Elves and Dwarves. They were carved so that the person on the throne appeared to be seated upon the four races. Great serpents were the arms and a starburst adorned the back of the chair. *The prince definitely thought highly of himself.* Thought Meka as she walked into the throne room.

"My prince, are your feelings the same as they once were? I have come to lay my wedding proposal at your feet. I hope that it has not fallen on deaf ears or on a stone heart," said Meka.

The prince stood and smiled inwardly. She had come around faster than he had thought. Maybe she did have some feelings that were covered by those for the now deceased Ragan. The prince kept the smile from his face as he rose from his throne and walked toward the kneeling Meka. He liked her in this position. He tried to suck in the humility that the woman emitted. It was nearly intoxicating for him.

He reached down, grasped the woman's hand, and paused. He stood there for a moment looking down on her and felt the woman's discomfort. He stood for a moment and savored the emotion. He then assisted her to her feet and said, "My dear Meka. You have made me extremely happy today. Of course, I will accept your proposal. You must never put yourself in that position again. You will kneel to no one ever again. I must have the carpenters erect another throne for my queen."

"I thought you were but a prince. I will be your queen or your princess. I do not mean to argue the point with you. However, what of your mother? Is she not still queen?" said Meka.

"Only just for now. A new world order is being born with our union and she either will move out of the way or be destroyed by it. Do you understand what I mean my love?" asked the prince.

"Of course. Forgive my ignorance. Maybe if you told me your plans, I could be of help," said Meka.

"Not yet my sweet. The time will come when I shall reveal my plan but not quite yet," said the prince looking down from the top step into his bride-to-be's eyes.

CHAPTER EIGHTY SIX:
MUTINY

Torlin strode into the city square and called everyone there to him. Using his abilities, he amplified his voice so he could be heard throughout the square. People and Metradon gathered close to hear his decision on whether to evacuate or stand and fight. He stood closer to the center of the square and began, "People of Metra. I include all of you in that if you are Dwarf, Gnome, Elf, Human, or Metradon. I have made my decision as to what we will do about the impending attack by the Dread Lords. Though we know little of them except that they come, I feel that with the aid of my brother we may be able to defeat them and send them back to the Dark Lands. I ask that a party of people from Metra go to Tetra to ask my brother to assist us in our defense. Do any of you wish to go on this mission?"

He looked around and saw several of the Tyris had volunteered. He went to each of them, shook their hands, and wished them well. Before they could leave though Two Horns made his way to the edge of the square and raised his voice so all could hear, "No one leaves. We stand and fight and then we go to Tetra and take what is ours. We obey the slaves no more. We now rule here again and we will make our presence here known."

Torlin went to speak and found that the Metradon had surrounded the massed population and had their fancy weapons pointed into the masses. Without thinking, Torlin raised his arms and started a shield around the square. Pan jumped in and added his power to the shield, as did Artitous. Soon the shield was high enough to keep the weapons from harming anyone. Two Horns again raised his voice, "Your shield will not hold forever. If you defy us now we will destroy you all faster than if you had just given yourselves over to us freely. Unruly slaves must be taught a lesson, and you all will be no exception. Now stop your resistance and allow yourselves to feel our rule."

"Two Horns. I have given your people all that they could have asked for. Do not do this. We can live together in harmony if we try. Please do not do this," said the Prince of Dracos.

At his words, Two Horns ordered the Metradon to open fire on the massed people in the square. Energy flared from the weapons into the shield repeatedly. For a time it seemed that, there would be a stalemate as the shield held and the weapons kept firing. Neither seemed to make much headway against the other, but as the fire continued the shield slowly began to waver. Two Horns glowed as if he had won when all of a sudden several of the Metradon opened fire upon the Metradon firing on the people. Quickly the two sides began to battle each other forgetting the humans and other races. When the firing stopped, Torlin lowered the shield and the Tyris and Rangers moved toward the Metradon who had fired upon them.

Men and women, Gnomes and Humans and Elves moved toward the battling Metradon and attacked with a fury. Two Horns waded into the mass of warriors and started ripping people in half as he waded through the mass of people. Warriors found that he had some form of shield, as their blows seemed to glance away without coming within an inch of the Metradon leader. The warriors kept attacking him hoping to bring him down and possibly end the fighting, but he quickly dispatched all those who got in his way.

Torlin raised his hand and fireballs leapt from his fingertips into the Metradon leader. These seemed to pierce the shield and inflict some damage as the Metradon leader slowed his forward motion. He turned toward the wizard prince and waded forward again. This time toward the prince. Pan jumped to the prince's aid and leveled lightning at the Metradon but it too only slowed the big Metradon. Looking around the Metradon leader put a whistle to his lips and blew three long blasts.

Slowly his people moved toward the gates of the city. Torlin was yelling not to pursue as the Metradon left the city. Roanda looked at Torlin with concern as the wizard fell to his knees with exhaustion.

The Metradon ran from the city leaving behind only the people of the races and the Metradon who had fired on their own people. The two groups eyed each other with suspicion as the battle finally wound down and ended. Metradon fingered weapons as they watched the approach of the prince and his commanders.

"You have aided us, why? I do not understand why you have attacked your own people. Please explain." said the prince.

"We do not agree with the methods and the ways of our brethren. They are overzealous and without scruples. Two Horns took command when another should have had it. We merely wanted to see justice served," said the Metradon.

"Your name sir? I would like to know whom I should thank for our salvation," said the prince.

"I am called Paulen, and I lead the resistance. Several of our members left with the others so we can monitor their movement. We have ways of tracking them that they will not know it is happening. As for your salvation, you worked at it just as hard as we did. Look to yourselves for the source of your victory." said Paulen.

"It is a pleasure to meet you Paulen. I hope that we can continue to live and work together. I do not know what the future holds anymore, but with your aid I hope we can save our city," said Torlin.

"It was our city before it was yours. Nevertheless, we understand that times have changed and things are different now. We will stand at your side and fight for the city but in the end, hopefully we will live here in peace," said Paulen.

"I could ask for no more. It is good to have you and yours as an ally. We are still grossly outnumbered by the Dread Lords' hordes, but maybe with your help and that of my brother, we may persevere," said the prince.

As the prince spoke the young dragon, Jasper, landed in front of the collected leaders of Metra. "You will find no help from your brother. He tried to destroy me just for entering the city. I saw a large number of the Metradon headed out of the city, has something happened?" asked the dragon.

"We have had ourselves a bit of a scuffle. However, true friends and allies have been revealed from the contest. What is this news of my brother?" asked the prince.

"Your brother had closed the borders of Tetra to anyone who dares to enter. It is Death to anyone who comes in as he sees anyone coming in as a spy. He has grown paranoid and distrustful of all. I did over hear that he is getting married though so he must not have gone all -bad," said the dragon.

"Married? To whom? Please sir dragon, tell me more of what has transpired. I need to know what I must do to get all of our people's together," said the prince.

"I have already told you that the dragons are not getting involved in this battle. You are on your own. As for the marriage of your brother, I know no more than it is going to happen. He was too busy trying to kill me for me to overhear anything else." said the dragon.

"Your kind cannot abandon us now. We have a long-standing alliance with your people. Surely that means something to your people, does it not?" asked the prince.

"I am merely a messenger. I will give your request to those who rule and return with our decision. I assure you, your brother's actions will be held in high consideration," said Jasper.

"They were the actions of one man. Do not condemn an entire people for the actions of one. Please reconsider your stand and accept my apology on behalf of our people." said Torlin as he fell down on his knees and bowed low to the dragon.

"Again it is not my place. Older and wiser minds than mine will decide the future of our relationship. Fare well Prince of Magic but do not look to the mountains for the aide of the dragons," said the young dragon messenger.

"Then please take our deepest regard to your elders. Moreover, fare well yourself. The world has just become a much more dangerous place," said the prince.

"Indeed." said the dragon as he filled his wings, launched himself into the air, and winged his way north toward the mountains.

"I hope we have not lost our way. It could cost us everything if we do not keep our allies. I have never been one for tactics but I think I will need a crash course. Roanda I need your assistance. Everyone else, get some rest. I fear we will need it. Moreover, dare I say it? Close the gates and post a watch, who knows what the night will hold," said the prince as he moved to the command tent that was used to command a restoration. Now it will house an army command.

Two Horns and the rest of the Metradon, who had fled, set up camp within sight of the city. It would be theirs again; they just had to wait their time. Two Horns called his top generals together and they talked for a long time behind the bodies of their guards. They had their weapons and they had some supplies. The rest they would have to work off the land. They spoke of finding the traitors still amongst them and Two Horns asked after the beacons. Surely, the resistance knew of them and had them working to track their movements. It would be a priority to scan all of the frequencies and destroy all of them. Once the city was blind, then they could attack at will. The city would be theirs again. Yes, it would.

CHAPTER EIGHTY SEVEN: LOCKDOWN

Thomas was also posting a watch and setting guards, though he was doing it to keep people in as well beyond the walls. The dragon escaping was troubling. How could he expect to make his plans and see them through with his brother's and his mother's spies coming in all the time? His time split as of late in planning his war and planning his wedding. He found out a little late that the Tyris did not plan their weddings. It fell upon the man to prepare the wedding.

Thomas was happy to plan the wedding though. He was still in disbelief that the young Tyris had come to him and asked him. He still believed it may be a trick but he had to trust someone. Why not her? Thomas entered the palace and went to the war room. His maps lay scattered and little notations all over them held the plans for his upcoming offensive. His brother expected him to believe that the Dread Lords were on the move again. Even if that were true, he had the firepower and the men to hold the city indefinitely.

Meka came into the room and looked around. "So this is how my husband to be spends his time. I had thought you would have been choosing floral arrangements. How goes your planning for the wasp people? Surely, we can dispose of them now that the Tetradon are using their energy weapons. I have never seen the like. How goes the planning for our day? I hope you are doing a good job of planning or I may be disappointed," said Meka with a sly smile on her lips. She knew of his plans and she approved. The wedding would be a grand event here in

Tetra. Too bad no one else from the outside could attend. She would have liked to have her new mother in law in attendance.

She moved beside the groom to be and looked over his shoulder at the map before him. It was a map of the Fields of the Pheni. What he was doing with that out was beyond her? Did he really expect to attack his brother? She placed a hand on his arm and asked him gently, "Do you really expect to assault the city of Metra? I would think we have enough to deal with here. Why the plans?" she asked.

"I must be ready for anything. My brother is crafty as well as powerful. He has the images of this world at his disposal. At least with those energy weapons I stand a chance against his magic. He will attack us if we do not attack him. I know it.," said the prince.

"Has he given the impression that he would be attacking us? As far as I know, he still works to unbury the city. Surely he would not be planning what you believe he is." said the Tyris.

"He is just cunning enough to do just that. He has kicked out the Metradon from his city and if I can get them to join with us I can take his city before he attacks ours," said the prince.

"How do you know this? Do you keep spies as you accuse your mother and brother of doing? I would like to know what is happening in the other city," said Meka.

"Of course I have spies. Why should I not? They spy on me so I spy on them. I have trusted Rangers watching the other cities. They relay all that occurs in the capitol as well as in the other ruin. If they meant no harm why build a wall to rival my own? Surely, it would not have been built if they did not expect to be attacked. The only way we would have attacked is if they planned to attack us. So they must be planning an offensive even as we speak," said Thomas.

"You realize that you sound paranoid. Surely just the construction of a wall is not enough to display intent to attack. We do not want to start a war neither of us can win do we?" asked Meka.

"Please let us not speak of this further. Let us speak of our wedding instead. The whole war business makes me cross and I would not like to be cross with you. So do you prefer blue or yellow?" asked the prince.

"Anything you choose will be fine. So what gossip of the court did your Ranger bring to you? I would love to hear It.," said Meka adjusting the conversation so as not to anger the young man.

"No gossip I am afraid, just tactical info. I hope that does not disappoint you too badly. After I take power, you may gossip with the other Tyris and the other women to your heart's content. You look tired my dear. Why do you not go and lay down in your chambers. I will see to it you are not disturbed," said the prince.

"I will go to my tents. It is better that way for now until we are wed. I do not need one of your trained lizards watching over me either. I appreciate the offer but I am capable of defending myself," said Meka.

"Never meant to imply that you couldn't. Just as my bride to be, you are a target for my enemies. I would not want anything to happen to you. I must plan but you take it easy and rest. Dagmar would not like to hear you call his people trained lizards though. You must get along with them. They are here to help us. Now go and rest and I will check on you soon." said Thomas as he guided her to the chamber door.

"I will look forward to it. Have you found out anything about the orders that got Regan killed? I would rest better if I knew more about that," said Meka.

"Nothing new on your lost love. I am truly sorry. Now go and rest. I will see you soon," said Thomas.

CHAPTER EIGHTY EIGHT: GOING TO WAR

Meka left and headed toward the tents but she did not go to her tent. When she realized she was not being followed she went to the tent of her sword sisters. Entering the tent, she took her place at their head and asked them again all that had happened while she was away.

"He prepares for a major offensive. He makes weapons and armor as well as those energy weapons of the lizard folk. They seem to have eyes on the back of their heads because we could not watch them long without them knowing about it. The human smiths and the dwarven smiths had no problems speaking of their orders to build more weapons. They did not see the need for secrecy. Just the lizards. Other people are collecting foodstuffs and other necessities for war. We believe he is planning an attack on the other city and then the capitol, Thalinburg. It is coming and coming soon. They say he is planning to leave before the next full moon. That is only three weeks away. By the time, we leave and reach Metra it will be the new moon and the skies will be dark. We believe he is planning to attack during the dark of night. Does he really wish to take both cities?" said the gathered Tyris.

"He does indeed plan on taking both cities. Nevertheless, he would not be cowardly and attack in the dead of night in the darkest part of the month. Surely your information is skewed." said Meka.

"He has the fletchers making night arrows. He also has people making torches and tinderboxes. It is possible he expects a night attack but it is more likely that the war will happen in the dark of night," said the Tyris.

Meka pondered the Tyris's words and just sat there listening. What could he be up to? She thought he would be honorable which is why she was marrying him. She stood up and started pacing the tent floor. This was not adding up. "Could there be any other reason for the construction of these items?" asked Meka.

"He could be making them for the night times during travel. He makes pitch and oil as well. Surely, he does not intend to burn the fields down around us. Maybe he just wishes to be prepared. But he is definitely planning an offensive and soon." said the Tyris.

"Then we must work to delay our departure. How can we sabotage the works that he is building?" asked Meka.

"We can't. The Tetradon have the whole place under strict scrutiny. The only way we can get to them is if the prince knows we were there. We can only delay our own leaving. Maybe delaying your wedding will slow him down?" said the Tyris spymaster.

"No, he looks forward to it so. I have come to genuinely care for the man. I have been careful not to show it too much but I think he knows. He would do anything for me and I have to be loyal to him. If we can do anything to prevent this war though, we must do it. Keep me out of the loop from here on out so that I can tell him I know nothing honestly. This way he will not suspect me of betraying him. Be well and do all that you can.," said Meka.

Meka did not realize she had been followed when she entered the Tyris's tent. Dagmar followed her at a distance to keep from being observed and he sat in the darkened corner of the tent to listen in on their conversation. Therefore, the women warriors were planning to disrupt his carefully laid plans. Dagmar left when he saw Meka rise and head for the exit. He must find a way to prevent the Tyris from sabotaging the offensive. He must have dominion over the two cities and then the world.

He quickly made it appear as if he were just walking up when he approached Meka. He would have to handle this carefully for the girl could ruin his plans. "Why I thought you had gone to your bed," hissed the Tetradon. "I was looking for your friends to go on a patrol for the city. They are needed to scout out the nests of the wasp people. They seem to be able to breach their defenses better than the men do. The prince needs more information on the bug people so he can clear their nests and rid us of their presence."

"They are resting now. They will be ready to do so whenever the orders arrive. Have yourself a nice day, I must go rest." said Meka.

"Thank you I will speak to the women now." said Dagmar. He left the young woman and entered the tent she had just left. Meka walked away and wondered how he had known where to find her. He could not have been following her. She would have to be more careful. Another order to scout out the wasps. She hoped that the women of the Tyris would have better luck than the men had. They, at least, would not go in stomping and banging. Stealth was something that the Tyris could do.

She continued to her tent but looked over her shoulder constantly to be sure she was not being followed. Now she felt paranoid and she did not like it.

Dagmar went into the Tyris's tent and gave them the order to investigate the wasp men's lair and left. A small smile came arose his face as he summoned several of the Tetradon. He wanted it to appear that the wasp people killed the women but they were not to return from the patrol. Meka would be alone and unable to stop his plans.

CHAPTER EIGHTY NINE:
WEDDING BLISS

Torlin left his tent and ran into Roanda and her Tyris standing before it. Roanda grabbed Torlin, the rest of the Tyris helped to bind and gag him, and they carried him to the command tent. Torlin looked wide-eyed and frantic to see what was happening but he could not and eventually he gave up trying. The women finally let him down at the command tent and unbound him.

"What is going on?" Asked Torlin.

"Be silent dear heart. All will be revealed in a moment," replied Roanda.

Torlin looked confused when he saw his mother walk into the tent. Excited to see her he hugged her and looked back at Roanda. His mother was wearing her best robes and it looked like she was trying her best to hide something or someone. Torlin walked over to her again and peered around her body and into her eyes, hoping to catch a glimpse of what had brought her here.

Athinina moved around her startled son, walked to the head of the tent, and called everyone over. Torlin again was dragged by the arms to the front of the tent in front of his mother and caused to stand there before his mother. When he looked at his side, Roanda stood there with a grin on her face. Still confused he was about to speak when his mother spoke. "My friends and peoples. My son is here to be wed today. Roanda, he seems to be a little surprised by this. Are you sure he was ready and willing to do this?"

"Of course. Let us begin." replied the Tyris.

"Don't I get a say in this?" asked the prince.

"No!" said Athinina and Roanda in unison. The prince looked around for support and found none. Even Pan Thor was looking forward and listening to the queen.

Torlin stood still and looked a little sheepish as Artitous came into the tent. He walked to Athinina, hugged her tightly, and began the wedding ceremony. Twice as they progressed through the ceremony, spiders attacked. Quickly dispatched, the spiders were removed from the area and the ceremony resumed. The whole time Torlin was grinning but looked for a way out of the room. No way to leave showed itself because the Tyris surrounded him and Roanda and his Mother and Artitous stood before him. As they progressed, he looked for escape less and less and gave into the festivities.

Finally, after what seemed an eternity the ceremony was over and Artitous was calling for him to kiss his bride. This he was pleased to do. She was always so soft and caring when he had stolen kisses before. Again, he was surprised when she grabbed him by the shoulders and wrapped her arms around him and dipped him back, kissing him deeply. After what seemed hours in that embrace, Roanda let him up and wiped her face. Torlin staggered around for a moment and finally leaned on Pan Thor to gain his feet again. Torlin looked around, found everyone starting the wedding feast, and saw Artitous and Athinina laughing and joking with one another. "Just remember that your family has a horrible record on wedding nights. You may want to set a guard and double the magical protections. You may need them," laughed the Druid.

"You would know, old friend. You were there for all of them. At least they will not have the giant spiders coming down from the ceiling. Too bad they only tried to crash the wedding." laughed the queen.

"Wait what? What about wedding nights? Tell me what is going on now," said Torlin.

"It is nothing. Just be wary after your wedding feast. Roanda may want to start a family sooner than later. Now go and be with your bride. Do not worry about anything," said Artitous. Artitous called the

Rangers over and had they set an extra guard on the walls and the royal tents. No need to tempt fate.

Two Horns and the exiled Metradon listened as the wedding feast finally died down. This would be their opening. The people in the city would be lax in their defense. This would be the prime opportunity to take back the city.

Two Horns called all of the generals of his people together and they sat and planned quickly. They would have to move quickly and strike hard. That would not be a problem. The Resistance within the city would be the problem. They had caused no end of trouble long ago and now they rear their ugly heads again. They would have to be dealt with first. Many of them knew about the tunnels that the Metradon had built and where now going to employ. Two Horns cursed himself for not keeping a better lid on those.

The Resistance would be waiting for them. However, this would be the ideal time to wipe them out with their human allies. Two Horns leaned over their maps and started his war plan.

The feast lasted deep into the night, with the bride and groom growing tired from all the well-wishing. Artitous entertained the crowds with light shows into the night air. The races of Metra looked on in wonder as the lights changed and danced across the night sky. Slowly all of the guests went to their respective tents and went to sleep for the night. Many of them heavy with drink.

Torlin and Roanda went to Torlin's tent and closed the flap. It would not be that night that they consummated their wedding. They were both exhausted from the festivities and all they wanted was to curl into each other's arms and sleep. Roanda went to his bed, stripped off the blankets and mats, and set them on the floor. A bed was no place to sleep in her opinion. So the two lay on the floor and soon went into a deep sleep.

About an hour later, a noise woke Roanda and she groggily grabbed her sword. Shaking Torlin, she woke to see two Metradon standing over the bed and raising their wicked looking blades. As fast as greased lightning the Metradon struck the bed with several well-placed blows and turned to each other after they received no response.

"Looking for something?" asked the Tyris.

The Metradon turned quickly just to fall to Roanda's blade and Torlin's fireball. Torlin ran out of the tent and into chaos. The would-be assassins were just the tip of a large iceberg. All around Metradon fought Metradon. Men and women fought the lizard folk as well, but were getting the worse of the battle.

Roanda ran to aid her Tyris as Torlin laid into the attackers with fireballs and the new lightning spell Pan Thor had taught him. Pan Thor was there back to back with Artitous fighting two of the Metradon wizards. Artitous was trying to talk them into joining their side but his words were lost on the ears of the enemy wizards.

Torlin tore into the backs of the enemy wizards and Pan Thor ran to his adoptive brother. "I heard about the after parties your family had on their wedding nights but I think this one takes the cake," said Pan Thor.

"Always a pleasure to entertain you. Might I suggest we continue to pay attention to those energy weapons? They seem to be dealing us a great injury," said the prince as he launched fireballs and lightning at the line of Metradon firing into the crowd of the races of Dracos and Metradon. Pan Thor launched his own attack but they seemed to not faze the attackers as they kept firing into the crowd despite the fact that they were taking injuries and casualties. The human and Dwarves pressed the Metradon firing down into them just for another group of Metradon to appear from nowhere and start firing at their backs. Torlin and Pan Thor attacked the new arrivals and were soon joined by Artitous and Roanda. Roanda went to her new husband's back and attacked any of the creatures that got close as Torlin sprayed fire and lightning repeatedly.

"Where are they coming from?" asked the prince as even more seemed to appear from nowhere. "Surely they cannot teleport themselves so tell me where they are coming from."

"They have a tunnel," hissed a voice next to them. Paulen and his troops of the Resistance had arrived and were attacking the ground in multiple locations. "We have been trying to collapse them but they are too well built by your Dwarves. They were supposed to be used for escape in the event of a siege but the enemy that knows of their existence can use them against you."

"Why was I not told of these tunnels? Who gave the order to dig them?" asked Torlin.

"I am afraid the order came from Two Horns. He said you wanted them built and no one questioned it. He knows where they all come out and where they all lead. He is the only one who knows about all the tunnels. But we know about some of them." said Paulen.

"Let them get into the city then have the Dwarves who built the tunnels destroyed them. It should not take them that long and then our enemy will be trapped within the city. We can then destroy them," said the prince.

"No group of Dwarves knew where each of the tunnels is. Each group had a section of each tunnel and did not know where or how they exited. I fear that we will have to face them with the tunnels intact." Paulen hissed.

"I wish my brother were here he would know how to fight this battle," cried the prince.

"Be still dear heart. We can solve this. Right now, we just fight. Plans come later. Now just fight." said Roanda.

"Have your people forget the tunnels and attack those who are in the city. Stay with a group of Rangers so that we do not accidentally attack you. Unlike your people, we cannot tell you apart," said Torlin as he once more started with his magic and lashed out about him.

Roanda saw a blade flying toward the prince and deflected it with her sword. Picking it up, she noticed that the blade was gnomish. Looking at it, she looked around and saw a young gnome running away from the combat to the Metradon.

"My heart we may have another problem. I think some of our people have gone over to the Metradon. A gnome just tried to kill you," said Roanda.

"Each of the races were approached and promised great riches to turn traitor to you and yours. Some took up the offer, most turned it away. Only a small group of Gnomes and Dwarves took up the offers," reported Paulen.

"And you are just telling me about it? Why did you not come forward sooner?" asked the prince as he hurled fireballs in all directions as they were now being surrounded.

"I could not come to you before they left. It was imperative that we stay hidden until we could be revealed for best effect. We still have people inside their hierarchy who are sympathetic to our cause. We use them as best we can but there is still a lot we do not know," replied Paulen.

The enemy had surrounded the people of Dracos and the fighting came to a temporary halt. The leaders of the Metradon headed by Two Horns came to the fore and asked to speak to the rulers of the people for the last time. "Come and speak to us. You will be the only ones hurt if you do. The rest will go back to slavery. Some for more glory than others. Those of you who turned on your brothers come forth, and receive your reward," cried Two Horns.

Torlin pulled his mother back and he walked toward the surrounding enemy. The rebels amongst the Dwarves and Gnomes came forward and stood proud before Two Horns. "As for you first. Destroy all of the traitors to their people. If they turned so easily once, they will do so again. Now as for your puny leader, you thought I was your equal. Now find out how superior I am to you."

The Gnomes and Dwarves fell to their knees to beg and plead for their lives but Torlin just stood there. He threw a shield up between the energy weapons of the Metradon and the races and watched as the energy weapons reflected off it. Torlin looked Two Horns in the eyes and smiled. "You want to believe your superiority then believe it but the fact is you are weak without your technology. How about I show you what happened to Horned Carl? I can show you how he really died."

Two Horns broke eye contact and shoved one of his generals in front of him. Torlin laughed as he watched the Metradon scurrying to avoid his power. The respite lasted only a moment though as the Metradon resumed their attack on the humanoid races of Dracos. Slowly the few thousand people in the city became a thousand. The shields that Torlin and Artitous made were slowly failing and the other Druids and

Wizards were attacking the enemy. Pan Thor tried to aid the shields but they still crumbled under the barrage of energy fire.

Just as they thought they were about to be finished a strange figure walked onto the field and raised both his hands. Athinina recognized the swords the man held immediately. She recognized the man a moment later. "Tanis!" She cried. The man charged the enemy. At first, it appeared he charged alone but as he moved forward, the aid he brought came into view. Dragons swooped down and attacked the surrounding enemies. Breaths of fire and ice, acid and lightning, came down upon the unprepared enemy.

The enemy broke after a couple minutes of this barrage and the people in the middle of the circle renewed their defense. The enemy fled to the tunnels and left the city again. Their numbers severely decreased by the attacks. Athinina ran to Tanis and slapped his face. Then she wrapped him in a deep and passionate kiss. After an eternity, she broke the kiss and asked him, "Where have you been for so long? You have missed your sons growing to men. Why did you not come back to us?"

"I tried for years, but do you know how hard it is to burrow out from under a statue. It took me a year to get unburied and find myself again. Then I had to find the swords you hid for me. Then it was a case that I felt I should arrive when I was most needed. That I did. What major things have I missed since I have been gone?"

Athinina and Tanis walked away talking as Roanda and Torlin looked over each other looking for injuries. Roanda planted a great deep kiss on Torlin and walked away toward their tents, but Torlin went to the dragons. "Good sirs and ladies. I was under the impression you were not going to assist us anymore. What changed?"

"We will not aid you against the Dread Lords, but these creatures are not Dread Lords. We will send them running and keep them running. Enjoy the rest of your wedding night, what's left of it, and be well." said the dragon elder and lifted into the sky followed by the horde of dragons.

"Be well and may you find a good horde of gold and jewels to lie on," said the prince.

As the dragons flew away, Torlin's mother approached with the stranger that assisted him. "And who is Tanis? My father was Tanis. However, he is buried in the heroes' field south of Thalinburg. So who are you?"

"I am he. It took me a few years to regenerate, the Demon had injured me, but the deathblow came from a Dread Lord. As an Askanitowa, the Dread Lord could not kill me and I was prematurely buried. I could not come back to you at first because I did not know who I was. Later I was gone so long I did not want to interfere in your mother's rule or your lives so I stayed away. I watched constantly but never interfered.

When you were in trouble I called in a favor owed me by the dragons and they came with me to assist you. I am sorry I have been gone so long but I am back now and ready to aid you however I can, Lord of Metra.," said Tanis.

"Do you mind if I do not seem overjoyed to meet you at this late point in my life. I need some time to process this. Does Thomas know? Of course, not he is not in trouble with the natives is he? Let me ponder this. I will be in my tent with my wife, please let me be." said Torlin and he turned to walk away.

"Your brother is in more trouble than you think. I go to him next, hopefully with the armies of Thalinburg and Metra at my back. Do not take too long. He needs our help too." said Tanis.

Torlin waved at the couple that bore him and walked to his tent. He needed sleep and some time to talk with his wife. Lord of Metra, he liked the sounds of that. However, he would not let it go to his head. Roanda would like being Lady of Metra. He could not wait to tell her all that she missed when she left.

CHAPTER NINETY:
A FATHER RETURNS

Torlin wrestled with the fact that his father lived. Here he was nearly twenty and the man decides to show himself. He spoke of this to his wife, but she said he would have to come to grips with his return. It was funny that the man did not want the throne of Dracos returned to him. He had earned it by right, but he was content to allow him and his brother to rule in his stead.

Torlin went to the walls and walked the circuit. The city was large but not so large that you could not walk around the entire wall network. It took him several hours in the darkness to complete the circuit but complete it he did. It tore at his being that the man had come back. Why could he not have stayed dead? Now he would need to find a means of coping with the fact that he was back.

Torlin approached some of the guards who lined the walls keeping watch for any signs of danger. Their numbers were much diminished after the battle earlier in the night. These men had not yet had the time to sleep, being put on duty just after the battle. Their relief was coming soon but these men were exhausted.

Torlin walked to each of them, thanked them for their work, and walked on. These men did not wrestle with Demons. They just moved on. After walking the circuit and debating a second round, he made the decision.

Walking down the stairwell, he walked to the tent his mother was using during her visit. The lamp was still lit and he could see the two of them in there and hear talking so he called into the tent. After a moment, the queen emerged from the tent followed by her husband. "Father, may we talk in private? I need to get something off my chest and I do not want my mother to think I am ungrateful. There is much we need to discuss," said the prince.

"As you have said there is much we need to discuss. Please lead the way, as I do not know the wonderful city of yours. You have grown to be quite a man.," said Tanis.

So father and son walked away into the night and his mother strained to hear the conversation between the two. After a moment, she realized that the conversation was being magically blocked from eavesdroppers so she walked to the tent of Torlin and Roanda.

"I did not intend for you to fall in love with my son when I sent you here, you know." said the queen to the prone form on the pallet of blankets and rugs on the floor.

"I did not intend to fall in love with him. It just happened. I hope you are not disappointed in me. This way I can protect him better. Though he could use a scar, he is too pretty." said Roanda.

"He does not need a scar, unless you have to give him one. He speaks to his father now and I hope the two can come to some form of peace. His father wants to reunite the world once more. He is saddened that the twin cities are at odds with Thalinburg and that the rest of the world is now looking toward the approaching Dread Lords. He promises to see that that threat is put down quickly. But he will need cities and Thalinburg as well as the nobles of the world to aid him." said Athinina.

"Why do you tell me these things, My Lady? I am merely a commander of a squadron. We go where you tell us, no more, no less," said Roanda.

"You are a noble woman now and a princess of the kingdom. You advise the head of the Mysteries of Dracos. My son listens to you and you have influenced him in a wonderful way. He has never been a pleasant person. He was always greedy for knowledge and power. Now he is kind and loving and I am sure he will make the right decision as far as his father is concerned. You have done that. Not him, you. My son has chosen well," said Athinina.

"I am not a noble woman. Nor am I one of those fluttering princesses. I am a warrior, My Lady. Nothing more and nothing less." said Roanda.

"A warrior, no doubt. A noble woman, now you are. You have married the Prince of Dracos. Like it or not you are a princess. You do not have to be fluttering or simpering. You just have to love him and see he does the right thing by the people," said Athinina.

"I was hoping that would not happen. I hoped that I would not be burdened with titles and court intrigue. I never even thought about being a princess until this very moment. I do not know how to be a princess. You will help me won't you My Lady?" said Roanda.

"Of course, but all you need to do is be yourself. You will figure out the rest as you go. I swear it to you," said the queen.

"I hope you are right. By the way, where are those men? Gossiping I suppose. You put two men together and all they do it seems is gossip. I hope they do not come to blows. Torlin could not face the weapons of his father, I do not think. I could be wrong though," said Roanda.

"I think they will be just fine. As for gossip, let them. They have much to catch up on," said the queen.

"You are right as usual and we both need rest if we are to keep those men of ours out of trouble. I will go to my blankets now and let you go to yours. Good night and rest well." said the princess.

"See you are getting the hang of it already. Good night and rest well my daughter." said the queen as she walked away into the night toward her tent.

CHAPTER NINETY ONE:
WRESTLING WITH FEELINGS

The two men walked a short way and Torlin cast a spell to prevent anyone from listening either magically or by hearing them. They walked in silence for a few more yards than Tanis spoke, "I know you have concerns about my return. Speak them and I will tell you what I told your mother."

"It has been nearly twenty years. You choose now to return. What has made you return? I have concerns about why you have come. You want to take over again and rule, don't you?" said Torlin.

"No, I don't. I have found out that I cannot rule. There was a prophecy that said that you and your brother were to rule this world. Not me and not your mother. I did not understand that until you were born. I have been gone because I could not interfere in your lives and decisions. You had to make your own ways. You have much to be proud of. You head the Mysteries of Dracos. By all appearances, you are a just man. That may not have been the case had I intervened. I was attacked and killed by the Dread Lords, but being as afflicted with life that I am, the Dread Lord could not kill me. I did take a long time to recover from my wounds from the Demon but that is another tale. I have no ambitions to rule Dracos. That is for your brother and you to share for as long as you live. Then your children to follow you. I will stay in the shadows where I belong." said Tanis.

"I have missed not having a father. I will listen to your council but I will not accept you as my father right now. That will come in time. We will see if you choose to rule. Right now, we have to help my brother. You say he is in trouble and needs our help. How do you know this? I will do whatever we need to do to assist him. Just let me know." said Torlin.

"Your brother has been corrupted by the influence of these reptilian creatures and plans to do harm to you and your mother. We must make him remember who he is. We need to make him remember so that he can rule at your side. If you two are fighting then the world will fall to the Dread Lords, and that would not benefit either of you. So how do you influence someone who is already being influenced? That is the question," said Tanis.

"I have some ideas, but they will need my wife to work. Let us all get together tomorrow and we will discuss how to influence my brother and win our war against the forces of evil. I just hope that we will not have to deal with the Metradon again. I have the Dwarves locating all of the tunnels and creating doors that open only one way. That way we will not have to wait for another attack through them. Now we must get some rest so tomorrow we can plan. Good night and sleep well." said Torlin as he dropped the shield and walked away toward his tent.

It was not the reunion that Tanis had hoped for but at least his son would take his council. He has years of missing time with his wife that he needed to make up for but that would have to wait until his battles were won. He just hoped he was not too late for his son.

Torlin returned to his tent torn about his father. He was happy to have his family coming back together, but he not being there for so long upset him. He spoke to his wife on this for hours and the sun was coming up as the two of them settled into sleep.

CHAPTER NINETY TWO: THE STORY

Tanis and Athinina spoke for a short time and they too found themselves drifting into sleep. Tanis explained why he had come back. "My heart. I know I have been gone a long time. I hope you can forgive me for being away. I have been working with the dragons to cement their aid in the coming frays, but was not able to do so. It took all that I could muster to get them to come now for the aid of my son. I do not think we will see them again for a long while. When I first got out of the ground and was getting my memories back, I rooted around looking for my weapons. I had thought it was hours but found out that it had been years. I found a well to wash and drink, but when I did, I tasted the magic of Warmonger. I climbed down the well and found Warmonger and Holy Avenger wedged not far above the water line. I collected the weapons and looked for scabbards. This was harder being me had no money and everyone believed I was dead. I sold my services as a caravan guard to earn a little money because I did not want to come back to the castle. I heard you had given birth to two strong boys and I did not want to confuse them if you had taken another husband.

I wandered the world and watched them from afar. And you. I was there when you opened the city of Metra. I saw what transpired and was so proud of the ingenuity of the boys and the power that they had together. I followed them when they split to work each of their cities. However, I did not allow them to know who I was. It was not until they fell in with the lizard folk that I decided I should return. I was too late to aid Thomas, but I was not too late to assist Torlin with his little problem. I was shocked to learn you were here. However, I felt it was a sign that I was meant to be back with my entire family, at least for a time. I will not remain forever because the pain of losing you and the boys would be too great. I am sorry. But I hope you will understand." said Tanis.

"If you think for a moment that you are walking away that easily you are sadly mistaken. I lost you once and I will not do so again. If it is pain that you are afraid of, just try to leave. I know why you will not rule but I do not understand why you think we cannot handle your curse to live forever. There are no more Demons, so I do not have to worry about you being killed again. I love you, Tanis Thalin and you do not get to make that decision for us. If we get sick of you we will send you away, but not until then. Do you understand?" asked Athinina.

"I do. I was concerned about you and the boys but it appears you are all stronger than I figured. I promise I will stay until you send me away, and not leave until that day. Does that suffice?" asked Tanis.

"Yes. It does. Moreover, I will keep you under lock and key until then. Come and kiss me so I can remember your touch. It has been so long.," said Athinina.

"As you wish My Queen." said Tanis as he moved to her and kissed her deeply.

CHAPTER NINETY THREE:
ANOTHER WEDDING

In Thomas's palace, the mood was somber as the bride-to-be prepared for her wedding. No giggling was taking place as the Tyris assisted her in getting ready. The bride had a quiet reserve more suited to a funeral than a wedding. She numbly worked the buttons on the gown her husband to be had found. 'It really is a beautiful gown,' she thought as she smoothed the fabric over her legs and thighs. She would be the talk of the city in that gown. Her heart was happy and sad at the same time. She was eager to wed Thomas but she would rather it had been Ragan whom she walked down the aisle to see. She still pined for her lost love but her new love should not have to know that.

She put a big smile on her face and looked into the mirror. She could not even convince herself that she was happy. However, she also knew what she was thinking.

"My Lady, It is time," said one of the Tyris with a giggle to her voice.

"That is something I will have to get used to. My Lady sounds like you are speaking to someone else." said Meka.

"Well, you will always be Meka to the Tyris," said the woman warrior. "By the way we have a patrol after the ceremony. Therefore, we may miss the feast. That creature said that was our orders. Your husband may be able to change them but we would rather be fighting giant spiders than dancing with these men anyway."

"I am surprised. No one mentioned it to me. I will get my husband to override the Tetradon and get you leave to remain at the wedding." True mirth finally making it to her voice.

"You would not do that to us would you? Dancing? Really? I would rather die than live through that." The Tyris joked.

"I can arrange that now I guess. I am going to be a princess now, am I not? I relieve you of your patrol this afternoon so you can attend the wedding feast," laughed Meka. "If I have to be there so do you all."

"As you say, my lady." laughed the Tyris as she walked away to tell the rest of the Tyris about the decision of the new princess.

Dagmar heard the exchange between the women and ran to the prince. His plans would be ruined if the princess to be had too much support in the city. He needed those women to go to their dooms.

He reached the throne room where Thomas stood pacing the floor. He seemed to be a little nervous before the wedding. *That was good.* Thought the Tetradon. *He would be easier to manipulate if he was distracted.*

"My Lord. The woman you are to wed countermanded one of my orders. I need you to give the order again so that it will happen," said the Tetradon.

"What order was that? I do not remember giving you any orders to give out. Tell me more about this order." smiled the prince as he walked over to Dagmar and started walking in circles with the lizard man.

"It is simply a patrol order for the Tyris, My Lord. It is only that the Tyris have not been on patrol for a while and I do not want them to get soft. So shall I redistribute the order?" asked Dagmar.

"No. If my queen says no patrol today, it is no patrol today," said the prince.

"But what of the wasp people, do you not want them eradicated?" asked Dagmar.

"No. Patrols will not go out today. I have spoken and I will not be disobeyed. Moreover, anyone disobeying my queen will answer to me as well. Do you understand my friend?" asked the prince.

"Of course, My Lord. I meant no offense. There will be no patrols today," said Dagmar as he slinked away thinking about the next day.

The hour came and Meka walked down the aisle. She was nearly to the altar when she stopped and looked around her. It seemed as if she may bolt for a moment but she continued to the altar. Placing her hand in the hand of the prince, she turned to the Druid and knelt with her husband.

The rest of the ceremony went without a hitch. The Druid was clear and proud to be doing a royal wedding. Both bride and groom knelt smiling throughout the ceremony. Everything went according to the prince's plans. Even the doves that they released flew beautifully from their hands. A storybook wedding would be jealous of this fine occasion.

After the ceremony, the prince and his bride danced the night away with her Tyris and his friends amongst the Rangers. The party was going full steam and all were having a ball. The bride and groom and their guests were drinking and carousing. All were having fun.

During the celebration, the Tetradon sat and planned. The skilled warriors of the Prince and the new Princess were a problem. He hoped that she would not countermand anymore of his orders. Slowly he would remove the warriors of the woman and the prince. Calling over his head of spies, he asked what the Metradon were up to.

The news from Metra was not good for the Metradon. Most of them had been chased from the city and the Resistance had reared its head. It was of interest to find out that the magical prince had also been wed on this day. He would put that in the back of his mind for now. It may come in handy later. The dragons had interfered in the battle against the Metradon and had saved the slave races. That could be a problem. In addition, a stranger had come with the dragons. One whom the people had rallied. This may be information that he could use to aid his cause.

He turned to his general and ordered that the walls be doubly guarded. It would be this night that the enemy may choose to attack. The slaves overdid their silly weddings, and would need clear heads to watch over them after the celebrations. He would inform the prince of his orders in the morning. It would make him smile. His brother and his mother both had weddings that were interrupted, but this prince would not. They would enjoy the day and keep their heads on until he was to remove them himself. He thought briefly of that day and smiled. He would rule both cities and even the slave races once more. That would be a day to remember.

Unbeknownst to the celebrants at the wedding a sinister plot was unfolding, as a traitor to the prince had infiltrated his ranks. The Dread Lords would move tonight. It would be fitting that they would interfere with his mother and his weddings. It almost made the man at the gate smile. He listened into the night and heard the birdcall the enemy had arranged to be the signal. He bent his back and pushed on the gates. Slowly they began to open and the man smiled dreaming of his reward. The gate got a fraction open when the Tetradon opened fire on the man pushing the gate. Quickly the man was slain and his last thoughts were of how it had all gone wrong.

The Tetradon moved to the gates quickly and tried to re-secure the gates but were stopped by the massed hordes of the Dread Lords. Many of the Tetradon moved to the gates and shoved with all of their might closing the gates but not before many of the Dread Lord's men entered the city.

Tetradon warriors swarmed the men who had made it in and sounds of battle soon floated to the wedding celebration. The prince and princess ignored the sounds but the seasoned warriors in the crowd could not. Quickly pulling on their weapons and armor, they ran toward the sounds of battle to find chaos in the streets as the enemy attacked. The Dread Lord Wars had begun again.

CHAPTER NINETY FOUR:
AN INTERRUPTED WEDDING

Thomas ignored the sounds of combat as the battle raged around him in the city. His Rangers and the Tyris had pushed back the enemy twice as the city layout was a death trap for intruders. The narrow streets and sharp corners allowed for defenders to stage ambushes everywhere and a few could defend against a larger attacking force with ease due to the narrow confines of the streets. It turned badly when the fighting got into the many squares and gathering places where the enemy numbers could be pushed to their advantage. These places dotted the city and made the defense a little harder. Getting the enemy to follow into the streets was difficult after a few successful attacks from the defenders. The enemy was learning from their mistakes.

Thomas finally found himself interested in the battle when it broke into the wedding plaza. Looking around at the Orc faces and the men in the Dread Lord armor, he screamed and drew his sword. Looking down at the blade, he realized his mistake. He had on a ceremonial sword, which was useless in battle. He was slipping if he could not remember which type of blade he carried. Looking around him, he found a bow and proceeded to open fire at the forces entering the plaza.

Thomas looked for targets and found that the energy weapons of the Tetradon were suddenly bringing them down. Dagmar and his people had finally entered the fray and the battle once more swung in the favor of the defenders. Dagmar and his people looked determined as they fired into the crowds of warriors. Thomas also noticed that they were taking no care as to whom they killed. Rangers and Tyris lay dead as well as the enemy troops. All fallen to the power and precision of the Tetradon energy weaponry.

Thomas looked on with no care for his own losses. He followed the enemy soldiers until they once more were pinned between the broad gates that now stood closed and the advancing armies of Tetra. The enemy commander lay down his weapon and fell to his knees and Thomas went to him and picked up his blade. "Is this the best you can do? You are pathetic. Surely, the great Dread Lords have more to offer than this measly attack. We will destroy your entire army in the morning as you are to be destroyed now," said Thomas as he swung the blade and removed the enemy commander's head before the man could answer.

In much the same way, he moved down the line of enemy troops and dared them to rise and attack him. He shouted taunts and accusations, threats and insults, but the enemy just knelt defeated afraid of the weaponry of the Tetradon. As Thomas slaughtered the last of the enemy's men, he threw down the blade and screamed into the night, "Do you have anyone worthy of facing me or have you broken your teeth against our walls already? Bring on your champions! I will lay them to waste as I have done to the rest of your drivel."

Meka ran to tend to the wounded in the wedding plaza. She was tending a dying Tyris when Thomas walked back into the square. Seeing he was covered in blood, she ran to inspect the prince who was now her husband. Her hands moved over the prince's body and searched for injuries, but the prince pulled away. "This is not my blood, Meka but that of our enemies. What a way to christen our marriage than with the blood of our enemies falling at our feet. The entire first wave enemy lay dead in front of the gates. I must think of what to do with all of them. We can handle this in the morning. Are you all right?"

"Many of my Tyris warriors were slain tonight. Not by the enemy but by those creatures you allow run free around here. Out of the five hundred I brought there are barely hundred left and thirty of those will never fight again. Therefore, I have seventy warriors in my personal bodyguard. That is unacceptable. What are we to do?" said the new princess.

"I will assign some of the Tetradon to aid the Tyris in your defense. You are the bravest woman I have ever known. Why do you need a large bodyguard? Has someone threatened you?" asked Thomas.

"No one threatens me now but as a princess I will be a target. I do not want those things watching my back. Please allow me to send for more Tyris or at least give me Rangers instead of them." said Meka.

"But the Tetradon are the best. Do you not want the best? You should have the very best of everything," said Thomas as he walked away, stepping on the dead and dying as he walked to the palace. Meka looked into the faces of her remaining warriors and followed her husband being careful not to step on anyone dead or alive. She was wondering if this had been a mistake after all.

Dagmar gathered the warriors and generals of his people and congratulated them on a job well done. They were slowly whittling away the prince and princess's forces. Soon they would have no warriors except the Tetradon and then the Tetradon would make their move for power. They needed to get the prince and princess down further on men and those evil women. The Tyris were the biggest threat to the Tetradon as they never found it to trust them. Those women always watched the Tetradon and followed them into their areas of the city. If anyone was going to uncover their plans, it was going to be those women.

Dagmar called his assassins to him and asked them to redouble their efforts to eliminate more of the women warriors. They could not kill a lot of them at once but they could whittle away at them one at a time. They were not to touch the new princess. She and the prince would be left to him when he took power.

It will be a shame to kill the woman he thought, but he needed to assert his authority over the people and he could not do that if they both lived. Even one of them could rally the races and interfere in his rule. Besides, the women slaves were a nice distraction at times. Yes, it would be a shame to have to kill them but it was after all a necessity.

The Tetradon moved to their part of the city and prepared to rest for the night. The races could stand watch tonight. After all what were the slaves for? Let them start to learn their place again.

The people on the walls watched as fire sprung up all around the city. Fires spread as far as the eye could see. Looking down from on high it looked like the fires covered the field. The men on the walls grew concerned as they watched the fires spring to life. Could there really be that many of the enemy out there? Smoke from the fires floated into the city and the men strained their eyes to keep the watch in the haze.

When morning came, the prince went to the gates and ordered the enemy dead to be brought to the top of the walls. Looking down at the enemy gathered around his city, he ordered them to release the prisoners. The men looked at the prince as if he had gone insane. There were no prisoners to release. Seeing the men's confusion, the prince grabbed up one of the corpses and threw it down onto the gathering enemy.

The men got the idea and followed suit, throwing down the dead bodies and severed heads of the enemy troops killed in the battle the night before. Meka watched from the ground as her husband and the men did their grisly work. She had no stomach for psychological warfare. They should have just buried or burned the dead.

The enemy screamed in rage as everybody fell to the ground. Soon the enemy war drums started beating again and the enemy brought forward great rams. The Rangers shot arrows down into the rams' operators killing them rapidly before they could reach the walls and the gates. As the arrows rained down on the enemy engineers, the enemy screamed in rage. How dare the people of the city resist them? Meka joined the defenders on the walls and fired into the engineers trying to build the siege equipment and work the rams. This she could do with a light heart.

The day passed with only the archers firing down on the invaders. No more attacks made it into the city and the Rangers found they were running low on arrows. Meka took her seventy Tyris and raided the camps of the enemy at night retrieving their arrows and stealing the arrows of the enemy. They worked in stealth not engaging the enemy unless they had to. Then they killed swiftly and silently not to arouse the suspicions of the enemy. They made it back into the city as the sun started to rise and they delivered their goods to the archers on the walls and rested the rest of the day, repeating their raids in the night.

Thomas was pleased to see the arrows. They would allow his men to fire on the enemy for the entire day. He was angry with Meka for going herself. That was not work for the princess. If she wanted to send her people, that was fine but she could not put herself in harm's way like that. The people needed her for morale.

Meka watched the darkness fall over her husband's features. He got this way when he was in combat and when he was directing his men. She went to him and leaned on his arm as the two watched the archers killing those who were trying to gain the walls of the city. There were just so many of the enemy. How could they survive this?

Meka saw it before Thomas did and she could not believe her eyes. In the distance, dust was rising as another army approached the city. Meka pointed it out to the prince and he laughed that they too would break their bodies on their walls.

It took her only a moment to realize it was the army of Lord Nargus. His battle standard raised into the wind as he attacked the rear of the enemy surrounding the city. The prince ordered the archers to be wary of the new army and not to open fire on them. They were to continue to prevent the walls from being breached. The heavy cavalry were pushing the enemy into the walls and the Rangers on the walls fired into the enemy as they ran from the horses.

They seemed about to break the enemy when the enemy rallied and the horse were pushed back. Later the same day, the Tyris saw another cloud of dust and saw it was the Elves. The Elven royal guard attacking the flanks of the enemy as their Rangers assaulted the enemy with precise arrow fire. Lord Nargus attacked again as the Elves attacked and again the enemy seemed on the point of breaking when once again the enemy commanders rallied their troops and pushed back the attacking Elves and horse.

The prince grew angry as the armies failed to break the enemy. Two of the finest fighting forces on Dracos now stood camped behind the enemy and they could not break the enemy siege. The Dwarves arrived shortly after with Perrick Alon at their head. The man looked ridiculous in his armor but the Dwarves fought hard and well only to once again be rebuffed and pushed back.

The army of Tetra felt it was doomed when once more dust showed on the horizon. The man leading that army was unfamiliar to the prince and princess but his stature spoke of one who was comfortable with command and warfare. He led the men of his army into the battle and the other three armies attacked with him. As the combined forces of Dracos attacked, the enemy the enemy pushed harder toward the city. The Rangers on the wall fired repeatedly into the enemy and soon the enemy was diminished and breaking from the field.

Thomas sat cheering but did not open the gates for his newfound allies. Meka ran down to open the gates but was caught by Thomas and told not to open them. The people out there would want to rule in their stead and may even kill them to do so. Meka said, "These are the Dwarves and Elves and men of Dracos. You grew up with these people. They do not want your city. They are here to help and to celebrate our great victory."

"They are here to take over. They are jealous of me. I have a beautiful wife and a beautiful city. They just want to take what is mine. I know it.," said the prince.

"Are you listening to yourself? These people just saved all of our lives," screamed Meka.

"You will see my love they will come and demand the city in a short while. I know it to be so. They will come in force," said Thomas.

As if on cue the people of the armies moved to the gates and demanded admission, the leaders calling up to the guards to let them in.

CHAPTER NINETY FIVE: NEGOTIATIONS

The combined leaders of the armies that had aided Tetra came to the gates and called up to the guards. Lord Nargus called up to them in greeting and asked for the gates to be opened. Thomas loomed up from behind the guard and called out to the massed leaders. "How dare you come here with armies at your backs? Did you think you could trick me into opening my gates so you could invade in the place of the Dread Lords? Be gone or I will show you what I had in store for the Dread Lords."

Nargus looked confused at the strange man and at Perrick Alon. "We are not invaders, we are saviors. We came in your hour of need and saved you all. Why are you acting this way?" asked Perrick.

"No one wants to help for nothing. You want what I have. Well you will have to take it from my cold, dead hands. I have no friends out in your world. Tell them my bride. I can trust only Dagmar and you. All others will be treated as the spies that they are. Do you hear me? I have no more time for any of you. Open the gates to no one," said Thomas.

The massed leaders of Dracos turned their horses and left toward the massed armies. As they, left Thomas looked out to see exactly who had come. He recognized Perrick and Nargus. He saw the Elven commander and he noticed the new man. He did not see his wicked brother who probably sent these people to him. He also did not see his mother. Strange that those two would not be there. Well maybe not that strange. They probably waited in the massed armies in case he became violent toward the spies. Those two had turned almost every one against him.

As he watched, a lone ranger under flag of parley came to the gate. "My Lord Thomas. I come from your father, the Lord Tanis Thalin. He seeks admission to speak to you. He awaits your response. What say you?"

"What say me? My father lies dead in the Field of the Pheni. You want to know what I say?" asked the prince as he grabbed up a bow and fired an arrow into the chest of the man in front of his gates. "That is what I say."

Meka watched in horror as the man fell. How could her husband be that way toward his own people? She walked to Thomas, put her hand on his arm, and led him away from the wall. There may be another war yet if her husband kept up his ways. She would have to work on him to bring him out of this. She looked into his angry eyes and smiled seductively. Maybe if they were alone she could soften his heart.

Thomas saw his wife's look, dismissed all of the people around him, and picked her up. He carried her to the palace and into his chambers where the two closed the door to the rest of the world and were together for hours.

After Thomas had exhausted himself, Meka dressed and went out to her Tyris. She explained to them the meeting on the wall and asked for help in getting a message out to the massed armies. They brainstormed for hours and no one seemed to have an answer as to how to get out of the city.   One Tyris asked, "What about the tunnels?"

"What tunnels?" Asked the new princess.

"The emergency tunnels of course. Did you not know about them? I followed one of the beasts to the entrances the other day. He seemed to be paranoid that he was being followed. He kept looking over his shoulder. I asked some of the Dwarves and they said that they had made them but had to report to Dagmar for some reason now that they were complete. He speculated that Dagmar had more building for them to do. I have not seen hide or hair of the Dwarves since then. Maybe you can find out something," said the Tyris.

"No, I did not know about them. I have not seen any of the Dwarves either in the last few days. I may be able to ask my husband as to their whereabouts. This Dagmar is making life for us in here dangerous; maybe we should arrange an accident for the beast. What do you ladies think of that?" asked the Tyris leader.

"I think that could be arranged. Now tell us about the last few hours that you and his highness. Do you think we do not know what you two were up to? Give us all the details," said the Tyris.

"You are dirty women. Where do I begin?" said Meka and the group of women put their heads together and whispered and laughed like schoolgirls the rest of the day.

Thomas listened to the reports from Dagmar. The Dwarves had turned on the city and were summarily dealt with. Dagmar reported that he had given the order of execution himself and that the Dwarves were being buried as they spoke.

"Dagmar. Do not bury the traitors. Hang them from the walls for the massed armies to see. Let them be a warning to them what waits for them if they defy me. Make it happen now," said Thomas, a dark gleam shining in his eyes.

"I had not thought of that my lord. Is it prudent to antagonize the enemies at the gates? I would have thought that not letting them know would be the better course of action," said Dagmar.

"I want it done that way. Did they finish anything that may have been sabotaged? Check all of the Dwarves' work for signs of sabotage and report back to me. I mean anything they worked on. Do it now," said the prince.

Dagmar smiled as he walked away. He had successfully disposed of the evidence of his tunnels; and made it that much harder for Thomas to resist him when the time came to take over. He would do as the man asked for now, but a time was coming when he would no longer be the servant. He would give the orders. He smiled again and trotted away toward the burial site. There would be no more errors.

One of the Tyris moved away from the gathering as they continued to speak of the day's events. She donned a cloak and grabbed her peach pit poisoned dagger from the side of her tent. She went out into the city, waited for darkness to fall, and then searched the city. Her target was not difficult to find. The big Lizard man made it easy to find him.

She stalked the lizard man into the night and finally found the opening she was looking for. Drawing the poisoned blade, she moved swiftly to close the distance between them. Just as he was about to stab her dagger into the back of Dagmar she felt a sharp pain in her back. Looking down she saw the end of a blade protruding from her chest. She tried to look behind her but found her body unresponsive. As she died, the last thing she saw was the faces of Dagmar and the lizard man that had protected him. She had not even seen the other one.

Dagmar smiled as the other Tetradon faded away again as his cloak covered him. This was an unexpected boon. The women were getting froggy. Good thing they did not know about the stealth cloaks. Otherwise, the woman would have killed them both. He would have to be more careful in the future. A plan was forming in his mind to eliminate the rest of those annoying women. They had apparently turned traitor too.

He would bring this to the prince and let him give the order to eliminate the women. It could not have been a better circumstance.

Dagmar gave the order to the Tetradon on the burial detail to change their orders and hang the corpses from the walls. The others just lay down their shovels, picked up the Dwarves, and placed them into carts. Dagmar warned them to be as discreet as possible, not wanting the new princess to find out before the work was done.

The others just followed their orders and worked mechanically at the mass grave to remove the bodies already interred there. It would only be a few hours to complete the task. Therefore, Dagmar went off to find the prince. He reported that his orders were being carried out. Then he went into the other tale. "Last night I was attacked by the Tyris. It was an unprovoked attack and I believe there will be more. We must do something about those traitors before it becomes too late. What do you say about that?"

"You expect me to believe that the whole lot of Tyris is after you and me? I am married to one of them. You probably got yourself attacked by a rogue. Bring me more than one attack and then I will personally disband the women warriors," said the prince.

Dagmar walked off fuming. It was not what he wanted but he would get his revenge. He noticed Meka leaving the women's tents and he entered. "I have new orders for all of you. You are to patrol the east side of the city with thirty Tetradon. We are to willow out some of the wasp men. Be ready to go in twenty minutes," said the Tetradon.

"As you say, we will be ready," said the Tyris.

"You will all have your reward when this is finished." smiled the Tetradon as he walked from the tent.

He walked to the waiting Tetradon and gave them the orders again. "Accompany them to the east side of the city, make sure that none survive."

He hissed as he walked away, one way or the other he would be rid of those infernal women. They would haunt his actions no more.

CHAPTER NINETY SIX:
WAR COUNCILS

Torlin paced the walls of Metra looking out over the fields surrounding the city. The Metradon had attempted attacks on two separate occasions and it was taking its toll on the moral of those inside. The Metradon had been frustrated once by the tunnels being blocked, the second time from the arrival of Lord Nargus and his cavalry. The heavy horse soldiers tore through the ranks of the Metradon and continued into the city.

The enemy was dispersed a third time by the Elves as they also returned to the city. The Dwarves returned but there was no enemy for them to face. As the gathered commanders sat in the command tents inside the city walls, they began to discuss the situation in Tetra. "The boy has got some serious issues, Athinina. He trusts no one but his bride and that beast of his. I am sure if she disagreed with the beast, he would take the beast's side. He was prepared to fire on us when we approached the city. What are we to do?" asked Perrick.

"We must gain his trust. Show him the deceit of the Tetradon. Only then will he listen to reason. The beast's hold on him is strong. We may have to work really hard to gain any iota of trust out of him and his bride may be our way to gain It.," said the queen.

"Who do you have in the city, beside the princess? It may not be as easy as you believe to sway the princess or the prince. They are both slowly falling under the manipulations of the Tetradon and we must do something to change this. How can we get someone into the city?" asked Torlin.

"May I suggest something?" hissed Paulen. "I have people inside the city and I have the means to communicate with them. It is a small device and it has a great range. I can communicate with the resistance inside Tetra and see to it that the people you need to speak to receive your messages," he said holding up the device. He pressed a button on the device and a small image of a Tetradon shone onto the floor.

"How can we help?" asked the Tetradon.

"We need to get a message to the Tyris stationed inside the city," said the queen.

"I fear that is going to be difficult. They have been sent to the east side of the city where there is an infestation of wasp like men. They are extremely powerful and Dagmar, our leader, sent them there to face these people. I fear they may not return," said the image in front of them.

"How about Paul Alon? Is he well and able to receive a message?" asked the prince.

"He is well. What shall I tell him?" asked the creature.

"Tell him we need him to open one of the tunnels for us in two weeks' time. We will meet him there and discuss what needs to be done. Thank you for your work and be careful. We do not need you to be caught," said Torlin.

"I will be careful. Be well." said the Tetradon as the device turned off.

"The device is traceable if Dagmar and his people think of tracing them. I will not risk our man inside without need and it will be only on rare occasion. Your suggestion of a meeting was a good one and we can use the device to set up meetings between us and the city," said Paulen.

"We will use it sparingly. We just need to start a communication with the other city. We also must see if we can save the Tyris from their fates," said Torlin.

"I am afraid that will not be possible. They will have to save themselves. Otherwise, they must be lost. It is too early to reveal we know what is happening in the city. I hope for their well-being but I am not going to be optimistic about their survival. The Tyris are a stubborn lot and will not give up even when over pressed and outnumbered. I am afraid we have to let them go," said the Queen of Dracos.

"Can we employ the dragons again? Maybe they can help save the Tyris and it would cloak our knowledge of what is happening inside the city?" asked Torlin.

"We will not be drawn into your wars and your intrigues, young one. Not even for Tanis will we do this, we are sorry." said the dragon elder.

"What says Mastol? Surely, he would say otherwise. He is the eldest and you would have to listen to him wouldn't you?" begged Torlin, genuine pain for his mother and bride showing in his eyes.

"No, we will not intervene, young one." said a booming Mastol from behind him. "I am sorry but this is not a Dracos' problem but a human one and we will not be drawn into it."

"I think I understand," said Torlin, "I just don't have to like it."

Roanda and Torlin sat and spoke for a while after the meeting broke about the loss of the Tyris in Tetra. Surely, they would retreat if pressed hard. They would not stand and die. Roanda repeated over and over that they would not but if they were, being set up they may face other challenges. Torlin was distraught as he fell into his wife's arms and he cried for the women even though he did not know them.

Roanda rocked the sobbing prince and assured him that the Tyris will not have died in vain and that they would be avenged. They just needed the advantage of surprise if they were to defeat the Tetradon. They would not have that if they intervened now. Torlin continued to argue but saw what his wife and family knew to be true. They must sacrifice those Tyris if they were to win this war.

It was two days later when the Dread Lords attacked the city of Metra. As dawn broke, the invaders approached the gates. Torlin stood like an oak on top of the gates and rained down lightning and fire, disorienting the attacking enemy. Nargus and his horses burst out of the gates and laid waste to the Dread Lords' engineers at the gates and the Elves peppered the invaders with arrows.

The enemy did not even realize there was not an attack from the Dwarves until the Dwarves attacked from the rear having taken the tunnels behind the advancing enemy.

The attacks at the front and rear disoriented the war hardened Dread Lord army, but did not break them. The defenders retreated to the city and the tunnels and waited for the next stage of the defense from Torlin. Torlin suggested a magical attack, but was shot down by Pan Thor when he reminded everyone that the Dread Lords could summon Demons to fight for them. Magic would force them to summon the Demons and then they would be lost.

Tanis suggested a winnowing of their troops by attacking from the walls with arrows and well placed magic. He said that the enemy would come to the walls the next morning. However, they would try to scare the night watch if they possibly could.

The Dread Lords set up camp around the city and lit their watch fires. The fires seemed to stretch as far as the eye could see. The vast armies of the Dread Lords seemed unbeatable from that view. The Tyris raided the enemy at night claiming arrows and weapons as well as killing some of the enemy. They made little dents but at least got the weapons and arrows.

The Dread Lords did not even attempt to breach the walls the second day. They merely banged on their war drums and screamed at the defenders. The defenders responded with well-placed shots from the Elves into the surrounding army. After brief exchanges, the Dread Lords continued with the drums and screams. The Elves had done their work well though as many of the enemy lay dead.

The enemy left their dead on the field as they left for the night. In the night, the Tyris went and recovered the arrows from the bodies and once more raided the camps for arrows and weapons. This time the enemy was waiting for them. As the Tyris collected the arrows from the fallen, a group of enemy equestrians attacked them. The collected corpses of the fallen prevented the horse from gaining any momentum and thus made them targets for the more agile Tyris.

Soon after the attack by the equestrians, the enemy lay dead and the Tyris was bringing in the horses as well as the arrows and weapons. The Tyris did suffer a loss, as one of their women was skewered by the lance of one of the equestrians. Her wounds overtook her as she returned to the city. She had just been wounded too badly.

The other Tyris carried her in as they returned to the city and she was buried with all honors. It was a regal affair in the night as the people in the city feared what the next day might hold and there might very well be more funerals to perform.

The Druids treated the minor injuries of the Tyris and Roanda thanked Torlin for burying her colleague. Torlin was touched by her sincerity and the two went off to consummate their new marriage as they had not had the time or the mood to do so.

In the early morning hours, the two royals were summoned to the walls as the enemy had left the field. Rangers sent out found that the enemy was headed back toward Tetra. They had apparently packed camp in the night and were now marching toward the city of Tetra. Torlin took this information and put orders out to prepare to move in support of his brother. He ordered all the warriors to prepare for a forced march to catch up to the Dread Lords before they could harm his brother.

Tanis quickly overturned his orders. The city was to remain on high alert and they were not to leave the city. Tanis explained to Torlin that the Dread Lords usually employed deception and it may be wise to give them a day or so to show what they were about.

Sure enough the next morning the city was once more surrounded by the Dread Lords and there were more of them than ever. Torlin ordered the Tyris to remain in the city and to avoid attacks from the enemy. The strange thing was that the enemy dead that still lay on the field was not being taken and buried. In fact, the enemy was taking a risk and was piling the dead on the base of the walls. Torlin ordered that the enemy piling the corpses be shot down, but a morbid curiosity kept him watching what was being done. More and more the corpses were piled and finally the last bodies were piled in front of the wall. Torlin ordered a doubling of the guard and watched even more trying to figure what they were about.

The Dread Lords ended the suspense as men carried casks of oil onto the dead and lit the bodies on fire. The archers brought down the enemy with the torches but it was not enough as the smoke started to block the archers view and began to choke the residents of the city.

People were walking around with their faces covered with rags soaked in perfumed water to drown out the smell of the burning flesh. Rangers dropped gallons of water down on the burning corpses but it just spread the oil and caused the fires to become worse.

As the Elves fired down on those working the fires, those bodies were added to the conflagration. After three days, Torlin ordered a cease-fire on the people around the fires outside the walls. He would give them no more fodder to fuel their smoke weapon.

So the Elves sat and watched as the men worked below and they fired only upon those firing up at the city or were building siege equipment. They fired fire arrows down into the siege equipment setting those on fire as well. The resulting smoke was nearly unbearable to those inside the city. People were moving as far as they could from the fires and still the smoke was there.

It would be the elder Thalin who would come up with a viable solution.

CHAPTER NINETY SEVEN: THREATS

Thomas got the report about his brother being under siege and he grinned. The troublemakers of Dracos would soon be destroyed. Meka listened to all of these reports with a passive ear and gave only fleeting advice. Thomas would listen to the advice and then turn to Dagmar. The beast was having more and more influence over the young man and it was getting scary.

Meka would take her husband for walks away from the beast and he would be warm and caring. In the lizard man's presence, he became cold and calculating. She went to the tents of the Tyris looking for some support. It had been several days since they had been there and she was growing concerned. One of those lizard men always seemed to be watching the tents and it was soon apparent that they were reporting all who entered or left the area. She was doing nothing wrong so she continued into the tents.

Shortly after she entered, Dagmar arrived. "My queen, why do you come here? The people here are away and they should not be back for several more days. You are better used being near your husband do you not think so?"

"I come to visit old friends. It seems dead here, as if they will never return. You gave them their orders and now it as if they are lost. If any harm comes to them, I will personally see you dead. Do you understand me? I will kill you myself," said Meka.

"I have an entire army at my back what do you have? You husband has fewer and fewer troops and now you have none. You will obey your husband and me and be a good little girl or I may arrange an accident for you as well as your people. Do you understand me?" said Dagmar, a smile cracking his reptilian face.

"Are you threatening me? I am the Lady of Tetra. You will obey me beast or I will kill you for your insubordination. Who do you think you are?" said Meka, fear coming onto her face as she spoke.

"No threats only promises. I run this city and I control your husband. I am the one who can and will destroy all of your people. Do not press me, My Lady. You have that title only because I willed it. Now go back to your husband and produce more people for me to rule," said Dagmar.

"You will not get away with this! I will get my husband back and we will kill you and all of your people," cried Meka.

"We shall see if you can sway him before I choose to destroy you and your husband. I only need him for short time longer. Then you and he will be destroyed." said Dagmar.

Meka reached down for the dagger she wore at her waist and found her hand being pressed into the sheath by Dagmar's heavy reptilian hands. He smiled as he twisted and she grimaced in pain. He twisted more and she went down to her knees. He was still grinning when he felt the sting of the second dagger enter his belly. Looking down he saw the smaller dagger she wore at her ankle deep into his gut. He rapidly let go and removed the dagger. Looking down at the wound, he rushed out of the tent and headed for the Druids for healing. Meka would require some watching it would appear.

Meka smiled as she retrieved her dagger from the floor. Dagmar knew enough not to accuse her in front of her husband of attacking him. However, she had no proof of what else happened in that tent. Dagmar was influencing her husband to do just as Dagmar wanted him to. Meka had to get message to Metra and Torlin, to prevent what was happening here from happening there. The danger from these creatures was real and now she needed to prove it.

Dagmar came into the palace with bandages around his abdomen. Thomas saw them and joked with him about hitting on the Tyris. Dagmar laughed and said he had run into an improperly stowed weapon. The wound was not bad but it would require time to heal. Meka walked in, saw Dagmar in the bandage, and smiled. The Druids had sewn him up instead of magically healing him. When she mentioned this, the lizard man shuddered and snarled at her.

Even the Druids disliked the lizard man. Thomas was oblivious to the snarl from the lizard man and started speaking of the upcoming war. He would start with the weakened armies of Metra. His weak brother would not even fire a shot in his defense against him. He would just walk in and take over. He may even let his brother live if he swore fealty to him.

The rest of Dracos would be more difficult. His mother would mass an army to rival his own. She did not possess his skills with tactics so the battles would not last long, but they would be a nuisance. The Elves would fall in line as soon as the city of Thalinburg was taken and Nargus practically worshipped him so that would be an easy win as well.

Meka asked him why they would attack their own people. Surely, there were other ways to gain the throne. Thomas looked at her as if he were explaining to a child and told her it had to happen this way. He told her she would have everything she could want including his mother's throne, she just had to let him and his advisors talk to make it happen. She found herself struggling not to pierce her husband as she had pierced the lizard man. The man was not really like this. She would have to do her best to eliminate the influence over him caused by the Tetradon. Until then she would simply swallow her pride and do as she must.

Thomas took Meka's hand, led her to the doors, and told her to wait for him in their chambers. He would make everything right then. She doubted this would be true, but she went anyway.

When she arrived, she found one of the beasts sitting in the chair in the room. It jumped to its feet when she entered and kneeled to her.

She eyed the beast with uncertainty as it knelt there and she asked what it wanted.

"My Lady, I am Warren, and I lead the resistance here in Tetra. I must make this quick or Dagmar will find out about it. We will help you and your people remain free. I just wanted to let you know that your women warriors return greatly diminished. By the time we were able to intervene most of the women were dead. I am afraid only twelve returns." Said Warren.

"Your aide is greatly appreciated. You say you are the resistance. I hope I can trust you. Dagmar had me followed here so I must let you out by the secret tunnel I had the Dwarves build into my chambers. No one knows of it but me and the Dwarves who built It.," said Meka.

"I am afraid the Dwarves are all dead and before they died they revealed the location of all the tunnels you ordered built. Dagmar will not be watching this one yet but if he feels you are meeting with people without his knowledge, he will begin to monitor them. From now on, I will communicate with you through notes written in the Elfish tongue. This should confuse Dagmar for a time as he felt it unnecessary to learn the languages of this time. It will not work for long if you leave them lying about. When you get them, read them, and then destroy them. I must go now. Be strong and we will win this." said Warren as he slipped into the tunnel and worked his way through it. He hoped he had not made a mistake by revealing himself to the princess but someone needed to be informed that there was help in Tetra.

He failed to see the cloaked watcher monitoring the tunnel, nor did he see the lizard man go off to report what he had seen.

CHAPTER NINETY EIGHT: SIEGE

The smoke around Metra continued to choke the city. More and more of the people were going to the Druids complaining of shortness of breath and burning skin and eyes. The worst they treated with magic, the rest were given whatever could make them more comfortable. Some received salves others received cloth masks to cover their mouths and noses.

Tanis and Torlin stood upon the walls and looked down upon the fires. The stones would not burn so they need not fear fire, but the smoke was getting dangerous. Torlin blew some of the smoke from around him with flows of air, cleaning the air for a few moments. Tanis looked at the clear air and smiled. "I know how to remove the smoke. Have all the Druids and wizards come to the walls. I will explain when they get here," said Tanis.

It took a couple of hours to collect them all but the walls were filled with the magical personnel just as Tanis had asked. He arranged them with wizards and Druids alternating around the city. Wizards used one kind of power while the Druids used another. The combination would allow for a constant breeze blowing from inside the city, pushing the smoke away from the city.

The Dread Lords saw the strange winds and saw the magical people on the walls. They deduced quickly what was going on and ordered their archers forward. They would end this intervention quickly. The archers loosed their first volley only to fall short of the summit of the walls.

The defenders saw the volley and archers of their own were brought to the walls to fire down on the attackers. Again, more and more of the attackers died but it did not slow the Dread Lords' assault. Once more, the dead were piled on the fires and the smoke rose once more.

The magical folk in the city continued the breeze, working in shifts to keep the air clear but soon the wizards and Druids found themselves growing weary from the constant magical use. Archers patrolled the walls and laid waste to the attackers whenever they appeared. The side effect of the breeze was the smoke covered the attackers' movements on the field. It became clear that this could not be a permanent solution to the situation. The new proposal had some merit as well. One of the wizards mentioned to Torlin that magical fire does not smoke. Torlin ignored this comment for a while then it dawned on him. They could magically burn the bodies being burned to stop the smoke.

Torlin called the wizard who gave him the idea and asked him to start the attack on the bodies. He would have all of the magic users move to the walls in a few moments to aid him in destroying the fodder for the Dread Lords' fires. It took an hour to gather them all, but they gathered and rained magical fire down on the bodies and sure enough, the smoke stopped as the bodies were consumed and reduced to ashes.

The Dread Lords came to the edge of the fire line, that line where archers could hit you if you crossed it, and stared at the defenders on the walls. The Dread Lords moved away and again grew silent in their siege of the city.

Several days after the fires were extinguished, the Dread Lords brought out the Trolls. The sight of them caused the defenders to run in fear until the brave Elves took the walls surrounding the gates and fired down onto the Trolls and their handlers. As the Elves fired down on the Trolls, Dwarves swarmed the walls and started flinging stones from slings. Human Rangers soon joined the other races with arrows of their own.

Torlin said, "They have Trolls. What next? I am about tired of this siege. Stand back and let me work."

Torlin drew back his arms and a wall of flames leapt up and moved toward the approaching Trolls. The Trolls balked at the coming flames and tried to run but their handlers pushed them forward. The flames hit the Trolls and they burst into flame. They fell to the ground and soon were all consumed by the flames. However, as one Troll fell to the defenders, another came forward and soon the field was covered with Trolls. Some died by the archers, others died by magic, and still others by the Dwarven slings.

Torlin kept putting out the walls of flame and they still attacked. After a time the attacks slowed down and the armies once more stood at a stalemate. The night was peppered with the fires of the enemy but something was strange in the field. As the defenders watched, balls of light began dancing around the enemy. Tanis and Torlin were quickly called to the walls and Tanis proclaimed, "Everyone remain in the city! Those are the Willows of the Wisps. They appear harmless but they are quite deadly. I believe the Trolls may have attracted them as they feed on the evil and the dead. Remain in the city, as they will not distinguish between them and you. They will not come into the city, so we should be safe for now."

"Willows of the Wisps? I thought they were legend. I hope you are right and they attack only them. But I will be sure to magically seal the gates just in case." said Torlin, as he watched in amazement as the wisps destroyed the enemy camp.

The Willows of the Wisps attack lasted for several hours. The screams of the enemy cutting the night like a sword as the creatures latched on to them and sucked the life force from their bodies. The enemy finally broke and ran at the break of dawn closely followed by the Willows of the Wisps.

For the first time in what seemed like forever to the defenders, their city was devoid of attackers. When they looked out into the field, they saw the left equipment and started the salvage process, collecting weapons and supplies in the event of another attack. Soon great wagons were full to bursting with the spoils being brought into the city. Great loads of arrows and weapons were distributed to the warriors and foodstuffs and medical supplies were distributed to the others in the city.

Tests on the foodstuffs to find out if it was poisoned were conducted and it was found fit to eat. The supplies were clean and ready for use.

Torlin told Tanis that he hoped it would not happen that they would have to use these newfound supplies, but they were ready now when it happened.

It would be three weeks of peace before the Dread Lords once more arrived at the foot of Metra's walls. The Dread Lords showed up once more with greater numbers and even more apparatus designed to penetrate the walls of Metra. Amongst their numbers were Trolls, Goblins, Orcs, and Men. Thrown in amongst the humanoid warriors of the Dread Lords Demons of all shapes and sizes were mixed in. These were all lesser Demons and not something to be gravely concerned about, but they were still a major problem. It indicated the presence of a necromancer amongst them.

Artitous took note of the Demons especially. He would watch their movements closely. One day he ordered the attack on a certain area of the enemy camp. He demanded that no one be left alive and no structures remain unburned. Torlin asked his mentor as to why he felt so strongly about this one part of the camp and Artitous replied to the inquiry, "That is where the necromancer is. We must lay waste to all of the necromancer's things and him if possible. This will eliminate the Demons. Remember kill and burn everything."

"It will be as you say. I understand the importance of what we are to do. I will send in two high degree wizards and a whole platoon of Tyris. That should do the trick," said Torlin.

"I will see no mistakes, I will go with them." said Artitous.

"I assure you that there will be no mistakes. However, I cannot stop you if you decide to go. Just be safe and return to us," said Torlin.

The raid on the necromancer was to happen two days after that conversation. It was about to commence when the first wave of attacks started on the city. Two great rams attacked the gates but found them solid and the rams were quickly dispatched. First one then the other attacked the gates of the city just to find magical assaults awaiting them. Next, it was the Trolls with their massive clubs and these fell to the well-placed arrows and sling stones of Elves and Dwarves. As each wave was repelled, the dead and dying were destroyed by magical fire and the ashes blown away on magical winds.

The necromancer showed herself the next day. She approached the city with a bodyguard of skeletons and undead creatures and directed the Demons to assault the city gates. Pan Thor was the hero this day as he threw lightning and fire at the necromancer and her bodyguard until she was forced to retreat.

They watched as she went back to her tent, proving Artitous's theory that she was indeed camped in that area. The assault team went out that night. They moved swiftly and silently through the enemy camp and dispatched the guards quickly. If they thought that the necromancer would be easily dispatched, they found that they were sorely mistaken.

When they attacked the tent, the first thing they found were two fighting Demons waiting at the flaps. After getting through them, they encountered an empty tent. They destroyed the tent but were confused. They had seen the necromancer enter that particular tent. Where could she possibly be?

They attacked several more tents in the area and still came up empty. The woman had disappeared. They were about to leave when two large lesser Demons blocked their path with the necromancer right behind. Artitous knew she was a female for the scantily clad woman exposed more skin than she hid. The metal and fabric she wore strategically covered the areas that should not be seen, but only just. There was also no doubt she was the necromancer from the black mist that swirled around her.

Artitous called out to the necromancer and threw several fireballs. He assaulted the Demons and they soon fell on the blades of the Tyris and to the wizard fire that attacked them. The necromancer seemed to be alone and undefended when she suddenly seemed to bend and swirl away. Artitous ordered the men back to the city with all haste and to prepare for more attacks.

Torlin asked what had happened and Artitous simply replied, "She has rediscovered traveling. She was able to dissolve herself into time and space and disappear. We are safe here for you cannot travel to places you do not know and you cannot travel with anything or anyone that is not attached to your person. She would not come here with just herself and a dagger or wand. I know her. She was once a great wizard but was tempted away from the side of light by the dark powers. She calls herself Elizarade now, but she was once called Claire of Monterbe. I had once hoped to save her but she is now so far gone we have little hope to bring her back. Our only hope will be to destroy her and all of her apparatus. However, if she can travel we will have to try to find her lair. It could be anywhere. I must consult with Marzioa. He knows the whereabouts of most of the known necromancers. It is just finding the man that is the problem. Nemeth, come here. Go to Marzioa and tell him of Elizarade. Get him to reveal the location of her lair for you and report back to me."

"How can a raven tell us anything? I don't understand," said Roanda.

"Artitous speaks the language of the Raven Lords. Nemeth will tell him all he learns as soon as he can learn it. Fly well Nemeth. Bring us back good tidings," said Torlin to Roanda. "Let us hope he can find Marzioa in time."

CHAPTER NINETY NINE:
INTERNAL CONFLICTS

As his brother struggled with the Dread Lords' attack, Thomas enjoyed a period of peace and prosperity. The Tetradon farmers had planted their crops again and the workers of different crafts had begun their work as well. The clearing of the city had come to a near halt due to the wasp men, but Thomas had a plan for them.

A couple of days after the Tyris returned from their ill-fated patrol, Thomas called his people together. They were going to make a last ditch effort to remove these people from the city. He ordered equestrians and archers to make ready. He gave the swordsman their tasks and the Tetradon he saved for last. He would send in the infantry and draw out the wasp men then he would have the Tetradon and archers pepper them with ranged fire and then finish them with the horses. It was a sound theory but no plan lasted beyond the first engagement.

The raid on the wasp men would happen in a day's time. All of the available warriors would be needed to make this work. Meka would remain behind of course and prepare for the wounded and dead. Warren left her a note informing her that there may be mischief afoot, but did not specify what that would be. She went to her husband and begged him not to run the assault until all could be found to be ready, but he insisted all was ready.

That night the Lady Meka and Lord Thomas spent their first night alone as husband and wife, and it was not until mid-morning that Thomas came out of his chambers. He moved with a new sense of urgency and a new conviction was seen in his eyes.

He strode out to the marshaling ground and jumped into his saddle. He called out to his warriors, "Today we free our city of the foul creatures that have plagued our existence here. If we all stay focused and do not allow there to be any horseplay or other nonconformity we will stand victorious today. Today we fight so tomorrow we rest and play. Are you ready to fight?"

A resounding response shook the walls of nearby buildings and dread filled Meka's heart as she watched her husband marching off to war with his people. She did a quick count of the troops and was amazed that there actually were twelve thousand souls in that army. Surely that many men and beasts should be able to defeat one colony of these creatures? She went back into her room and donned the Mytan, though she had not worn it since she was a young warrior. Picking up a short spear and shoving two more behind her straps on her back, she picked up her shield and went out to the marshaling ground. The remaining Tyris, all ten of them, waited for her and they all moved behind the main army. Eleven more souls would not make much of a difference but they would at least show themselves at the battle.

They arrived just in time to watch the infantry moving into position and a flood of yellow and black creature swarming from the building they occupied. Archers fired flaming arrows into the building and it burst into flames bringing forth even more wasp men. The men of Tetra stood fast as the wasp men attacked and the first wave of wasp men were cut down. The second wave rushed the infantry but was also cut down by the archers and Tetradons' energy weapons. Soon the wasp men pulled back to the burning building and regrouped themselves. The enemy was strange having broken into waves and planning strategy. These things had more intelligence than Meka had thought. This could pose a problem for her husband, who had believed them to be primitive and without sense.

She watched the equestrians move into position and waited to see what would occur. She was amazed to see them bunch around an individual that appeared slightly larger. Meka seemed to believe that it also looked somewhat feminine. The warriors of the wasp men kept a tight circle around this individual and the fighting was most intense there.

The equestrians started their charge and the ranged weapons covered their movements. The equestrians made it to the protected individual and there the charge was halted by the sheer weight of numbers surrounding that being. The fighting had wound down except for that location and Meka and the Tyris waded into the fray. They fought their way to the prince, who had been unhorsed, and just as a large being was about to kill the prince who was distracted by several other wasp men, Meka rammed her short spear deep into the belly of the beast. The other wasp men saw this one fall and swarmed to get to it. However, the battle had gone poorly for the wasp men. Soon there were only a couple of them left to mop up and the equestrians and infantry left to be treated for wounds and to bury their dead. The battle had claimed two thousand soldiers, but they had in turn slaughtered at least thirty thousand enemies.

Thomas marched proud in front of the troops while Meka remained behind to collect the wounded and the dead. She had made a promise after all. She was surprised that Thomas said nothing about her Mytan. *He may have been too distracted by the combat*, she thought. After all, the fighting had been heavy. She walked with the wounded and dead to the marshaling ground and found her husband.

"What are you wearing, my heart?" asked the prince.

"My Mytan. It is about time I resume my duties as a Tyris commander. Besides I thought my husband might approve," said Meka.

"You think wrong. You are a married woman now and should dress as such. That is more for the bedroom than for the battlefield. Now go and change." said Thomas.

"Since when do you restrict the Tyris manner of dress? Alternatively, is it just mine? Be careful with your words or you may be the one in trouble here," said Meka.

"I am not restricting anyone's manner of dress I simply ask you to act the part of princess and not dress in the uniform of your prior station. You must be a leader to all of Tetra not just to those women of yours. How can a man take a woman seriously when she is scantily clad as you are now?" asked Thomas.

"Very easily if he knows what is good for him? If he watched the face as you should with a commanding officer, what was worn would not make a shred of difference. But to make you happy I will change my clothes." said Meka as she shed her clothing and walked naked from the field toward the palace. Several guards moved their cloaks around her as she walked, but it was obvious to all there that she was naked.

Thomas shook his head but watched until his view was blocked. He would have to make this up to her later. The men quickly averted their eyes when they realized they were looking at their princess but some still took the opportunity to gawk at the naked woman walking amongst them to the palace.

When Meka made it to her chambers surrounded by the Tyris, they all burst out laughing at the huge joke she had played on her husband. She quickly donned her usual garb of Rangers' clothes and leather armor, and sat talking to the women of her encounter with her husband earlier in the day. They quickly began speaking of children and how she would have to give over her command if she became pregnant. She balked quickly and said, "Who's getting pregnant? I just had some fun with my husband."

They continued to talk of little things for another hour and then they left and the prince came in. He walked into the room waving a bouquet of flowers in the doorway before entering.

"The flowers may stay, but I am not sure of the man bearing them," said Meka.

"That was harsh. After all, I was not the one who walked naked through the men. Do you forgive me then?" said Thomas.

"Harsh? You have not begun to see harsh. But all is forgiven, come in and we can settle this matter alone and together." smiled Meka. "That walk has made me desire you a little." They spent the rest of the night together and most of the next day. It would be the banquet in the prince's honor for the destruction of the wasp men that would draw them out, but it was reluctantly and not without them being late by half an hour.

CHAPTER ONE HUNDRED: DARK MAGIC

Nemeth returned the first day without any news. He was sent out again the next day and he returned empty handed. They continued to keep the enemy from the walls as Nemeth kept trying to find the missing wizard.

On the fifth day, they sent Nemeth out he finally came back with tidings of the wizard. Marzioa sent word via Nemeth that he would be there in three days' time with aid for the city. In the meantime, he sent word that Elizarade set up her workshop in Thalinburg. She kept her lair in the red light district, Elf Street and Main Street. She would not be hard to find once you knew where to look.

Rangers were dispatched to her lair and wizards went to see that there was nothing there of a caustic nature to the Rangers. When they raided the lair, Elizarade attacked with a pair of Demons and attempted to flee. The wizards knowing she could travel had placed wards around the building preventing such things and soon she was being taken away in chains. Her powers blocked by powerful spells by the wizards.

A small smile lit the necromancer's face as she was led away. It was all going according to her plan.

As the necromancer was being captured, the Demons on the battlefield went crazy. They attacked the soldiers of the Dread Lords with a vigor that belittled their previous zeal for battle. The Demons were dispatched but not before killing a full third of the enemy soldiers.

The men on the walls cheered at the sight of the enemy being laid to waste by their own creatures.

Torlin saw the opening and ordered the equestrians to charge into the enemy and the archers to fire into the enemy horde. The ensuing chaos brought the enemy losses to half their population before they once more regained control and began their counter attack.

Torlin pulled the equestrians out and the archers covered their retreat. The armies of Metra were jubilant at the victory of the equestrians and small celebrations ensued at the return of the victorious troops. Torlin looked nervously out onto the surrounding field looking for the next surprise. He need not wait long for the surprise as soon an army of skeletons and other manners of undead troops marched to the gates of the city and began to attack them. How this was possible without their necromancer he did not know, but here they were attacking the city. Necromancers rarely ever worked together but it would appear that there was another necromancer at work here.

Nemeth was once more sent out and he returned without any word of any other necromancers. As far as the bird saw all were Orcs, Goblins, and Trolls. He reported a large group of humans gathered on the far flank as well, but none of them was magical as far as the bird could sense. Roanda once more asked how a bird would know if any of them possessed magical training, and Torlin explained that the ravens could sense magic. Roanda looked at the bird, stroked his feathers, and whispered to it, "If you think of betraying us for them I will use you to stuff a pillow."

The bird squawked and jumped to Artitous's other shoulder as he and Torlin laughed at the bird's ruffled feathers. Roanda smiled as she moved away from the bird. Tanis and Athinina just took each other's hands and walked away chatting like schoolchildren. All seemed right with the world, but Torlin was still concerned about the possibility of another necromancer. If Elizarade could travel so could anyone she worked with. They would be sharing secrets.

The fire elementals came early the next morning. The flaming humanoids came to the gates and attacked them with concentrated flame attacks. The wizards on the walls rained down water and ice attacks neutralizing the enemy attacks. Torlin finally defeated the elementals with well-placed ice storms. He had hoped not to use that because it weakened the gates.

The ice elementals came next as soon as the fire elementals were defeated. They attacked the frozen gates with more ice attacks and the defending wizards had no choice but to attack with flames and fireballs. The concentrated flames defeated the elementals but left the gates glowing in the heat. The gates started to warp slightly as the gates cooled. Carpenters and metal smiths rushed to the gates and had to wait for them to cool in order to fix the damage.

The enemy tried to come with rams as the gates cooled but were chased off by the concentrated fire of the Elves' and Rangers' arrows. "It was a solid plan," said Tanis as the leaders spoke of the day's assaults. "Too well orchestrated to be that of Orcs and Trolls. I believe that they still have many wizards over there we will have to dispatch. We have to get word from Thalinburg as to who allied with Elizarade and see if we can find and kill them. She should be willing to tell us anything to prevent her powers from being stripped from her. But we cannot be there to hear her story since we are stuck in here."

"There are the escape tunnels if they are not being watched by the Metradon. It would get us beyond the attackers but we would be seen soon after emerging, so we would have to move very swiftly," said Torlin.

"No. We cannot risk using the tunnels. The enemy would find them and then use them to breach the walls. I am afraid Nemeth will have to report what the wizards have found in Thalinburg to us," said Tanis.

"Nemeth will leave as soon as we break this meeting. I will see to him getting to Thalinburg, but I fear for his safety. Surely they have learned of the raven's spying eyes by now." said Artitous.

"We must attempt it once more though. I hate to put him through it but we need to know what she has said. I hope we can get him through. It is our only hope," said Tanis.

"We will send several ravens and hope at least one makes it through to Thalinburg. We must also hope they can get back without incident," said Artitous.

Artitous excused himself from the meeting and went to the walls with several ravens on his arm including Nemeth. After speaking to them briefly, he let them fly. The enemy stood and watched the ravens go without incident. *So far, so good.* Thought Artitous.

After what seemed an eternity, the ravens were spotted heading back from Thalinburg. Artitous stood on the parapets looking for the birds when he saw the first of them fall to Goblin arrows. They had laid a trap for the birds. Nemeth lifted himself high above the enemy but was still hit in the wing by an arrow. He managed to make it to the edge of the walls and Artitous caught him on a flow of air.

The other two ravens fell dead by arrows fired from the ground. Nemeth cawed pitifully as the arrow was removed, Sucking up all the sympathy from the human women. Artitous healed the wound after the arrow was removed and he spoke to the bird asking for his report.

"Elizarade is dead by her own hand. She committed suicide after being stripped of her powers by the wizards there. Before they stripped her powers, she gloated on how she was still able to control the Demons and elementals even when her powers were blocked. She gave up no allies but she did give up the well she had on her person. For you not magically inclined a well holds magic for times when you cannot otherwise use the power. It was probably enough to coordinate the attacks but not enough to free her. Maybe there is no ally. Maybe we just faced her.," said Artitous.

The attacks started again in earnest the next morning. Goblins, Orcs, and Trolls attacked the walls directly trying to bring them down. As they tried the archers and wizards on the walls rained down destruction upon them. The Goblins had just gotten ladders to the edge of the walls when war horns were heard in the distance. Looking out into the horizon there appeared the larger than life army of the Ogre. These large humanoid creatures were dedicated to peace and learning, but were ferocious in battle. They wielded swords twice as long as they were tall, and cut swaths through the Goblins and the Orcs. The Trolls turned from the gates to face the new enemy just to be peppered with arrows and fireballs.

At the fore of the Ogre army, rode Marzioa, who laid about him with his staff, knocking Goblins senseless with well-placed strikes to the head. He rode laid back in his saddle and lit his pipe, striking the Goblins on occasion with his staff. The Ogres kept the wizard safe, but his laid-back approach to this battle was almost humorous.

The equestrians and archers covered the approaching army and soon the enemy was broken on the pincer of Ogres and equestrians. The Ogres and equestrians entered the city victorious, the enemy routed. The soldiers inside the city cheered the Ogres and Marzioa and soon celebrations were breaking out throughout the city. Marzioa rushed to the leaders of the city and reported on the necromancer's demise.

"She was found with two daggers cutting her wrists. They were put there by a rough hand. I do not believe she killed herself. The wizards who were to guard her said no one went in and no one left. I do not know how but I believe someone killed her.," said Marzioa.

"Did she reveal anything before she died? We must know what we are up against here. The enemy was routed today but they will return, and next time the Ogres may not be there to face the Orcs and Goblins," said Artitous.

"A contingent of twelve hundred Ogres will remain with the city. They are aware of your other potential problem and are ready to face these lizard men as well," said Marzioa.

"And grateful we are for that. We must figure out though how to help Thomas. He does not realize the danger he is in. How do we help someone who does not realize they are in danger?" asked Torlin.

"That is a problem for another day, Torlin. For now just bask in the thought that you are free from assaults and sieges for a time. Now it is time to celebrate." said Marzioa as he made a glass of wine materialize from out of thin air. "Anyone else want one?"

The laughter continued long into the night and the watch reported all clear for the first time in weeks. Metra was finally at a temporary peace.

CHAPTER ONE HUNDRED ONE:
A FAMILY DISPUTE

Torlin and the leaders of Dracos sat in conference over ale. They were celebrating their victory over the Dread Lords and discussing what to do about Thomas. Torlin suggested that he and Roanda go to Thomas to try to get him to see sense. Roanda could speak to Thomas's wife and between the three of them convince Thomas of the error of his ways.

Tanis disagreed. If Thomas was willing to anger the dragons by killing one of them, he would not stop at killing his brother. Tanis felt that it would be suicide for Torlin to go. Tanis said, "I will go to Thomas. He cannot kill me, and I may be able to get him to see what is going on. If these creatures are as evil as you say they are, it is imperative that we move quickly to get these creatures out of the city."

"They are cunning and very intelligent. You must take care. If the Tetradon are anything like the Metradon, their leader is probably glued to Thomas. Your best bet is going to be to approach his wife. She may be able to get them apart long enough for you to talk to Thomas and set things back to right. You will need troops to back you after you have separated them. The Tetradon will not go without a fight," said Torlin.

"Then we must leave a defensive force here in Metra and mobilize our armies to go to Tetra." said Tanis. "That way we can be there to save the day."

"I fear that the sight of our armies will act as a catalyst all right. But one for him to attack and fight. He will assume we are there to take over and he will defend his own violently. Of this, I have little doubt.

As children, we would do different things in town and he would always play the benefactor but the truth of the matter was he was paying people off to keep their silence about his violent temper. I fear the Tetradon leader may be playing on those emotions. We must keep the armies out of site of the city and then our plan may work," said Torlin.

"Then let us prepare for battle, my son. What will be will be." said Tanis as he walked from the gathering and headed to the Elves to prepare for the march to Tetra.

As Tanis left, Torlin noticed something at the gates. Farmers, tradesmen, and other citizens of the area had come to the city. They asked for admission to the city to make their new home. They had heard of the benevolence of Lord Torlin and were looking for a new start in the ancient city. Torlin told the guards to open the gates for the refugees but to check closely for saboteurs and spies.

A large man and a small Elf woman came to the command tent and introduced themselves. They were the leaders of the refugees and she was a weaver looking for permission to open her shop in one of the old buildings. The man claimed he was an innkeeper and would like to use the inn on the main plaza as his inn. Torlin welcomed the pair and all of the refugees who came into the city bidding them help with the reconstruction of the city.

The innkeeper offered a bit of knowledge about Tetra. The prince was going berserk. He allowed no one entrance and was killing off his people. Reports had it that thousands had died in the city already. The city was locked down tighter than a drum. No one was fool enough to go there. His princess was benevolent and kind but he was very dangerous at the best of times.

Torlin thanked him for the information and went to the rest of the leaders of Metra's armies. He related the information to the rest of the leaders and all agreed that something would have to be done. The decision was made to go to Tetra and try to resolve this issue. They would leave as soon as the armies could be prepared and their plan put into place.

It would take three days to get the armies ready for the journey to Tetra and to sober up the leaders. Lord Nargus was still a little tipsy when he mounted his horse, but recovered the rest of the way on the road. The armies went out with great fanfare and all of the soldiers in the armies felt like heroes. Their newfound citizens were busy setting up shop after the parade of troops, and the remaining troops closed the gates and prepared for the eventuality of another attack.

On the road, Torlin and Tanis got the opportunity to talk and bond. Tanis learned from Pan Thor and Torlin different magic and Tanis taught them magic that they had never seen before. Athinina watched the men and smiled. Her family was coming together, if a little later than she had hoped. Now if they could only get Thomas here at this reunion all would be right.

Tanis and a small bodyguard left and rode ahead to Tetra. The main body of the army remained behind so that there would be no cause for Thomas to be alarmed. However, Tanis did not receive the welcome he had hoped. Thomas called down to the approaching people that they were to turn and leave. There was no welcome here for them and if they approached, they would be shot down where they stood.

Tanis called up that he was Tanis Thalin and he needed to speak to his son. His request was answered with arrows that rained down on the men at the gates. Fortunately, none were killed but they got the idea. There would be no communication between father and son. Dagmar appeared on the parapets with his energy weapons and fired down on the men as they left for the rest of the army. Dagmar felt that Tanis might be the threat to the Tetradon's plan for conquest. He would have to be silenced before he made it to Thomas.

Dagmar sent out runners and soon found the army of Metra and saw them all poised at the edge of Tetra territory. The runners returned with word of the army and Dagmar called Thomas into counsel. He revealed that he had sent out the runners and Thomas became angry. Thomas had said no one in or out. Dagmar apologized and brought up his father's betrayal. He had brought an army to his city. It lay just over the horizon. Surely, they should send their army to confront them.

Thomas called Meka to him and spoke at length of the army and what should be done. After an hour of discussion, the two appeared before the Tetradon and men left of Thomas's army. "We march to war!" screamed Thomas, "They dare to bring an army to my gates, I will teach them all!"

The preparations for war began in earnest and the men and lizard folk worked hard together to gather all they would need to confront the army. It would take them several days to prepare but they went to the gates four days later ready to face the rest of Dracos.

CHAPTER ONE HUNDRED TWO: BROTHER VERSES BROTHER

Thomas rode at the fore of his army. The war drums thundered as he marched the army toward the rest of Dracos' armies. The Tetradon marched in front of the men and Elves of Thomas's Rangers who were in front of the Tyris and fighters from the other races. The horse rode at the fore with Thomas. The whole would have been something to remark about had the other armies of Dracos not been there. Thomas's large army was dwarfed by the size of the other army.

Thomas looked at them and saw many battle weary faces. However, they all fingered weapons ready to fight for what they believed was right. Thomas thought them fools to stand against him, but they did only follow orders. His brother and mother should have to pay the price for defying him.

A strange man made his way out to the front of the army and moved toward Thomas. The Tetradon with Thomas raised their weapons to fire but Thomas waved them off. Let their messenger come and offer their terms of surrender. "I am Tanis Thalin. I come to see my son and seek to preserve him from this folly," said the stranger.

Thomas just stuttered and stammered at the man's introduction. How dare he use his father's name? "My father lies dead in the Fields of the Pheni. I should kill you where you stand for your impertinence. If this ruse is the best you can come up with, then I will accept your surrender now," said Thomas.

"I am your father, Tanis Thalin. And I beg you to end this without bloodshed. There is no reason for it.," said Tanis.

"Father or no. I declare this world is mine and all of you who bow to me now will be spared. Do not make me destroy all of you. As you see I have energy weapons and I am not afraid to use them," said Thomas.

"We have Ogres. However, that does not mean anything to either side. Our weapons mean nothing, just sit with us and we will see what can be arranged," said Tanis.

"There is no more to be said here. Return to your armies and I will return to mine and we shall see who will reign supreme," said Thomas.

"We will not fight you, Thomas. So there can be no battle with only one side wanting to fight," said Tanis.

"If you will not fight then you will all die. I have no problem with either solution. Now if you do not mind I must prepare your demise," said Thomas.

Tanis rode back to the army and gave the order for them to step off for Tetra. However, as they began moving Thomas's equestrians came barreling toward the army. Tanis called for the wizards and Druids to erect a barrier of air between the two armies. They managed to get the barrier up just as the equestrians were about to collide with the right flank. Several of the equestrians were trampled as they ran into the barrier and had their fellows run into them, unable to stop in time.

Thomas reared up his horse and bellowed in rage at the barrier and the departing army. Thomas ordered the energy weapons be brought to the fore and used against the barrier, but it was so massive due to the number of wizards and Druids that the weapons made no difference against it. Again, Thomas bellowed in rage, went to the barrier, and started striking at it with his sword. One of Thomas's lieutenants tried to pull him away, but Thomas struck him down in a fury.

Thomas stopped swinging his sword long enough to call for his bow. If they could not get to them directly, they would go over the top. Thomas was once again frustrated as the arrows bounced off the barrier and fell harmlessly to earth. He could see the enemy army and could not reach them. He tried repeatedly, but was unable to penetrate the barrier. Finally, the last of the armies of Dracos was moving away and the Dwarves at the rear saw Thomas's army and Thomas trying to attack them. In response to Thomas's attempted attack the Dwarves stopped and mooned the army of Tetra. After but a moment they continued and soon no one held the field.

Thomas made a decision to make for Metra. His army being smaller would overtake the larger force and destroy them before they made it to the safety of the city. The only problem they faced was the barrier that traveled with the enemy army. Thomas cursed himself for not keeping some of the magical folk with his army. He had always thought he had no need for them but he was slowly seeing the error of his ways.

Tanis saw the army following and ordered the barrier to be maintained. It would be necessary for as long as the enemy followed them. He hoped that Thomas would give up the chase and go home. However, this was not to be the case as Thomas followed the army all the way back to Metra. The city was under siege again.

Torlin stood on the walls and looked down at his brother's army. This was not like the Dread Lords who had recently laid siege to the city. He would not fire down onto them as he would the Metradon or the Dread Lords. He needed to find another way to prevent them from entering while no one was injured in the process. He finally decided to erect the barrier of air at the gates so they could not get to the gates themselves.

Tanis and Torlin tried repeatedly to call down to Thomas to ask him to lift the siege and to meet with the leaders of the city. The siege they would say is worthless because they had running water in the city and had plenty of food for all of those in the city. These pleas fell on deaf ears as Thomas continued day after day to attack the barrier. He got no closer to the actual gates but he continued to attack.

These attacks would last for two weeks before the horizon was darkened once more by an army. This time it was the Dread Lords and their minions returning for another attack on the city. The horns were sounded and people were taken to safety within the city. They now had civilians in the city that needed protecting and Torlin moved to see them all moved to safety.

Thomas did not turn to face the incoming army, continuing his assault on the city. The Dread Lords seeing this attack brought forth their Trolls and Demons and proceeded to attack the barrier, which still held. Thomas seeing this unexpected ally attacked with renewed fervor. Torlin with a heavy heart gave the order. Fire upon the attacking Trolls and Demons and if they accidentally hit the humans then they hit the humans.

At first the Demons and Trolls alone fell to the arrows and fireballs, but they realized that they were avoiding the humans. So they used the humans as shields to protect the Demons and Trolls. Torlin gave the order to do what they had to do and the first blood in the brother verses brother war was spilled.

CHAPTER ONE HUNDRED THREE: FLANKING MANEUVERS

Arrows and fireballs rained down on the troops of Thomas and the Demons and Trolls of the Dread Lords. Soon twenty men and twelve Demons and Trolls lay dead at the foot of the gates. The wizards on the walls used magical fire to burn the bodies so that they could not be used to choke the city.

It was strange that the assault stopped so rapidly. The enemies of Metra seemed to be distracted by something. Using his gifts Torlin gazed at the horizon and saw the battle going on there. Soon the battle approached close enough that no magnification of vision was needed to see the combat. Torlin knew his brother would not want any assistance, but his brother did not see the second Dread Lord army heading toward his flank. He was trapped between the two and Thomas's army would not last the day.

Torlin ran to his leaders and shouted to prepare for battle. They needed to march as soon as physically possible. The Elves jumped to the fore and prepared to leave the city with the Ogres and Dwarves close behind them. The humans brought up the rear and the magical folk brought up the tail end. They would work from as far away as was possible from actual combat.

Torlin was half hoping for another attack by the Willows of the Wisps. He could get his brother's and his army into the city before they settled in. He charged his army forward toward the battle, which had moved even closer to the city. He reached the Dread Lord army just as the second Dread Lord army closed the pincer on Thomas. Torlin let fly with fireballs and lightning bringing down the largest of the Demons approaching his brother's army. The falling Demon crushed the life out of several Orcs and Goblins, causing others to turn and face the new threat.

The Elves crashed into the Orcs and Goblins, combat ensued hot, and heavy for what seemed an eternity until the Elves fell back between the dwarven lines and the Dwarves moved forward. The Dwarves laid about them with axe and sword not about to be outdone by the Elves or humans. Again after a long period, the Dwarves fell back between the lines of men and Gnomes and the men and Gnomes proceeded to attack and kill with the vigor of those on a rescue mission. Soon the men and Gnomes moved back through the Elven line and the process continued until the second Dread Lord army broke on the army of Metra's teeth.

To clean up the remaining Dread Lord troops the Ogres moved forward and took the field. Torlin had held them in reserve until the last just so they could handle anything large that attacked from the first Dread Lord army. After cleaning up the troops of the secondary force, the armies of Metra moved forward to assist with the primary force from the Dread Lords.

As Torlin approached, Thomas split his forces and charged the Metra army. Torlin sent wave after wave of air barriers at Thomas's army and the other magic users attacked the Dread Lords. Torlin would shove back Thomas's army and Torlin's army would fire into the gap toward the enemy army. Thomas's generals finally realized that Torlin was not in fact attacking them and turned to face their common enemy. Soon Thomas's armies and Torlin's armies were fighting side by side with the exception of the Tetradon and Thomas. These attacked anyone who came close.

Thomas roared as he laid about him with an energy weapon he had picked up from a fallen Tetradon. In his fury, he killed several of his own men and Tetradons. Thomas raged and roared and attacked without any kind of rhyme or reason. Even Meka could not get close to her husband. It was finally an Elf with a dummied arrow that brought down Thomas. The blunt arrow hitting Thomas just behind the ear knocking the young man out.

Torlin moved quickly and recovered his brother's prone body as the Tetradon moved to take it. Torlin and his forces made it first, picked up the fallen prince, and carried him toward the city. The Tetradon seeing Thomas was down attacked with a renewed fervor. The Dread Lord army had retreated into the distance but the Tetradon continued to assault the armies of Metra.

Torlin had his magic users create a barrier so that the forces could escape and he took his brother and his wife to the city for treatment and to get them to talk to him and his father. The barriers went up quickly and the Tetradon helplessly threw themselves at it. Thomas and Torlin, Roanda and Meka, all moved to Metra and the safety of the walls.

Meka hugged Roanda as the gates closed behind the last of the Metra army. She cried as the Tyris welcomed her into their home and they spoke at length of Tetra and the loss of the Tyris there. Thomas lay prone on the bed still unconscious from the arrow as Torlin joined the conversation. He hoped he would not have to restrain his brother but his armor and weapons were taken as a precaution.

Torlin introduced Meka to Tanis and the two exchanged pleasantries. Torlin then asked them to sit and he began, "Father, I believe an explanation is in order. Now that both of your sons are here, you need to explain why you were not there. You owe us that much."

"When your brother wakes I will explain all. I promise. You handled this battle well. However, you have a greater one now. You have these lizard folk at the gates beating at them and attacking them. However, the battle I refer to is the one for your brother. Before we can tell him our tales, we must first get him to listen. The battle is over, but it has really only just begun," said Tanis.

"We will tell you boys everything I promise that," said Athinina walking into the room. Pan Thor followed closely into the room and embraced his brother as he greeted him.

"Where am I?" came a voice from behind the gathered family. Everyone turned and faced Thomas, Tanis and Torlin both grasped the power ready to bind him if necessary. "Hold your hand, I am beaten. I swear I will not come against you."

"You are in my home," said Torlin. "And you are not a prisoner, you are my brother and I would like to speak to you."

"I am at your mercy. Speak if you wish. I will not try to stop you. I do not know how you did it, Torlin. However, you defeated the greatest general in the world. Now what do you wish to speak of?" said Thomas.

"A blunt arrow brought you down. Shot by Martin himself to stop your rampage. I had little to do with the strategy that won the battle. That was our father and Artitous's genius. I just said to do It.," said Torlin.

"Aren't you forgetting something, my heart?" said Roanda.

"By the way this is your new sister-in-law. Roanda Thalin meet Thomas Thalin. Thomas Thalin meet Roanda." said Torlin.

"That was not what I meant. Some of that strategy was mine. Give credit where it is due. Surely Tanis and Artitous would say the same," said Roanda.

"Of course you were involved in the battle plan. I did not mean to omit you. I have already met your wife, Meka. A very lovely girl she is too. May you both be happy and blessed." said Torlin.

"My wife is prisoner as well? I am sorry my love, but it appears as if we may be staying in a cell for a while. It will not be as grand as our palace but we will at least be together," said Thomas.

"You are not prisoners, neither of you. Just sit at the table and we must find out where our father has been and why he stayed away for so long.," said Torlin.

"Then a story it is. A great work of fiction I will wager but please let it begin." said Thomas as he sat down at the table and faced Tanis.

"Then let us begin at the beginning." said Tanis.

CHAPTER ONE HUNDRED FOUR: STORIES OF OLD WARS

"My story begins at the battle on the Fields of the Pheni. As I killed the great Demon, Potiutios, and it injured me badly when a sword pierced me from behind. That is when I fell and the Demon fell upon me looking like it had killed me when in fact it had just wounded me severely. The deadly wound had come from a Goblin's sword so I could recover from it. As you know, only Demons can kill an Askanitowa. Well, I fell into a deep recuperative sleep. It lasted nearly a year before I finally awoke in the ground of the Fields of the Pheni.

"When I awoke I did not know who I was. I simply knew I was missing something. Therefore, I left and went in search of who and what I was. I was found by an old traveling peddler and offered a job as a bodyguard for him. I did not know who I was so he named me Ibris. I did not know then that I had magic and did not recover it for nearly a year after that. For nearly ten years, I traveled with that peddler, searching for something I did not know.

"I settled down in a village near the Dark Lands. I fought to keep off the armies of Goblins and Orcs that tried to ransack the village. It was there that I met Claire. She was kind and gentle and offered me a home and later a new life. We were married and all was right with the world.

"She was a good woman and bore me two children, fraternal twins. A boy named Garren and a girl named Almedda. The woman died in childbirth and I raised the children on my own for a time. The boy showed skills in arms and fighting. He was a difficult boy and fought often. Almedda is a skilled magic user and follows the arts of the Druids. It was not long after their birth that I began travelling again. I packed them up into a peddler's wagon and searched once more for what I felt was missing and then I saw the statue.

"The statue on the Fields of the Pheni shook loose the memories that I had for so long tried to recover. I searched for several days looking for my lost blades. It took me another couple of days before I finally found them at the bottom of the well. I had sent down the bucket and tasted the magic in the water. I crawled down the well and reclaimed my swords, Warmonger and the Holy Avenger. After that, I went to the dragons and again settled down with the children. When I heard of the situation here with the two cities and the Dread Lords, I left the dragons and headed here with an army of them at my back.

"Your armies were at odds and I had to do something to end the fighting. Now I am here to help and guide you. I will be bringing the other children here shortly. They should get to know the rest of their family," said Tanis.

"That's it? You traveled for twenty years and had two children? Surely there was more to this story that you are not telling us." said Thomas. "How anticlimactic!"

"I will go into more details another day. I just need you two to be even and square. I do not need to see you two at odds any longer. If it will aid the healing process, I will leave and take the other two children with me. It is totally up to you." Said Tanis.

"No details are needed right now and you are welcome here in Metra for as long as you desire. We have the room even with the locals moving in. I hear we have gained another smith and two more farriers. We have also gained several new fletchers as well. We will be in need for nothing soon," said Torlin.

"You let civilians in your city? You truly are weak. What next, women, and children? When will you learn this is a battlefield? And one I will take from you because you are weak." said Thomas.

Meka walked over and cuffed her husband behind the ear and Torlin said, "We have had women and children for a couple of months now. Whom do you think takes care of the livestock and the day-to-day tasks of Metra? Surely your army has better things to do than make its own weapons and armor? Raising its' own food?"

"It is still a bad idea," said Thomas.

Meka walked over, hugged Thomas, and said, "Only because you did not think of it first, my dear."

"That is not why it is a bad idea. But what about the Tetradon at the gates. If you have forgiven and forgotten with me what about them? Surely they are worthy of it as well?" said Thomas.

"I still fear them, Thomas," said Meka.

"They are a good race. Unlike their counterparts here. Let them in and see." said Thomas.

"Those beasts fired on us and your troops during the battle. It seemed to us that the only ones they were not firing on were the Dread Lords.," said Torlin.

"Surely it was a mistake. Bring them in so they can explain. Dagmar has been a loyal servant to me, these last few months. Give him the opportunity to explain," said Thomas.

"I will go to speak to them." said Tanis as he headed toward the door and went to the walls.

Tanis called down from the walls to the Tetradon below and awaited the leader of them to come forward. Dagmar came forward and then fired on the man on the wall. "Did you fire upon us by accident as you do now? Or do you have ulterior motives for my son?"

"You are all slaves of the Tetradon and as far as we are concerned you are in revolt. We will put down the revolt and then take both of these cities as our own. Give up now and we may allow some of you to live," said Dagmar.

"What are you saying? We are friends, Dagmar. Surely you do not mean this." said Thomas. "I sacrificed so much for our friendship. What about Ragan? And the Tyris? I followed your suggestions with my orders," said Thomas. Meka's face went red at the mention of Ragan and she fingered her dagger.

"So you know, we are with child," said Meka. "I tell you so you know before you die. I am going to destroy you for destroying him. I must go. I cannot stay here with him."

"Then stay with Me." said Roanda "Surely an order does not mean he destroyed your first love. He may have truly meant him to perform a task for him."

"I will stay with you sister, but do not defend him to me. Not right now." said Meka.

Thomas moved to follow the women from the wall but Tanis stopped him. "Let them go. Surely, you are not stupid enough to walk into that hornet's nest. We will try to speak to them later."

"She is my wife." began Thomas.

"But she is Tyris as well. And right now, you are a marked man. Do not give her the opportunity to harm you for she surely will. Let her cool down, then you may have a chance of getting through to her." interrupted Tanis. "Come and we will have an ale while these good men and women fire down on these lizard folk."

And fire they did, and soon the Tetradon were moving away to regroup and plan their new angle of attack. Unbeknownst to them they were being watched by yet another army.

Chapter One Hundred Five: The Enemy of My Enemy

The Tetradon pulled back from attacking the city and spied another army. The Tetradon grew wary as the other army approached. It was the Metradon approaching and the Tetradon were hoisting weapons. Two Horns and a contingent from the Metradon approached under a white flag. Dagmar cautiously allowed them to enter and the two groups sat and talked.

"We can help each other," said Two Horns. "Surely we are stronger together than apart."

"Why would we trust a Metradon? Do you think us fools?" asked Dagmar.

"We have a common enemy and a common problem. The enemy is the humans, Elves, and Dwarves. The problem is they have our cities. We can help each other regain control, and then we can settle our rift. Surely they could not stand before our combined might." said Two Horns.

"Maybe we can do this. I must confer with my people. We still possess our city. That is our difference," said Dagmar.

"You possess nothing, just as we do not. The gates are closed to you since the ravens flew. Only the resistance and the humans live there now. Our few troops who are left have been forced from the city. So now what do you do?" Two Horns remarked as he sat at the table and looked around at the Metradons and Tetradons surrounding it.

They were convinced for now, but Two Horns was not going to lean on his laurels. He needed them to strike and strike now. "We must attack at once with both of our armies. Their puny barricade cannot stand our combined weight. Let us put them down while they are sitting on their hands," said Two Horns.

"Then let us do this. Why do we linger here?" asked Dagmar.

The two armies combined for the first time and moved toward the city. As they moved the Wizards and Druids on the walls began to launch fireballs and lightning. Soon the two sides were firing back and forth the lizard folk with energy weapons that struck the barrier and dissipated and magic which seemed to hit every time. Arrows joined the fray as the Elves came onto the walls to help in the defense of the city.

The Dwarves moved to the tunnels in case they attempted to use them again and all drew weapons and waited for the enemy. It did not take long for the enemy to attempt to use the tunnel network again. Soon a battle raged at the mouth of the tunnel complex and the Dwarves held back the combined army of Tetradon and Metradon.

The equestrians joined the fray by leaving the gates and charging through the barrier. They had been warned that they could leave but could not return unless they dropped the barrier. The horse had been happy to take the chance to break the siege. The Ogres fought side by side with the Dwarves and the equestrians. Their giant swords clearing great swaths with each swing.

The armies of the Tetradon and Metradon pressed forward and at first seemed to be winning the battle. The horse and Ogres fell back as the battle raged and the Dwarves and archers seemed to be slowing down. When it appeared the lines would break, Tanis appeared on the walls, started raining down his own fire, and balled lightning. This was the catalyst that Torlin and Thomas's armies truly needed. They pressed back and soon the Tetradon and Metradon were falling back.

As they fought, another army approached. The Dread Lords figured on taking advantage of the battle weary armies on the field and soon the battle was being fought on three fronts. Thomas and his Rangers exited the city, attacked the two armies, and joined the fray bolstering the troops' morale and raining arrows into the Dread Lords, Metradons, and Tetradons' armies. Again, the enemy surged and the forces of Dracos fell back to the barrier.

As they fought, yet another army came forward. This time it was the dragons arriving at the battle. Attacking the rear of the Dread Lords and the Tetradons and Metradons, the enemy split its attention between the lizard folk and the armies of Dracos and the dragons. Split four ways the Dread Lords fell to a man to the surrounding armies.

Dragons using breath weapons attacked the Metradons and Tetradons as the armies of Dracos attacked with arrows, magic, lances, and axes. Giant swords pushed forward as the Ogres fought with renewed vigor at the sight of the dragons.

After what seemed like an eternity, the battle was over and the remainders of the Metradons and Tetradons moved away from the field and dispersed into their own peoples. Both groups of lizard folk found themselves severely diminished. They would leave for now, but they would recoup and return. They limped away and left for wherever they were hiding.

Tanis rode out to the dragons and embraced the elders of the dragon army. "My friends, Thank you for the impromptu rescue. I had hoped you received the raven about our situation. I also hoped you would respond. The Ogres were a great boon, but your efforts were the turning point," said Tanis.

"We honor our treaties Lord Tanis. You needed our aide and we came. Some day you and yours will have to honor the treaty by aiding us. But for now, at least, may peace reign in the land." said Mastol.

"You old ham, you just could not stay away. I knew you would come and bring friends," laughed Tanis as he led the way to the city and was followed by the great wyrm and the armies of Dracos.

All enjoyed the hospitality of Torlin and Metra for a two-week celebration. The Druids healed those who needed it and the others just rejoiced in the new peace. Marzioa reported that the ravens from the Dark Lands were reporting a new brightness in the land. It could have been nothing or it could be that they had truly destroyed what was left of the Dread Lords.

The Metradon and Tetradon resistance fighters came to the fore, revealed they still had men within the armies of their people, and would be informed if there were anything to worry about from them. Peace had come to the cities for the first time in what seemed like an eternity.

CHAPTER ONE HUNDRED SIX: FORGOTTEN REVENGE

Meka snuck down to the building where Thomas was staying. She was feeling queasy from being with child but that could not prevent her from getting revenge for Ragan. She pulled her dagger from its sheath and moved into the room where he was sleeping. She walked to the disheveled bed and stood over it looking down at its occupant.

Suddenly the rage she had been feeling was gone. She lowered the dagger and looked down at her husband. He was to be her child's father when it was born. She sat on the bed and a tear came to her eye. When had she grown so weak? She reached down and stroked the brow of the man in the bed. He stirred but did not wake which was just as well. She threw the dagger down and lay on the bed with her husband being careful not to wake him, even staying out of the covers so the draft would not make him uncomfortable.

Winter was coming and soon the world would be covered in white and travel would difficult. She would have to arrange for them to leave for Tetra soon. The young twins of Tanis had finally made it from the dragon's cove. Garren and Almedda had already met their older siblings and some bad blood rose from the girl Druid and the older wizard. Druids felt that they alone respected the power of magic and all those who practiced magic should be trained and raised by the Druids. Wizards were power hungry and did not respect the abilities that the Creator had given them.

Wizards believed that the opposite was true. They believed that the Druids had too many rules and regulations. There were many types of both the Druids and the wizard folk, but they split on this point. They would work together when needed but they were not the best of friends. The only exception seemed to be Artitous, Marzioa, and Torlin. These three got along together well and it showed what the two groups could do together.

Almedda was an old school Druid. She believed all wizards were corrupt. She was one of the Guardians of the Groves. And she took the role seriously. Torlin tried to speak to her but she had decided already that he was no good. Pan Thor tried to intervene but that got them nowhere. She was just as skeptical of the Catarel as she was of Torlin. She was smitten with her brother Thomas though and would try to come into his tent and talk at all hours of the day and night.

Thomas drew his sword on her several times but she still did not get the message. Thomas did not know how to be a big brother. His other sibling was his age. The boy Garren would not even go to the training grounds when Thomas was present. The boy had heard of the atrocities that the man had committed and wanted nothing to do with him. Thomas was impressed that he was such a good equestrian even at his age.

Torlin was seen often in the company of Garren. The older man and the ten-year-old boy seemed to hit it off quite nicely. Garren would be seen riding with Torlin often around the walls as Torlin inspected them. Garren always had a sword on his back, but it was as large as he was.

The younger children were as different as twins could be. Besides one being a girl and one being a boy, the girl was dark haired and had brown eyes. She was tall and lanky and looked the part of a Druid. She would often be in the company of Artitous so that she could learn his magic. She could eat the city out of house and home and not gain an ounce.

Garren was fair-haired like the twins, but he was not built like them. He had blue eyes and a rosy complexion. Seeing Torlin with the start of a beard, Garren wanted one as well. His father and his brothers picked on him as he tried to show the peach fuzz growing on his lip and chin. "Let the cat lick that off. No need for a razor yet." would be Tanis's remark to the boy when he would show his attempts at a beard and mustache.

This would only agitate the boy but he would take it in stride. Although he tried to learn magic, he found he had no talent for it, just like Thomas.

Meka was thinking about all this when Thomas awoke beside her. Feeling around he felt her leg and turned to her. "You may get under the covers with me, if you so desire. Or is the blanket the only thing staying your hand?"

"You are insufferable but I am not getting under there with you. That is how we got into this mess. You men think that women can bear a child and run the businesses and keep their husbands in line all at the same time. I cannot do it. I am always ill to my stomach and I am grouchy and irritable. Try and touch me and I will ram this dagger so deep into you, you will be passing arrowheads for a week. Do you understand my husband?" said Meka.

She suddenly burst into laughter and looked at Thomas's shocked face. Thomas had retracted his hand as if it had been bitten. However, a smile came to his lips as he kissed her and pulled her to him.

Roanda had some news for Torlin. He too was to be a father. The wizard was in shock as she relayed the news from the Druids. She had thought it was just a stomach complaint and found out she was going to have a child. Torlin was ecstatic and was going around giving pipe tobacco and ale to his friends and family.

Roanda looked fondly on her husband and his youthful response to the pregnancy. He would make a good father. Nevertheless, she would now have to make plans for their families to leave now. Winter was coming, and the roads were treacherous at the best of times. They did not have the wagons to spare to send them out with a wagon, but she would make do with what they had.

Tanis, Athinina, and the kids left that morning, heading back to the capitol. Meka and Thomas would leave a couple of hours later. The animosity between the brothers cooled but was not completely resolved.

Thomas would keep an eye on Torlin and Thalinburg. However, he would not close the borders either.

The men and women of Thomas's army marched out to great fanfare from the civilian population. They had missed Tanis and the Ogre army that morning, but that was just as well. Tanis did not like the fanfare anyway and would shy away from it. Better, that it was just not there.

Torlin watched the armies of the Ogre and Tanis move away from the city from the wall. He waved to them as they left until they could not see him anymore. Then he used his power to produce fireworks for them. It was the least that they deserved.

He repeated the scene later that day when his brother left. The waving was returned by Meka but not Thomas, and the fireworks were wasted on the man, but it made Torlin feel better. His brother may not be the same as he was but he was getting there.

Torlin turned to Roanda and took her hand. "We truly have grown haven't we?" asked Torlin.

"More than we will ever know my heart. More than we will ever know."

It would be years in the coming but another war and another rift would appear in Dracos, but that is the story for another day. For now, let us just leave the tale a happy one, one where brothers no longer fought and a father returned from the great abyss. What could be better?

The End